Has Anyone Seen My Husband?

Also by Kathleen Whyman

Wife Support System
Would You Ask My Husband That?

Has Anyone Seen My Husband?

Kathleen Whyman

embla
books

First published in Great Britain in 2024 by

Bonnier Books UK Limited
4th Floor, Victoria House, Bloomsbury Square, London, WC1B 4DA
Owned by Bonnier Books
Sveavägen 56, Stockholm, Sweden

A CIP catalogue record for this book is available from the British Library.

ISBN: 9781471416408

This book is typeset using Atomik ePublisher.

Embla Books is an imprint of Bonnier Books UK.
www.bonnierbooks.co.uk

For my agent, Emily Glenister, and Helen Lederer,
founder of Comedy Women in Print.
Without you two this book may not have happened.
Thank you for believing in me.

PS Enough of the schmaltz – when are we
going out drinking?!

Chapter 1

'No French woman would wear Lycra other than for sport. Out of respect for themselves and, *plus important*, out of respect for those around them.' My mum, or Maman as she preferred to be called, patted her chignon and grimaced at my black leggings. 'I thought you and Scott were going to a restaurant, not the gymnasium.'

'We are.' I stood back to let her through the front door.

'Then why are you wearing exercising clothes, Marie?'

The boring answer was: practicality. I spent so much time kneeling down – playing with Anna or measuring the brides I made gowns for – that I needed to wear leggings under my shift dress to ensure I didn't constantly flash my knickers. Boring was better than brazen.

'Don't get your *culottes* in a twist, I'm about to change.' I looked at my watch. 'Better hurry, Scott'll be home any minute. Thanks for babysitting.' I gestured to the living room. 'Anna's watching CBeebies.'

Maman muttered something in French under her breath, which, roughly translated, meant 'not that shit again'.

Grinning, I ran upstairs to get ready. There wasn't time to shower, but as I hadn't been exercising, despite apparently being dressed for it, I reasoned that a once-over with Anna's potty-training wet wipes would suffice. I'd need a shower later, anyway. Date night with your husband was, after all, code for guaranteed shag. My leggings wouldn't be needed for that particular form of exercise.

I changed into a jade-green wiggle dress with a keyhole neckline that I'd made for the occasion and braided my dark hair around the back of my head, so that the plait fell over

1

one shoulder. Before I had a chance to refresh my makeup, the front door opened and Scott's footsteps hurried up the stairs. My stomach fluttered with excitement. It was our first night out in months and I couldn't wait.

Scott came through the door and I caught my breath. Even after four years together, his piercing blue eyes, thick sandy hair and dazzling smile still gave me the instant horn. Except, I realised, he wasn't smiling. In fact, he looked positively grim.

He looked me up and down, and took in my dress. 'Shit. Didn't you get my message?'

I shook my head. 'I had clients all afternoon, so my phone's been on silent.' My excitement did a quick assessment of the situation and scarpered.

Scott groaned. 'I'm so sorry.'

'What's tonight's reason?' I asked, flatly.

'Her car's broken down. She needs me to pick the kids up from football.'

That was better than usual. Liz was only hijacking cocktail hour, not the entire evening. 'It's fine. We'll go when you get back.'

Anna burst into the room. 'Daddy?' She looked at Scott quizzically, surprised to see him home before her bedtime. He ruffled her dark curls and angled his face away from her.

'She hasn't got any food in,' he mouthed, not noticing Anna's outstretched arms. 'So I said I'd take them for pizza.'

'Pizza?' Anna squealed, attempting to scale Scott's leg, as he hadn't taken the hint to pick her up. She grabbed his crotch and the penny dropped. Judging by the tears in his eyes, he probably wished his balls hadn't yet.

I scooped Anna up while Scott composed himself. 'You've already eaten, chick.'

'Who's Daddy having pizza with, then?'

I looked to Scott for an answer. Anna had no idea she had a half-brother and a half-sister, or that Daddy had been married before. Unfuckingbelievable, as my cousin Brigitte astutely put it.

Scott squirmed, which was the correct response when lying to your child about something other than Father Christmas, the Tooth Fairy or why Mummy and Daddy's bed sometimes squeaked. 'Someone from work,' he told Anna, tweaking her nose. 'I'd rather have pizza with you.'

We could all have pizza together if his ex-wife allowed Anna and me to meet their children. But every time Scott broached the subject, she reared up like Maleficent at the end of *Sleeping Beauty* and stopped him seeing Harry and Bella for a while. Also unfuckingbelievable.

I kissed Anna's cheek. 'Go downstairs and say goodnight to Mamie.' Anna did as I asked. It'd be nice if this was out of respect for me, but it was purely because the TV was downstairs.

I closed the door and turned to Scott. He'd taken off his shirt and was rubbing his armpits with one of Anna's wet wipes. I should never have introduced him to the idea. Getting intimate with Scott wasn't as arousing as it should be, when he smelt the same as Anna's bottom.

'Liz can't keep pulling this crap.' I unzipped my dress and stepped out of it. 'The whole point of pre-arranging evenings with Harry and Bella is to stop this happening.' It took a lot to get me cross, but I'd really been looking forward to tonight and was sick of Liz controlling our lives. I pulled my leggings back on. No exercising for me tonight, regardless of my Lycra apparel. This added insult fuelled my anger. 'She has to let us meet them, too. It's wrong to lie to Anna about where you're going. And Harry and Bella deserve to know they have a sister.'

Scott stared at the floor, a muscle pulsing in his cheek. Why wasn't he angry too? He should be furious at the way Liz treated him. I wanted to shout at him. To bellow in his ear that Anna wasn't a dirty little secret and he had to make Liz accept her existence. But anything louder than the gentle hum of an electric razor would be heard downstairs, so I went for aggressive whispering instead.

'It's time for an ultimatum,' I hissed. 'Either Liz tells the kids about us, or you will. If they don't want to meet me and Anna that's their choice, but Liz can't decide that for them.'

Scott shook his head. 'An ultimatum would get her back up. She'd stop me seeing them and I'd have to threaten legal action again.'

'Threaten it, then.' I jabbed a finger at him, realised with horror that this was something my mum did and crossed my arms instead. 'The law's on your side. She can't invent excuses to keep the kids away every time you challenge her irrational rules. It's not on.'

Scott sank down onto the bed and put his head in his hands. He was silent for several moments before releasing a long, shaky breath. 'Harry's night terrors are back.'

I sighed inwardly. It wasn't that I didn't care – I wouldn't wish night terrors on any child, especially Scott's son – but it was hard to drum up yet another bout of sympathy for a stepchild I'd never met.

'I promised I'd sit with him till he's asleep,' Scott said. 'Liz said it takes hours some nights.'

How convenient. Brigitte and I suspected that Liz wanted to get Scott back. She was probably scaring Harry deliberately to get Scott over so she could try and seduce him. I could just picture her in a pink baby-doll nightie and fluffy mules, beckoning Scott into her room. Actually, that was bullshit. I couldn't picture her at all, as we'd never met, but in my imagination she was basically a slut.

'Why do you have to stay when she's going to be there?' I asked.

Scott went quiet again. My frustration grew and I was on the verge of asking if he was in training for a sponsored silence marathon – and could I sign my mum up for it too – when I realised he was crying.

I dropped to my knees in alarm. 'What's wrong?'

'These night terrors are petrifying for him.' Scott's shoulders shook. 'He's scared to go to sleep. It's heartbreaking, watching him thrashing around and screaming, unable to help him.'

I wrapped my arms around him, guilt replacing my earlier anger. How could I be so selfish? Prioritising a night out over Scott's son's wellbeing. Of course he had to help Harry through it.

'I feel responsible,' Scott sobbed. 'If I hadn't left, maybe he wouldn't get them.'

I squeezed him tightly. 'You mustn't blame yourself. Liz is the one who had the affair.'

'I know, but it still feels as though I've let him and Bella down. And now I've let you down.' He looked up at me with watery eyes. 'I'm sorry about tonight. I don't blame you for getting angry, but what kind of a dad would I be if I wasn't there for Harry when he needs me?'

I felt another surge of guilt. My own parents were divorced, and I'd barely seen my dad once he met someone else and started a new family. One of the things I loved about Scott was that he was still very involved with his kids. I could hardly take umbrage when he spent time with them.

'You're not letting me down. We'll go out another time.' I smoothed down his thick sandy hair, which always stuck up slightly on one side, courtesy of a second crown at his hairline. Brigitte joked that he'd had plugs. Liz certainly gave him enough grief to cause hair loss, but her maintenance demands barely left enough for a haircut, let alone hair-replacement treatment.

Scott wiped his eyes and shook his head. 'You must think I'm pathetic. Crying like a baby.'

'No,' I said firmly. 'Being upset about Harry is nothing to be ashamed of. I'm glad your children are so important to you.'

Scott cupped my face. 'Thank you for being so understanding.'

I clasped my hands over his. 'I just want everyone to get along and for the children to be proper siblings. I don't want

Anna to be an only child.' My last comment was slightly passive-aggressive. I was desperate to have a baby, but Scott couldn't cope with more emotional, physical and financial stress while Liz was so unreasonable.

'I know,' he said softly.

'Liz doesn't have to worry that I'd make Harry and Bella feel excluded,' I said, pre-empting the usual defence. 'They'd be part of our family unit.'

Scott nodded. 'I'll tell Liz it has to happen as soon as Harry's over these night terrors.'

'But how long will that take?' My frustration was building again. 'They've got to find out some time, and the longer she puts it off, the harder it'll get.' I decided to get it all out. 'And we need to start trying for another baby. I'm already forty and—'

'Please stop.' Scott released my face and stood up. 'I'm worried about Harry, stressed with work, guilt-tripped by Liz. I'll lose it completely if I don't have you on my side.'

My heart went out to him and I jumped up. 'I'm always on your side. Nothing will change that.'

Scott put a hand to his chest. 'Thank you.' He smiled and warmth flooded through me. Nothing else mattered when he smiled at me like that. Never mind that he smiled in the same way when Scarlett Johansson came on the screen. He was only human, and it meant I could lust over Idris Elba without feeling guilty.

'I wish I could help,' I said.

'You can.' He took my hand. 'By trusting me to sort it out and letting me switch off from her crap when I'm at home. You'll be the first to know when I've got through to her, I promise.'

I walked him to the front door, then went into the living room where my mum was playing with Anna. Unfortunately for my daughter, my mum's interpretation of playing meant sitting on the sofa, reading a magazine, while Anna entertained herself.

'Good news, Maman. You're off the hook for babysitting. Scott's had to go out.'

'I am not surprised, Marie.' My mum closed the magazine. 'What man wants to be seen with a woman who wears exercising clothes?'

I returned her scathing look with a withering one. She was in no position to criticise anyone's dress sense. While most French women were chic – think Clémence Poésy and Marion Cotillard – Maman, for all her Frenchness, eschewed this tradition and instead dressed with the colour, flamboyancy and delusion of a clown. Her favourite outfit was a patchwork jacket teamed with red-and-pink striped harem pants, and lime-green trainers. By contrast, her twin sister, Francine, was the epitome of glamour, in crisp white shirts, tailored trousers and ballerina flats. They might have identical faces and figures, but no one would mistake them in a line-up.

'What I'm wearing has nothing to do with why we're not going out.' My eyes flitted to Anna to make sure she wasn't listening, but she was transfixed by a rerun of *Get Well Soon* on TV. I could relate. I often got transfixed by Dr Ranj myself. 'It's the usual reason,' I told Maman quietly.

'You should be pissed off,' Maman said, not quietly. I widened my eyes to remind her that her highly impressionable three-year-old granddaughter was in the room. Maman shrugged. 'It is a wonder you are not placing an advertisement asking: has anyone seen my husband? He spends more time with them than with you and Anna.'

'They're his children. It's only right he's there for them,' I whispered nobly, even though I was in fact a bit pissed off.

Maman tutted loudly. 'You have been together for four years and never met. *C'est ridicule.*'

I agreed, but would never admit that to her. It'd only go to her head. 'There's nothing I can do about it,' I said, with a lightness I didn't feel.

'You are enabling this situation by not doing anything

about it.' Maman jabbed a finger at me. 'You must insist on meeting them, for Anna's sake.'

'It's not that straightforward,' I murmured.

'*Connerie*,' Maman snapped.

Anna looked round. '*Connerie*,' she mimicked.

I glared at Maman. I wanted Anna to speak French, but would prefer that 'bullshit' wasn't part of her starter vocab.

Maman smirked, unable to hide her pride at Anna's immaculate pronunciation. She stood up and put my magazine in her bag. 'I'll go home, as you don't need me.'

'Stay for dinner if you like,' I said. 'It'll be healthy – I'm sugar-free now.'

Maman tutted. 'Marie. Food is an occasion to be enjoyed. Cutting out an element is like cutting out part of your soul.'

'You didn't say that about the chicken goujons and croquettes the other day. You were very happy to cut out those elements.'

'It was ready-made.' She visibly shuddered. 'With no presentation.'

'Sorry,' I said, not meaning it. I'd rustled up dinner in the half hour between collecting Anna from nursery and getting back to my studio for a client. Cooking from scratch and providing silver service hadn't been an option.

My mum smoothed back her dark chignon, her one concession to style. It really didn't go with the leopard-print dungarees she was sporting. 'I'll eat at home,' she said, kissing me on both cheeks. 'Stop with the sugar-free. You are thin enough.'

'It's to make me healthier, not thinner,' I said. Not that having a splitting headache most of the time felt very healthy. Apparently, that was normal when first giving up sugar. I'd been forced to take this drastic action after scoffing four large Easter eggs the previous week. They weren't even my eggs; they were Anna's. I tried to kid myself I was protecting her from future obesity-related health issues, but in truth I was just greedy.

'Well, be *keefy*.' Occasionally, my mum came out with

words that were neither English nor French. Or from any other language used on the planet known as Earth.

'If you mean be careful, then yes, I will.' I picked Anna up. 'Say bye to Mamie.'

Anna waved and my mum patted her on the head. She made no secret of the fact she didn't 'do' young children. She'd come into her own when Anna was old enough to drink espresso and go shopping. Which would be when she was about five if she'd inherited her grandmother's genes.

After I'd bathed Anna and put her to bed, I couldn't be bothered to cook, so finished off Anna's leftover jacket potato with cheese and beans. Then remembered the beans had sugar in them. Bugger. I'd have to start again now.

I sighed as I loaded the dishwasher. Scott would be having pizza with Harry and Bella now. I wondered what they were like. Hopefully, nothing like their mum. It was unbelievable that she acted like the wounded party when it was her who'd had an affair. She must have known Scott would leave if he found out. His dad had cheated on his mum repeatedly and Scott wouldn't tolerate infidelity. A year later, he met me. To say Liz took umbrage at this was like saying Henry VIII had a slight issue with commitment.

I sank down into a kitchen chair and massaged my temples. My head was pounding, either from the lack of sugar or the frustration at Liz's refusal to meet me. I hated not knowing my stepchildren. I hated that Anna was unaware she had a brother and sister. And I hated that Scott was dealing with all of Liz's stress on his own. The look of despair on his face when he'd described his guilt about Harry's night terrors was heartbreaking. If Liz let them come here, rather than Scott always having to go there or take them out, that'd be one less pressure on him. And once Liz met me, she'd see I was a decent person and only wanted the best for the children. That I wasn't out to replace her by being a super-cool stepmum. There was definitely no chance of that. Only aged three, Anna was already pretending she didn't know me when I picked her up from nursery. But how could I get Liz to give me a chance if she was determined to keep me away?

If this were a television drama, I'd engineer a meeting, confront her head-on, and say something incisive and clever that cut to the core of her insecurity. In the next scene, we'd be sharing a bottle of wine, and discussing child-share options and joint family holidays. I didn't need it to go that far – joint holidays were definitely off the table, as was my ability to say anything incisive and clever – but a conversation could potentially resolve everything.

I thought back to Maman's earlier words. She'd said I was enabling the situation by letting it happen. Was that true? If so, then it was down to me to *dis*able it. And the only way I could do that was by meeting Liz and proving that she could trust me.

I shot a guilty look towards the door, as though Scott might come through it and somehow know what I was thinking. He'd asked me to trust him to deal with it, but how long would that take? I'd waited four years already. I couldn't risk it being another four.

I swallowed hard, my heart pounding. I wasn't sure how, but I was going to find Liz and resolve this ridiculous situation once and for all. It was the only way we'd all be able to move on with our lives.

I bit my lip. I just had to hope it didn't backfire. And that Scott never found out what I'd done.

Chapter 2

'No, Maman. I am not going to ask the doctor to re-educate my vagina,' I said into the phone with an exasperated sigh.

'*Pourquoi?*' my mum asked, as though we hadn't had this conversation a hundred times before. '*En France*, all mothers have *la rééducation périnéale.*'

'The NHS's resources are stretched thinly enough without finding extra money to tighten everyone's fannies. Or employ Michelin-starred chefs,' I added, before she started moaning about the standard of meals she'd received in hospital when having a hip replacement the year before.

'They laughed when I asked for a cheese board and the wine list.' She winced at the memory. 'And they call themselves civil.' I raised my eyes to the sky. 'Why are you going to the doctor?'

'Just a routine smear test.' My tone was light, but my stomach tightened. There was nothing routine about having a stranger insert what looked like a shoehorn into a region that was most definitely not a shoe, and scrape out some cells with a very long cotton bud.

'Why do you have the doctor for this? I see a nurse.'

'The nurse can never reach the cells. My cervix tilts backwards, apparently.'

'Another affliction your brute of a papa gave you.' My mum was determined to blame him for everything.

'What are you doing today?' I asked.

'*Occupe-toi de tes oignons*,' she said huffily. Occupy yourself with your onions was the French way of saying mind your own business. Which probably meant she didn't have plans, but wanted to appear elusive.

11

'I'm at the doctor's now, I've got to go,' I said.

'Wait!' she instructed. 'Have you insisted to Scott that you and Anna meet his children?'

'I'm working on it,' I said, glad she wasn't there to see me rub my nose – a sure-fire giveaway that I was lying. My enthusiastic determination to meet Liz had fizzled out faster than a sparkler in the drizzle, as I had no idea how to go about it. I'd ask Brigitte if she had any bright ideas when I saw her after my appointment.

Minutes later, I sat waiting to be seen by Dr Greene, a new GP to the surgery. There seemed to be a very high turnover of doctors. I hoped the frequent departures were nothing to do with my mum. Her impatience with the British embarrassment about nudity meant that she'd strip off the moment she entered the doctor's room, without waiting to be ushered behind the curtained area. In her eyes, this saved time and awkwardness – the doctor was going to see it anyway, so why be bashful? I'm not sure the GP always saw it like that. Especially when she'd gone about an ingrowing toenail.

I scanned the other patients in the waiting room. Could one of them be Liz? I side-eyed a couple of women around my age, straining to see if there were any clues to their identity – a witch's hat or the number 666 tattooed on their wrist, perhaps – then gave myself a reality check. Liz lived in Guildford, so wouldn't be registered with a GP here in Horsham.

'Marie Dubois to room three,' a man's voice said over the tannoy.

I leapt up and hurried along the corridor, as though afraid my appointment would be given to someone else if I didn't arrive within seconds of being called. So, the new GP was a man. Not that it mattered who did my smear. They were there to do a job. To get in, get it done and get out, so to speak. Their gender was irrelevant. The door to room three was open and I stepped inside.

Dr Greene looked up and smiled. 'Hello.'

I froze. There was nothing irrelevant about this doctor's gender. He was gorgeous. Dark skin, broad shoulders and warm, deep brown eyes. If I hadn't known Idris Elba was an only child, I'd swear the actor's brother was sitting in front of me.

He stood and shook my hand. 'Dr Greene. Nice to meet you.'

'You too.' He had a firm grip, but his skin was soft to the touch. His hand was as perfect as the rest of him. I swallowed hard. Lying down semi-naked for an Idris Elba lookalike was the stuff fantasies were made of. Having a smear test by one was not. It was way too embarrassing. I didn't want Dr Greene thinking of soiled shoehorns every time he saw me from now on. I pressed my thighs together tightly. I couldn't do it. I just couldn't.

'Take a seat.' Dr Greene gestured to the chair by his desk, sat back in his own and smiled. 'Would you like a female chaperone present?'

'No.' This was mortifying enough without a witness.

'Don't be nervous. It's a quick procedure and shouldn't be too uncomfortable.' He plucked a pair of surgical gloves from a box on his desk. 'Is there any possibility you could be pregnant?'

I hesitated. I could lie and say I was. Hopefully, I would be in the not-too-distant future, and it'd get me out of having a smear today. I started to nod, then realised he'd have to log it and appoint me a midwife. I turned the nod into a shake.

Dr Greene looked understandably confused by my head jiggling. 'Can I clarify: are you or aren't you pregnant?'

'No. Not yet. We're trying. Or we will be soon.' I cringed. 'Not that you need to know that.'

'Do you want to do a test just to be sure?' Dr Greene asked.

I sighed, wishing that was why I was really there. 'No, there's no need.'

'OK.' Dr Greene stood and tugged a curtain around a bed

in the corner. 'Please remove your clothes from the waist down and lie on the bed with your knees bent.'

I didn't move. My mum would be lying on the bed stark naked by now, demanding canapés and an aperitif. However, despite being half-French, I was also half-British and that half very much wanted to keep my underwear on.

Dr Greene cleared his throat. 'I do need you to lie down for the smear test.'

I swallowed hard. I would not lie down. I would lie instead. 'Smear test?' I feigned a look of confusion. 'I'm not here for a smear test.'

'You're not?' Dr Greene frowned, which did nothing to reduce his attractiveness, and checked his computer screen. 'It says here that the nurse was unable to get any cells on your last test due to your tilted cervix, so she recommended you see a doctor.'

I had visions of Dr Greene with one foot up on the bed and his arm inside me up to his elbow, in a desperate attempt to retrieve some of my elusive cells.

'Someone else's notes must have been put on my record.' I scratched my nose.

Dr Greene looked perplexed. Another expression that had no negative impact on his looks. Putting a bag over his head was probably the only way I could ever view him as a normal human being. 'Sorry,' he said. 'I'll get that amended.' He smiled. Make that two bags. 'So, what are you here for?'

Good question. I stared uncomfortably at my hands in my lap and noticed smudges of red felt-tip from a picture Anna had drawn earlier. I say picture, but it was more of a scribble. Partly because she was only three and partly because she'd been too engrossed in the TV to give it her full attention. I mentally high-fived myself as I recalled the programme she'd been watching. It was *Get Well Soon* again and the little boy on the show had earache.

'An ear test,' I shouted with delight.

Dr Greene jumped.

'Sorry,' I laughed nervously. 'Sore ear. That's why I'm here. The receptionist must have thought I said smear, but I said ear. E-A-R. Easy mistake to make.'

'OK.' Dr Greene took an otoscope from his desk and attached a funnel to it. 'Which ear?'

'Which ear?' I repeated, my delight dissolving.

'Yes.' Dr Greene's laid-back manner was also dissolving. 'Which ear hurts?'

I prodded each ear. If I prodded really hard, could I make one of them hurt?

'Never mind. I'll look in both of them.' Dr Greene stood up, tilted my head to one side and thrust the otoscope into the exposed ear. I winced. Just as well I hadn't gone ahead with the smear test if his technique was this brusque.

'Nothing wrong here.' He tilted my head the other way. 'Or here.' My cheeks burnt with shame. Removing the funnel, he tossed it into a recycling bin and sat down heavily. 'Ms Dubois,' he said, double-checking my title on the screen. I'd kept my maiden name, as my business was established in that name, but had changed from Miss to Ms as an acknowledgement of my married status. 'Are you sure your ears hurt?'

Oh God, I was going to have to lie even more. 'You thought I meant *my* ears?' I flapped a hand, as though batting away this ludicrous assumption. 'No, it's my daughter, Anna, whose ear hurts.'

Dr Greene's eyes narrowed slightly. 'Why didn't you bring Anna?'

I widened my own eyes innocently. 'Was I supposed to?'

Dr Greene covered his face.

This was mortifying. I'd have to change surgeries. Except that I really didn't want to go to the other practice in town. I used to go to school with the receptionist and she was such a gossip that, once she'd read up on my history, it'd be common knowledge in no time that I'd once had to have a tampon surgically removed. At least Dr Greene hadn't been involved with that.

I cleared my throat. 'Should I make another appointment and come back with Anna?'

'That'd be helpful,' Dr Greene said tightly. I admired his professionalism in not telling me to fuck off. 'Wasted appointments cost the NHS money. Feel free to see another doctor if you'd like a second opinion.' He turned to his computer and typed something in. I couldn't see the screen, but I could see the keyboard and was sure he hit the F key more than was necessary.

Chapter 3

'I must have seemed such an idiot,' I told Brigitte later that day. Her beauty therapy centre was adjacent to my studio. This made it cost-effective, as we shared the rent on the property, housed above a shop. More importantly, it meant we could nip in and out of each other's rooms to chat in between clients.

'Should have let him do his job, then,' Brigitte said. 'You've only yourself to blame.'

My stomach plummeted at the suggestion. 'I'd rather he thinks I'm a twat than let him see mine. It would have been mortifying.'

'If he's that good-looking, I'd let him give me a smear.' Brigitte fiddled with the button on her salon uniform, seemingly in readiness for her imaginary appointment.

'You've got Sanjay!' I said. 'If you look up the dictionary definition of good-looking, Sanjay is top of the list. It's no wonder you two are always at it.'

'Not at the moment, we're not.' Brigitte pursed her full lips, an act that would make most men, and no doubt countless women too, weak at the knees. 'Sundeep and Ammo stayed last night. Pooja told them not to speak rudely to me, so they didn't speak at all. Not a single fucking word.'

Pooja was Sanjay's ex-wife. Their break-up had been amicable – they'd married too young – and now raised their teenage children, Sundeep and Ammo, jointly. Pooja was lovely, and she and Brigitte got on brilliantly. The situation would be ideal, except that Brigitte had never wanted children, and Sundeep and Ammo didn't want her.

I searched for a positive spin. 'Isn't that good? Everything they say annoys you.'

'It was actually quite creepy. Asking someone a question and them acting as though you're not there. I felt like Bruce Willis in *The Sixth Sense*.' Brigitte tossed her dark hair over one shoulder, something I'm sure Bruce Willis wished he could do. 'Sanjay keeps saying he'll tell them off, but doesn't want to spoil the time he has with them, so they get away with murder.' Brigitte tutted. 'He needs to man up and give them a good talking-to. They can't stay at ours every week and behave like that.'

'He can't get any more manly,' I protested. 'He makes Dwayne Johnson look effeminate.' Sanjay was a firefighter, and was broad, tall and ruggedly handsome, with jet-black hair and a neatly cropped beard. It took all my self-control not to reach out and stroke him whenever I saw him.

'Looks can be deceptive,' Brigitte said grimly. 'I love that he's a gentle giant, but he's got to toughen up with them. If I'd wanted to be taken for granted and treated like a doormat, I'd have had my own kids. I chose not to for a reason.'

She pulled her long, dark hair back into a tousled ponytail. Like her mum, my aunt Francine, she was effortlessly stunning. Well, semi-effortlessly. She had permanent eyeliner, tinted eyebrows and lash extensions. Consequently, she didn't have to make much of an effort each day, but there had been behind-the-scenes effort carried out at some point. She'd have looked stunning anyway. The treatments she had just enhanced her natural beauty. She'd even inherited our mums' classic French physique – petite frame, prevented from looking scrawny by softly rounded hips and a cracking pair of knockers. Sadly, I'd inherited my dad's genes. Not the Adam's apple or ball sack, thankfully, but broad shoulders, with an athletic frame. My dad had been a runner in his younger years. Possibly in an attempt to get away from my mum.

Despite the differing physiques, people often commented on how similar Brigitte and I looked. We were as close as sisters, biologically as well as emotionally, due to the fact that both our mothers and our fathers were identical twins.

The French sisters had come to England for the summer back in the early 1980s and had romances with my dad and Uncle Rod. Maman and Francine didn't realise till they were back in France that they were knocked up. They phoned my dad and Rod, and explained the situation. A few days later, Dad and Rod turned up at their house, whisked them back to Blighty, married them and set up home in neighbouring streets. They gave birth to beautiful (I liked to think, although Maman had never specified) baby girls a few days apart. It was a really romantic story.

Well, it would have been if Maman and Francine hadn't quickly realised that security and level-headedness bored them, while my dad and Rod discovered that passion and wild abandonment were all very well for a one-off fling, but were a totally different kettle of fish for a lifelong commitment. The fact that my dad and uncle used the phrase 'different kettle of fish' should have been a clue. They stuck it out for a while to give me and Brigitte the illusion we were part of stable families, but admitted defeat and divorced when we were both eight. They even did that in unison. The marriages were, according to our English grandparents, a flash in the pan. Or, as Maman said, a flash in the pants. Despite living in the UK for forty years, she still hadn't completely grasped English phrases.

The sisters never remarried, but both brothers did, launching Brigitte and me into blended families with stepmothers and step-siblings and half-siblings. Our mums were bitter and resentful, and our dads got absorbed into their new families. Brigitte and I saw them less and less, until they barely featured in our lives. We vowed we'd never get involved with anyone with any baggage. Which is why it was so ironic that we were both now second wives, with exes and stepchildren of our own to deal with. Quite frankly, it was pants. Without any flashes in them to increase their appeal.

'I know you're desperate to meet your step-kids,' Brigitte

said. 'But at least you don't have to put up with them hating you because you're married to their dad.'

Would they automatically hate me? If they did, that'd be heartbreaking, particularly after waiting so long to establish a relationship. I shook myself. I'd worry about that later. They had to meet me first. Which reminded me: I needed to speak to Brigitte about my Find Liz plan.

'I've got something to tell you,' I said.

Brigitte smiled. 'And I've got to come up with a new makeup look for my Insta grid. Can I practise on you while we talk?'

'What kind of look?' I asked, remembering the time she'd got over-enthusiastic with the glitter. It had looked as though I'd fallen into the craft table at Anna's nursery. 'A new client's coming in twenty minutes. Don't want to scare her off.'

'Don't worry, I'll be subtle.' Brigitte forced me to sit back and patted primer onto my eyelids. 'What do you need to tell me? Does it concern the hot doctor?'

'No! And he's not *that* hot.' I rubbed my nose.

Brigitte swept powder across my eyelids. 'Bullshit.'

I ignored her and steered the conversation back on track. 'Scott had to cancel our date last night to help out with Harry and Bella.'

Brigitte jabbed the brush into my eye socket. 'Again? Liz does this every time.'

'I know! Maman said the same and you're both right. This can't go on any longer.' My stomach tightened. 'That's what I need to tell you – I'm going to meet Liz.'

'Scott's convinced her at last? Thank God.'

I winced. 'Not exactly. I'm going to have to engineer a meeting.'

Brigitte gasped. 'Covertly? Like in a secret-mission way?' I could tell she was already planning what colour PVC catsuit to wear.

I rolled my eyes, but as they were closed, it had very little impact. 'No, nothing sneaky.' I could sense her disappointment. 'OK, maybe a bit sneaky,' I admitted. 'Scott mustn't know. He's stressed enough as it is. He's even asked me to stop talking about it because home is the one place where he can escape her.' I realised Brigitte had paused, so opened my eyes. 'When I "bump into Liz",' I used air quotes, 'I'll pretend we got chatting, not knowing who the other person was. By the time we "realise",' more air quotes, 'she'll have seen for herself how normal and non-threatening I am. She'll drop her defences, and we'll all get along and live happily ever after.' I smiled triumphantly.

Brigitte sounded unconvinced. 'How are you going to bump into her?'

My triumphant smile wavered. 'Not sure yet.'

Brigitte thought for a moment. 'We could tail Scott next time he goes round.'

I shook my head. 'Too risky.'

Brigitte instructed me to look up as she applied liner to my lower lashes. 'How are you going to find her, then?'

'Google.'

Brigitte arched one eyebrow, a skill I was very jealous of. Why couldn't our near-identical genes have shared that talent rather than deciding to make it a Brigitte exclusive and granting me the ability to wiggle my ears, a party trick that lost its cool factor after the age of ten.

'We googled her the day you and Scott got together,' she said. 'There were about eight zillion women called Liz Bradford.'

'Liz Clark,' I corrected. 'He changed his name after they split up.'

Brigitte nodded thoughtfully. 'Why was that again?'

'He didn't want any link to his dad. He hated him for cheating on his mum. Then Liz cheated on him. The name was tainted, so he changed it.' I sat poker-still as she came at me with a mascara wand. 'Kind of like we did. Using our mums' surname rather than our dads'.'

Brigitte snorted. 'Let's not romanticise it. We'd love to

distance ourselves from our mums, but Dubois is far cooler than our dads' surname.'

She was right.

'Anyway,' she said, dabbing gloss onto my lips. 'There were eight million of whoever we googled.'

'Yes, but that was in the whole world.' I massaged my lips together. 'We didn't look into her properly, because we assumed I'd be meeting her soon. This time I'll narrow my search to Guildford.'

'You need to refine it more than that. Tailor it to her job or her interests. Or find her on social media through someone she and Scott have a connection with.'

'Scott's not on social media,' I said. 'Doesn't want clients he shows around homes snooping into his private life.' Brigitte shuddered. Social media was her life. 'I'll try and find out more about her,' I continued. 'Discreetly, of course.'

'It'd be quicker to tail Scott,' Brigitte said.

She was probably right, but I felt bad enough engineering this meeting behind Scott's back, without adding stalking to the mix. I sighed and pressed my fingertips into my eye sockets.

'Stop – you're ruining your makeup.' Brigitte grabbed a bottle and, without warning, spritzed me with setting spray. I sneezed and she passed me a tissue so I could blow my nose. It was a good job Scott wasn't there. He had a phobia of nose-blowing and retched whenever anyone used a tissue. I'd caught him googling hazmat suits the time Anna and I had both had colds. I admit, the phlegm dribbling down Anna's chin was grim. Even Maman hadn't been able to stomach it – and she ate snails.

When I'd sorted myself out, I posed reluctantly for a photo, then peeked in the mirror. Brigitte had smudged charcoal liner around my eyes, which, with a peach shadow, made my grey irises stand out against my dark hair. I had to admit, she'd done a good job.

'I love it. Thank you.' I licked my lips, then froze. 'Shit. This gloss hasn't got sugar in it, has it?'

She slapped my shoulder lightly. 'Stop worrying about sugar and start worrying about what you're going to say to Liz when you find her.'

'I'm not worried,' I said. No need to rub my nose, because I wasn't lying. I genuinely wasn't worried. I was bloody petrified.

Chapter 4

'Hi, I'm home.'

Anna and I exchanged a look of surprise. Scott was rarely home before her bedtime. For once, they could have a father-and-daughter bonding experience over her bath and story, then Scott and I could watch a few episodes of *Game of Thrones*. We were massively behind – the show had finished ages ago and we were still only on series four – because by the time Scott got home, we were usually too tired to focus for an entire hour on a programme, even one as compelling as *Thrones*. By compelling, I meant violent and rude. Neither of which was usually my thing, but the story was great fun and the nudity had toned down since the show started. The first series was almost pornographic in places. I'm not a prude, but I felt very uncomfortable watching it, not least because it was Maman who'd recommended it.

Scott picked Anna up and tweaked my plait. 'You look nice.'

I chose not to mention that Brigitte had given me a makeover. Much better that Scott thought I was naturally attractive.

'You're in time for Anna's bath,' I said.

'Daddy can do it.' Anna pushed me away. 'Don't want you.' She was punishing me for cooking a nutritious dinner that would help her grow into a healthy, strong adult rather than giving in to her tantrum and getting a McDonald's. I was such a bitch.

Scott grimaced and my heart sunk.

'Go on . . .' I forced a smile while fighting the urge to shout: *remember us? We're your family too!*

24

He tipped Anna upside down so she couldn't hear him. 'Harry's struggling with his maths homework and has asked me to help,' he whispered.

'He's only eight,' I whispered back. 'Surely Liz can help with the more taxing elements of adding and subtracting.'

'Sorry, babe, but I've got to go.' He glanced down to make sure Anna wasn't listening, but she was giggling away. 'You'll understand when Anna's older and gets stuck with her homework.'

'If she does, *I'll* help her.' I couldn't resist adding: 'She can already count to 100 – in French.' Implying that I was a better mother than Liz was a cheap shot, but it was frustrating that Scott didn't seem to realise how much time and effort I put into Anna's development. And by frustrating, I meant fucking annoying.

'Harry and Bella aren't as lucky as Anna.' Scott spun her the right way around and handed her to me. 'They deserve one parent who cares about their education.'

Guilt coursed through me. 'Of course you should help Harry,' I said softly. Then, louder, 'Daddy's got to work. He'll do your bath another time.' Anna responded by blowing a raspberry at Scott and punching me in the boob. She was such a charmer.

After Scott had left, and I'd got through Anna's bath and bedtime, I sat down on the sofa with my laptop. I had a stack of sewing to do, but that would have to wait. Finding Liz was more important. I fought the urge to snack on chocolate buttons while I looked. If I was going to wean myself off my sugar addiction, I needed to get through a month without any sugar. So far, I'd managed forty-five minutes. Absentmindedly licking the lid of Anna's yoghurt pot hadn't helped.

I entered Liz Clark into Google and twenty-seven million results came up. Not quite up there with Brigitte's estimate of eight zillion, but it may as well have been. I narrowed the search to Liz Clarks in Guildford, hoping I was remembering correctly which town she lived in. She'd moved twice in the four years Scott and I had been together, and it was hard to keep track. It was probably yet another excuse to have Scott around, while he found her a new house – which he was paying for, of course. My revised search did indeed limit the number of Liz Clarks found. To three million. I wasn't sure how long Harry's homework would take, but even if he had to crack Einstein's theory of relativity, it wouldn't allow enough time to trawl through all of those.

I scanned through pages and pages. There were loads on LinkedIn, but I discarded those, as Liz was a full-time mum. I didn't judge her for that. I fully respected women who chose to focus on their children while they were little. It was different for me because I had my own business, which I absolutely loved and wanted to keep going. Besides, there was a shitload of other stuff for me to judge her on.

Many Liz Clarks had Facebook pages, but a photo of a pet or a flower seemed to be the preferred profile pic. None of the actual Liz Clark photos matched what I believed Scott's ex would look like. For one thing, they were smiling. I'd once asked Scott what Liz looked like. After he'd stopped grimacing, he'd disclosed that her only similarity to me was our dark hair. That wasn't enough info to pick her out in a line-up, let alone a multi-million list of websites. I scrolled through the Liz Clark pages on Google, passing chefs, cake makers, barristers, NHS workers, dermatologists, a window cleaner – even a Liz Clark sailing around the world with her cat. We didn't need any other people in the world. There were enough Liz Clarks to keep us fed, healthy, crime- and wrinkle-free, and provide a plentiful stream of cat memes. Could Marie Duboises have the same impact? How many of us were there?

Abandoning my futile search for Liz Clark, I entered my own name into Google. There were significantly fewer of us. A French (unsurprisingly) actress from the 1960s dominated most searches, but there were also a smattering of artists and models. We might not keep the world turning, but we at least made it look nice.

'Hi.'

Scott's voice made me jump and I slammed my laptop shut. 'You're home early.'

Scott flopped down next to me. 'It's gone ten.'

'Is it?' I'd disappeared down a rabbit hole of Liz Clarks and the evening had whizzed by. I really needed more info to have any hope of tracking her down. 'Harry's homework go OK?'

'Yes, thanks.' Scott picked the remote control up.

'Is it Guildford they live in now?' I asked, as casually as I could. 'Brigitte asked and I wasn't 100 per cent.'

'Yep,' he said, switching the TV on. 'Are you going to bed?'

I hid a yawn. I was tired, but needed to find out more about Liz. 'I could stay up a bit longer. Fancy a *Game of Thrones?*'

'Why not?' As he searched for the next episode, I searched my mind for a subtle way to extract information about Liz, without arousing his suspicion. I opened and closed my mouth a few times, unable to think of a single question that wouldn't sound like a bungled interrogation. Scott scrolled past *The Wire*, one of my favourites of all time, thanks to Idris Elba's role as Stringer Bell. My encounter with Dr Greene flashed up and I felt my cheeks flush. I'd have to be at death's door to ever ask for an appointment with him again. In fact, the encounter had been so mortifying that death was more appealing. I forced myself to stop thinking about Dr Greene and get back to my investigation.

'You watched *The Wire* when it came out, didn't you?' I asked.

Scott laughed. 'Bet I know why you want to watch it again.'

'I don't want to watch it again,' I said, truthfully. There was no need now that I could watch Idris as the leading man in other dramas, rather than having to wait for his co-stars to have their turn. 'I was just wondering if you used to, er, watch things at home together, like we do.'

'What do you mean?'

I fiddled with my plait. 'It just occurred to me that this is how we spend our evenings, and I wondered if you and Liz used to do the same or if you had separate hobbies.'

Scott frowned. 'Why? We've been together for four years and you've never asked before.'

'Don't know, really.' I laughed self-consciously. 'Because you were round there, I suppose. Curious to know if she sits with you and the kids or is off doing her own thing.'

Scott scoffed. 'She never sits with us. Never sat with me back then, either. Too busy with her career and her clubs to be a mum and wife.'

I tried to conceal my surprise. 'I thought she didn't work,' I said, recalling the numerous times Scott had complained about her demands for extra money, when she wasn't contributing herself.

'She did back then. Arranged parties and mothers' meetings. That kind of thing.'

I ignored the sexist reference. I needed to stay on track, not detour into a conversation (or lecture) about gender equality. 'What were the clubs?'

'What weren't they?' Scott tutted. 'Yoga. Some sort of dance. Book club. Any excuse to get out of looking after the kids.'

'I didn't know she was so active.' My impression of Liz had altered dramatically from a slovenly siren to a supple, twinkled-toed, literary hostess. I'd never felt threatened by her before, not seriously, but now she sounded like quite a formidable woman. 'And she stopped doing all of that? Doesn't she miss it?'

Scott rubbed his jaw. 'Funny you should say that. She told me tonight that she wants to go back to work and her clubs, so I'll need to babysit more.'

'More?' I gasped. 'If you do more, we'll never see you.'

'Don't worry. I told her I couldn't.' Scott patted my knee.

I fumed silently for a moment, then realised that, actually, this could be the answer. 'If she's going to be out a lot of the time, she'll have to let the kids come here.' I grinned. 'It's the logical solution.'

Scott gave a little laugh. 'You're forgetting that there's nothing logical about Liz. But you're right – it could be our way in. Once she's found a job and settled into it, I'll talk to her.' He put his arm out, encouraging me to snuggle into him. 'Enough about her. Let's watch this.'

He pressed play and I rested my head on his chest, holding in my frustration. Every time I thought we were getting somewhere, I got knocked back. It could take months for Liz to find a job, then months for her to settle into it, all of which ate into my remaining baby-making time. I couldn't wait that long. I had to find her. But how? It wasn't physically possible to accidentally-on-purpose bump into three million Liz Clarks and enquire if they had two children named Harry and Bella, then either woo them or hotfoot it onto the next one. I'd have to close my business and put Anna up for adoption to fit it in. My head throbbed with the enormity of it and I forced myself to focus on the TV to relieve the pressure. A few scenes later, Jon Snow was injured and required to remove his shirt, which helped to reduce the forcefulness of my focus. Liz who?!

Forty-five minutes later, the episode finished, and the essential-to-the-plot violence and nudity had left me feeling a little hot under the collar (by collar, I meant crotch).

I gazed up at Scott. 'Want to go to bed?'

Scott ran a hand across his eyes. 'Sorry, babe, I can't. Too tired.'

'To sleep, I mean. Don't worry, I'm not going to pounce on you,' I said lightly, as though the prospect hadn't crossed my mind.

Scott hauled himself up and we crept upstairs so as not to disturb Anna. She could sleep through a fire alarm (as proved when I once closed the grill door on a shepherd's pie and the glass dish had exploded, sending plumes of smoke wafting through the house), but step on a creaky floorboard and she was as alert as if someone had thrown cold water over her. Scott hurriedly cleaned his teeth, pulled off his clothes, tumbled into bed and was instantly asleep. As I changed into my PJs, I noticed that my leggings had left an unflattering elasticated print around my midriff and ankles. Perhaps my mum had a point about them.

Scott's phone beeped from somewhere on the floor. I found it in his jeans pocket and turned it to silent. As I did, a message flashed up on the screen.

Why R U with her? U should be with me, it read. My stomach lurched. It wasn't the first of Liz's texts I'd seen, but they always unsettled me.

I looked down at Scott, full of sympathy for the stress he had to put up with just so he could see his children, which he had a legal right to do anyway. He looked so peaceful and handsome with his thick, sandy hair and chiselled jaw. Why Liz had cheated on him was a mystery. I placed his phone on the bedside table.

He sat bolt upright and grabbed my arm. 'What are you doing?'

I squealed. 'Your phone beeped. I just turned it to silent.'

Scott released my arm and flopped back on the pillows. 'Sorry, babe.' He rubbed his eyes. 'Was having a weird dream and you made me jump.'

'It's OK.' I sat down and put my hand on his chest. His heart hammered fast beneath it. 'Liz sent another of her charming messages.'

Scott snatched the phone up. His jaw clenched as he read it. 'That's not on.' He put the phone in his bedside drawer. 'I'll talk to her again.'

'Thanks.' I took the chest-stroking up a notch. Scott seemed quite awake now and, thanks to a combination of Jon Snow's topless antics and not having had sex for a couple of weeks, I was, to coin a phrase, well up for it.

I ran my fingers down his torso to beneath the duvet and leant in for a kiss. Our lips met and a warmth swirled around my stomach, before plunging between my legs. My fingers crept downwards, brushing over Scott's pubic hair. He pulled sharply away and I toppled forward into the headboard.

'Sorry,' he said. 'We're out of condoms.'

'Oh.' I straightened up, panting slightly.

He gave me an apologetic smile. 'I'll get some more tomorrow.'

'You don't have to,' I whispered. 'We can't keep waiting for Liz to turn into a normal human being or it'll never happen.' I reached down again.

Scott took my hand out from under the duvet and placed it firmly on top of the covers. 'Let her get this job first. Then I'll speak to her, set some boundaries, and we can focus on us.'

I nodded, reluctantly, and clambered over to my side of the bed.

Scott kissed the tip of my nose, snuggled down under the duvet and fell asleep. I sighed, trying to ignore my disappointment. The phone in Scott's bedside-table drawer vibrated. I tried to ignore that too, but couldn't. Annoyed with myself for caring what the message said, I crept out of bed and carefully slid the drawer open, only to read a reminder for Scott about a meeting the following morning. Relieved, I put the phone back in the drawer and was about to close it, when I noticed something. It was a packet of condoms.

Chapter 5

'Why are you messing around with condoms?' Brigitte asked. 'Just go on the pill or get the injection, like me.'

I gave her a sideways look as I pinned a bodice onto my tailor's dummy. 'Have you met Anna?'

Brigitte slapped her forehead and her long, dark ponytail swished with the exuberance of a prize-winning show pony. 'Course. Sorry.'

Scott and I had only been together eight months when I fell pregnant, despite being on the pill. I took it every morning with my breakfast and had not missed a single one. Forgetting to take it wasn't possible, as I never *ever* forgot my breakfast. Scott and I were massively freaked out and I almost got a termination, before we decided that we should just go for it, especially as I was thirty-six at the time and, in my mum's words, *un certain âge*. That is, getting on a bit. Of course, we were extremely glad we had, because Anna was gorgeous. Demanding, rude and knackering, but gorgeous. All she was missing was a little brother or sister, but hopefully she'd have one in the not-too-distant future, before I was past *un certain âge*.

I sighed. 'Not having sex is the most effective contraception. Maybe he wasn't in the mood, so pretended we'd run out.' I jabbed a pin into the dummy. 'But why wasn't he in the mood? Do you think he's gone off me?'

'Don't be silly,' Brigitte said. 'He'll have forgotten they were there. You'll be back at it again soon. Not sure when Sanjay and I will.'

'Is he making excuses too?' I was astounded. I'd seen Brigitte in her underwear, and just one flash of those bazoomas should have Sanjay not only thanking his lucky stars, but donating his entire salary to NASA and doing voluntary work at the nearest planetarium.

Brigitte shook her head and said bazoomas quivered. 'Pooja's away with work, so the kids are staying all week. No chance of any hanky-panky with them around.' She fiddled with a scrap of lace on my desk. 'I know the kids didn't want us to get married, but I thought they'd have accepted it by now. I didn't expect them to still resent me eight years later.' She pulled a face. 'How did we both end up dealing with stepchildren and exes, when we swore we wouldn't?'

I pinned the skirt of the gown I was working on to the bodice. 'We weren't to know it would be so challenging.'

'You've got a short memory,' Brigitte said. 'Our mums wouldn't let our dads come to the door when they picked us up and dropped us off. They had to wait at the bottom of the path for at least ten minutes. Longer, if it was raining. Don't you remember your dad was almost arrested for loitering once?'

I grimaced. 'Mmm. That was bad, wasn't it?'

Brigitte snorted. 'Yes, it was bad. Especially as it was your mum who called the police.'

She had a point. Definitely should have thought it through more.

I stood back to check how the dress looked. Brigitte clapped her hands. 'It's beautiful. You should put a pic on your Insta page.'

'Posting a photo of the groom's dick would be less controversial,' I said. 'The Big Reveal is the most important part of the bride's wedding day.'

Brigitte looked at me questioningly. 'I thought committing to one another for the rest of their lives was the most important part.'

We burst out laughing. It was *so* about the dress.

'Speaking of Insta . . .' Brigitte took her phone from her pocket. I stepped protectively in front of the dress and she held her hands up. 'Don't worry, I won't take a photo. No, I was thinking, social media's got to be the best way to find Liz.'

'How, when I don't know what she looks like?'

'Finding a mutual connection through Scott's the obvious way. I know he doesn't do social media, but he must be on LinkedIn. If Liz is job-hunting, she will be too.' She opened an app on her phone, typed Scott's name in and scrolled for a few moments. 'How can he not have a LinkedIn account?' She couldn't have looked more appalled if she'd just discovered he didn't know how to read.

'Don't ask me,' I said. 'I'm still disappointed that Threads isn't a dressmaking network.'

Brigitte rolled her eyes at me. 'I'll have to find Liz through her employment history. Do you know which companies she's worked for?'

'No, only that she used to do party planning and wants to get back into it. Is that enough?'

'It's a start,' Brigitte said. 'I'll look up job ads for that sector in Guildford.'

I fiddled with my plait. 'How will that help? I can't hang outside and accost everyone who goes for an interview.'

Brigitte raised an eyebrow. 'You're not usually this negative.'

'Sorry.' I sighed. 'Just feeling a bit frustrated.'

'Should have had that smear test.' Brigitte grinned. 'That would have sorted you out.'

The bell at the foot of the stairs leading up to her salon and my studio chimed, signalling the arrival of someone. I was dressing it up when I said 'studio'. Really, it was just a small collection of rooms. One good-size room that I worked in, one tiny waiting room, an even tinier kitchen and a miniscule loo that didn't have a window. Off-site poos only, when working at the studio. I'd had to ban Brigitte from sneaking in and going, so as not to sully her own toilet. Even if she did bring her fruits-of-the-forest air freshener.

'That'll be Beth,' I said.

'I'll go and continue my investigations next door.' Brigitte headed to her studio, pausing to greet Beth on the stairs. 'Marie let me have a sneak peek and your dress looks amazing.'

Beth let out an excited squeal and practically ran inside, followed by her daughter, Izzy, who was quite possibly the most beautiful five-year-old ever. She had her mum's dark skin, but fair Afro hair and blue eyes, presumably inherited from her dad. Beth also had a son, Henry, who was dressing as Superman for the wedding. My needlework services weren't required for his outfit.

This was Beth's second marriage, and apparently her first one – and the wedding day itself – was so disappointing that she was making up for it with a spectacular dress, with reams of tulle and lace. Not only was such an elaborate dress a dream for me to make, but Beth was a dream client, enjoying the build-up without being a bridezilla.

I'd thrown a sheet of muslin over the mannequin and now carefully lifted it off to reveal the dress. Beth gasped. 'I love it!' She clasped her hands together. 'It's perfect. Thank you.'

I smiled broadly. My chosen career might not make me a contender for a Nobel, but it made a handful of people very happy, and that was good enough for me.

'Do you like it, Izzy?'

Izzy nodded and gave a gappy grin. The loss of some of her teeth made her look even more adorable, unlike some kids who made the Gruffalo look like child-model material.

I started unpinning the bodice. 'Try it on and see how it feels. I won't put the zip in till nearer the wedding, to make sure it's a perfect fit.'

Beth hesitated then shook her head. 'I can't. Got to get back to the office for a meeting. Did I tell you about the holiday park I'm doing the PR for? It opens in a few weeks and the sales team are blaming their lack of bookings on me. I've got to go and justify what I've been doing. Believe me, I'd much rather stay here.'

Kneeling down, she hugged Izzy. 'Uncle Michael will be here soon. He'll bring you home after you've tried on your bridesmaid's dress.' She turned to me. 'Is that OK? I didn't want Izzy to miss her fitting. My brother will stay out of your way.'

'Of course.' I wiggled my ears at Izzy and she giggled. Not as cool as raising one eyebrow, but not an entirely wasted skill.

The bell on the door downstairs chimed.

'That's probably him now,' Beth said.

We heard Brigitte come out of her treatment room. 'Hello,' she called down the stairs in a breathless tone that even someone who was completely deaf would be able to decipher as sultry. Clearly, Uncle Michael was ticking a few boxes for Brigitte. A deep voice murmured something I couldn't hear.

'Come on up,' Brigitte said. 'She's through here.' I could picture exactly how she must look: framed in the stairwell, her long legs drawing the eyes up to her curves, her fingers toying with the end of her ponytail. Uncle Michael was probably feeling a ticking in his own box. 'I could give you a treatment while you're waiting, if you like?' she said. 'A mini facial or head massage maybe?' I hoped whoever she was talking to could see her wedding ring, otherwise they'd be forgiven for misinterpreting the meaning of head massage.

'No, thank you. Got a couple of calls to make.' The voice grew more distinct as it came up the stairs. It was deep and smooth, and vaguely familiar.

'I'll be in my salon if you change your mind.' Brigitte's heels clicked away. Always leave them wanting more was her motto. It didn't go down well when she was doing her tax return.

Izzy ran to the door. 'Uncle Michael!' A pair of hands scooped her up and she giggled. 'Come and see Mummy's dress.'

'No!' Beth said. 'I want it to be a surprise.' She ushered Uncle Michael into the tiny space that was my pathetic excuse of a waiting room before I even saw him. 'Do you mind covering it up again?' she asked, coming back in.

'Course not.' I put the muslin back over Beth's gown and took Izzy's from the rail. Beth's mouth dropped open when she saw the jewel-green dress. Made of satin, it was high-waisted, sleeveless and ankle-length. It was a joy to work with such a vibrant colour; I couldn't understand why most people dressed flower girls in white, when surely one of the perks of being five was wearing bright colours. The only adults that got to dress so boldly were children's TV presenters. And my mother.

'It's gorgeous.' Beth smiled, then looked at her watch and groaned. 'Can't believe I've got to go. I've asked Michael to take a photo of her in it for me.' She gave Izzy a big hug. 'Be good. I won't be home late. Thanks, Marie. See you soon.'

Izzy looked at the dress in my hands. 'Is that for me?' she asked shyly.

I nodded and her arms shot up in the air. 'Yes!' she squealed.

'Let me ask your uncle if he wants a drink, then you can try it on.'

Izzy started pulling her clothes off and was down to her pants by the time I reached the door. Maman would be proud.

'Hi,' I called out, taking the two steps it took to cross the landing separating my studio from the waiting room. 'I'm Marie. Can I get you a . . . ?' I tailed off when I saw Uncle Michael. My stomach lurched.

Uncle Michael was Dr Greene.

I stared at him, two thoughts racing around my mind. Firstly, thank fuck the smear test hadn't happened – the mortification would have been too much to bear. Secondly, he was even more handsome than I'd remembered: very Stringer Bell in *The Wire*. No wonder Brigitte had been drooling.

'Hello,' I said nervously. For some unknown reason I had to stop myself from curtseying, as though his being a doctor gave him some sort of royal status. 'I didn't realise you were Uncle Michael.'

Uncle Michael, or Dr Greene, looked at me quizzically. 'No reason you would,' he said.

'No.' I stood there, feeling foolish. 'Not really the thing you announce when meeting a new patient.'

He frowned, then recognition dawned. 'Of course. We met at the practice.' His frown deepened, no doubt as he remembered my ridiculous behaviour. 'How's your daughter?'

'Fine,' I said. 'Why?'

He looked confused. 'She had earache. Did you take her to another GP to check it out?'

I considered lying – Neglectful Parent wasn't a label I wanted. But he might ask which GP we saw and what the outcome was.

'It cleared up by itself,' I said. 'So I didn't have to waste anyone's time bringing her in unnecessarily.'

Dr Greene didn't say anything but, judging by the expression on his face, I was pretty sure he was recalling that I'd wasted his time unnecessarily.

'Tea or coffee?' I asked brightly.

'Neither, thanks. I need to make a call, so I'll get on.' He turned his back on me.

I had a feeling we weren't destined to be friends.

Back in my studio, Izzy almost pounced on me. Her excitement was contagious, and I pinned darts in place to get the right fit as we chatted about important matters, such as why there was a singer called Lady Gaga, but not a Man Gaga.

'How does that feel?' I asked Izzy. 'Not too tight or too loose?'

Izzy shook her head. 'It's a bit scratchy.'

'That's the pins. Stay still and I'll get you out.'

'Ouch!' Izzy said loudly.

'Sorry, chick.' I rubbed her arm, where a pin had scratched her.

'What are you doing?' Dr Greene's voice bellowed through the door and I jumped. 'We should sue you.'

Sue me? I examined Izzy's arm. The pin hadn't drawn blood. It was hardly GBH. And how could he see me anyway?

I slid the dress up and over Izzy's head very carefully to avoid another pinprick.

'Don't make it worse,' Dr Greene shouted.

How was he seeing this? I hung the dress up while Izzy pulled her leggings and T-shirt on, then opened the door nervously, expecting to see Dr Greene looming in the doorway, waiting to give me a bollocking for puncturing his niece. Or take a leaf out of Stringer Bell's book and do something with slightly more impact. Such as killing me.

Dr Greene wasn't standing there, though. Instead, he was pacing up and down the waiting room like a caged animal. Given the room's tiny proportions, he could only pace a couple of steps before having to turn. His jaw was clenched and his phone was pressed to his ear. I breathed a sigh of relief as I realised that it wasn't me he'd been shouting at.

'Enough of these excuses,' he snapped, turning sharply as he reached the sofa. 'I'm done with it.' Pivot. 'If I don't get a satisfactory outcome,' turn, 'I'll come down there,' swivel – I was starting to fear for the life expectancy of my carpet – 'and deal with you personally.'

Dr Greene was a bit scary. What had the person he was speaking to done? Set fire to his house? Broken his heart? Forgotten to pick up his dry cleaning? He spun on his heel as he reached the sofa again. I backed away towards my door but the movement must have caught his attention, because he looked across and met my eyes. For a moment we stared at each other. I tried to assume a nonchalant expression but had no idea what a nonchalant expression looked like, so chewed on my lip instead. Dr Greene's eyes narrowed and he stopped pacing – probably thankful for the excuse, before he became dizzy.

'Do you mind?' he snapped, gesturing to his phone, and, for the second time, turned his back on me.

I inhaled sharply. How rude. Stringer Bell may have been a

sadistic, ruthless murderer, but he had manners. I relabelled Dr Greene in my mind. Stringer Bell was out. Bell-end was in.

I strode back into my studio – as much as one can stride two steps – and shut the door firmly. Izzy was twirling a ream of red ribbon like a rhythmic gymnast, oblivious to the fact her uncle Michael was a complete tosser. I smiled and made appropriate oohing and aahing sounds as she danced, while inwardly fuming. How dare he talk to me with so little respect? Or make such a scene? What if Brigitte had a client with her? It was unlikely her zen track of Tibetan chimes would create a sense of calm, with him going off on one outside.

'Do you mind?' I muttered, shaking my head. What a pompous, arrogant, bell-end kind of thing to say.

The door to my studio swung open.

'Uncle Michael.' Izzy grinned and whirled a blue ribbon at him.

Dr Bell-end took a deep breath and smiled at her. 'Ready to go?' He didn't even acknowledge me.

'Nearly,' Izzy said. 'Just need to do a dance with the yellow ribbon.'

His smile tightened, but he nodded and leant back against the doorframe, studiously not looking at me. His rudeness was shocking. And he was a doctor – responsible for the wellbeing of vulnerable people, who were too weak to stand up for themselves. Well, I wasn't weak, and I could stand up for myself.

'Yes, I do mind,' I said quietly, so Izzy couldn't hear.

He frowned and crossed his arms. 'Sorry?'

'You said, "Do you mind?" just now, in the waiting room.' I crossed my arms, realised I was mirroring him and dropped them to my sides. 'Yes, I do mind. If you want to have an argument with someone, do it in private, not here. I wouldn't behave like that at your place of work.' My arms hung awkwardly by my sides. I cursed Dr Greene for crossing his, so I couldn't.

'You shouldn't have been eavesdropping.'

'I wasn't.' My arms twitched. 'You were being very loud, right outside my door.'

Dr Greene uncrossed his arms. Relieved, I crossed my own. He tucked his hands into his pockets. Frustratingly, I now longed to thrust my hands into the pockets of my dress. Why did he keep taking all the good positions? Selfish sod.

'You're not setting Izzy a good example of how to communicate with people,' I added.

'And you are, right now?'

'Don't try and turn the tables,' I snapped. 'You're the one acting like a self-righteous—'

'Prick,' Izzy said loudly – and very astutely. 'Marie pricked me with a pin,' she continued.

How did I ever think she was cute?

Dr Greene frowned.

'It was an accident,' I said quickly. 'It didn't bleed. I don't think your esteemed medical intervention's needed.' My hands found their way into my pockets. My damn, duplicitous body seemed intent on mirroring his. 'It was your fault anyway. Your shouting distracted me.'

He opened his mouth as though to say something, then turned to Izzy. 'I think it's time to go.' She nodded and followed him to the top of the stairs, waving as she went.

I smiled – at Izzy, not her uncle – turned on my heel and went back into my studio. The bright green bridesmaid's dress hung on the clothing rail. He'd forgotten to take a photo of Izzy in it. What a bell-end.

Izzy had been my last client of the day so I packed up and said goodbye to Brigitte, who had back-to-back clients for the next three hours, before she could go home.

'I don't mind,' she said when I pulled a sympathetic face. 'Sundeep and Ammo are over. I'd rather be here.'

Given that her appointments for the evening included a back, sack and crack wax, and a skin tag removal (not, thankfully, for the same client), she must have been really desperate to avoid going home.

I ran down the stairs, pulled the door shut behind me and headed towards home. It only took ten minutes and I walked quickly, my head full of ideas for my new client Rebecca, who wanted a 1950s-style gown.

I turned towards the church and craned my neck to see if any 'youths' were hanging around the gravestones. Cutting through the churchyard shaved a few minutes off my journey, but I avoided it if there were gangs of potential muggers in there. I felt guilty, as they probably weren't muggers at all. They were likely perfectly well-mannered young adults who liked the churchyard for its historical architecture and tranquil setting. Fortunately, there weren't any groups seeking solace in the church grounds that evening, so I strode through, playing with variations of Dior's New Look dress in my mind.

As I reached the corner of the church, I glanced over my shoulder to make sure a gang of muggers – sorry, brass-rubbing enthusiasts – weren't loitering, before I ventured down the narrow walkway that came out the other side of the building.

The low branches of a tree near the entrance quivered. I squinted to get a better view and a dark shape shifted behind the trunk.

My stomach tightened, but I was determined not to overreact. It's just a shadow, I told myself. My stomach was having none of my bravado and churned nauseatingly. It's sugar deprivation, I told it. The drop in glucose is causing paranoia. I slowly turned away. As I did, a flash of light came through the trees, as though someone had switched a torch on and off. Or the sunlight was reflecting off someone's glasses.

Fuck. My stomach was right. Someone was there. And whoever it was, didn't want to be seen. Fine by me – I didn't want to see them either.

Pulling my bag close to my chest, I ran, not daring to look back in case I tripped. The muscles in my legs burnt as I pushed myself forward as fast as I could. A crunch of gravel behind me drove me on and I pelted down the walkway, across the stretch of green to the exit and out onto the populated road the other side. Still, I kept running, ignoring the pain in my legs and the bewildered expressions on the faces of the people I passed. I swerved round corners till I reached our road, and only then did I slow down, panting and checking no one was behind me. When I was sure they weren't, I slumped onto the ground by my front door, my legs trembling with exhaustion.

The door swung open and Maman looked down at me.

'What are you doing out here, balancing on your laurels?'

'Resting,' I said shakily. 'Not balancing. Resting.'

'*N'importe quoi.*' Maman flapped her hand at me to come inside. 'Anna's on the toilet and needs wiping.'

I hauled myself up. 'Has it just happened or has she been sat there since you collected her from nursery?'

Maman didn't answer, which told me everything I needed to know. I just hoped Anna hadn't wriggled around too much.

I glanced up the street before closing my front door. No one was there. Of course they weren't. This sugar withdrawal was making me paranoid. I hoped.

Chapter 6

'Hello, Dr Jones,' I purred, slipping into the booth opposite Scott.

The Dr Jones address was a reference to my long-standing love of Harrison Ford in *Indiana Jones*. Admittedly, Harrison was a lot younger when my crush started, but even now, when he was dressed as Indy, I still would.

'Hello, Elsa,' Scott replied and we both cringed. Elsa was the hot German architect Indiana had a fling with in *The Last Crusade*. Our role-play cool rating had plummeted since *Frozen* came out.

'Maybe it's time we came up with new names,' I suggested, picking up the espresso martini waiting for me. 'James Bond and Moneypenny?'

Scott nodded enthusiastically. What man wouldn't want to be likened to the greatest secret agent of all time? Moneypenny had become much more kickass of later years, so I wouldn't mind being her. Especially as she shot Bond once, and there had been a few occasions when I'd wanted to shoot Scott. Not with an actual gun, I didn't want him to die, but when he annoyed me – leaving a puddle by the kitchen sink, even though I'd warned him it would warp the wood, for example – shooting him out of a cannon had a certain appeal.

'Thanks for the drink.' I took a sip. 'Is it decaf?'

'Of course.'

I smiled gratefully and ignored the fact Moneypenny probably wouldn't decaf her espresso martinis. Although she might, if she had a three-year-old who woke up at five every morning.

'How was work?' I asked.

Scott opened his mouth to reply and his phone rang. He glanced at it and I could tell, from the way his jaw tightened, that it was Liz.

He switched it to silent and slipped it in his shirt pocket. 'Don't want her spoiling our night.'

I grinned. A rare night out and an even rarer night of having his full attention. Usually, he was on constant standby, in case Liz called to insist he went round immediately to tend to something urgent, such as rescuing the hamster from behind the sofa, when I hadn't even known they had a hamster.

He started to tell me about work. He'd forgotten we were in character so went into more detail about the latest legislation affecting estate agents than I suspect Bond would have, but I didn't mind. At least we were together. I sipped on my cocktail and admired him as he talked. He was so good-looking. His thick sandy hair showed no sign of thinning, but was starting to grey around his tufty second crown. To be expected now he was mid-forties, as were the faint crow's feet around his blue eyes. Like Harrison, he'd still do it for me when he was eighty. Even though I'd be a sprightly spring chicken in my late seventies. I dismissed the thought. I didn't want to envisage being older than Maman was now.

'How was your mad mum tonight?' Scott asked, somehow guessing that the slight look of terror on my face had something to do with her.

'Fine.' I took another sip of my drink and was gutted to realise it was the last mouthful. Why did cocktails come in such small glasses? A vase would be a much more suitable receptacle. 'Although,' I added, 'she couldn't understand why Anna had eaten and needed to be in bed by 7.30. She'd brought olives and bread and cheese for them to have together.'

'She does know Anna's three?'

I nodded. 'Yes, but *en France . . .*' I didn't need to finish the sentence. Everything Maman did, said, bought and thought was French. She drove a Citroën 2CV, only used French brands and seized every opportunity to tell us how much better things were in France, from their eating habits, and healthcare, to the state of their *vagins*.

During the course of the half hour that Scott and I had been out, his phone had vibrated constantly. He hadn't mentioned it, but I could see it quivering in his shirt pocket. He'd end up with jogger's nipple if it didn't stop soon.

'A weird thing happened when I was walking home,' I said. Although it was ridiculous to think I'd been followed, it'd still be nice to have Scott's reassurance. 'I cut through the churchyard—'

His phone vibrated again.

'I'll put it on flight mode.' Scott took the phone from his pocket.

'Good idea. In the churchyard, it really felt as though . . .' I trailed off. Scott was staring at the screen on his phone, his face completely white. 'What's happened?' I asked.

Scott didn't speak.

'Is it one of the children?'

He stared at me numbly.

'What's happened?' I asked again. 'Is someone hurt?'

'Bella's been sick.' He shook his head. 'I feel terrible. She's been asking for me and I just ignored the messages.' He took my hand. 'I'm so sorry to do this to you, but I've got to go and see her. I can't enjoy the night, knowing she's ill and needs me.'

Disappointment coursed through me. 'Of course.'

Scott stood up and I followed, trying to pretend I didn't mind cutting the evening short.

'You don't have to leave as well,' Scott said.

I felt my ears wiggle. One raised eyebrow would have worked so much better.

'I'm not going to stay on my own, like some lush who's so desperate for a drink she goes out solo.'

'Could Brigitte join you?'

I looked at my cocktail glass longingly. I didn't get out often. Plus, Brigitte did fall into the lush category. She'd be finishing work now and had already told me she didn't want to go home. Nor did I, particularly. Anna was going through a phase of insisting I stayed in the room till she fell asleep. Some nights I'd be convinced she'd gone off, only to have her shout, 'Not yet!' when I tried to creep out. Maman had looked horrified when I explained the routine. 'I will not sit on the floor like a dog,' she'd huffed. 'It's because you put her to bed so early.' If I went back now, I'd be lumbered with the night watch, while Maman hotfooted it home in her neon trainers.

Scott nipped to the gents while I called Brigitte, who didn't hesitate in agreeing to come.

'She's on her way,' I said to Scott when he got back to the table.

He gave me a thumbs up. 'How long will she be?'

'She said fifteen minutes, but I've known her to spend longer than that applying lip liner.'

Scott checked the time on his phone. There must have been another message from Liz, because his jaw tightened.

'Go.' I stood to kiss him goodbye. 'I hope Bella's OK.'

'I don't like leaving you on your own.' Scott looked helplessly around the bar. 'Is there anyone you know who can sit with you till she arrives?'

The door opened and we both looked across. I sat down quickly when I saw who was walking in. Dr flipping Bell-end.

'No, no one I know.' I held the cocktail menu up in front of my face. 'Go. I'll be fine.'

'If you're sure.' Scott leant down to hug me, an action made rather clumsy by the fact I wasn't prepared to put the menu down in case Dr Bell-end saw me. 'I'm so sorry about this, babe.' His voice cracked and I lowered my menu to see a pained expression on his face. 'I'm always letting you down. I don't mean to.'

I put a hand to his face. 'It's not your fault Bella's sick. She needs you.'

Scott pressed his lips to my hand. 'I love you so much,' he whispered.

'I love you too. Now go.'

He swallowed hard and gave me such a look of affection and tenderness that my thighs quivered. It really had been a while.

My phone beeped as he left: *On my way. Line 'em up. B x*

I walked to the bar and waited to be served. Another message from Brigitte appeared on my screen: *Make mine a large stiff one.* A photo immediately followed of what could only be described as a massive cock. I hoped it wasn't Sanjay's.

'What can I get you?' a voice asked.

I jerked my head up so fast, it actually hurt. 'Two decaf espresso martinis, please.' I placed my phone face-down on the bar. 'And a tap water.'

While the mixologist worked her magic, I rested my elbows on the bar and massaged my temples. Bloody sugar-free diet. I'd felt healthier before I started. Now I felt ill or on edge all the time. As though I'd forgotten to do something or had made some sort of mistake that was going to have huge repercussions. Such as presenting a bride with a bone-white gown instead of the ivory she'd requested, or making three bridesmaids' dresses when there should be twelve. I was fastidious in checking details, though – 'measure twice, cut once' was the mantra I lived by – so this was definitely paranoia. As was the ridiculous notion that someone had followed me through the churchyard. As if anyone would.

Someone to my left cleared their throat. 'Hello.'

I turned to see Dr Greene leaning against the bar a few feet from me, a pint of beer in his hand. As if I didn't feel crap enough already.

'Hello,' I said coolly. 'Didn't see you there.'

'Possibly because your head was in your hands,' he said. 'How many have you had?'

'None,' I said indignantly.

'I'll just take your empties,' the bartender said, leaning over and moving mine and Scott's empty glasses before replacing them with two full ones. Dr Greene raised his eyebrows at me. Not cool enough to raise just one, I noted with satisfaction. Not that I could either, but Brigitte was practically an extension of me, which upped my cool rating considerably.

'OK, I've had one.' I tapped the card machine. 'But it was decaf.'

'That doesn't make it non-alcoholic.'

'I know,' I said petulantly. 'But I'm not pissed. Just got a headache.'

'You'll probably have another one tomorrow.' Dr Greene nodded at the two cocktails in front of me.

'One's for my cousin.' Deliberately ignoring the espresso martinis, I took a sip of water to demonstrate how virtuous and self-controlled I was and, hopefully, to help my headache. A thought struck me. 'Can I ask for some medical advice?'

'No,' he said flatly. He was charm personified.

'But you're a doctor.'

'If there's something wrong, go and see a GP at the surgery.' He didn't suggest I saw him, I noted, not that I ever would.

'It's a very quick question,' I said. 'It'd make up for your shouting the other day.'

He picked up his pint glass. 'I didn't shout. I merely pointed out that it would have been easier to diagnose your daughter's ear infection if you'd brought her with you.' He spoke calmly and rationally, which made him sound even more condescending. Especially, as he was right.

'I meant when you shouted on the phone at my place of work. So unprofessional and disrespectful.' No idea why I used the phrase 'place of work' in the manner of a detective interviewing a suspect. Dr Greene had a natural ability to make me act like a bit of a knob.

'Anyway,' I said. 'I'm quitting sugar and keep getting

headaches.' I decided not to mention the paranoid feeling of being followed. His demeanour didn't exactly scream: *share*. 'How long do you think they'll last?'

Dr Greene sighed. 'These fad diets never do anyone any good. An all-round, balanced diet combined with regular exercise—'

'I know, I know.' I didn't need to listen to his TED talk. I ran, did workout routines from YouTube and ate healthy meals, but couldn't shift the thickening around my middle. Possibly because I got through several giant bars of chocolate a week, hence the need to quit sugar. 'But cutting out processed sugar's got to be good, hasn't it?'

He gave a curt nod. It seemed to pain him to agree with me.

'So how long till the headaches stop?'

Dr Greene shrugged. Did he get taught that reassuring gesture in medical school or was it something he came up with himself? 'Two to three weeks, on average.'

I looked at him sceptically. 'Mine have been going on for over a month.'

'Have you cut out sugar completely?'

'Pretty much. The odd bit in Anna's leftovers when I'm not thinking.'

Dr Greene rolled his eyes theatrically. Something else he'd learnt at medical school? 'You can't say: "I didn't mean it, it doesn't count." Every time you eat sugar, you're going back to square one. There's no point doing it if you're not committed.'

I bristled. 'I've switched from Dairy Milk to 85 per cent dark chocolate. That's commitment.'

'What's in the other 15 per cent?'

'Antioxidants,' I said defiantly.

'No. Sugar.' He pointed at the two espresso martinis in front of me. 'What's in there?'

'Coffee. *Decaf* coffee – healthy. And vodka – the purest of the spirits.'

Dr Greene reached over, picked my glass up and took a

sip. My mouth dropped open. How rude, not to mention unhygienic. He was a doctor; he shouldn't be spreading his germs around. Who knew what disease-infested patients he'd tended to that day?

'There's something sugary in there,' he said, oblivious to my aghast expression. 'It'd taste like a bull's scrotum without something to sweeten it.'

I didn't ask how he knew what a bull's scrotum tasted like. Maybe that really was something they learnt at medical school.

'It's Kahlúa,' the bartender said, smiling up at Dr Greene.

I gave Dr Greene a sideways glance. I could understand why the bartender was flirting. He *was* very good looking, but that didn't compensate for his personality, which was, at best, shit.

'It's a coffee liqueur and contains eleven grams of sugar per ounce,' she continued. 'Lot more to mixology than just bunging the ingredients in a glass. There's a science to it.' She finger-combed her blonde fringe. 'I'd be happy to teach you a few things, if you like?' This was not directed at me.

Picking up the glasses, I turned towards my table. 'Thanks for your help,' I muttered under my breath.

'You're welcome,' Dr Greene replied. No need for an ear test for him, then. 'You could always get a second opinion,' he added, as I walked away.

I retreated to my bar stool and was just about to take a much-needed mouthful of my cocktail, when Dr Greene walked over. What now?

'You forgot this.' He held out my phone.

'Thanks,' I said stiffly. The screen lit up as I took it, displaying the dick pic that Brigitte had sent me. Horrified, I slammed my hand over it, but not before Dr Greene had seen. Lips tightly pressed together, he turned and went back to the bar, where the mixologist waited with a smile.

Bollocks.

I slid my hand down and had another quick look. No, no bollocks – just a cock. Did that make it slightly less offensive?

'You still looking at that?'

I jumped as Brigitte sat down opposite me.

'Don't ever send me porn again.' I tried to look disapproving but was too pleased to see her to be cross. 'Thanks for coming.'

'Thanks for asking.' Brigitte sipped her cocktail, leaving a red lipstick mark around the rim of her glass. 'You look nice,' she said, then narrowed her wing-lined, grey eyes. 'Actually, do we more or less look the same?'

I realised we'd both tonged our dark hair into beach waves, and wore heels, skinny jeans and a sleeveless, black top. The only difference was that Brigitte's boobs were spilling over her black silk vest, whereas mine were covered up by my high halterneck. Purely because they didn't have the volume required to spill over anything. If they were the same size as Brigitte's, I'd dress like a Victoria's Secret model.

I laughed. 'Does this mean we're on trend or unimaginative?'

'We look hot. That's always on trend.' She raised her glass, clocked Dr Greene at the bar behind me and whistled. 'Where do I know him from?'

'Beth's brother. He came to the studio. He's a complete bell-end,' I added.

As though sensing he was being talked about, he turned, looked over and did a double take. Looking as similar as we did, it happened often to me and Brigitte. I suspected it happened to her quite often when I wasn't there, too. Brigitte grinned and waved. He gave a tight, awkward smile and turned back to the sugar-expert know-it-all bartender.

'See,' I said. 'Bell-end.'

'I'd forgotten how gorgeous he is.' She sighed theatrically. 'Can't believe you turned down a smear test.'

I cringed at the thought. 'I should start a smear campaign against him. He practically told me off when I asked his advice about giving up sugar.'

Brigitte smiled mischievously. 'Wish he'd tell me off.'

'He took a sip of my drink without asking.' I frowned at my cocktail, wondering which part of the rim to avoid. 'He actually put his lips on my glass.'

Brigitte let out a small moan.

'It's disgusting!' I said. 'I don't know where he's been or what he's got.'

Unable to resist my drink any longer, I wiped the rim nearest to me with a napkin and took a mouthful.

'If that's where he drank from, you're practically kissing him,' Brigitte said wistfully.

I pulled a face and put the glass down.

'What's wrong with you?' Brigitte rolled her eyes. 'You've shared a drink with one of the hottest men I've ever seen outside of my fantasies and you're complaining?'

'He might be hot, but he's an arrogant dick.'

Brigitte arched an eyebrow. 'You sound like Elizabeth Bennett in *Pride and Prejudice*.'

'I'm pretty sure she didn't call Mr Darcy a dick.'

'Bet she was thinking it.' Brigitte leant forward. 'And look what happened to them. You may as well accept now that you're going to fall madly in love with him.'

My ears wiggled. 'Even though he's a bell-end and I'm happily married?'

'Mere details.' Brigitte tossed her dark hair over her shoulder, causing her boobs to quiver enticingly. A car screeched to a halt outside and I doubted it was because the traffic lights had turned red.

'Can we talk about something else?' I asked.

'Yes.' Brigitte picked up her phone. 'I've found a few potential Liz Clarks.' She opened an app and handed it to me.

My eyes widened at the photo of a woman wearing a cropped top and what were basically large pants, doing the splits, upside down, while hanging from a pole.

'Someone you know?' I asked, taking a sip of my drink.

'No, but her name's Liz Clark.'

My mouthful of espresso martini deposited itself back into

the glass. I blinked manically at the photo. This toned, strong woman was the picture of empowerment, with a slightly slutty appeal. This couldn't be Scott's ex. It just couldn't.

I shook my head. 'She's nothing like how he described.'

'She's got dark hair.'

'So has the Princess of Wales,' I snapped. 'You're not suggesting she's a contender too, are you?'

Brigitte tutted. 'I haven't purely searched for women with dark hair.'

'There's nothing pure about this photo.' I glared at the woman who, in fairness, had committed no crime other than bearing the same name as Scott's ex and having moves that'd make Dita Von Teese blush.

'Scott said she used to go to some sort of dance club,' Brigitte said. 'Pole dancing is a form of dance. Supposed to be brilliant for strengthening your core.' With the woman's legs akimbo mid-air, it wasn't her strong core that was drawing the eye. 'Full credit to whoever does her bikini wax,' Brigitte said, peering closely. 'She's been given a thorough going-over.'

The possibility of Scott also having given her a thorough going-over turned my stomach. I put the phone down and pushed it away from me. 'That's not her. Scott's ex isn't capable of doing that. He's had to do the vacuuming on more than one occasion because she's put her back out. No way can she shimmy up a pole and do a burlesque routine.' God, I hoped she couldn't. Unless that was how she'd put her back out. I took a large mouthful of my drink and swallowed fast, in case Brigitte produced another jaw-dropping image. 'Did you find any other Liz Clarks?' I asked in a small voice. 'Preferably, less agile ones.'

'Loads,' Brigitte said. 'But I'm starting off with ones that have some link to the information we have.' She ticked off her fingers. 'She's dark-haired – but not royalty.' She winked and I giggled, despite the churning in my stomach. 'She has two primary-school-age children. She used to be in a book club and some sort of dance class, and her career's in party planning.' She didn't point out that Kate Middleton's family had run a party-supplies company, and I was thankful for that. 'Do we know anything else?'

'Yes,' I said confidently. 'She's a controlling, money-grabbing, unreasonable cow.'

'Unfortunately, they don't give you the option to select those skill sets on LinkedIn.' Brigitte picked up her phone and showed me another profile she'd found. 'This Liz Clark lists reading as her top hobby and includes the hashtag "book club". She used to work for a charity that helps children learn to read.'

I snorted. 'We can dismiss her. Scott's Liz doesn't help her own children with their homework. Can't imagine she'd help other people's.'

Brigitte traced the outline of her lips with a fingertip. A habit she had whenever she was thinking. I didn't want to know what about. 'She might not have been on the frontline. Could have been an admin role.'

I shook my head. 'Charity work is nothing like party planning. Got any others?'

'Well, I don't want to brag, but . . .' Brigitte tossed her hair back. 'I've saved the best till last.' She scrolled to another profile and held her phone out for me to take. 'Think this might be The One.'

I drained the remains of my cocktail, then reached for Brigitte's phone.

The LinkedIn profile on the screen revealed a woman roughly the same age as me, with dark hair cut into a severe bob. She had sharp features and a stern expression. So far, so Liz. Despite the hostility oozing from her photo, she was attractive. Although, she looked as though she'd stab you if you told her so. Or indeed told her anything. Meeting her and revealing that I was 'the other woman' suddenly seemed a very ill-advised approach.

'Why do you think she's the one?' I asked. 'Aside from the fact she makes Bellatrix Lestrange look mumsy.'

'Her career history and status.' Brigitte angled the phone so that she could read it. Liz's eyes seemed to follow me as her image tilted to the side. 'Her previous role was for a company called Prestige Party Planners. She's not worked for several years and is now actively seeking employment.' My stomach clenched. It all fitted. This must be her. I snuck another look at Liz's photo. She was definitely giving me a side eye. 'And,' Brigitte continued, 'she's registered her interest for an event showcase at Hermitage Hotel tomorrow evening, here in Horsham. We should go.'

'Tomorrow?' I yelped. 'That's too soon.'

'Thought you wanted it to happen soon.'

'I'm not mentally prepared.' I gripped my glass. 'Didn't realise you'd find her this quickly, or that she'd be so mean-looking.'

'She's not that bad.' Brigitte's head wobbled slightly, a sure sign she was lying.

'I can't ask my mum to babysit again.' I seized my get out of jail free card. 'If Scott's not working, he'll probably be looking after Harry and Bella, so that she can go to this thing.'

'I'll ask *my* mum,' Brigitte said. 'She'd love to see Anna.'

I wasn't sure she would. My aunt Francine had even less clue about child-rearing than Maman. She'd wanted to take Anna to the Moulin Rouge for her third birthday to give her some *bonne culture française*. Not the film or the stage show, which would have been inappropriate enough – the actual club in Paris where women dance topless and whose culture derives from prostitution. Not very *bonne* in my opinion.

I picked up my glass, realised with disappointment it was empty, and put it down again. 'Not sure that's a good idea. She hasn't looked after a three-year-old since you were three.'

'She'll be fine.' Brigitte paused, clearly recollecting her own childhood, which included Francine leaving her home alone while she popped out on an essential errand. That essential errand being a game of bingo. 'It's only for two hours,' she added quickly. 'We're unlikely to get another chance of knowing exactly where Liz is at a specific time. We have to go for it.'

I leant back in my chair, suddenly full of doubt that this was the right thing to do. Not only did Liz look much more menacing than I'd anticipated, but ignoring Scott's request to let him deal with it was a betrayal of his trust. Tracking Liz down and engineering a meeting was going behind his back. Did I really want to do this? I wasn't sure anymore.

Brigitte's phone beeped, reminding me of the countless times Scott's phone did the same. Liz hounded him. As she had tonight, on our precious night out. OK, there was a genuine reason on this occasion, but there wasn't usually. I thought back to all the times he'd had to dash off when she clicked her fingers. How she used access to their children as a way of controlling him. How she took that access away every time he stood up to her. How she wouldn't let them meet their sister Anna. It was all so wrong.

I looked again at the photo of Liz. I really didn't want to go to this event tomorrow and confront her. But, for the sake of my family, I had to.

Chapter 7

The following evening, I waited nervously outside the Hermitage Hotel for Brigitte to arrive. No way was I going in without her. We'd manged to find out what Liz looked like – perhaps she'd done the same. My image could be hardwired into her brain with instructions to kill. I told myself not to be silly. Being a devious, manipulative cow didn't make her a murderer. I wouldn't be going to the toilet alone, though, just in case.

At least I didn't need to worry about Anna's welfare. Scott had a rare evening at home, so thankfully Aunt Francine's babysitting services weren't required. It was interesting that Liz hadn't asked him to look after Bella and Harry. She obviously had another babysitting source that he wasn't aware of. Not that I could discuss this with him. Not yet, anyway. I'd told Scott I was going to a wedding fair. I'd never lied to him before and hadn't been able to meet his eye when he kissed me goodbye. Liz must have lied all the time when she was having an affair. How did some people do it and still sleep at night?

Sanjay's car pulled up opposite and Brigitte got out of the passenger seat. Dressed in navy cigarette pants, a fuchsia silk blouse and dark-framed non-prescription glasses, she looked sophisticated, professional and beautiful. And, thanks to the undone top buttons of her blouse, like every straight teenage boy's teacher/student wet dream.

Sanjay and I waved at each other as Brigitte strode across the road. His children must have been in the car; I could see the outline of two people jostling in the back. That would explain Brigitte's speedy strides away from them.

'I'm so sorry,' she said as she reached me.

'What for? You're not late.'

'For that.' Brigitte nodded in the direction of Sanjay's car. I turned to see Maman and Francine clamber out, bickering furiously, and leaving the doors wide open for Sanjay to get out and close.

My already nervous state went up several bars. 'What are they doing here?' I yelped. 'Please tell me they're going somewhere else.'

Brigitte shook her head and grimaced. 'My mum was already on her way to yours when I rang to say she didn't need to babysit after all. She was right near my road, so popped in to use the loo.' Course she did. Neither Francine nor Brigitte could last ten minutes without needing to go. 'I was in the loo myself,' Brigitte continued, proving my point. 'So she asked Sanjay where I was going tonight and he stupidly told her. Next thing I know, she's on the phone to your mum, wanting in on the action and insisting they come too.'

'No!' My hands flew to my face. 'They can't get involved. They'll ruin everything.'

Brigitte gave me an apologetic look. 'Bit late for that,' she said, as Maman and Francine reached us, still bickering.

'*Ma chérie*. This is so exciting,' Francine said, kissing me on both cheeks.

'Stop! She is my daughter.' Maman practically pushed Francine back into the road and kissed my cheeks much more noisily than her sister had. I was under no illusion that this came from a place of love. It was pure one-upmanship. When Maman and I were on our own, the closest I got to a display of affection was acknowledgement that she knew me.

'You two need to leave,' I said firmly. 'Sanjay misunderstood. Brigitte and I are here to work.'

'Work – at a hexclusive 'otel?' Maman asked. Usually, her inability to use the letter H in the correct way made me smile, but not today. 'You do not fool us, Marie. You are here to find Scott's ex-wife.'

'Shush.' I grabbed her arm, proud of myself for not grabbing her throat. 'We need to be discreet. You two don't know the meaning of the word.'

'We know the meaning of all the words,' Francine said indignantly. 'Which we shall now demonstrate. Come, Magali.'

She looped her arm through Maman's, all animosity forgotten, and they darted through the entrance door before Brigitte or I could stop them. We exchanged a look of alarm and darted after them. We didn't have to dart far, as they'd been stopped in the reception area by a woman asking to see their entry ticket to the event. I breathed a sigh of relief. Brigitte had only bought two tickets, so they wouldn't be allowed in.

'Our daughters have our tickets,' Maman said, gesturing in our direction, before marching past the woman with Francine. They hesitated, spotted a sign directing them to the event and ran, actually ran, along a corridor and out of sight. I pressed my lips tightly together, sure that plumes of smoke were streaming from my nostrils.

'So much for discreet,' tutted Brigitte.

It took several minutes to purchase another two tickets, which cost £40 each – £10 more than the online price Brigitte and I had paid the night before. At a total cost of £140, I had better find Liz and make contact to justify it. And get a shitload of free stuff.

'You didn't show them the photo of Liz, did you?' I asked Brigitte as we hurried down the corridor to The Redcoats Suite, where the event was taking place.

'Course not. They have no idea what she looks like.'

That was one small mercy.

'So they'll be accosting every woman they see, not just the ones with dark hair,' Brigitte added.

My stomach churned. This had disaster written all over it.

We entered The Redcoats Suite and scanned the room. Each wall was lined with stands showcasing hospitality products, such as glassware, floral arrangements and photography services. Maman and Francine had ignored all these and made a beeline for the bar, where they now stood, holding glasses of fizz. In both hands. At least they'd be getting our money's worth out of the event.

'Hello and welcome,' said a smiley man standing at a table covered in lanyards. 'Can I take your names please?'

'Brigitte and Marie Dubois.'

The man's smile turned into a frown. 'I'm afraid those lanyards have just been claimed by those ladies.' He pointed to Maman and Francine, who were draining the first of their glasses. 'Are they with you?'

The urge to disown them was very strong, but I resisted. 'Our mothers have picked our name badges up by accident. Shall we take theirs and swap over?'

'Perfect solution,' the man said. 'Their names are . . . ?'

'Anastasia and Drizella,' Brigitte said.

The man hesitated, then wrote the names in bold capitals on blank labels.

I scanned the lanyards on the table that were yet to be claimed, while we waited. One caught my eye and I almost squealed out loud. Liz Clark. Brigitte had been right. She was coming tonight. I was going to meet her.

'She's not here yet,' I said, my legs feeling decidedly shaky as we walked across the room, clutching our freshly made lanyards. 'But she is coming.'

Brigitte nodded. 'I noticed that too. Let's sort these two liabilities out, then watch and wait.'

Maman and Francine had another two full glasses on the go.

'This isn't a piss-up,' Brigitte hissed. 'Slow down.'

'But there are so many glasses poured,' Maman said. 'It will go to waste if we don't drink it.'

'They're for *all* the people coming, not just you.' I tried to take one of the glasses from her, but she held on tight. 'Don't have any more. We're here to do a job, remember, not have fun.'

'*C'est possible* to do both, Marie. You are too uptight. You get that from your papa.'

Francine growled a few expletives at the mention of my father and I sincerely hoped no one within hearing distance could speak French.

Brigitte handed me my own glass. 'Let's leave them to it. If they drink enough they might pass out. They'll do less damage if they're unconscious.' I wished I could get drunk and pass out with them. It was a much more appealing prospect than dealing with Liz. We walked away without telling Maman and Francine, in case they decided to come with us. Although, as we didn't have a portable bar, it was unlikely.

'Why would Liz come to this event?' I asked, deliberately not catching the eye of the enthusiastic exhibitors as we passed them. Guilt and sympathy would force me to first engage with them, then subscribe to whatever they were selling regardless of whether I needed it or not. And unless it was some sort of protection against Liz, I didn't need it.

'She's looking for a job in the hospitality industry. This event caters for all elements of that industry.' Brigitte shrugged. 'Maybe she's going to give her CV out to the suppliers.'

'Sounds a bit too resourceful for Scott's Liz,' I said. 'She can't even change the time on the microwave when the clocks go back.'

One of the event organisers handed us a goody bag as we passed by, and we welcomed the excuse to stop at a tall bar table and examine our wares, while keeping a beady eye on the door.

'Here you are,' Maman shrilled next to me. Christ, she was pissed already. 'What are you doing?' she asked loudly.

'We're undercover,' I whispered. 'That means we need to keep a low profile. Not stand out.'

Maman tapped one finger against the side of her nose.

'Go back to Francine,' I instructed. 'We'll let you know how it goes with Liz.'

'Liz Clark is here?' Maman bellowed.

'Stop shouting,' I hissed. 'I'm nervous enough without you drawing attention to us.'

'Pffft.' Maman batted her hand. 'There is nothing to be nervous about. Just tell the silly woman to stop being silly and the problem is solved. I will tell her if you will not.'

'Do not say a word,' I snapped. I pointed to the bar area where Francine stood glaring at people who dared try and help themselves to a drink, as protective of the glasses of fizz as a lion of its cubs. 'Go back and stay there till we get you. Now.'

Maman pursed her lips, put down her empty glass, picked up my full one and wobbled away, back to Francine's habitat.

Brigitte reached across the table and squeezed my arm. Her eyes hadn't left the door the whole time. 'Don't let her get to you. Keep your focus.'

'You're right.' I opened the pack of mints in my goody bag and popped one in my mouth without thinking. It wasn't until the sugar hit my taste buds that I realised what I'd done. 'Not again,' I groaned.

'There's a tonne of sugar in the prosecco,' Brigitte said. 'Give yourself a night off.'

'I haven't had any prosecco,' I sighed. 'Maman took my glass. Hopefully, that'll keep her quiet.'

'Liz Clark?' came a loud voice, with a heavy French accent, from the direction of the bar. Brigitte and I spun around. Maman was squinting up at a tall redhead. 'Liz Clark?' she asked again. The woman shook her head. Maman dismissed her with a wave of her hand and turned to the next woman. 'Liz Clark?'

At the other end of the bar, Francine was doing the same.

'For fuck's sake,' Brigitte and I said in unison, before sprinting across to exercise some damage limitation.

Reaching Maman, I took her arm and turned her around, away from the line of people waiting for a drink. 'Stop this now,' I whispered, a forced smile on my face for the benefit of the people watching. 'I told you to be discreet. *Discrète*. Asking everyone if they're Liz Clark is *not* discreet.'

Maman tutted loudly. 'You will never find her and get your solution by being quiet. Be bold and put an end to these foolish games.'

'I know who she is. I don't need or want your help.'

'You know who Liz Clark is?' Maman shrieked. 'Who is she?'

Someone behind us cleared her throat. 'She's me.'

We all spun round. She was right. It was her. The woman in the photo on Brigitte's phone. Jet-black hair in a bob. Dark eyes. But, somehow, she looked nothing like that woman. She was much shorter for one thing, possibly about five feet tall. I'd always envisaged a statuesque, towering beast of a woman. And she was softer in the flesh, her features less angular. And instead of being hard and accusing, her eyes conveyed anxiety. As well they might, given that her name was being bellowed around the hall in the manner of selecting one of the Tributes in *The Hunger Games*.

'Are you looking for me?' Her accent was Northumbrian, soft and warm, full of uncertainty. Scott hadn't mentioned that she was a northerner, although, in fairness, he hadn't said she was a southerner either.

'You are Liz Clark?' Maman frowned, clearly on the same train of thought as me. Too bad it wasn't a high-speed train with her on board.

Francine leant forward, just one step away from poking her with a stick. 'Are you sure?'

'Yes.' Liz Clark laughed nervously and held up her lanyard, where her name was clearly printed. 'Can I help you with something?'

'It's my daughter you need to help.' Maman shoved me with surprising force and I lurched towards Liz Clark, who stepped sideways to avoid being stampeded. I grabbed hold of a tall bar table to steady myself but, designed merely as a pop-up event accessory rather than a support aid, it lacked the strength to hold me up. The table and I tumbled to the ground, and empty plastic champagne flutes rained down on me, most of which were marked with Maman's and Francine's coral lipstick.

I stared up to see a textbook example of freeze, flight or fight play out before me. Brigitte stood rooted to the spot, a stricken expression on her face. Francine sped off to the other end of the bar, where she adopted a wide-eyed air of innocence. And Maman went into full-on, finger-jabbing, telling-off mode.

'Marie,' she snapped. 'Get up this instance. You are making spectacles of yourself.'

I glared at her. 'I wouldn't be sprawled on the floor if it wasn't for you.' She looked slightly, *very* slightly, chastised, and sloped off after Francine.

Liz extended a hand. 'Are you all right, pet?'

'Yes. Thank you.' I gazed in disbelief as she helped me up. Liz Clark was kind and thoughtful and helpful. I didn't think she was capable of such behaviour. My own flesh and blood clearly weren't. 'Thank you,' I said again.

Brigitte snapped out of her horrified trance and stepped forward. 'Marie, are you OK? You went over so fast. I couldn't stop you.'

I could have gone over in slo-mo and Brigitte wouldn't have been able to stop me, rooted to the ground as she had been, like a D-list celebrity in a spotlight. I didn't say this, though. Instead, my mind whirred, as I tried to think how I could explain to Liz Clark why we were looking for her.

'Marie, is it?' Liz said.

Now it was my turn to freeze. She knew my name. Would she make the connection? Was this friendly façade about to dissolve to reveal her true nature?

'Yes,' I squeaked.

'That's my middle name,' she said. I snuck a glance at Brigitte, who looked as bewildered as I did. Scott would surely have mentioned that coincidence? 'Named after my mum, Mary.' Liz's eyes welled up. 'Sorry,' she sniffed. 'She passed away recently. Still coming to terms with it.'

'I'm so sorry,' I said, exchanging another look with Brigitte. This Liz couldn't be more different to who I was expecting – sensitive, emotional, kind, not covered in scales or breathing fire.

Liz took a tissue from the sleeve of her cardigan. Another surprise – I didn't have Liz down as a cardi-wearer. 'I was her carer. Ended up leaving my job for a few years to nurse her.' She dabbed her eyes. 'Need to get back into work now, especially with my son at uni. We want to help him out a bit if we can. That's why I'm here tonight. Hoping to make some connections that could lead to a job.' She blew her nose and tucked the tissue away. 'Don't suppose that's why you were looking for me, was it?'

I shook my head numbly, the earlier anxious churning in my stomach slowing to an ache – part relief, part disappointment. No wonder she was nothing like who I'd been expecting. This Liz Clark wasn't Scott's ex. Their name and vaguely similar career path were the only things they had in common.

'No, can't expect to land on my feet that easily.' Liz gave a small smile. 'So why were you looking for me?'

I swallowed hard. A rational explanation had yet to form in my mind.

'School reunion,' Brigitte said. Liz and I both looked at her in surprise. Brigitte nodded enthusiastically. 'We went to school with a Liz Clark and thought you might be her, but you're not. Really sorry to have troubled you.'

'Oh.' Liz looked as disappointed as I felt. If she were Scott's ex, we'd have a perfectly amicable relationship with none of the crap that we had to deal with. 'Nice to have met you anyway. Let me know if you hear of anything. You can find me on LinkedIn. Excuse my photo, though. I wasn't in a good place at the time. Really need to update it.'

'Of course,' I said, sorry that I genuinely didn't know of a job opportunity I could pass on to her. It sounded as though she could do with a break after the hard time she'd had.

Liz gestured to the rows of exhibitors. 'I'd better get out there.' She took a deep breath. 'Got to be in it to win it!'

'You go get 'em,' Brigitte said, with a smile.

'Good luck,' I added.

We turned to each other as she walked away and Brigitte pulled me in for a hug.

'Sorry that wasn't her,' she said.

'Me too.' I sighed. 'Back to the drawing board.'

Brigitte grinned. 'Pole dancing?'

'Are you mad?' I felt my ears wiggle. 'You saw what just happened. If I can't get enough purchase on a bar table to keep me upright, hanging upside down from a pole is not a good idea.'

Brigitte swallowed a smile. 'That was quite a sight. Or a spectacles, as your mum put it.'

I wanted to be cross and affronted about it for a bit longer, but a giggle burst out of me. 'At least she's stopped calling it "making a testicles of yourself".'

Brigitte snorted loudly and we both bent over double with laughter, almost sending the bar table crashing to the floor again.

'I'll have whatever you're having.' Brigitte and I straightened up to see Beth grinning at us. 'How are you having so much fun? I've had back-to-back meetings with suppliers and not one of them has made me smile, let alone belly laugh.'

'Beth!' I reached out and hugged her, realising mid-hug that although we got on well, she was a client and perhaps this was overstepping boundaries. She hugged me back, then Brigitte, so clearly hadn't taken offence. 'What are you doing here?' I asked.

'The soft launch of our latest holiday destination is coming up,' she said. 'I go to loads of these events to get the best products and deals I can. How about you?'

'Thought it was a wedding event. Must have got the date wrong.' I rubbed my nose. Beth would probably think I was really stupid now, but the truth would make me sound stupid *and* bonkers, and I wanted Beth to like me.

'Easily done when you're juggling work and a family.' Beth gave a nervous smile. 'Please don't get the date of my wedding wrong, though.'

'It's 14th August.' I tapped the side of my head. 'Your dress will be ready, I promise.'

Beth smiled broadly. 'Thank you.' She looked at her watch. 'I'd better go if I want to get back to see the kids before they go to bed.'

'Who's looking after them?' I asked. 'Your ex?'

'No. James, my fiancé.' Beth's jaw tightened. 'Their dad has nothing to do with us. Hasn't even seen them for four years.'

'What a wanker,' Brigitte said.

'You got that right.' She patted Brigitte's arm. 'Lovely to see you both.'

'I can't believe her ex is so horrible,' I said to Brigitte after Beth had gone. 'She's so lovely.'

Brigitte winked. 'So's her brother.'

I gave her a withering look. 'Her brother is a bell-end. Unlike Sanjay – he's the full package.'

Brigitte nodded. 'He does have a full package.'

'Including being a hands-on dad,' I said, ignoring her smutty comment. 'He and Scott might do more with their kids than we want sometimes, but that's much better than having nothing to do with them. Beth's poor kids don't know their dad.'

There was a shriek from the bar area of the room.

'Wish we didn't know our mums right now,' Brigitte said tightly.

'Shall we go?' I whispered.

'Definitely.' Brigitte slipped her arm through mine and steered me towards the exit before guilt or a sense of duty stepped in and I felt obliged to go back for them.

As we hurried towards the door, I caught sight of Liz Clark talking animatedly to a supplier. She glanced up as we passed and gave me a thumbs up. I smiled back, happy for her. With all the commotion Maman and Francine had caused, I'd temporarily forgotten the reason for this visit. To meet Scott's ex. His Liz Clark was out there somewhere, manipulating and controlling our lives. And I still needed to find her.

Chapter 8

I slumped down in my seat at the doctor's surgery, holding a bridal magazine in front of my face. Theoretically, for research purposes – to see what styles and fabrics were currently on trend – but actually to ensure Dr Greene didn't see me if he happened to pass through. I was back for my smear test and had requested a female doctor this time. I was so determined to see anyone other than Dr Greene that if one of the receptionists had offered to do the procedure, I'd have taken them up on it.

It had been a week since the event showcase. Brigitte had spent hours trawling social media and the internet – she had a lot of time on her hands, as Sanjay's kids were staying, preventing those hands from being otherwise occupied – but hadn't found any other Liz Clarks with a possible connection. She was desperate to try the pole dancing class and/or tail Scott next time he saw Harry and Bella. I was desperate to avoid both of those, so had come up with another option that wouldn't risk breaking any bones or the law. I'd have a sneaky look through Scott's paperwork to try and find Liz's address. We would then plot our next move. Brigitte was already planning a stake-out. There would *not* be a stake-out, but planning this stopped her going on about the pole dancing class.

It wasn't until I started looking through Scott's things that I realised he didn't really have anything. His bedside drawer contained a phone charger, the box of condoms that we *still* hadn't used, some plastic things that slot inside shirt collars and some fancy-looking hair products. Our house wasn't big – I'd bought the Victorian terrace on my own (it was how we'd met – Scott was the estate agent who'd shown me around) – so there wasn't much room for 'stuff'. Unless your name was Anna, in which case you had a tonne of crap that covered every single surface and floor space. I kept most of my dressmaking paraphernalia at work, but there were still stacks of wedding magazines in every room, a huge bag of sewing that I carted to and from the studio, and a pile of life-admin paperwork in the kitchen that never seemed to go down. Scott didn't have anything, not even any books on the shelves. Guiltily, I wondered if he felt he'd be imposing by adding his own clutter to an already overfull house. Even though it was technically my house – his name wasn't on the deeds, as I paid the mortgage, and he paid the bills and ludicrous maintenance payments – it was his home, as much as mine. I needed to reiterate that and encourage him to leave his belongings lying around. Preferably documents with Liz's address on, if that wasn't too much to ask.

The door leading to the doctors' rooms opened and, to my surprise, Scott walked through.

'Scott?' I stood up. 'What are you doing here?'

Everyone in the waiting room looked at Scott expectantly and his cheeks flushed.

'Sorry,' I whispered, walking over and kissing him. 'Is everything OK?'

'Fine. Just renewing my hay fever prescription.'

'I didn't know you had hay fever.'

'That's because I take medication.' Scott took my hand and led me to the side of the waiting room. 'What about you?'

'Smear test,' I mouthed.

Scott grimaced. He wasn't a fan of *downstairs* procedures. 'How long will you be?' he asked.

I shrugged. 'How long's a piece of string?'

Scott paled. 'They use string?'

'No, I mean, I don't know how long I'll be. Depends when I go in.' I giggled. 'How do you think they get the cells? Send a harpoon up there?'

71

Scott looked as though he might gag.

I laughed again, but stopped abruptly when a door behind the reception opened and Dr Greene walked through. I whipped my magazine up to cover my face.

'What are you doing?' Scott pulled the magazine down.

'Don't want to lose my page.' We both looked down to see an article profiling pubic hair shaping stencils for honeymoons. Scott's eyes widened. Mine watered. A bikini wax was painful enough without adding feathering to the mix.

'Marie Dubois to room three,' a woman's voice said over the tannoy.

'I'll wait for you,' Scott said. 'Want me to look after your magazine?'

'No, you're all right.' I tucked it into my bag – didn't want him getting any stencilling ideas. 'See you soon.'

He gave me a quick peck at the exact moment Dr Greene looked across. He frowned and his eyes darted between the two of us. I pretended not to see him, mumbled a goodbye to Scott and rushed towards room three.

'Sorry I couldn't take you out.' Scott took a bite of the Spanish omelette I'd cooked us. 'Just paid for football and drama club, so money's a bit tight this month.'

Money seemed to be a bit tight every month, thanks to his children's many extracurricular activities. I hoped they'd remember Scott when they were an Oscar-nominated actor and first-league footballer, or professional dancer and martial arts champion, or Olympic speed stacker and internationally renowned recorder player.

'Shouldn't Liz pay for half of their classes?' I asked.

Scott squirted tomato sauce onto his plate. 'She bought Harry a new taekwondo uniform and Bella an outfit for dance, so it evens out.'

I was pretty sure two terms' worth of fees cost considerably more than a leotard and what were basically pyjamas, but didn't want to ruin this rare moment of time together, so kept quiet.

My lack of input must have spoken volumes.

'I know.' Scott shoved his plate away, most of his omelette untouched. 'But whenever I push back, she makes seeing the kids so difficult.' A muscle pounded in his cheek and my heart went out to him. The way Liz used Harry and Bella as bait to keep him at her beck and call was so wrong, as was demanding extra money on top of all the maintenance he paid. It was painful to witness Scott being reduced to a doormat just so he could see his own kids. I appreciated that being a single mum must be tough, but that was no excuse for using the kids as pawns or demanding more than Scott physically and financially had to give.

Frustration coursed through me. 'I can't bear to see her treat you like this. We have to do something.'

Scott's face drooped. 'Yeah, but remember what happened last time I put my foot down.'

The previous Christmas, I'd told him something had to be done when he'd missed Anna performing in her nursery's nativity play. Liz had insisted he take her and the kids to some festive market in the middle of nowhere because she was scared to drive through the country lanes. He'd done it, worried that she wouldn't let him visit the kids on Christmas Day if he didn't. I'd been furious. Anna would only ever be a three-year-old angel once in her life (she certainly didn't act like one at home) and he'd missed it. I'd told him he had to stand up to Liz and say no to her demands if they affected Anna. He'd agreed, told Liz she had to be more reasonable, and suddenly she and the kids were going away over Christmas, so he couldn't see them. It hadn't been our best Christmas Day. Scott was quiet and withdrawn, Brigitte and Sanjay had clearly had a row, and Maman and Francine got pissed on grappa and slagged off all the presents they'd been given.

I wasn't prepared to give up, though. 'She can't keep doing

this. Surely, she wants what's best for the kids, which is for them to see their dad happy.'

'You're talking about her as though she's a reasonable person. She's not. She's a manipulative, lying bitch, who wants to cause trouble.' He pressed a fist to his mouth.

'But it's crazy that you're living by her rules, and Anna and I can't even meet them. We have to—'

'Stop!' Scott jumped up from his chair. 'You have no idea how much stress I'm under right now. I can't even have a break from it in my own home.'

My cheeks grew hot. 'I just want to help. I hate seeing you go through this.'

He thrust his hands in his hair. 'You can't help. It's a fucking mess.'

Scott had got frustrated and annoyed before, but this was the first time I'd seen him so vulnerable, so helpless. It worried me.

'Don't go back to the office,' I said. 'You need a break.'

Scott nodded glumly. 'I could do with some air. I'll go for a drive.'

'Good idea.' Scott's new car was his pride and joy. Going for a spin was exactly what he needed to do to unwind.

'Be back soon.' He gave a half-hearted smile and left.

I stayed at the kitchen table, wondering what to do. He'd been out of sorts ever since Bella had been sick. Maybe he had a virus. If he was feeling below par, it was bound to have a knock-on effect. I absentmindedly picked at his leftover omelette, licked his fork, and then realised I probably shouldn't be sharing his cutlery if he was ill. I put it down quickly, as though acting with speed cancelled out my mistake. Tomato sauce hit my taste buds and I groaned, as my sugar detox faced yet another epic fail. I'd been doing so well too. It had been . . . I checked my watch. Almost twenty-four hours since I'd eaten the home-made rock bun that Beth had brought into the studio for me. I knew I shouldn't have done, but was too polite to say no. All four times.

Sighing with frustration, I picked up the plates and carried them to the dishwasher. My foot knocked against something and I looked down. Scott's briefcase. The only place I hadn't searched for Liz's address.

I shoved the plates in the sink, pushed the kitchen door shut and knelt down on the floor. I was secretly a bit embarrassed about Scott's attaché briefcase. It was so stuffy compared to the leather satchels most men under the age of ninety used now. I slid the catches to the side and it sprang open with a very satisfying click. OK, maybe I could see the appeal. Inside were stacks of A4 card wallets embossed with the estate agency's logo, and papers detailing houses for sale or to let. Thanks to the rigidity of the briefcase, they were in pristine condition. The corners would be bent inside a leather satchel. I took back my previous snobbery. Perhaps I'd get one to keep my dress designs in. Actually, no, Brigitte would never allow that.

Aside from Scott's laptop and a notepad, there was nothing else in the main body of the case, but there were a number of pockets within the lid. One was for pens, another business cards. The main large pocket contained a trade magazine so dull I almost fell asleep just looking at the cover. One small pocket was clearly designed for a phone to slot into, but Scott always had that on him. The corner of a piece of paper was poking out. I eased it out with my fingernail. It was a beautiful black and white photo of Harry and Bella. He'd shown the same photo to me on his phone when we'd first got together, and it was clearly professionally taken. It was a wonder Liz had given him a copy. Although it was on very flimsy paper, so she hadn't forked out on a high-quality version for him. My heart ached for Scott. She controlled every element of his contact with his own children: when and where he saw them, who he saw them with, what photos he could have of them. It was cruel and unfair. No wonder he'd snapped earlier. He was living on a knife-edge through no fault of his own.

I slipped the picture back and opened his laptop. Unsurprisingly, it was password protected, so all I could do was stare blankly at the screen. Frustrated, I put it back, closed the case with another satisfying click and went back to clearing the plates. I was scraping Scott's omelette into the bin, when the front door opened. My stomach flipped over with relief that I wasn't still snooping through his case. His ex-wife was a devious cow. He didn't need me to be one too.

Scott came over and wrapped his arms around me. 'Sorry,' he said. I cringed. It should be me apologising, given that I'd just been going through his briefcase. 'None of this is your fault,' he continued. 'I don't want us to row about it.'

If Scott thought that was a row, he should spend more time with my mum. During one argument with my dad, she'd thrown all our breakfast bowls at the kitchen wall, one after the other. We'd had to eat cereal out of mugs afterwards. And all because he'd left the toilet seat up. 'Don't think I will be playing legs in the air with you later!' I'd heard her shout after him, as he'd scuttled into the garden to escape, followed by, 'You can take Popol to the circus yourself.' For months I'd eagerly awaited a trip to the circus – I didn't care if Popol came or not – to see Maman perform her legs-in-the-air trick. It was only when I later became fluent in French that I learnt 'Faire une partie de jambs en l'air' was slang for shagging and that taking Popol to the circus meant to masturbate. Really wish I'd studied Spanish instead.

I wrapped my arms around Scott. 'I was wondering if you've picked up Bella's bug,' I said. 'Everything seems worse when you're not feeling well.'

Scott rested his forehead against mine. 'You're so lovely. I don't want this crap – my crap – to come between us.' He ran his hands up and down my forearms. 'I don't want to lose you.'

I smiled into his eyes. 'You're not going to lose me, silly. None of this is your fault. Apart from having some sort of personality bypass ten years ago and accidentally marrying a crazy person.'

Scott screwed his eyes up. 'I'm such an idiot. Everything's a mess.'

'We'll sort it out somehow,' I said gently. My resolve to meet Liz went up a notch.

Scott buried his face in my neck. 'I love you so much.' His body trembled in my arms.

'You're shivering.' I pulled back and placed my palm on his damp forehead. 'I was right – you're ill. Phone work and get someone else to cover your viewings. You need to go to bed.'

Scott wiped his brow with the back of his hand. 'I'll be all right, only got a couple to get through.' He took his phone from his pocket, glanced at the screen and grimaced. 'Actually, you know what? A couple of days away from it all will do me good.'

He called the office while I put the plates in the dishwasher.

'Have you got any clients this afternoon?' he asked, as he hung up.

I shook my head. 'Sewing day today. Why?'

'I'm going to bed.' Scott slapped my bottom. 'Fancy joining me?'

'You're ill,' I said regretfully. An afternoon in bed sounded idyllic, especially as I'd been gagging for it for weeks.

'Ill, yes. Dead, no.' Scott walked over and took my face in his hands. 'It's not often we're in the house alone. We should make the most of it.'

I grinned and met his lips. At long bloody last – a session of legs in the air.

After what could only be described as a very tender love-making session – Scott had showered me with more kisses and declarations of love than ever before (hopefully, we'd be back to legs in the air next time) – he fell asleep. I watched his face soften, the tension that seemed omnipresent evaporating. Liz was causing that tension. I wanted more than anything to free Scott of her control, and the stress and misery that came with it. My heart sunk. There was only one thing for it. I was going to have to do that bloody pole dancing class.

I eased myself out of bed, went downstairs and texted Brigitte. *I'll do the class,* I typed. Brigitte phoned immediately.

'That's brilliant!' she said. 'Especially when you were so against it.'

'I'm still against it,' I said. 'But needs must.'

'Are you talking about your sexual needs now?'

'No,' I said smugly. 'You know I went to the doctor's this morning for a smear test.'

Brigitte inhaled sharply. 'You didn't? With Dr Dishy?'

The mere thought made me cringe. 'Of course not. I had it with another doctor.'

'You had sex with another doctor?' Brigitte's voice was so high, I could barely hear it.

'No! I had the smear test with another doctor, not sex.'

'Who did you have sex with, then?' Brigitte asked breathlessly.

'Scott, of course.'

'Oh.' Brigitte sounded disappointed.

'I bumped into him at the surgery and we went home to have lunch, then went to bed.' It all sounded a bit flat after Brigitte's false assumptions.

'That's . . .' Brigitte searched for the right word. 'Nice,' she settled on.

'Yes, it was nice,' I said defensively. It had been nice. Not great, not setting the world on fire, but nice was OK.

'What was he doing at the doctor's?' Brigitte asked.

'Getting some tablets.'

'Tablets?' I sensed her interest growing. 'Viagra?'

'No! For hay fever.' I frowned, as doubt crept in. 'Although, he's never mentioned hay fever before.' I bit my lip. 'Maybe it was Viagra.'

'Would it matter if it was?' Brigitte asked. 'He's doing it so he can have sex with you.'

I wasn't comforted by this. 'My husband needing drugs to get it up feels a bit insulting.'

'Don't think of it like that,' Brigitte said. 'You're always saying how stressed he is. Perhaps it's affecting his libido, so he thought he'd get some help.'

'He needs help to fancy me?'

'You wouldn't be shagging if he didn't fancy you. Stop worrying about it.'

I couldn't help but worry.

'Better go,' Brigitte said. 'My client won't have a face left if I leave her acid peel on any longer.'

'Do you really think he's taking Viagra?' I asked quietly.

'No, I was joking. Love you, bye.'

I suspected she was saying that to make me feel better, but it didn't work. The seed had been sown. Sadly, not literally. Scott's vigilant use of a condom had seen to that.

Chapter 9

The phone was ringing when I let myself into the studio the next morning, even though it wasn't even nine and I didn't officially open until 9.30. I ran up the stairs, my thighs burning despite the fact I did this several times a day.

'Marie Dubois Bridalwear,' I panted into the receiver.

'I'd like to make an appointment,' said a female voice. 'To get a wedding dress.'

I unhooked my bag from across my body and managed to wrap the strap around the phone cord so that it dangled like a sporran. Brigitte always took the piss out of me for having a retro phone. Maybe it was time to upgrade to avoid wardrobe malfunctions. 'Thanks for calling. Can I take your name?'

'Cleo.'

'And when's the wedding?' My chair was piled high with magazines and swatches, so I knelt down on the floor to use my desk.

'August.'

'Great.' I checked my calendar. 'Fifteen months gives us enough time to play around with ideas, make up a toile, have fittings—'

'No, this August.'

I choked. 'As in three months away?'

'Yes.'

'Sorry, but I can't design and make a dress in that time.' I hated to turn down work, but had to be realistic. 'Not with all the other dresses I'm making.'

'What if it's really plain?' Cleo asked. 'Doesn't have to be embellished, or have sleeves even.'

'You could buy something like that a lot more cheaply from one of the high-street shops that sell wedding attire,' I said gently. 'There are some lovely dresses out there.'

'It's not that straightforward.' Cleo paused. 'I'm pregnant.'

'Congratulations,' I said. 'I'm very happy for you, but it doesn't change—'

'Can we at least meet to talk about it?' Cleo interrupted. 'I could come in this afternoon.'

'Sorry, I've got a full day.' It was true. Beth would be in shortly for a fitting, two brides were collecting their finished dresses, then Brigitte and I were taking Maman and Francine out for their birthdays.

'Tomorrow, then?' Cleo asked.

'I can't. I don't mean to be rude, but it's hectic in the run-up to summer. I physically don't have the time. Sorry.'

'I see.' The quiver in Cleo's voice was replaced with a different tone. One which implied I could go fuck myself. 'Sorry to have bothered you.' The line went dead.

I hung up and, still kneeling on the floor, lowered my head to the desk. The conversation with Cleo had drained me and it was only five past nine. The front door chimed, as someone opened it. Beth wasn't due in till 9.30, so it had to be Brigitte.

'Please bring me caffeine,' I shouted, my head still resting on the desk. My eyes were exactly level with the crotch of the person who'd just come in. But it wasn't Brigitte's. It was a blue-suited crotch with, if I wasn't mistaken, a definite bulge. My own eyes bulged and I sprang to my feet, forgetting that the telephone cord was still wrapped around me, and my bag was dangling between my legs. The phone crashed to the floor, taking a long length of the phone cord with it so that the remaining cord tightened across my chest, making my boobs stick out either side of it. It wasn't a great look.

'Morning,' Dr Greene said.

It would have to be him, wouldn't it?

'Morning,' I said stiffly, picking up the phone and releasing some of the tension on my chest. 'How can I help you?'

'Shouldn't I be asking you that?' Dr Greene said, the corners of his mouth twitching as I wiggled my bag over my hips and up my body, before hooking it over my head.

'I can manage.' I busied myself untangling the phone cord and bag strap.

Dr Greene stepped forward. 'Would you mind giving this to Beth, please?' He took a small toy giraffe out of his pocket. 'I took the kids out yesterday and Izzy asked me to look after this. I forgot to give it back.'

I finally separated the phone cord and bag strap, and placed both on the desk. 'Sure. She's in later.'

'Yes, she said. I didn't call in on the off-chance.'

'Good.' I checked that he didn't have his hands on his hips, so I could claim this pose without mirroring him again. His were tucked casually in his trouser pockets, which emphasised the visible-bulge issue. I completely forgot where to put my hands and tugged at the neckline of my shirt instead, feeling suddenly warm.

Dr Greene put his head to one side. 'I saw you in the surgery last week. Talking to Scott Bradford. Are you two . . .?' He trailed off.

'Married? Yes. I use my mum's surname.'

Dr Greene rocked back and forth on his heels. I deliberately didn't look at his crotch area, in case the motion had an effect on the bulge in his trousers. Then I deliberately did. I was only human. And yes, there was movement.

He cleared his throat and my eyes snapped up. Fortunately, he wasn't looking at me or he'd have thought I was a massive perve. With good cause.

He fiddled with the giraffe. 'There's something I want to talk to you about.'

My face grew hot. Did he know I'd been in for a sneaky smear?

He studied the giraffe intently. 'It's unethical for me to

discuss a patient with anyone, even their spouse.' His eyes flitted to mine then back to the giraffe. 'But you told me you wanted another baby.'

'I shouldn't have done.' My cheeks burnt. 'It's private.'

Dr Greene nodded. 'Even if I wasn't aware of that, I feel it's my duty of care to point out that you're both young.'

I frowned, not sure what he meant, then I remembered Brigitte's diagnosis. I withheld a whimper. She was right. Scott *had* been prescribed Viagra. And it was so unusual at his age that the doctor was questioning it. What did that say about me? That I was so repulsive, Scott couldn't get it up? If Dr Greene could draw that conclusion just from looking in my ears, thank goodness he hadn't looked in anywhere else.

'Forty's not that young,' I protested.

'Clinically, it's geriatric.'

I bristled.

'But it's young enough,' he said. 'How many children have you got?'

'One,' I said stiffly. 'But Scott has two from his first marriage as well. He sees them a lot and his ex is very demanding. He's under a lot of pressure and is exhausted.' I hoped I was right and Scott's need for Viagra was because of external influences, not because he no longer found me attractive. We'd had sex again last night. He wouldn't if he didn't fancy me, would he?

Dr Greene looked directly at me.

'And you?' His large brown eyes bore into me. 'Are you OK with it?'

'Yes,' I snapped. 'Not that it's any of your business.' I picked up my diary. 'Can you go now? I'm very busy.'

He placed the giraffe on the desk, gave me a tight smile and left.

The bell chimed as he was making his way down the stairs.

'Hello,' Brigitte said coquettishly. The door closed and she ran up the stairs. 'Dr Dishy isn't very sociable, is he?'

she said, coming straight into my studio, her dark ponytail swinging.

I clutched my diary in an attempt to stop myself shaking. 'He's *not* Dr Dishy. He's Dr Bell-end.'

Brigitte took the quivering diary out of my hands and put an arm around me. 'What's happened?'

I swallowed hard. 'He came to drop something off for Beth, but then asked me about Scott. You're right – he's taking Viagra.'

Brigitte gasped. 'He told you? I didn't think that was allowed.'

'He didn't actually say it, but he intimated it and said Scott was too young to need it.'

Brigitte glowered. 'Who does he think he is? He can't judge people.'

I shook my head. 'I'm so embarrassed. And sad – why didn't Scott talk to me?'

'Probably because he's embarrassed too,' Brigitte said.

'I'm his wife. He should be able to tell me anything.'

'Do you tell him about that hair on your chin you have to pluck?'

'No!' I ran a hand over my chin, checking if the little critter was growing through again. 'I want to keep some illusion of romance and mystery.'

'Maybe it's the same for him.'

That made sense. What man would want to admit that he was struggling in the bedroom? If it were me, I wouldn't want to turn it into a big deal either. I'd respect his privacy and pretend I didn't know.

Brigitte slid her jacket off and smoothed down her black uniform. 'Are you going to make a complaint about Dr Greene?'

I shook my head. 'It'd make things awkward with Beth. It's not like he was discussing it with a stranger. I will if I catch him gossiping about it in the corner shop.'

'You should make a complaint about him if he's in the

corner shop, full stop. All they sell is top-shelf mags – on all the shelves. The sleazy shop owner threw himself in front of them when I took Anna in to buy a comic.'

I laughed and smoothed my own skirt down. Except that it wasn't there. I looked down in horror. When wriggling myself free of the phone lead and bag strap, the hem had folded up on itself, turning my skirt from an acceptable mid-thigh length to a very unacceptable fanny-skimming one.

'Dr Greene must think I'm a right slut,' I wailed, tugging my skirt down. 'I've got my husband on Viagra, I stared at his cock, then I practically flashed him.'

Brigitte's eyes widened. 'He got his cock out? What sort of a doctor is he?'

'No!' I lowered my voice, even though no one else was in the building. 'I accidentally saw the outline through his trousers.'

'There are no accidents,' Brigitte said, pressing her palms together. 'Only purpose we haven't yet understood.'

'Well, I don't understand Dr Greene's purpose in life.' I tutted. 'Unless it's to humiliate me.'

Brigitte nodded solemnly, then smirked. 'So how big are we talking? If you could see the outline, he must be well-endowed.' My cheeks burnt. 'Well?' she insisted.

The door downstairs opened and Brigitte reluctantly went to greet Beth. I breathed a sigh of relief. Saved by the bell-end's sister.

Chapter 10

'It's gorgeous. Thank you.' Beth turned from side to side, admiring her reflection. Her toned shoulders and back were on display through the tattoo-lace over an illusion Sabrina neckline and barely-there open back. Her waist was nipped in and would, when finished, be accentuated with beaded trim over the white skirt made up of layers of light, floaty tulle. I still needed to sew it together and stitch three million microscopic beads onto the bodice. It'd be a busy three months, given that I had another eight brides getting married between May and August, half of whom had bridesmaids. Oh, and a three-year-old to lovingly raise, nurture and convince that just because the swear words my mum taught her were in French, didn't mean they weren't rude.

I couldn't complain, though; it was the nature of the business. Worryingly quiet during the winter months and punch-yourself-in-the-face-to-stay-awake frantic in spring and summer. Or punch someone else in the face if they decided that the plunging neckline they'd insisted on, ignoring my advice, wasn't the look they wanted after all. I didn't actually punch the bride in question in the face, although – as she decided this two days before the wedding – I'd have been justified. Instead, I'd gritted my teeth, palmed Anna off on my mum and worked forty-eight hours straight to replace the hand-embroidered bodice with a more suitable one. Apparently, the marriage only lasted six months. Less time than it took to make the bastard dress.

Beth gave an excited shimmy. 'Wish I didn't have to wait three months to wear it.'

'I'm glad you do, or I wouldn't be getting any sleep before

the wedding.' I smiled at her reflection, unable to miss the resemblance to her brother. They were both tall, with large, deep brown eyes and smooth, flawless skin. But that was where the similarities ended, because Beth wasn't a knob.

Beth pulled her hair off her face and put her head to one side questioningly. 'Up or down?'

'Up. Show off those gorgeous cheekbones.'

'That's sweet, thank you.' Beth smiled. 'The plus side of not having time to eat at work. Speaking of work . . .' She reached into her bag, took out two red envelopes and handed them to me. 'Invites for you and Brigitte to the soft launch of the holiday resort I'm doing the marketing for. You can bring your husbands and kids too.'

A free holiday? Wow. I opened my envelope, took out a stick of rock and postcard-style invitation, and scanned the details. Friday to Sunday, self-catering accommodation and access to all amenities included.

I grinned at Beth. 'Thank you. This is so generous.'

'It's the least I can do when you've made me this.' Beth held the skirt of the dress out and twirled around. 'But you must give me your honest opinion of the resort and let me know if anything needs improving, no matter how minor.'

Unless I had to build our lodge before we could sleep in it, I couldn't foresee any complaints. Reading the invitation again, I absentmindedly unwrapped my stick of rock and took a bite, then spat it out into my hand.

'What's wrong?' Beth's face was aghast. 'I've sent a hundred of those out.'

'Nothing, sorry. I've given up sugar. I keep forgetting.'

'But it tastes OK?'

'It tastes bloody lovely,' I admitted.

Beth put a hand to her chest. 'Thank Christ. Thought I'd poisoned everyone then. The reviews wouldn't be up to much if I had.' Beth's phone vibrated in her bag on my desk. 'I'd better answer that, then get back to the office.' She reached for her phone and spotted the toy giraffe. 'Is this Izzy's?'

'Yes. Dr Greene dropped it round just before you came in.'

'That was sweet of him. I said I'd go into the surgery to get it.' Beth smiled. 'You can call him Michael.'

I had a wealth of other names for Beth's brother, and Michael was not among them.

While Beth answered her call, I opened my diary to the weekend of the launch. It was only two weeks away, but I could juggle my appointments to allow me to go. It might be trickier for Brigitte, as she was usually booked solid on Saturdays. I then opened the Calendar app on my phone. An exercise class was scheduled in for the day before and I frowned, wondering where that had come from, before remembering that it was the dreaded pole dancing class. I entered the details of the weekend away and was about to invite Scott, when I noticed he was already scheduled at a conference. Crap.

'I'd better go.' Beth checked her watch. 'Need to be back by twelve at the latest.'

I unpinned the back of her dress. I couldn't believe Beth drove all the way from Brighton to me in Horsham, which took about forty-five minutes, when there were countless bridal boutiques closer to where she lived.

She changed into a green, floral dress and swapped her silver sandals for wedges. 'Let me know how many of you are coming, and if you and Brigitte want to share a lodge or have separate ones,' she said, blowing me a kiss as she hurried out of the door.

'I will. Thank you again,' I called after her.

I'd just hung her dress up when I heard Brigitte say goodbye to her client, then the loo door closing. When it reopened, I presented her with her invitation.

'Pack your cossie,' I said. 'Beth's given us a free holiday!'

'Really?' Her eyes lit up. 'Barbados? Mauritius? Hawaii?'

'Tamworth.'

'As in Tamworth, an exotic island off the Bahamas that I've never heard of?' she said hopefully.

I gave a sympathetic smile. 'No, it's in Staffordshire. But it'll still be great.' Her expression indicated that it wouldn't be. 'Come on,' I said. 'When was the last time we went away? We'll have a laugh, and it's free.'

She opened the envelope and immediately put the stick of rock in her mouth, twirling it salaciously around with her tongue. She was only one step away from tying a knot in it as though it were a cherry stalk.

'You're right,' she said. 'A weekend away is just what we need. Who needs sunshine when we have . . .' She hesitated.

'Each other?' I suggested.

'Alcohol,' Brigitte corrected.

'It's a family resort, not Ibiza.'

'All the more reason to drink.'

Good point. 'Scott's at a conference so it'll just be me and Anna. What about Sanjay?'

Brigitte shook her head. 'We've got Sundeep and Ammo that weekend.' She grinned. 'Perfect timing. Girls' weekend, here we come!'

Chapter 11

'They'd better not drink as much as they did last week,' Brigitte said, as we walked to the hotel where we were meeting our mums. 'They can't remember getting home.'

'Wish I couldn't remember them being there at all.' I looped my arm through hers. 'Don't mention the pole dancing class. They might try and come to that too.' We exchanged a look of pure horror.

'Any other topics to avoid?' Brigitte asked.

'Scott's Viagra. They don't need an excuse to tell us how Frenchmen are so much more virile than Brits.'

Brigitte cringed. 'Wonder what today's beef about our dads will be. Could be anything from avocados being out of stock in the supermarket to an inflation increase on tampons.'

'They've always got Brexit to fall back on,' I growled, still furious that our dads had voted Leave. We suspected they'd done it in the hope their ex-wives would be shipped back to France, despite having lived in the UK for forty years. I had to admit, even though I was a fierce Remainer, there were moments I fantasised about this too.

The hotel foyer was so small that we walked straight into the reception desk, almost knocking a silk flower arrangement off onto the woman sitting behind it.

'Welcome to The Regal.' She smiled brightly. I admired her professionalism. Not sure I could have mustered up such warmth if forced to wear a maroon cravat.

'We're meeting our mums for afternoon tea. They might already be here.'

'Yes, they arrived half an hour ago.' Great. We were on time but would still get told off for being late, because they'd

90

chosen to get there early. 'The restaurant's along the corridor, second on the right after the ladies. Enjoy.'

We nodded our thanks and walked down the corridor towards the sound of piped music. The carpet was so worn in places that it was shiny, and the embossed wallpaper had bald patches. Claridge's, it was not.

I glanced at Brigitte. 'It's a bit . . .' I searched for the right word.

'Shit?' Brigitte ventured.

She'd hit the nail on the head. Unlike whoever was responsible for hanging the pictures, judging by the many holes in the walls.

Brigitte pushed open the first door we came to. 'I'm going to the loo. See you there.'

I followed. 'Can't face them on my own. They'll have a right moan about this place. The website said shabby chic.'

'It was half-right.' Brigitte wrinkled her nose as she went into one of the cubicles.

The door opened and a woman with a blonde bob and razor-sharp cheekbones came in. She physically jumped when she saw me and scuttled into a cubicle.

Brigitte came out, washed her hands, shook them dry – obviously, the hand dryer wasn't working – and we ventured out to meet our mums. The restaurant was fairly well decorated compared to what we'd seen so far, in that the paint wasn't peeling off the walls. Our mums sat at a table by the window, their signature dark chignons and coral lipstick in place. From the neck up they were identical, but below the neck was a very different story. And it wasn't one with a happy ending. Francine wore a navy, square-neck dress with a slim red belt and red court shoes. She was the epitome of chic. Her sister was not. Maman's brightly coloured, spaghetti western-style patterned poncho clashed horrendously with the black-and-white striped skinny trousers she wore under it. Although, I couldn't think of a single item of clothing that wouldn't have clashed horrendously with it.

91

'*Bon anniversaire*,' we chorused.

'*Merci*,' our mums replied in unison, offering both cheeks for us to lean down and kiss before we sat opposite them.

'We began to think you wouldn't come,' Maman said.

I smiled apologetically. If she was criticising my timekeeping, hopefully she wasn't going to mention the shithole I'd booked for their birthday. 'Though we wouldn't blame you for not turning up,' she continued. 'This hotel has no *joie de vivre*.' OK, she was going to mention it.

To change the subject, I gestured to the large cafetière on the table. 'You went for coffee, rather than afternoon tea?'

'Yes, but it is not pleasant. The English are not good at coffee. Unlike *en France*.' She passed hers and Francine's cups to me and Brigitte. 'You girls can have it.'

'So, what is news?' Francine asked.

'Nothing,' Brigitte and I said. Brigitte's head wobbled slightly, while I rubbed my nose.

'Nothing?' Maman laced her fingers together. Her elbows stuck out at right angles, making her poncho look like a giant triangle with her head balanced on the top. I wished she'd take it off. Either the poncho or her head – I wasn't fussed which. 'You ladies have your own businesses,' she said. She and Francine were very proud of the fact we'd set up on our own, without any help or input from men. 'And children,' she added. They weren't so proud of this, as it had required some input from men. 'You must have news.'

'They're Sanjay's children, not mine.' Brigitte picked up a menu. 'I'm counting down till they go to uni.'

I remembered some news that didn't involve Viagra or pole dancing. 'We've been given a free holiday,' I said. 'One of my clients is doing the PR for a family resort in Staffordshire and has invited us to the soft-launch weekend.'

Francine looked suspicious. 'Who is this client and what do they want?'

'Nothing. Her name's Beth. I'm making her wedding dress and have got to know her pretty well. They have to fill the resort so the staff can have a test run of what it'll be like when it opens officially. There'll be journalists doing reviews, the staff's family and friends, and some minor celebs.'

'Celebs?' Brigitte peered over her menu. 'Please say it's the Hemsworth brothers.'

'More like the Pussycat Dolls, and Torvill and Dean.'

Brigitte pouted, clearly disappointed. I, however, was hoping for a flash mob *Boléro* routine at the roller disco.

A waiter in a maroon waistcoat appeared and asked if we were ready to order.

'We will all have the French afternoon tea,' Francine announced. I looked at my menu. There was no French afternoon tea. He left, a confused look on his face.

'Will Sanjay and Scott go on your free holiday also?' Francine asked.

'No, just us and Anna.'

'You know what they say,' Maman declared. 'While the mice are away, the cats will dance.'

'No one says that.' I crossed my arms. 'Scott and Sanjay don't dance, anyway.'

'I meant you two,' Maman said. 'Who will be stopping you dancing while you are away?'

'We don't need stopping,' I said. 'It's a family holiday centre. Dancing isn't an option.'

'Where there is a holiday, there is always dancing.' Maman and Francine exchanged a knowing look, which was totally unjustified, as they knew fuck all.

'Here's your birthday present,' I said, thrusting two envelopes at them before they invited themselves along.

'*Parfait*,' they exclaimed when they opened day passes to a spa. Brigitte and I breathed a sigh of relief. Maman and Francine had no qualms telling us if they didn't like a present, and it was a bit galling to be told the thing you'd spent hours carefully selecting was as welcome as a gift-wrapped dog turd.

'I have a present for Marie also.' Maman reached under the table and handed me a Jiffy bag with a courier logo blazoned across it. The presentation left a little to be desired, but I still felt a thrill at getting an unexpected gift.

'What's this for?'

'It is necessity for your happy marriage,' Maman said.

My cheeks flushed. Was Scott's need for Viagra that obvious?

Before I could open it, the waiter arrived with a trolley laden with finger sandwiches, scones and an assortment of manufactured sweet treats, including Mr Kipling French Fancies. Under normal circumstances, I'd be pissed off at the lack of freshly baked fare, but if the kitchen was anything like the rest of the hotel, the fact it had been made in a factory, rather than on the premises, was a blessing.

The waiter placed two small bottles of tonic water on the table, followed by two glasses of clear liquid.

'Is that gin and tonic?' Brigitte asked. 'Another two,' she said, when the waiter nodded.

'I don't like gin,' I said.

'I know.' Brigitte grinned. 'They're both for me.'

'Open your present,' Maman urged.

I tore along the perforated opening and warily took out the box that was apparently necessary for my marriage. What would it be? A book on how to bake the perfect croissant? Agent Provocateur underwear? A DVD of *Emmanuelle*? The word *sonde* on the box gave no clues, so I read the text, which gave far too many. A *sonde*, it transpired, was an electronic vaginal re-educator that promised to deliver a 'youthful vaginal tone'. I thrust the box back in the bag.

'What is it?' Brigitte asked.

'Nothing.' I picked up one of the plates and offered it to her. 'Sandwich?'

She shook her head. 'What's the present?'

'Doesn't matter. It's going back.'

'Marie!' Maman grimaced. 'It is not returnable.'

I glared at her. 'You have it, then.'

'I do not need it. I had *la rééducation périnéale* at the hospital in France.'

Despite living in the UK, she and Francine had flown back for mine and Brigitte's births. They'd spent an entire week in bed while nurses carried their babies to them, brought them three-course meals with wine – including breakfast, probably – and re-educated their *vagins*, before returning to their husbands in Blighty.

I picked up a French Fancy, put the whole thing in my mouth and took another. Fuck the sugar-free diet, I needed a hit. Ideally, one that involved my mother's face. While I was foraging for cakes, Brigitte took the opportunity to slide the package off my lap and read the box.

'Safely and effectively reduce incontinence.' She snorted. 'What is this?'

'A Kegel pelvic toner,' my mum said matter-of-factly. 'To tighten up the *vagin* after giving birth.'

'Bit late, isn't it?' Brigitte said. 'Anna's three.'

'It doesn't need tightening,' I snapped. This wasn't strictly true. I couldn't go on a trampoline or skip without a few droplets escaping, but there was no need to make a song and dance about it. Especially, as that resulted in me wetting myself too.

Another two gins arrived. Perhaps I could develop a taste for them. Once the waiter had left, Brigitte opened the box. 'It's a dildo with electrodes attached,' she said, taking out the instructions. 'Place the probe in your vagina,' she read. I crossed my legs. 'Gentle electrical nerve stimulation is delivered to the pelvic-floor muscles, so they create the perfect Kegel exercise,' she continued. Maman and Francine listened intently, nodding as though at a poetry reading. 'Used regularly, it will strengthen pelvic-wall muscles, increase desire and enhance intimacy.' Brigitte arched an eyebrow. 'Maybe I should get one.'

'Have that one,' I said. 'I'm not sticking electrodes up me.' I shoved another cake into my mouth.

'Marie,' Maman scolded. 'Food should not be hurried.'

I allowed myself a brief fantasy about my mum being

exiled to France and took a large mouthful of water, then gagged. It wasn't water; it was gin.

Choking, I took a mouthful of coffee and almost spat it back into the cup. Maman was right: it wasn't pleasant. Especially, now it was cold. My stomach churned. 'Just going to the ladies,' I muttered, standing up. 'Be back in a minute.'

I made my way unsteadily to the toilet. The consumption of so much sugar after weeks of cutting back, and an unexpected shot of gin, had left me decidedly nauseous. I leant against the sink and took a deep breath. One of the toilets flushed and the glamorous blonde I'd seen earlier came out of a cubicle. Had she been in there all that time? She hesitated when she saw me, then washed her hands quickly and left. In fairness, I'd do the same if I'd just done a forty-minute poo.

I took a few more deep breaths, splashed cold water on my face and returned to the table, hoping that the cakes would have been taken away. Sadly, they were still there. Even more sadly, so were my mother and aunt.

'How is your mission to find Liz Clark?' Maman asked.

'Mind your own business.' It wasn't a polite response, but she'd forfeited such niceties by giving me a contraption to tighten my fanny.

'You can tell us.' Francine smiled.

'Tell *you*?' Brigitte snorted. 'After the other evening?'

Maman and Francine inhaled sharply. 'You should be thanking us,' they said in unison.

Brigitte and I inhaled equally sharply. 'Thanking you for what?' we said together.

'We found Liz Clark,' they harmonised. Maman elbowed her sister, keen to be the dominant voice. 'If not for us, you would have searched all night like a needle in a haycock.'

'Hay*stack*,' I said.

'A stack is not what your papa called it.'

My earlier nausea returned with force.

Francine leant forward. 'We will help find the real Liz Clark.'

'No need,' I said. 'I've aborted the mission.'

'You cannot give up so easily, Marie.' Maman wagged a finger at me. 'This is poppystack.'

I pressed my fingertips to my eyes. I didn't have the energy to correct her.

'Cock,' Brigitte said. She not only had the energy, but was clearly delighted for an opportunity to say the word out loud. 'The word is poppy*cock*, not poppy*stack*.'

'Make up your minds,' Maman snapped.

'*Ce n'est pas important*,' Francine said. 'Finding Liz Clark is.' She rubbed her hands together. 'I have an idea.'

'No, you don't,' Brigitte said quickly.

'Next time Scott visits his children, I will follow him.'

Maman glared at her sister. 'That was Brigitte's idea, not yours.'

Brigitte gave me a sheepish smile. 'Sorry. I said it flippantly when we were on our way to the event last week. I didn't mean for her to actually do it.'

'You are not to follow Scott,' I said sternly. 'It's called stalking and it's illegal.'

'Marie is right,' Maman said. I almost fell off my chair in surprise. '*I* will follow him,' she continued, ruining the moment. 'He is *my* son-in-law.'

'It's still illegal,' I spluttered.

'Scott knows your car,' Francine said to Maman, ignoring me completely. 'He doesn't know mine.'

'You don't drive. You only wanted the car to get more in the divorce settlement.' Maman tried to look condescending, but pride won out.

'I don't drive,' Francine agreed. 'This doesn't mean I can't. Scott has never seen my car or seen me drive, so I will not be a suspect. You can come with me, in case I forget what to do.' She smiled triumphantly. 'I am the perfect person for the job.'

Brigitte raised an eyebrow in my direction. 'Never thought I'd say this, but she has a point.'

I looked around the group, at their eager faces. I wasn't comfortable with the thought of Francine tailing Scott, but my mum and aunt were so stubborn that they'd do it with or without my blessing. Easier to agree and tell them when Scott would be going, rather than have them following his every move.

'Fine,' I said wearily. 'He's seeing them on Thursday, before his curry night. He'll go straight from work at 5.30. His car will be parked round the back of the estate agent's. You can follow him from there.' I bit my lip. 'It'll be rush hour. Will you be OK with the roads so busy?' Maman and Francine nodded. I pressed my hands together. 'Don't let him see you. And go straight home once you've seen where Liz lives. All I need is the address. Don't hang around and, whatever you do, don't take any photos of Liz or the kids. You really would get arrested for that.'

Francine and Maman nodded solemnly, then put their heads together and whispered in French at high speed. No doubt making a pact to do the exact opposite of what I'd just instructed.

'It's a crazy plan,' Brigitte said, 'but it might just work.'

I exhaled loudly. 'I'm already regretting it. The only shred of hope I have is that it'll get me out of the pole dancing class.'

Maman's head snapped round. 'Polish dancing?' she said. 'Why not French dancing?'

I groaned inwardly. This situation had 'stack' up written all over it.

Chapter 12

The following morning, I was unlocking the front door to work – and looking forward to a green tea to try and counteract the gin, bad coffee and sugar overload from the day before – when I became aware of someone watching me. A shiver ran through me, as the fear of being followed the previous week returned. You're being paranoid, I told myself. Don't be silly. There's no one there. I spun round, then jumped a metre into the air when someone *was* actually there.

A woman stood on the edge of the kerb, staring at me. I swallowed hard, not sure how to react. She didn't look dangerous. In fact, she looked vaguely familiar. Her blonde hair was cut into a sleek bob, with a fringe that perfectly framed her face and emphasised her razor-sharp cheekbones and very pale blue eyes. Those eyes were trained on me, expectantly.

'Have we met before?' I asked.

'No.'

I frowned, then remembered where I'd seen her. 'You were in the toilets at The Regal Hotel yesterday.' For a very long time.

'Yes, I had a meeting there. Sorry, don't recall seeing you.'

'That's OK.' We looked at each other awkwardly for a moment then I gestured to my front door. 'Better get on. Bye.'

'I'm Cleo.' She stepped closer. 'We spoke on the phone yesterday. I know you said you were too busy to make me a dress, but I was passing and hoped you'd give me some advice.'

Oh crap. This was an ambush. My toxin-infused body couldn't handle this right now. It was working overtime just to keep me alive.

I gave what I hoped was a sympathetic smile. 'Sorry, I can't. Got back-to-back appointments all day.' I pushed the front door open. 'My advice is to go to one of the big department stores, try some on and see what you feel good in.' I tried to slip inside, but one of the dress carriers I had looped over my arm slipped to the floor.

Cleo picked it up and held on tight when I tried to take it back. 'Please,' she said. 'Just five minutes. You don't open for another half an hour.'

I gritted my teeth. 'OK, but only five minutes. I need to get ready for my first client.' I turned, and she followed me up the stairs and into my studio.

As I hung up the dress carriers, Cleo sat down on the small red sofa in my studio. Most bridal salons went for a décor of creams and pale pinks in satin and silk, but I loved vibrant colours. And Anna's spilt Ribena didn't show up so much.

'Do you know what type of dress you'd like?' I asked.

Cleo placed her hands on her stomach. 'What do you recommend for pregnant brides?'

'It depends how pregnant they are,' I said.

Cleo crossed her legs, as though afraid I might try and peek up her skirt to work it out. 'I'm five weeks now.' She smiled at the obvious surprise on my face. 'I know it's early. Only you and the father know so far.' I felt my ears wiggle under my hair. 'He's really excited,' she continued. 'It wasn't planned, but sometimes that's the best way, isn't it? To move things along to the next level.'

I nodded. It had worked with Anna. Maybe we should try that approach again. Just go for it and see what happened. We didn't know for sure that we were even able to have another baby. Especially, as my *vagin* hadn't been re-educated.

'He's much happier with me than he was in his last relationship,' Cleo continued. 'His ex was very controlling.'

'Well, I'm glad he's found happiness with you,' I said. 'Now, about your dress . . .'

'He *has* found happiness.' Cleo sat up tall, her porcelain chin in the air. 'And she should know it.'

This declaration didn't sit comfortably with me. I'd never gloat about how much better off Scott was with me than Liz. Not out loud anyway.

'A high-waisted dress with a loose skirt would probably be best,' I said. I picked my portfolio folder up off my desk, turned back and jumped another foot in the air. Cleo was standing inches from me.

'Is that you?' She pointed at a photo on the wall, of me on my wedding day.

I nodded and tried not to look proud, because that was arrogant and vain. But I did look bloody good. I'd exercised like mad to lose all the baby weight – running with Anna asleep in her pram and doing gruelling Jillian Michael routines. Whenever I wanted to stop, I'd picture the 1920s-inspired *Vogue* dress pattern of my dreams and it'd keep me going. The slender satin wedding dress had a delicate tulle overlay adorned with Swarovski crystals and pearl beads. The back plunged almost to my waist, the neckline was scooped, and the sheer cap sleeves were embroidered with a web of tiny pearls to make my shoulders look less broad and more feminine.

Cleo stared at the photo for so long that I began to feel nervous. Even I didn't look at it that intently. Not every day, anyway.

'You must swim a lot,' she said eventually. Those damn broad shoulders. Should have used more pearls. 'It's a pretty dress, though.' Cleo sat back down and crossed her legs neatly again. 'What was your wedding like?'

'Very low-key, just my immediate family and close friends,' I said. 'My cousin was bridesmaid and my daughter was a flower girl, although she was only six months old. Just an excuse to make a tiny dress, really.'

'Only your family?' Cleo asked.

'Er, yes.' We were slightly veering off track here. 'My husband's an only child and his parents passed away before we met.'

Cleo propped her chin up with one hand. 'Have you had any more children?'

'Shall we focus on your gown?' Enough with the interrogation. I opened my portfolio to show her some dresses with a high waist to allow for a baby bump. Some were traditional, with a stretch lace fabric and a full floor-sweeping skirt; others were modern and relaxed, with a shorter length.

Cleo flicked through the folder, barely registering any of the dresses I'd spent hours designing and making.

'There are so many,' she said.

'I've been doing it for twenty years, so yes, I've dressed a lot of brides.' I willed her to slow down and actually look at the photos. 'Seen any styles you like?'

'Nothing's jumping out at me.' Cleo turned the pages so quickly that her perfect hair fanned out around her face, as though she were walking down a runway. 'Do you live in Horsham?'

'Yes. Do you?'

Cleo shook her head. 'Eastbourne.'

Eastbourne was over an hour away from Horsham, which was a long way to come for dress advice. I still couldn't believe Beth travelled forty-five minutes from Brighton to see me, although I knew she coordinated her visits to see her brother. If Dr Greene were *my* brother, I'd drive forty-five minutes in the opposite direction.

'I travel around the area with work and have a client in Horsham at the moment.' Cleo turned the pages of my portfolio, but she was looking at me rather than the brides smiling out at her, the album balanced precariously on her lap. 'I might move here. It's a nice town.'

I nodded. 'I grew up here and love it. My husband's an

estate agent. I could give you his number if you like?' I wasn't sure why I was encouraging this strange woman to move to my home town, but the words were out before I could stop them.

The album slipped off Cleo's lap and fell to the floor. I swooped down on it protectively. It took many gentle reminders (actually, constant nagging) to get brides to send me a photo and I knew I'd never get another if anything happened to these. Statistically, half of them were probably divorced now anyway.

'Sorry.' Cleo rested her hands on her stomach. 'It was getting heavy.'

'That's OK.' I looked at the clock. Fifteen minutes till my next client, and I needed to give her dress a quick press, lay out a selection of beads for her to choose for the waistband and, most importantly, have a mug of tea. 'Sorry I can't help,' I said, trying to end the meeting.

Cleo held her hands out. 'Let me have another look.'

I hugged the album to my chest, not sure what she expected from me. I'd made it very clear I couldn't help. I didn't have time to consume a hot beverage, let alone knock up a wedding dress. 'Don't mean to be rude, but I need to get ready for my next client.'

Cleo stood up abruptly. 'I'll go, then.' The words 'thanks for nothing' hung in the air unsaid. She turned to leave and I took a sharp intake of breath. The back of her skirt was spotted with blood.

'Don't panic,' I said, uttering the very words that were guaranteed to incite instant panic. 'There's blood on your skirt.'

Cleo swivelled round to look at it. 'No.' Her voice broke. 'No.'

'Spotting isn't unusual in the early stages of pregnancy.' I tried to sound calm. 'I'm sure it's nothing to worry about, but best to get it checked out. There's a surgery down the road. I could take you.'

Cleo shook her head, her eyes swimming with tears. 'I'll go to my own doctor.'

'That's an hour away. And you probably shouldn't drive.'

'My partner can take me.' Tears streamed down Cleo's cheeks.

'Let me at least walk you to your car.' I went to place a hand on her arm and she flinched.

'Don't touch me.' Cleo walked slowly down the stairs, clutching the handrail. I followed, desperate to help, but being completely useless.

'Drive carefully,' I said when we reached the front door. 'Please let me know how you get on.'

Cleo didn't register me or my words. The door banged shut and I sank down onto the stairs, wishing there was something I could do. One thing was certain: if Cleo ever came back, I would somehow find the time to make her a wedding dress.

Chapter 13

The church clock struck 5.30 in the distance as I left work to go and collect Anna from nursery. My stomach plummeted. It was Thursday. Scott would be leaving work now and, unbeknown to him, Maman and Francine would be following. At least I hoped it'd be unbeknown to him. Francine's car was a fluorescent green Citroën 2CV. Hardly subtle, and its occupants were even less so. I wouldn't put it past them to beep and wave at Scott, and everyone else on the road, as though taking part in a carnival parade.

If Scott saw them, my instructions were to act surprised, claim it was a coincidence, and drive home immediately. Admittedly, it'd be one hell of a coincidence if he saw them on the road where Liz lived, but presumably other people lived on that road too. Maman and Francine could be visiting one of Liz's neighbours. Provided she hadn't driven them all out.

My phone beeped with a message on our family WhatsApp group. Usually I ignored it, as Maman and Francine discussed inane topics at length, seemingly unaware that, as Brigitte and I weren't involved, they should have a private conversation. As they were seemingly unaware of most things in life, this wasn't surprising. Tonight, however, I was very much involved. Unfortunately.

I read the first message.

Maman: *We see him.*

Five seconds later.

Maman: *We are following him.*

Ten seconds later.

Maman: *He is stopped at traffic lights.*

Thirty seconds later.

Maman: *Now traffic is moving.*
Maman: *We are going straight.*

I phoned Maman.

'*Oui*,' she whispered.

'You don't have to message every movement,' I said.

'But is important to know where he is going, *n'est-ce pas?*'

'The final destination is the important bit. Liz's address. I don't need to know every time you stop at a traffic light on the way there.'

'Oh.' Maman sounded surprised. 'We don't need to stop at traffic lights,' she said at normal volume, her voice slightly away from the phone.

'*Bien*,' Francine replied in the background. '*C'est énervant.*'

'That's not what I said.' I stopped walking and tucked myself into a shop doorway. 'You *must* stop at traffic lights, no matter how annoying they are, but you don't need to tell me every time you do. *Tu comprends?*'

Maman tutted. 'Your accent is very poor, Marie. *Tourne à droite*, Francine. *À droite*, Francine. *À droite*, Francine!' She bellowed the final instruction and I held the phone away from my ear, then nervously listened again. A cacophony of car horns sounded out in the background. Maman sniffed. '*À gauche. Tourne à gauche.*'

'Is everything OK?' I asked.

'*Bien sûr*,' Maman said. 'Francine is confusing right with left.'

It sounded very much like Maman was the one doing the confusing. Francine's stream of expletives echoed this observation.

'I think it's best we stop talking, so you can concentrate on navigating,' I said. 'Remember, come back as soon as you see where he parks. And keep well back. Drive *keefily*.' She had me at it now. 'Scott hasn't seen you, has he?' I added.

'Or course not,' Maman snapped. 'Do you think we are fools?'

I declined to comment.

* * *

I had to wait a full hour for the next instalment. I collected Anna and we did our usual push-me-pull-me thing with the buggy, so the five-minute walk home actually took twenty. I didn't mind, as it kept her entertained and it was a warm evening – the activity could wear a little thin on cold, rainy days. But my ears pricked up every time I heard a siren in the background, and I envisaged Maman and Francine screeching around corners in hot pursuit of Scott, with the police in hot pursuit of them.

I grabbed my phone when Maman eventually rang. 'What happened?'

'That is not how you start a conversation, Marie,' Maman scolded. 'You must enquire for my health first.'

I couldn't hear any clanging bars, prisoners screaming or food trays being slammed down on steel tables, so assumed she hadn't been arrested. Did that mean they'd been successful? '*Ça va?*' I asked, immediately followed by: 'Now tell me what happened.'

'*Rien.*'

'What do you mean nothing?'

'I mean what I say. There is nothing to tell.' Maman yawned down the phone.

'Am I boring you?' I asked.

'A little.'

I shook my head. 'Something must have happened. When we last spoke, you were following Scott. Did you see where Liz lives?'

'Yes and no,' Maman said.

I raised my eyes to the ceiling. 'It can't be both. You have to choose one.'

'In that case . . . *non.*' A wave of disappointment washed over me. 'We did not see where Liz lives,' Maman continued. 'Scott drives very fast and there were many cars.'

'I understand.' My disappointment segued into relief. I'd never wanted them to follow Scott. They'd insisted, and failed. We could cross that option off and they couldn't criticise me for not allowing them to try. 'Glad you're all right,' I said.

'All right?' Francine shrieked. I hadn't realised I was on loudspeaker. 'I am not all right. There are maniacs on the road. Many of them tried to crash into me.'

'I did warn you it was rush hour,' I said.

'I cannot believe you made us do this.' OK, they could still criticise me. Francine took a shaky breath. 'I am never driving again.'

At least one good thing had come out of this.

'Sorry to hear that,' I lied. 'Thank you for trying.'

'Is that all you have to say?' Francine snapped. 'After I risked my life for you.'

'Anna's calling me,' I lied again. 'She's just done a poo.'

The line went dead.

I put my phone down with a sigh. It would have been great to get Liz's address, but the whole operation had always been too risky for my liking. This was by far the best outcome.

Although, I realised with a sinking feeling, now I was going to have to do that bloody pole dancing class.

Chapter 14

'Hi, babe,' Scott slurred, sliding into bed next to me and bringing with him the aroma of Cobra, garlic and cumin. 'Didn't expect you to be awake this late.'

Turning my head to look at the clock, and escape his breath – much as I loved Indian food and the accompanying lager, the smell wasn't so appealing second-hand – I realised it was almost midnight. I'd been lying there for two hours, worrying about what to wear to pole dancing, how to get out of pole dancing, how to befriend Liz at the class, how to befriend her without attending the class, and how Cleo was. It had been two days since she'd come to the studio. I didn't have her number, so could only hope that she and the baby were OK.

The incident had highlighted my own fears about miscarriage, especially as I was *un certain âge*. I understood Scott's concerns – Liz was demanding, financially and physically. Money was tight and Scott's time was limited, so adding a baby to the mix would just add to his stress. But I didn't want Anna to be an only child. Brigitte and I weren't technically sisters, but we were as close, and I couldn't imagine not having that bond in my life. I wanted Anna to have it too. The longer we left it, the higher the risk it'd be too late.

My plan to get Liz on my side was littered with flaws. She could take an instant dislike to me, which was very likely, given that she was a complete cow. She might not be fooled by the 'complete coincidence' of the meeting and would then be even more wary of me. Also, pole-dancing Liz Clark might not be Scott's Liz Clark. There were several million of them, after all.

Scott had asked me not to talk about Liz, but there was no avoiding this conversation any longer. I had to grow a pair and tell Scott it was time to start trying. Actually, if I could grow a pair that'd be a massive help. I could just get on with it without having to involve him at all.

I opened my mouth to speak, as Scott wrapped his arms around me. 'Did you see the local news?' he asked.

'Er, no.' I was all fired-up to talk about our future, not the latest council meeting outcome, or how the Horsham Hornets had fared in their last game.

'There was a massive pile-up on the outskirts of town.'

I froze.

'No one was hurt, luckily.' Scott hiccuped. 'I only just missed it. Saw some of it happen in my rear-view mirror. This bright green car was skidding all over the place.' I held my breath. 'Must have been a system failure at the crossroads traffic lights, 'cause the cars all piled into each other.'

'That's awful.' I swallowed hard, knowing only too well what sort of system failure it was. 'Are you sure no one was injured?'

'I'm sure.' Scott nuzzled my neck. 'This is one of the reasons I love you,' he murmured. 'So caring. Always thinking of others.' My cheeks grew warm. I *was* thinking of others – Maman and Francine to be precise – but those thoughts definitely weren't caring.

I forced Francine's Wacky Races antics out of my mind and focused on the conversation I needed to have with Scott about trying for a baby. His curry night had clearly put him in a good, if drunken, mood, so I should strike while the madras was hot.

'I've been thinking—'

'You know Andy from work?'

I suppressed a frustrated groan. No, I did not know Andy from work. I'd only met Scott's colleagues once, four years ago. On one of our early dates, we'd bumped into his work friends having a night out. Scott had introduced me, but as they were all called Andy or Dave, I couldn't remember any of them.

I gamely tried to recall Andy. 'Is he the one who said his wife could get me a discount at the Pound Shop?'

'No, that's Dave. She works at B&M now. Andy's the one who looks like a spacehopper.'

'Oh, him.' I still had no idea, but it was easier to go along with it.

Scott tapped his thumb against my shoulder. 'Andy said something really profound tonight.'

'What was that?' I asked, wondering if in Scott's drunken state he'd mistaken the meaning of the word profound for complete bollocks.

Scott paused. 'Can't remember exactly,' he admitted. 'But the gist of it was about the importance of being a good dad and how important that is. Made me think about my dad,' he added quietly.

I turned to look at his profile, illuminated by the clock radio. Scott's parents had divorced when he was fifteen, after years of rowing caused by his dad's constant affairs. Scott had been named after his dad, but was so disgusted by his father's behaviour, and then Liz's betrayal, that he'd discarded both his given first name (Richard) and surname – Clark – just before we'd met. Even without this very understandable reason, it wasn't a bad idea to change a name that could be shortened to Dick.

'The fights were horrible,' he said. 'Having to listen to them at each other's throats.' He sighed loudly and I very nobly didn't spoil the moment by wafting his breath away with my hand. 'Don't know why he didn't leave earlier. Why make me put up with twelve years of that?'

So he'd been twelve, not fifteen. Unless Scott was so pissed that he'd lost the ability to count. It was possible.

'Because he didn't want to leave *you*,' I said softly. 'He might not have loved your mum anymore, but he wouldn't

111

have stopped loving you.' This was pure speculation on my part. His parents had died before we'd met, but it seemed the best explanation.

'Does Anna think I'm a good dad?' Scott asked quietly.

'Course she does.' I squeezed his hand. 'You're a *great* dad.'

He might not be around much, but he was very sweet with Anna and never got cross with her. Unlike me. Before Anna was born, I'd believed myself to be extremely patient – I had to be, when making gowns for brides who believed I was available exclusively to them 24/7 and expected me to double up as their wedding planner, free of charge. Anna, however, could cause me to flip from stable, caring parent to irrational, screeching demon with one throw of a bread roll. She didn't just know how to push my buttons, she also knew how to hammer them with a force Thor would be proud of.

'Don't doubt yourself,' I continued. 'Just because your dad was . . .' I searched for the words, unwilling to label his dead dad a cheating wanker. '. . . Wasn't a great role model, it doesn't mean you're like him. We're not replicas of our parents.' I winced at the prospect of morphing into my mad mother. 'If we were, you'd be completely justified in leaving me.'

'I'd never leave. You mean the world to me.' Scott's voice cracked. 'I don't want Liz to ruin what we've got. I'm going to stop running round there every time she rings. I won't answer the phone even.' His eyes shone with tears. 'She'll probably try and stop me seeing the kids, but I've got to take a stand. You're my priority, not her.'

My heart went out to him. He was trying so hard to please everyone – me, Anna, Liz, Harry, Bella, his dead parents. All on top of a stressful job.

'Things are going to change, I promise,' he whispered.

I bit my lip. 'Does that include trying for another baby?' Scott tensed. 'I don't mean right now.' I was perfectly OK with us not having sex tonight. It was late and his biryani breath really wasn't doing it for me. 'But soon.' Scott nodded.

'Really?' I clutched his hand. 'It could take ages, might not even happen, so it needs to be soon. *Very* soon.'

'Soon – I get it.' Scott smiled sleepily. 'Soon.'

He fell asleep and I snuggled into him, wondering why I wasn't more elated. He'd said everything I wanted to hear – he'd stop pandering to Liz and, most importantly, we could try for a baby soon. But it wasn't fair that Harry and Bella would be penalised while Scott took a stand against their mother. Also, we were no closer to me and Anna meeting them. If anything, this would make Liz resist it more.

Scott began to snore and I rolled onto my other side. If I wanted us to be one blended family, not two isolated ones, I was going to have to go to the bloody pole dancing class and forge a union with Liz. I wouldn't be able to do that when I was pregnant, so the sooner, the better.

I smiled at the memory of Scott agreeing we could start trying soon. The burning question was, how soon was soon?

Chapter 15

Brigitte and I watched the rain hammering against the car windows and the steps leading to The Pole Hub entrance door.

'Perhaps it'll get rained off,' I said. 'No one else has arrived.'

'That's because the class doesn't start for another twenty minutes.' We hadn't been sure how long it'd take to get to Guildford, especially if either Maman or Francine happened to be on the roads, so had allowed plenty of time. As it turned out, there was very little traffic and not a pile-up in sight, so we'd arrived far too early. Brigitte checked the Instagram page. 'No post to say it's cancelled. You're not getting out of it that easily.'

I was so desperate to get out of it that I'd almost hoped Scott would get a call from Liz telling him he had to babysit Bella and Harry, but he hadn't. He'd stuck to his word and hadn't taken a single one of Liz's calls over the past week. And he hadn't questioned me when I said Brigitte and I were trying out a new exercise class and would get something to eat afterwards. Why would he? I'd never given him cause to doubt me. Which made me feel even guiltier.

'Stop worrying,' Brigitte said. 'Worst-case scenario, we have a laugh and a bit of a workout; best-case scenario, it's the real Liz and you can start your action plan of getting her onside.'

'No. Best-case scenario, I merely make a fool of myself. Worst-case, I seriously injure myself. Or, even worse . . .' I swallowed hard. 'It *is* her. I don't want Scott's ex to be some incredibly flexible, sexy, femme fatale. How can I compete with that?'

Brigitte shook her head. 'You're not competing with her. He left Liz before he met you. If he wanted back in, he'd have done it long ago. Not that he would, because he loves you. And she's a total bitch.'

'I'd still prefer it if she was a frumpy, unattractive bitch.' I exhaled loudly, then pulled myself together. This was my chance to make things right with Liz, and get a healthy balance for Scott and his children, rather than an all-or-nothing arrangement. Plus, I should make the most of this time – it could be my last twenty minutes on Earth if I fell on my head mid-aerial or ankle hang. I'd made the mistake of googling some pole dancing moves. Many of them contained the word mount, which didn't seem wise when they were at pains to market this as a form of exercise, not prostitution.

A movement outside caught our eye: a woman, dressed in a hoodie, joggers and trainers, carrying a large sports bag, ran across the road and up the steps to The Pole Hub.

'Let's do this.' Brigitte took the key out of the ignition.

I wished desperately that we weren't doing this. I'd got lucky with the first Liz Clark; she'd been sweet and shy. Going by the photos on Insta, particularly the ones in which she had her thighs wrapped around a pole or her arse in the air, this Liz Clark was definitely not timid.

We got out of the car and I pulled my mac tightly around me. Partly to keep me dry, partly to hide the fact I was dressed like a hooker underneath. Albeit quite a low-rent one – the rich and famous wouldn't be risking their marriages or reputation for a night with me in my Primark cycling shorts and vest top.

'Is this the class that Liz Clark goes to?' Brigitte asked, as we followed the woman through the door she'd just unlocked.

'That's my name, don't wear it out,' said a voice so gravelly, she must have got through forty cigarettes a day. Quite possibly forty a night too. My stomach lurched. Meeting Liz was scary enough without her actually being scary. Her hood was up, pulled so far forward that her face wasn't visible. If it matched her voice then I would run screaming from the building.

Liz, whose name I had no intention of using so often it wore out, unlocked an internal door and reversed in, flicking light switches with her elbows. 'I don't go to the class, though,' she said.

I breathed a sigh of relief. Scott's ex wasn't a nubile hottie and we didn't need to put ourselves through this torture.

'I'm the teacher. I run the class.'

Fuck.

Brigitte gulped audibly. 'We've signed up for a beginner's class,' she said. 'Be gentle with us.'

'That's between you and the pole,' Liz said. 'Nothing to do with me.'

Her manner reminded me of a rancher in a Western. One of the tough, wizened types with missing teeth and a propensity for killing anything that crossed their land, be it rabbits, bears or Father Christmas.

Liz kicked off her trainers, pulled her hoodie over her head and rolled her joggers down, revealing hot pants and a crop top. Brigitte and I gasped. Her body was phenomenal. Every inch of her was toned and supple, her abs looked as though they'd been spray-painted on, and her skin was smooth and lightly tanned and not remotely wizened. Was this the body that Scott had married and slept with for years? I took my trainers off, but did up every button on my mac, feeling more inferior than I ever had before in my life.

'Names?' Liz barked. Her voice contrasted drastically with the magnificence of her physique.

'Anastasia and Drizella,' I said. I hadn't used our real names, in case Liz recognised them.

Brigitte rolled her eyes.

Liz opened her bag and took out some forms, which she handed to us. 'Health questionnaire and liability waiver. That means if you injure yourself, it's not my fault. It's 'cause you didn't listen properly. Follow my instructions and you'll be all right.'

I hesitated at the point on the form where I had to put my address. Would Liz know Scott's home address? Not wanting to take the risk, I used Maman's and hoped Liz didn't petrol bomb it in the night. Or the day, for that matter. It took me longer to complete the forms than it should have done, because I couldn't take my eyes off Liz, as she rolled out mats, checked the poles and did a few stretches. Her body was that of a twenty-year-old. Her face was harder to ID. She'd clearly had some work – there were no lines on her forehead and around her eyes, or a number eleven between her brows, and her lips were plump. But her neck and hands weren't treated. Scott was five years older than me. It made sense that Liz might be too. Whatever age she was, she was extremely attractive. Bugger.

Women started to wander into the class, and chatted among themselves as they warmed up.

'I'm going to talk to Liz,' I whispered to Brigitte. 'Might not get a chance once the class has started.'

I took my form over. Liz scanned the health questionnaire and gave a satisfied nod. 'You look amazing.' I gestured to her physique before patting my stomach through my coat. 'I've not been able to lose my tummy since I had a baby and she's three now.'

Liz nodded. 'This class is perfect for you, then. Pole work is primarily core strengthening.'

'Do you have children?' Not very subtle, but needs must.

'Yep, two.'

That ticked that box.

'Boys? Girls? Both?' I asked.

'One of each.'

Tick.

'And you live in Guildford?'

'Yep. All my life.'

The field was narrowing.

'Are you married?' Was this pushing it?

'Used to be.'

I ran a hand down my plait. 'Hope it was an amicable separation.'

Liz cackled. 'Not really. I cheated on him and he didn't like it.'

My pulse quickened. Everything fitted. It was her: I'd found Scott's ex-wife.

'Grab yourselves a pole and get to know it,' Liz said. 'We're about to start.'

I darted over to where Brigitte was guarding two poles next to each other.

'It's her,' I whispered. 'What do I do now?'

'Take your mac off,' Brigitte said. 'The class is starting.' She'd taken off her own coat to reveal shiny, tiny shorts and a matching bra top. With her hair in a high ponytail and her lips painted red, she looked like a pro. In both senses of the word.

I reluctantly unbuttoned my coat and tossed it to the side of the studio, where it knocked over two water bottles that didn't belong to us.

'Sorry,' I mouthed, my hands up, in case the owners were watching. Tugging my cheap shorts down, I focused on what Liz was doing at the front of the studio. Standing behind her pole, she was holding it with both hands at shoulder height.

'Up on tippy-toes and take your right foot back,' she instructed. 'Now sweep it around to the front, keeping contact with the floor, and step forward. Then sweep your left foot to the front, keeping contact with the floor, and repeat.'

Her hips sashayed sensually as she performed the steps slowly. Beside me, Brigitte did the same, as did the other members of the class. As did I! This wasn't so hard. Next came a body roll. I didn't roll as deeply as Liz, but I was keeping up and not falling over, which was an improvement on my last encounter with a Liz Clark.

'Now we're going to add a fireman's spin,' Liz shouted. 'Inside arm is extended. Take three sexy steps.' I faltered. What was a sexy step? 'Connect the inside ankle, lean, cross and rotate around the pole.' Wait, what? Liz smoothly spun around the base of the pole and straightened up using a body roll. 'Now do the same on the other side.'

How was everyone keeping up with this? Determined not to be the only one not spinning, I threw myself at the pole, whacking my shins sharply against the steel, before falling hard onto my bottom.

'Don't worry if you don't get it the first time,' Liz said. 'Keep practising and you'll get there.' As everyone else had got it, this was clearly for my benefit.

I hauled myself up, ignoring the throbbing in my shins where they'd hit the pole. All it took was practice. I would not give up. I could do this.

I could not do this.

An hour later, my head was spinning with instructions – 'point your feet', 'wrap around the pole', 'roll down', 'drop to a diamond', 'add a hair toss' – and Liz's favourite chant: 'It don't count, if the booty ain't out.' My brain was exhausted and my body battered. Muscles that I didn't know I had, ached, as did all the ones I did know about. My shins and the tops of my feet were covered in bruises. My palms stung. The soles of my feet throbbed. I didn't dare examine my inner thighs – the skin felt red raw. And I was drenched in sweat.

'That was amazing,' Brigitte said. 'Hard work, but amazing. Let's sign up for the rest of the term.'

My muscles quivered in fear at the prospect. 'I doubt Scott'll be able to babysit every week.' Especially, if I didn't ask him to.

Brigitte wound her damp hair into a top knot. 'How will you get Liz to know and like you, without coming to the class?'

'Anyone fancy going for a drink?' Liz called out.

I grinned at Brigitte. 'That's how.'

None of the other students came, so it was the perfect opportunity to talk to Liz and prove my worth as a stepmother.

'What did you think?' Liz asked, opening a large packet of peanuts and gesturing to us to share them.

Brigitte smiled her thanks and took a handful. 'I loved it.'

'You did great. You're a natural.' Liz nodded at me. 'How about you?'

'It was hard work,' I said. 'Really hard. And I definitely wasn't great.'

'I've seen worse,' Liz said. 'And you stuck it out for the whole hour. Not everyone does.' That wasn't praise exactly, but I still felt a small glow of pride. 'Have a soak in Epsom salts tonight if you've got some,' she added. 'And get some arnica for your pole kisses.' She laughed at mine and Brigitte's puzzled expressions. 'That's what we call the bruises. You'll get them for a few weeks, till that part of your body desensitises. Then we'll learn a new routine and you'll get them someplace else.'

I had no intention of coming back and getting pole kisses on yet more parts of my body. I needed to manoeuvre this conversation towards the shock discovery that we had a connection and then I'd never have to go near a pole again.

'So, you've got two children,' I said.

'Yep,' Liz said, stirring Tabasco sauce into a tomato juice.

With her voice, I'd assumed she'd be necking pints of ale. Or oxen blood. 'Not that they're children anymore.'

Brigitte and I exchanged a surprised look. 'What do you mean?' I asked.

'They're grown-ups now. Got kids of their own. I'm a grandma five times over.'

'You can't be,' I spluttered. This didn't tick any boxes. In fact, it un-ticked them.

'How old are you?' Brigitte asked. 'If that's not too rude a question.'

'Fifty-five.'

Brigitte gazed at Liz in awe. 'You're my hero. How do you look so amazing?'

Liz blushed, not something I expected to see. 'Pole dancing, obviously. A bit of Botox and fillers. I'm very strict with my diet. Lots of water, protein, very few carbs, no alcohol.' Brigitte's look of admiration was slipping. Liz put her hands up. 'Sounds boring, but I had throat cancer ten years ago. Wasn't sure I was going to make it, so now I want to be as healthy and strong as I can be.'

I put down the lager I'd been chugging my way through, ashamed for being so judgemental. When I'd heard Liz's gruff voice, I'd assumed she was a heavy smoker. Instead, she was a clean-living cancer survivor.

I picked up the water I'd also got and clinked my glass against Liz's, then Brigitte's spritzer. 'Lovely to meet you, Liz. Here's to healthy living.'

'That was an unexpected turn of events,' Brigitte said half an hour later, when we got into her car to head home. 'I'm not sure what surprised me more: Liz being fifty-five or you agreeing to come again next week.'

'If I've recovered.' I wriggled in my seat. 'Even sitting down hurts. I believed her when she said we'd ache for several days.'

'It don't count if the booty ain't out,' Brigitte sang. 'It'll be worth it to have a strong body like hers.'

I nodded. 'I'm glad we came. She's a very inspirational woman.' I sighed. 'But she's not Scott's ex. That Liz Clark is still out there and I've no idea where.'

Chapter 16

'Oh, I do like to be beside the seaside,' Brigitte sang beside me.

'The seaside?' Anna shrieked from the back of the car.

I glared at Brigitte as best I could without taking my eyes off the road. 'No, chick. No seaside.'

'But Auntie Brigitte said seaside.'

'She got it wrong,' I said gently. 'Again,' I hissed, much less gently. 'The whole point of this resort is to provide a beach-like experience with wave pools and artificial sand.'

'Why?' Brigitte asked.

'So you don't waste precious holiday time travelling hundreds of miles to the coast, then spend the whole time pretending to have a good time even though it's freezing cold and seagulls are pooing all over your fish and chips.' Anna giggled behind me. I should have stuck to the professional wording. Beth's marketing literature hadn't mentioned pooing.

'Let me get this right . . .' Brigitte said. 'We're travelling hundreds of miles *away* from the coast to escape the authentic experience in favour of a manufactured one?'

'Yes,' I admitted. 'But it's to support Beth, and it's free and it's an excuse to get away and—'

Brigitte put a hand on my arm. 'No need to justify it. I hate the seaside. They never have toilets.'

'If you must wee every fifteen minutes, you've got to learn to go in the sea,' I said. 'You made such a fuss last time we went to Brighton.'

'I wasn't being unreasonable,' Brigitte said. 'You try changing a tampon underwater.'

'What's a tampon?' Anna asked.

'It's a French word,' I said. 'It means tiny towel.'

Brigitte tutted in the exact same way our mums did. 'I'm with the French on this one. You've got to tell her how it is.'

'I will when she's older,' I said. 'Three's too young to understand periods.'

'What's a period?' Anna said.

'It's another word for a school lesson.' I held a finger up to Brigitte. My forefinger, rather than the one I wanted to hold up, as Anna was being so enchantingly observant. 'It is in America.'

'They call bottoms "fannies" in America,' Brigitte said. 'Going to start using that word too?'

Anna giggled again. 'Auntie Brigitte said bottom.'

'And fannies,' Brigitte said over her shoulder.

Thankfully, Anna was laughing about the word bottom too much to add fannies to her repertoire. I was starting to wish Brigitte hadn't rearranged her appointments so she could come away. We reverted to squabbling-siblings mode when cooped up in a car together.

'Don't be facetious,' I snapped.

'What are faeces?' Anna asked. Her dark curly bunches bobbed about in the rear-view mirror as she craned forward. She was adorable and this thirst for knowledge needed to be encouraged but, quite frankly, she was doing my head in.

'Why don't you have a nap?' I suggested. 'Save your energy for swimming when we get there.'

'Oh, I do like to be beside the seaside,' Brigitte sang.

'Seaside?' Anna squealed.

I gritted my teeth.

'Thanks for coming to my presentation.' Beth hugged me. I withheld a yelp as she unintentionally put pressure on my post-pole-dancing battered body. 'I'll try not to go on too much.'

'Take as long as you like,' I said. 'This is my child-free break for the weekend.'

'Doesn't have to be the only one. We have a babysitting service.' Beth handed me a green folder. 'All the information's in here.'

I smiled my thanks and took a seat at the back of the room. Inside the folder was a key ring, a pen that doubled up as a torch and a packet of Love Hearts. Anna would be thrilled. Before I had a chance to read any of the leaflets, Beth cleared her throat into a microphone.

'Welcome to Heavenly Hideaway.' A broad smile hid a slight tremble in her voice. She was either nervous or suppressing a laugh at the name, which she'd confided to me sounded more like a porn film than a family resort. 'Thank you for being our guinea pigs for the weekend. Our staff are fully trained, and everything has been tested and trialled, so your stay should be perfect. But please do say if there's anything that you feel would make it even more enjoyable. Before I go into details of everything available to you, a few housekeeping rules.'

I switched off. If there were an emergency, I'd follow all the people running to the nearest exit rather than try and recall their location from this meeting. I was enjoying some outfit-watching – the same as people-watching, but I analysed their clothes – when a person I definitely didn't want to watch walked in. Dr Greene. I put my head down and unwrapped the Love Hearts with the stealth of a sniper to avoid making a noise. The message on the sweet was EAT ME. It'd be rude not to.

'Hello,' Dr Greene said quietly.

I frowned. Why pick the chair next to me? There was a room full of them. Looking around, I realised all the other seats had been taken, but there was floor space. He could have sat cross-legged at Beth's feet. I gave a tight smile and put another Love Heart in my mouth.

'Giving up sugar's going well, I see.'

125

I sniffed. 'Your sister's giving an important talk about housekeeping. You should be listening.'

'You're right,' Dr Greene said. 'Although, she's actually talking about horse riding lessons.'

'House, horse. Potato, potahto.' I shrugged.

'Potahto?' Dr Greene put his head on one side. 'Who says that?'

I shook my head. Hadn't this man heard of Michael Bublé? 'Please stop talking over Beth's speech.'

Dr Greene nodded and faced the front. Even that annoyed me, which didn't make sense, as he was doing exactly what I'd asked him to do.

I focused on what Beth was saying.

'At Heavenly Hideaway you have the choice to spend as much or as little time with your family as you like.' She gestured to a screen behind her, which showed a photo of children laughing with a Heavenly Hideaway entertainer. 'Our fun clubs run every day, freeing you up to have important me-time.' The screen changed to show a woman having a massage, then to a photo of a couple sitting outside a café in the sun. A third image showed two women with cocktails in their hands. That was more mine and Brigitte's style, although I could hardly pick Anna up from fun club pissed. 'We're offering 50 per cent off all food and beverages this weekend,' Beth said. Maybe I could get a little bit pissed.

Beth went on to list the more adventurous activities the resort offered and I switched off again. Pole dancing was dangerous enough. Dangling suspended from wires while scaling an artificial wall or crossing rickety rope-bridges connecting trees wasn't for me. Not because I was scared of heights. Heights didn't bother me at all. It was the falling from a height and hurtling to my death that unnerved me.

Dr Greene shifted in his chair next to me and I involuntarily turned my outfit analysis onto him. It was the first time I'd seen him in anything other than a suit. Today he was wearing a navy short-sleeved shirt, tailored mustard-coloured shorts and navy Converse. I had to give him credit for his colour coordination. And, reluctantly, for his physique. Everything, from his calves to his arms, was firm and toned, and his shirt sat flat across his stomach, without any straining at the midriff, as Scott's had started to lately. Dr Greene clearly worked out. Poor Scott didn't have time to exercise because of Liz's demands. Hopefully, that'd change now. Maybe we could even start running together.

Romantic visions of me and Scott bounding across buttercup-strewn meadows ran through my head. It was like something out of a 1970s chocolate-box advert until my *Game of Thrones* addled brain upgraded it (or downgraded it, depending on your way of thinking) to a full-on romp in the grass. It was just getting interesting, when I realised everyone was applauding and Beth had finished her talk. Guiltily, I clapped so enthusiastically that my folder slipped off my lap and the Love Hearts rolled away under someone's chair.

Dr Greene reached down and handed me my folder. He wasn't gentlemanly enough to go delving under the chairs in front for my sweets, but I couldn't hold that against him. Much as I wanted to.

'Have a good weekend if I don't see you,' he said, striding to the front to talk to Beth. It was more likely to be good if I *didn't* see him.

Chapter 17

'How long do we have to do this for?' Brigitte asked, as we swam Anna round the whirlpool river for the eightieth time.

'Forever,' shrieked Anna, an arm tightly looped around each of our necks, ensuring neither of us could breathe properly.

An Amazonian cry came over the loudspeakers and there was a flurry of activity to get to the main area of the pool for the wave machine.

'Let's play in the waves, Anna,' Brigitte said.

'No.' Anna stuck her lower lip out determinedly. 'Like it here.'

Brigitte pouted even more impressively.

'You go,' I said. 'I'll stay with Anna.'

'I can't go on my own,' Brigitte said. 'I'll look like a loser.' She kissed Anna's cheek. 'Please, Anna. Do it for Auntie Brigitte.'

'I will if you pay me,' Anna said.

Brigitte looked impressed by her niece's devious tactics. 'How much?'

Anna wiped her nose on my shoulder while she considered her answer.

'One hundred,' she announced.

'One hundred what?' Brigitte asked cautiously.

Anna considered the question. Her answer could be anything from pounds sterling to unicorn tears. 'Pennies,' she said eventually.

'One hundred pennies? Done.' Brigitte scooped Anna under one arm and we swam in the direction of the main pool before she could up her fee.

Brigitte's hot-pink swimsuit stood out among the mumsy tankinis, my own included, as we walked across to the shallow area of the main pool.

'Is your costume going to survive the waves?' I asked. 'The back's so low, I can see your arse crack.'

'It's called bum cleavage,' she said airily.

'We're at a family resort, not a pole dancing class,' I hissed. 'It very much does count if your booty's out.'

'Be thankful our mums aren't here.' She grinned. 'They'd be sunbathing topless by now.'

I was saved from dwelling on this hideous thought by the sight of Beth waving from one of the artificial beach areas at the side.

'Go and chat if you want to,' Brigitte said.

She didn't need to ask twice. If she was about to lose her costume, I'd rather not be there, in case she tried to pinch mine.

'Thank you.' I kissed Anna. 'Try not to drink the water, chick. It'll give you a tummy ache.' Anna obliged by spitting out the contents of her mouth in my face. Being a mum was great.

I navigated my way up the slippery steps, which was made even trickier by every muscle in my body screaming in agony after last night's pole dancing class. I hobbled towards Beth, wishing my towel wasn't on the other side of the beach complex. I couldn't expect her to wait while I went and found it, so sucked it up – my stomach as well as my pride – and tried to pretend I wasn't really in the equivalent of my underwear.

We sat down on deckchairs beneath a parasol and immediately a waiter brought over two non-alcoholic strawberry daiquiris.

I smiled my thanks and took a sip. Delicious. 'Are you pleased with how it's going?' I asked. 'Everyone seems to be having fun.'

Beth nodded. 'So far, so good. Some people will always find something to complain about, but most of the feedback's been very positive.'

'We're having a great time. Thank you for inviting us.'
I took a long sip of daiquiri through my paper straw. It
instantly began to disintegrate. Good excuse to drink fast.
'What could anyone complain about, especially as it's free?'

Beth looked around to make sure no one was listening.
'Utter crap mainly,' she whispered. 'A spider in the bath,
two birds mating outside their bedroom window, that kind
of thing.'

I snorted. 'What do they expect you to do? Exterminate
all insects and chaperone the wildlife?'

'Probably.' Beth eased her feet out of her shoes and rotated
her ankles. 'This is the first time I've sat down in the last
eight hours. I'm shattered and it's only day one.' She caught
sight of my legs and gasped. 'You're covered in bruises.
What happened?'

My face grew warm. 'Please don't judge me.'

Beth shook her head.

'Brigitte and I went to a pole dancing class.' I shifted in
my lounger and winced. 'I wasn't very good.'

Beth grinned. 'I tried burlesque once. Now, that was
embarrassing.'

We leant closer, united by our risqué exercise routines.

'Tell me everything.' I giggled.

'I used to go to Jazzercise and it was the instructor's hen
do,' Beth said. 'Izzy was only six months old. I was still
breastfeeding and had to squeeze myself into a basque.'
She covered her eyes with one hand. 'They made us climb
into giant cocktail glasses and dance in the windows of the
club. It was on a Saturday afternoon and everyone walking
past, doing their shopping, could see us. I've never been so
humiliated in my life.'

'OK, you win,' I said. 'But I bet you looked amazing. Your
husband must have loved the basque.'

Beth lowered her hand. 'The marriage was over by then.'

I gasped. 'When Izzy was only six months old?'

Beth shrugged. 'He was barely around anyway. Had no

interest in Izzy and Henry.' She fell silent and I didn't like to pry any further.

'Are they here?' I asked.

Beth visibly brightened. 'Michael and Dean are looking after them.'

It took me a moment to remember that Michael was Dr Greene's first name – it was Bell in my mind. Did that mean . . . ?

'Is Dean Dr Greene's partner?' I asked.

Beth nodded. 'Did he mention him? He's always going on about how inspiring he is.'

I shook my head, cringing at how foolish I'd been about that stupid smear test. Dr Greene probably felt the same way about women's bodies as I did about Scientologists. Nothing against them personally, but wouldn't want to take one home with me.

'And call him Michael, not Dr Greene,' Beth added, with a smile. 'He's off duty this weekend.'

'You kept your maiden name,' I said, realising that Beth's surname was Greene, like her brother's.

'I went back to it after the divorce,' Beth said. 'I'd used Greene at work anyway.'

I nodded. 'I didn't take Scott's name. It's a bit complicated because he changed it, but even if he hadn't, I'd established myself as Marie Dubois and didn't want to risk losing customers by going under a different name.'

'Dubois is a great name,' Beth said. 'Sounds French.'

'It's my mum's surname. More memorable than Wright, which is my dad's. I like that it's my mum's heritage too.' Not that I'd ever admit that to Maman.

A shadow crossed Beth's face. 'Wish my name was my family's heritage.'

I sipped my drink. 'Isn't Greene your parents' surname, then?'

'Yes. And my grandparents', and great-grandparents', etcetera. But the name belongs to the plantation owners, who enslaved my ancestors. We'll never know what our real family name is.'

I swallowed hard, ashamed to realise that although I abhorred slavery and racism, I hadn't considered the long-lasting impact it still had. 'That's horrible. And so sad.'

Beth sighed. 'Yeah, it's hard knowing that my name came from a slave trader who abused and exploited my ancestors. What's more worrying is that people don't want to recognise this history, and the fact that the slave trade made millions and a lot of people got very rich from it.' Her brow furrowed. 'The foundations of modern capitalism at its worst.'

'I'm so sorry.' I wished I could say something more substantial. I didn't come from money, so hopefully my own ancestors hadn't profited from such a disgusting legacy.

'It's not your fault.' Beth smiled. 'And my family are really close. The bastard slave owners didn't destroy that.' She leant over and swapped my empty glass for her full one. 'Have mine. I've got a wedding dress to get into in ten weeks.'

'Thank you.' I settled back on the lounger. I wanted to ask more about her heritage, but wasn't sure if it was too personal. 'Have you and Dr Greene, I mean Michael, always got on?' I asked instead.

'Yes. It's such a relief to have him back.'

'Where's he been?'

'Syria. He went on a twelve-month placement nine years ago and didn't come back till January. Said it didn't feel right leaving, when so much help was needed and he was in a position to provide that help.' Beth sighed. 'It was horrible not seeing him for so long. He missed my first wedding, and didn't meet Henry and Izzy in the flesh till recently, although we Skyped as often as we could.'

I worked my way through Beth's daiquiri, unable to imagine not seeing Brigitte for years or for her to be absent from the most important moments of my life. 'Must have been really hard.'

'It was,' Beth said. 'Constantly worrying something might happen to him. It helped when Dean joined him, knowing he wasn't on his own, but it was still tough. I had to keep reminding myself that he was doing something that made a difference in the world. I'm really proud of him.'

It was hard to reconcile this heroic man with the one who'd shouted outside my studio and been condescending at the wine bar. I sucked hard on my new straw and it disintegrated in my mouth.

'Here he is, with Henry and Izzy.' Beth straightened up and waved.

Picking paper-straw segments from my tongue, I steeled myself for polite chit-chat while wearing a tankini, as Dr Greene – *Michael* – approached us. His chest was broad and his arms toned. He wore bright blue swim shorts, which clung to his muscular legs. Not that I was looking.

'Mummy!' Izzy skipped over. 'Did you see me swimming?'

'You were amazing.' Beth smiled. A clever tactic – she wasn't lying or acknowledging that she'd been talking to me rather than watching. I needed to learn from her. 'You too, Henry. That backflip was Olympic standard.'

Oh, she had been watching. It was just me who forgot they had a child the moment someone else took responsibility for them. Guiltily, I sat up to look for Anna and Brigitte in the pool. My view was obscured by Michael patting himself down with a towel. I had to admit, there were worse views to be had. His skin shone even after he'd wiped the drops of water away, and his body was firm and defined. Had he really been helping sick people in Syria for nine years or had he been competing in consecutive Ironman challenges? His back was to me, and my eyes roamed up and down his body, absorbing every detail. Not in a sordid way – more in an appreciative way, as one would study a work of art. That's what I was telling myself, anyway.

'Dean's a personal trainer,' Beth whispered in my ear.

'Had a career change after Syria. Michael's a pretty good advertisement for it, isn't he?'

I blushed so violently that it brought tears to my eyes. Beth had just caught me leering at her brother. Explaining that I was admiring him in the same way I would Monet's expressive interpretation of water lilies was unlikely to sound plausible. My cheeks burnt with shame.

'Are you ill?' Beth looked at me worriedly. 'You've gone really red and your eyes are watering.' Before I had a chance to reply, she called her brother over. 'Michael, can you check on Marie? She doesn't look right.'

'No!' I yelped. 'I'm fine. He's off duty, remember?'

Ignoring my protestations, Michael squatted down in front of me. I squirmed in my lounger, as he placed a cool hand on my forehead. 'You're very warm,' he said. 'Do you feel hot?'

'Yes,' I admitted.

'Is the heating too high?' Beth asked. She plucked a walkie-talkie from her bag. 'I'll radio maintenance and get them to adjust it.'

'No, don't,' I said. 'It's just me.' I didn't want to be responsible for everyone else freezing their nuts off.

'You're forty, aren't you?' Michael asked. 'Could be perimenopausal.'

The look I gave him could have frozen his nuts off.

'I'm not perimenopausal,' I snapped. 'Just because I'm a bit warm doesn't mean—' Michael smirked and I stopped talking. What I wanted to say wasn't suitable for a family resort.

He ran his hands down my neck and gently felt my glands. Then he took my face in his hands and stared into my eyes. Under very different circumstances, this would be the stuff dreams were made of, but there was nothing arousing about having a public examination from a man who, despite his charity work, was an annoying prick.

'Look down for me,' he said. I obeyed and he pulled my

upper lids up. 'Now look at the ceiling.' He did the same to my lower lids. 'Experienced any dizziness, drowsiness or headaches recently?'

'I had a headache earlier, but it's gone now.'

Michael looked at me thoughtfully with his big brown eyes. He didn't deserve such beautiful eyes. My face flushed again under his watchful gaze. Nervously, I took a sip of my drink, only to discover the glass was empty.

'Strawberry daiquiri?' he asked.

I nodded. 'It's alcohol-free.'

He put his head to one side with a concerned frown.

Maybe I'd got him wrong. Maybe he did care about people. Maybe he was a decent guy.

'There's your answer.' He gave me a condescending look. 'Sugar.'

Or maybe he was a bell-end.

'I'm on holiday,' I protested. 'I can't be sugar-free on holiday.'

'Never said you had to be.' He put his hands up, as though I had a gun trained on him. If only. 'Just giving you my diagnosis. Your withdrawal headache's gone and you've had a blood surge to your head. Classic sugar overload symptoms.' He shrugged. 'Feel free to get a second opinion.' He went to stand, then noticed the bruising on my feet. His eyes travelled from my ankles to the tops of my thighs. I tugged the hem of my tankini top down to cover the bruises on my midriff. His earlier stern expression softened.

'Are you all right?'

'Yes.' My already hot face felt as though it were going to burst into flames. 'Dance class,' I muttered.

Michal frowned. 'Were you being used as the dance floor?'

Beth put her walkie-talkie away and crouched down next to me. 'Sure you're OK?'

I nodded. 'Fine, thank you. Apparently, I drank the daiquiris too fast.'

'Don't apologise. They've passed the taste test, which is

great.' Beth squeezed my arm and stood up. 'Nothing to see here,' she told the onlookers straining to see if there was any drama. They looked disappointed, then a murmur ran through the crowd.

'Let me through,' a voice cried. 'That's my cousin.'

The crowd parted and Brigitte hurried towards us. Her wet costume clung to her bouncing breasts, and her nipples were so erect that she'd stab someone if they brushed up against her. Several googly-eyed dads looked as though they'd be happy to risk their lives trying.

'What's going on? Is Marie OK?' Brigitte leant over Michael's shoulder.

He encountered a face full of cleavage and quickly looked away.

I looked up at her helplessly.

Brigitte frowned at me. 'Why do you look like Violet Beauregarde?'

I glowered, which probably made me even redder. 'Where's Anna?'

'Here, Mumma.' Anna let go of Brigitte's hand and glared at Michael. 'Who's he?'

'He's a doctor,' I said, putting an arm around her.

'No, he isn't.' Anna looked Michael up and down critically. 'Doctors wear white coats and have steth-ah-scopes.'

Michael's mouth twitched. 'I usually wear more than this,' he said. 'Impressive use of the word stethoscope. Plenty of adults don't know it.'

'I watch Dr Ranj on TV,' Anna said, clambering onto my lap. I suppressed a shriek of pain as her little heels dug into my bruised legs.

'Good for you.' Michael stood up and turned to Beth. 'I'll take Henry and Izzy to find Dean. See you for dinner?'

'I'll walk with you. Haven't had a chance to check in on the gym yet and it'll be nice to see Dean.' Beth turned to me and Brigitte. 'I booked a sitter for Anna for eight o'clock. See you in the main bar later?'

'Thank you and yes, please.' Brigitte and I exchanged a grin. A night out was an unexpected bonus. We watched Beth and her brother lead the children out through the beach area to the changing rooms. Beth in her yellow, bodycon dress, Michael in blue shorts moulded to his uptight arse. Brigitte sank into the lounger next to me.

'Wow,' she breathed. 'I know he's a bit up himself, but he's seriously hot.'

'You're not his type,' I said, tickling Anna's feet. 'He's gay.' I winced as Anna kicked me in my already bruised shin.

'Good,' Brigitte said. 'You can talk to him normally now. Do you worry you're being disloyal to Scott if you talk to another man?'

'No.'

'Why do you act so weird around him, then?'

'I don't!'

She raised one eyebrow. I ignored her.

Chapter 18

'What a waste.' Brigitte sighed as we watched Michael chatting at the bar.

'Not to a gay man,' I said. 'Provided being devoid of personality isn't an issue for them.'

We were sitting at a table in the corner of the resort's main bar, people- and outfit-watching. Instead of the shiny black shoes with jeans and a polo shirt favoured by most of the men, Michael wore a green fitted T-shirt, ink-blue jeans and white Converse. He was undeniably the best-looking man in the room. And the resort. Quite possibly the entire British Isles. Which made him even more annoying.

Brigitte stood up. 'Just going to the loo. I'll get us another drink on the way back.'

I smiled my thanks and checked my phone again in case the babysitter had called. I'd never left Anna with someone I didn't know before, but Beth assured me that the sitters were thoroughly checked and college-trained. They were probably more qualified to look after Anna than I was.

My phone pinged and a message from Scott came through.

Miss u x

I missed him too. I was used to doing things with Anna on my own, but seeing all the dads with their children made me wish Scott were here with us; that we were spending time together as a family. And that I had someone to snuggle up to in bed. Not that it had to be in bed. I'd be well up for—

'Sex on the beach,' a deep voice said.

Jumping, I looked up to see Michael standing by our table. Could he tell I'd been about to embark on a *Blue Lagoon* fantasy? Were there telltale signs that doctors could pick up? Enlarged pupils maybe? Flushed cheeks? Drooling?

'Excuse me?' I longed to raise one eyebrow indignantly, but instead felt my ears wiggle. Was it my imagination or did Michael's eyes flicker towards them? I ran a hand through my hair to cover them.

'Sex on the beach.' Michael placed two cocktails on the table. 'Brigitte asked me to claim them if they arrived before she got back.' He rubbed his neck. 'Surprised you didn't hear the barman shouting: "Who's waiting for sex on the beach?" Everyone else did.'

I laughed and picked up the nearest glass. 'Thank you for bringing them over. Never had one before.' I went to take a sip and almost gagged as the scent of peach schnapps hit me. Peach schnapps was, to me, what kryptonite was to Superman, but it involved more use of the toilet. It had been my shot of choice as a student and I'd thrown up on it so many times that the mere smell had my insides quivering in fear. I put the glass down and swallowed hard.

'Something wrong?' Michael asked.

'No,' I said quickly, in case he saw it as a cue to carry out another public examination. He didn't look convinced so I changed the subject. 'Beth said Dean's a personal trainer. Must be handy.'

Michael shrugged. 'Not when he's making me feel guilty for having a pizza instead of a chicken and quinoa salad or telling me to go for a five-mile run when all I want to do is watch *Game of Thrones* with a beer.'

'I love *Game of Thrones*!' I said, astonished we had something in common. 'Who's your favourite character?'

'Ned Stark,' Michael said. 'Sean Bean's a bit of a hero. Could have something to do with watching *Lady Chatterley* when I was a teenager.'

I nodded, remembering being shocked by the nudity. It was the first time I'd seen a naked man on TV. None of my friends had been allowed to watch it, but to Maman, who'd grown up in a country where topless dancing girls performed on family shows – couldn't quite imagine it on *Pointless* – a bit of nude frolicking was *rien de conséquence*. To a young, gay teenager, Sean Bean's naked body must have been a bit of an eye-opener.

'Great moral compass,' Michael added.

That was one way of describing it.

Brigitte slid into the seat next to me. 'Thank you,' she said to Michael, raising her cocktail. 'Do you want to sit down?'

There was an awkward pause in which I felt guilty for not having invited him, while at the same time desperately hoping he wouldn't accept. Admittedly, this was the most amicable conversation we'd ever had, but we'd happened upon a shared interest. Expanding our repertoire beyond the realms of Sean Bean's arse was asking for trouble.

'No, I'll get back.' Michael gestured to the bar. 'It's my turn to get the beers.'

'I thought the drinks were free.' Brigitte took her purse from her bag. 'I never meant for you to pay for them.'

Michael put his hand up. 'It's fine. The first were complimentary and these were on me.'

'Thank you.' Brigitte smiled broadly and ran a fingertip around the rim of her glass. She just couldn't help herself.

Michael looked at me. 'Can I get you another drink? A decaf espresso martini, perhaps?'

'Peach schnapps,' I said to Brigitte, as she opened her mouth, either to point out that she'd just got me a drink or to mime the act of fellatio. There was no knowing with her. 'No, I'm OK,' I said to Michael. 'Thanks anyway.' It was kind of him to offer, and impressive that he remembered my drink of choice, but I didn't want to get into a round and have to talk to him at regular intervals during the evening. 'Have a good evening.' I waved, and he nodded and walked away.

Brigitte motioned to Michael's retreating back. 'Are you sure he's gay? I swear he looked at my tits.'

'The Pope would look at your tits in that outfit.' Even I found it hard not to ogle her cleavage in the strappy top she was wearing. 'Michael's definitely gay. He has a boyfriend *and* he just told me he fancies Sean Bean.'

'Fair enough.' Brigitte took a sip of her drink. 'Sorry about the peach schnapps. I didn't realise.'

'That's OK.' I picked up the glass of water I'd got as an accompaniment to my first cocktail. 'Can't get too pissed. Anna wants to go swimming first thing.'

'Think I'll skip it,' Brigitte said. 'Nice as they've done the beach area, it's hardly Mauritius. Not that I'd know,' she added glumly. 'We've just paid half of a £1,200 school trip for Sundeep to go to Iceland.' She sighed. 'Iceland, for fuck's sake. What happened to coach trips to the local pencil museum?'

'That was our family holiday, not a school trip,' I reminded her. 'Which made it even more shit.'

Brigitte didn't laugh. 'I'm a bit fed up of it, to be honest. Not being able to afford the holidays we want because Sanjay spends all his money on the kids. Having to cancel a night out at the last minute because Pooja's asked if we'll have them and Sanjay won't say no. It wouldn't be so bad if they were nice to me but they're not, they're vile.' She blinked hard. 'I love Sanjay, but this isn't the life I signed up for. I'm resentful and snappy, and it's not me.' She dabbed delicately under her eyes with her fingertips. Even when upset, she was careful not to smudge her makeup.

I squeezed her hand. 'It'll get better. They're hormonal teenagers. In a few years they'll be adults and won't stay over or need money, because they'll be earning their own.'

Brigitte gave a small smile. 'The countdown to uni starts here. Then we'll be wishing we only had to pay halves on a trip to Iceland.' Picking up my abandoned cocktail, she took a large mouthful. 'Let's change the subject. What's next in the Locate Liz project?'

'Nothing.'

Brigitte's eyes widened. 'You can't give up.'

I crossed my legs under the table and winced as my bruised thighs grazed each other. 'We've tried everything. Don't know what else I can do.'

'But you can't carry on as you are.'

'He hasn't seen them at all this past week,' I protested. 'He said he was scared of losing me and Anna, and things were going to change.' An image of Scott's imploring eyes came into my mind. 'I've never seen him so upset. He really meant it.'

'I'm sure he did at the time,' Brigitte said. 'But he's done this before and after a few weeks he's back to jumping through hoops to make her happy. Getting to the root of the problem – Liz – is the only way to stop this vicious cycle.'

'I know it's frustrating, but—'

Brigitte snorted. 'Frustrating is needing a poo when you've just painted your nails. The way Scott puts Liz's demands ahead of yours is unacceptable.'

Brigitte had never been so negative about Scott before.

'I know you're looking out for me,' I said. 'But after everything he promised, I have to give him a chance. If it goes back to how it was before, then I'll do something. I won't let him take the piss.'

Brigitte gave a small smile. 'He'd better not.' She wrapped her arms around me.

'You two OK?' Beth asked, appearing at our table.

'Yes, thanks.' I gestured to one of the empty chairs. 'Join us for a drink. Or are you still working?'

'No, off duty now.' Beth ran a hand over her brow and flicked imaginary sweat away. 'Sure I'm not intruding?'

'Not at all,' Brigitte said. 'We're just slagging off our husbands.'

Beth sat down and signalled to one of the bar staff. 'I'd better not moan about James till after we're married, but I'll happily slag off my ex.'

She smiled at the barman, who placed a bottle of cava and three glasses on the table. 'Fancy some fizz?'

'Yes, please,' we both said.

Brigitte downed the remains of her cocktail so quickly, I was surprised Beth didn't ask her to perform magic tricks at the fun club.

'Is James here?' I asked, eager to meet him. It was always interesting to see what my clients' fiancés looked like.

'He arrives tomorrow,' Beth said. 'Couldn't get out of work today.'

'Scott couldn't either,' I said. 'He's at a conference all weekend.'

'My ex worked every weekend,' Beth said. 'It's hard solo parenting.'

I hadn't thought of it like that, but with Scott at the estate agent's or with Harry and Bella each weekend, I was solo parenting most of the time.

'Is that why you broke up?' Brigitte asked Beth. 'Because of his work?'

Beth shook her head. 'I wasn't happy about his long hours, but I accepted it.' She hesitated. 'His affair wasn't something I was prepared to accept, though.'

'No!' I gripped my glass. How could anyone cheat on Beth? She was kind and warm and fun, not to mention beautiful. 'That's horrible.'

Brigitte leant forward. 'How did you find out?' I nudged her with my elbow. This wasn't a bit of gossip; it was raw and sensitive and real.

'You don't have to tell us,' I said. 'It's personal.'

Brigitte's expression indicated that that was exactly why she'd asked the question. Where was the fun in learning something impersonal? She could get that from watching *University Challenge*. Although, as she had a crush on Amol Rajan, she could make even that personal.

Beth clicked her tongue against the roof of her mouth. 'I caught him having sex with a woman he worked with, in our car.'

Brigitte and I gasped. 'I'm so sorry,' we said in unison.

Beth smiled. 'James is much better for me than he was.' She took a sip from her glass. 'I thought I was happy, but I was fooling myself. He did whatever he wanted, whenever he wanted, and I looked after the children and ran the house. If ever I was ill or snowed under with work and asked him to make dinner or put some laundry on, he'd react as though I'd asked him to donate a kidney.'

Brigitte gave me a sideways look. Scott wasn't great if I was ever ill. Aside from his snot phobia, the prospect of entertaining and feeding Anna single-handedly filled him with such panic that I tended to get on with it even if I felt crap. That was where the similarities with Beth's ex ended, though.

'Now I'm with someone who wants to spend time with me and the kids, I realise how lonely I was,' Beth continued. 'It wasn't a great way to find out, but it was for the best. I'm so much happier now than I'd have been if we'd stayed together.'

I shook my head. 'But catching them like that. Must have been hideous.' I couldn't begin to imagine the horror of seeing Scott being intimate with another woman.

'Was at the time, but he did me a favour, really. Especially, as he's turned out to be such a bastard.'

Brigitte's eyes widened. 'More of a bastard than cheating on you?'

'Yep.' Beth's jaw tightened. 'He hasn't seen Henry and Izzy for four years.'

'Four years?' Brigitte and I said at the same time.

Beth nodded. 'At first he came over every weekend. I think he was hoping we'd get back together, but I couldn't.'

'Too right.' Brigitte tossed her hair over her shoulder. 'He doesn't deserve you.'

'No, he doesn't.' Beth pulled herself up tall. 'As soon as I started divorce proceedings, he moved out of Brighton and stopped seeing them. Doesn't even acknowledge their birthdays.'

My throat tightened. 'How can he not want to see his own children?'

'He's remarried. Apparently, his new wife wanted a fresh start without any baggage so . . .' Beth trailed off.

Brigitte's eyes narrowed. 'And he's just gone along with it? What an absolute shit.'

Beth nodded. 'Now he's saying he shouldn't have to pay child maintenance, because I'm remarrying.'

I couldn't believe it. Poor Henry and Izzy. How old were they? Eight and five? Their dad had been absent for half of Henry's life and most of Izzy's. What damage would knowing that one of their parents didn't care about them do?

'This is so wrong.' I gripped the table. 'The way he treated you was disgusting, and then to desert his children? He should want to see them and provide for them.' I had a sudden rush of pride for Scott for doing the right thing; for sacrificing so much of his time to make sure Harry and Bella never felt they'd been rejected in the same way that Beth's children had.

'I know.' Beth sighed. 'It breaks my heart if I let myself think about it. So I don't. He's ruined enough of our lives. He's not going to ruin any more.'

'What does James think?' Brigitte asked.

'That one man's loss is another man's gain.' Beth smiled. 'He gets on great with the kids. Probably easier for him to be a proper dad without someone else getting territorial and telling them how he wants it done.'

Was that how Liz felt about me? That I'd try and take ownership of Harry and Bella, and change how she was bringing them up?

'I've got the opposite problem,' I said. 'Scott sees his kids all the time, but his ex won't let me and Anna meet them. He has to split his time between two lots of children, when we could all be having fun together.'

Beth frowned. 'That sounds complicated.'

'It's shit, that's what it is,' Brigitte said. The three cocktails she'd consumed in quick succession were making their presence known. 'We've tried meeting up with his ex to show her that Marie's a nice, normal person who she can trust with her kids, but we can't find her.'

Beth put her head to one side. I could see that from an outsider's viewpoint, this wasn't standard behaviour for a nice, normal person.

'I know that sounds a bit desperate,' I said. 'But that's because I am. I so want us to be a happy, blended family, but she won't give me a chance and it breaks my heart that Anna's missing out on her half-siblings.'

Beth topped up my glass. 'Those kids are lucky to have someone who cares so much that they'll go to extreme measures to meet them,' she said. 'Unlike my ex, who rejected his own flesh and blood.' Her phone buzzed on the table. Brigitte and I automatically checked our phones too. Me for an alert from the babysitter. Brigitte for another dick pic, probably.

'It's from Michael.' Beth looked over her shoulder towards the bar, where her brother had been standing. 'He's gone to the gym to find Dean. Says he'll see me back at the lodge.' She looked at her watch. 'I should mingle a bit. Sorry I offloaded on you. That's not why I came over.'

'No, it's fine,' Brigitte and I said. We had to stop talking in unison or we'd morph into our mums. And I wasn't ready to start dressing like Ronald McDonald.

'Sorry you've been through so much crap,' I said.

Brigitte nodded. 'You're definitely better off without him.'

'I know.' Beth stood up and gave us a big smile. 'Enjoy the rest of your evening.'

'You too,' Brigitte and I said together. I might as well accept my fate and start shopping for extra-large shoes.

'Can't believe that about her ex-husband,' Brigitte said, once Beth was out of earshot. 'What a wanker.'

I nodded, determined to stop moaning about Scott. Being overly involved with his children was so much better than not being involved at all. And I knew for a fact he'd never shag another woman in his car. He wouldn't even let Anna eat breadsticks in there.

Chapter 19

'Thanks for a great weekend,' I said, pulling up outside Brigitte's house. 'Glad you could come.'

She leant over and hugged me. 'Me too. It's been fun.'

It had been lovely to have someone to talk to and share experiences with. Anna's three-year-old conversation was rather limited and, no matter how hard I tried, she wouldn't be drawn on matters such as climate change or the #MeToo movement, or whether Robbie Williams regretted leaving Take That.

Scott didn't enjoy talking about topical issues either. Or anything non-topical. He was so drained by the time he got home that all he could manage was, 'Sorry, babe. Rather not talk, if you don't mind.'

By contrast, Brigitte and I hadn't stopped talking all weekend and I'd miss that. Tears filled my eyes and I blinked hard to contain them. This was ridiculous. I'd see her at work tomorrow.

'Love you.' Reluctantly, I let her go.

'You too. Say bye to Anna for me.' She smiled over her shoulder to where Anna slept in her car seat, her head lolling to the side.

Sanjay opened their front door and jogged up to the car. Brigitte got out, one eyebrow raised.

'Sundeep and Ammo?' she asked.

'At their mum's.' Sanjay grinned. He went to the boot and took her case out, then they practically sprinted into the house, only just remembering to wave before they shut the door. It wouldn't take a wave machine pool to get Brigitte out of her clothes tonight.

I turned the car around and headed home.

When we got back, I carried Anna into the house and nudged the front door shut with my hip.

'Marie?' Scott called. A few moments later he shuffled out into the hall.

Anna slid down me and sleepily walked towards the living room.

'Careful, sweetheart.' Scott stepped back, as Anna neared him. 'Daddy's a bit fragile.'

I smiled. 'Hungover, you mean.'

'I wish,' Scott said in a small voice. 'Had a bit of an accident.'

My stomach lurched. 'What's happened?'

'Groin strain.' Scott grimaced. 'Pulled it in the team-building game of football.'

'Ouch. You poor thing.' I hugged him gently, then crouched down by Anna.

'Daddy's hurt himself, so we must be very gentle with him.'

Anna blinked up at Scott. 'Does your fanny hurt?'

Scott gave me a bewildered look. Anna must have been taking notes in the back of the car.

'No. It's Daddy's . . .' I hesitated. How could I describe Scott's groin region to Anna without being graphic? She'd recently noticed that his naked body was different to ours, when she'd wandered in on him getting changed and had exclaimed with delight, 'Ooh, Daddy's got a tail.' A story she then shared with all the staff at her nursery. There was no need to give them any more detail about Scott's anatomy. 'Daddy's leg's sore,' I settled on.

Anna patted Scott's thigh. With her fist.

He backed away before she could demonstrate any more affection. 'I'll go back to the sofa. Need to rest it.' He hobbled, wide-legged, back into the living room, then lowered himself carefully onto the sofa and clicked the remote control to restart the motor racing he'd been watching.

'Can I get you anything?'

'Go on, then. Beer please.' He winked. 'Medicinal purposes. And some frozen sweetcorn,' he added. 'The peas have defrosted.'

The rest of the afternoon passed quickly. Anna played happily with her toys, her bedroom seeming to her like Santa's Grotto after having been limited to one box of Lego and a colouring book while we'd been away. I busied myself with laundry, housework, keeping Scott's beer and vegetable ice-pack refreshed, and trying not to resent how much food was being wasted to keep his groin at optimum temperature.

By early evening, Anna was settled, the clothes airer could hold no more and I'd tidied away all the toys. I opened another couple of beers and handed one to Scott.

'Thanks for looking after me.' He flashed me a smile and I felt a stirring.

I fiddled with the wrapper on my beer bottle. 'How long do groin strains last?'

'Couple of weeks.' Scott looked forlornly at the bag of frozen peppers on his lap. 'It's pretty sore.'

'You poor thing.' I knelt by his side, ashamed that while he was in pain, I was thinking about my own needs. And the hygiene implications for the frozen veg. 'What can I do to help?'

'Just stay here,' he said softly. 'It's nice to have you home.' He stroked my hair, massaging my scalp with his fingertips. I tried to relax into it but, having seen him rearrange his tackle earlier, I'd be more comfortable if he'd washed his hands first.

'How was the conference?' I asked.

Scott shrugged. 'The usual seminars and networking.'

'And team-building activities,' I added.

'Yeah. Won't be doing them again.'

I edged away from his hand. I could feel the dirt building up. 'Were the evenings fun?'

Scott removed his hand. 'I've already lost most of my weekend to work, babe. Last thing I want to do is talk about it.'

'Course, sorry.' I followed his gaze to the TV and tried to care about the motor racing but, quite frankly, the washing on the airer was more interesting to watch. I wasn't ready to give up on the notion of a conversation yet, either.

'The resort was nice,' I said. 'Huge pool, loads of activities, five different restaurants.' I glanced up. 'We should go some time. I can get a discount.'

Scott nodded. 'We should. Sounds great.'

I waited for his usual follow-up of: 'We can't afford it till Liz becomes more reasonable,' but it didn't come.

I swallowed a smile. He *had* changed. It wasn't just talk, as Brigitte had claimed. He'd taken a stand with Liz, which meant more time at home and a little more money for things such a family holiday. Surely, the next step was meeting Harry and Bella. Having witnessed the crap Brigitte endured, I knew we wouldn't go from being strangers to skipping through bluebell woods – especially not with Scott's groin strain. We'd take it slow. Grow our relationship gradually. Start with a couple of hours a week before, eventually, sleepovers some weekends.

My excitement grew as I pictured our family Christmas. Maman and Francine would hate the noise and chaos – Brigitte wouldn't be overly enamoured by it either – but it'd be wonderful to see the children together, squealing with excitement as they opened their stockings, Scott giving them piggyback rides around the Christmas tree. Again, groin strain permitting.

'What are you grinning at?'

Scott's voice hoisted me out of my rose-tinted daydream and I realised I was staring into space, a huge smile on my face.

'Just happy we're back together,' I said. No need to reveal my vision for the future just yet. Baby steps.

His phone beeped and I tensed.

'If it's Liz, I'll ignore it,' he said, easing the phone from the pocket of his jogging bottoms as I retreated to the armchair. He looked at the message and his jaw tightened. 'As predicted.' He turned it to silent and put it back in his pocket.

It vibrated instantly. We both ignored it and stared at the TV, drinking our beers. I tried not to let the constant vibration from Scott's pocket bother me. He wasn't leaping up and racing round to Liz's, as he always had before. He wasn't answering the messages. He wasn't even reading them. But still, his phone vibrated.

Chapter 20

'When did you start wearing briefs?' I asked Scott, placing the pairs I'd just laundered in his underwear drawer. I used a comedy voice for the word briefs, rolling the R. Not that there was anything remotely comedic about briefs. They were hideous. Bordering on offensive. Brigitte and I had made a pact in our early twenties to never get involved with a man who wore pants, rather than boxers. Not sure how we'd glean this information without getting fairly involved with said man in the first place, but thankfully neither of us ever had to turf a boyfriend out on account of his underwear choices. Until now.

Scott lay on our bed, scrolling through his phone. 'It's only till my groin strain's healed.'

That was a relief. I loved Scott and didn't want to divorce him, particularly not on such a flimsy technicality, but a pact was a pact.

'Might not even need them anymore. It's been two weeks.' Scott put his phone down. 'Is Anna asleep?'

I nodded, the edges of my lips creeping up into a smile.

Scott grinned. 'Come here, you.'

'Are you sure?' I said, almost running to the bed. 'It's actually been one week and six days.' Not that I was counting.

'Very sure,' Scott said, kissing me.

I straddled him, pulling my top up and over my head, then doing the same with his.

He grinned at my enthusiasm. ''Fraid you're going to have to do all the work. Doctor's orders.'

'Fine by me, Dr Jones,' I laughed, arching down towards him.

'Hang on.' Scott dodged my kiss and reached into his bedside drawer.

My heart sunk when I saw the packet of condoms in his hand. 'But you said when you'd spoken to Liz, we could start trying. And you've spoken to her.'

'I have and we will.' Scott took a foil wrapper from the box. 'In a couple of months.'

'But it might take a couple of months to—'

'Stop talking. That's another order.' He pressed his lips against mine, and I tried to ignore the knot in my stomach and relax into the kiss. At least he hadn't had to pop a Viagra to perform.

Scott ran his hands up and down my back, before unhooking my bra and cupping my breasts, massaging me in the way that always sent sparks shooting between my legs.

Except that the sparks weren't shooting tonight. Not even when he trailed his fingers down my stomach and slipped them inside me. Or when I mounted him and moved back and forth, watching the pleasure on his face increase until he climaxed.

Scott fell asleep afterwards, thankfully oblivious. He'd be so upset if he knew I hadn't enjoyed it. Sex was our thing. Some couples went to concerts or the cinema. Others shared a passion for hiking or restoring antique furniture. Scott and I didn't need any common interests, because sex was our hobby. If conversation dried up or we were disgruntled with one another, a shag soon sorted us out. Sex was the very core of our relationship.

Scott's breathing deepened beside me and I turned my head to look at him. He was so handsome. I definitely still fancied him. Tonight was just a blip. I'd been working hard and it was bound to have an impact. Everything would be fine.

An hour later, unable to sleep, I crept downstairs and FaceTimed Brigitte.

'Scott been summoned away by Liz, has he?' she said.

'No,' I said defiantly. 'He's upstairs, asleep. Told you he meant it about standing up to her.'

Brigitte's eyes flicked to the top of her screen. 'It's nine o'clock on a Friday night. Why is he asleep?' I shrugged and she nodded knowingly. 'Nice work.'

I laughed half-heartedly.

'Something wrong?'

I hesitated. Given the state of our political system, the climate crisis and the plight of millions overseas who were genuinely suffering, whinging that I hadn't had an orgasm didn't seem justified.

I rubbed my nose. 'Just a bit bored.'

'Watch that film on Netflix I told you about.'

'Not really in the mood. Can we talk instead?'

Sanjay appeared over Brigitte's shoulder and waved at me. He wasn't wearing a shirt and was so easy on the eye that just one glimpse of him could cure glaucoma.

'Actually, I'll let you two get on,' I said, sensing that the two of them had plans. 'Night.'

I picked up the TV remote and started flicking through the channels. The sound of a milk bottle being knocked to the ground outside made me jump. Probably just a cat, I told myself. Or a fox. Obviously, it wouldn't be a psychopath with a machete. However, I would not be opening the front door to verify this.

I tried to settle on a programme, but another sound of glass clinking made me freeze. First thing tomorrow, I was cancelling the milkman. Sod the fact it was supporting a local business and helping the environment. I couldn't handle this stress. A third noise outside made the hairs on my arms stand up. Trembling, I crept to the window, pulled back an inch of curtain and peered out, poised to leap back screaming if anything vaguely resembling a human being was out there.

The neighbour's tabby cat sat on the pavement outside the window. I released a long, shaky breath. I really needed to get a grip. The tabby sauntered away, neatly sidestepping the milk bottles this time.

Relieved, I lowered the curtain, turned off the TV and scampered upstairs. After checking on Anna, I crept into bed and, surprisingly, given that I'd had such a scare, felt myself drifting off immediately. I was about to go under, when a thought struck me. My eyes snapped open.

The milk bottles hadn't been lying on the floor. Whoever had knocked them over had stood them back up again.

Chapter 21

'Where's my blue shirt?' Scott hollered down the stairs.

'The airing cupboard,' I hollered back.

'Where's my red cup?' Anna hollered from the kitchen table, knocking aside the pink one I'd given her, as though re-enacting a brawl in a Western saloon.

'Don't shout at me,' I hollered.

Anna pouted. 'You and Daddy shout.'

She was right and I instantly felt guilty. What sort of an example were we setting?

'Sorry, chick.' I kissed the top of her head. 'We all need to be kinder to each other.'

In the past week there had been a lot of shouting. Shouting or silence. Scott seesawed from getting frustrated by the simplest of things – he had a meltdown one day because we only had mint-flavoured Club biscuits and he wanted orange – to being incapable of speech at all. 'Too tired, babe,' was all he could muster some evenings.

He wasn't too tired for sex, though, and we'd done it every night. Another reason to hope he wasn't on Viagra – the NHS was struggling enough, without him draining their funds. Worryingly, my heart wasn't in it and I wasn't convinced Scott's was either. We seemed to be going through the motions and I had no idea why. I couldn't blame it on Liz's negative energy – Scott hadn't seen her since promising me he was going to make a stand.

I had a moment of clarity, and realised why he was grumpy and withdrawn. He was missing his children.

'You haven't seen Harry and Bella for a while,' I said quietly when he came downstairs. 'Why not pop round after work?'

'Trying to get rid of me?' Scott put his mug down heavily by the sink.

'Course not.' I mopped up the coffee that had spilt out of his mug. 'I've just realised that you haven't left the house for three weeks, apart from for work. You must miss them.'

Scott's jaw tightened. 'Thought that was what you wanted. Said it wasn't right I spent so much time with them when I should be here.'

I glanced at Anna to see if she was listening, but she was busy sprinkling eggshell onto the floor.

'That's not how I meant it to sound,' I said quietly. 'I've never begrudged you seeing them. Just wanted more of a balance.'

A muscle pounded in Scott's cheek. 'I can't win.' His body was taut, as though holding every emotion in, his fists clenched by his sides. My heart ached for him. He must be in agony. Feeling torn between two sets of children. Wanting to do the right thing by all of them. Always feeling disloyal to the ones he wasn't with.

'I'm sorry if I gave the wrong impression,' I said softly. 'You mustn't stop seeing Harry and Bella; just don't let Liz take advantage and get you round every night. That's what I objected to.'

Scott smoothed his hair. 'If that's what you want.' There was a note of sarcasm in his voice. 'Guess I'll be late home, then.'

I forced a smile. 'Have a nice time.'

Scott walked out into the hall. I followed, but he'd shut the front door before I could even say goodbye, let alone kiss him.

What the hell was all that about?

'It's like that saying,' Maman said, as we took a seat at the artisan café across the road from my studio.

'Be careful what you wish for?' I guessed.

Maman shook her head and her purple lightning-bolt earrings ricocheted off her angular cheekbones. 'Turn your tongue around your mouth seven times before you speak.'

'What?' I spluttered.

'*Il faut tourner sept fois sa langue dans sa bouche avant de parler.*' She gestured in the air. 'Don't speak until you have turned your tongue around. Stops you saying the wrong thing.' She dropped her hands and tutted. 'Your papa's language has ruined it.'

'He didn't invent the English language.'

Her glare suggested otherwise.

We picked up the menus. Maman read it cover to cover, grimacing as though reading her own death warrant. I began to regret my choice of venue. Brigitte and I came to this café regularly, usually for takeaway coffees, so to eat in was a treat. If my mum was going to be her usual charming self, I'd never be able to come here again.

Our waiter, Luke, greeted us with a smile – poor, deluded, fool.

I smiled back. 'The salmon and quinoa salad, and a tap water, please.'

'Double espresso,' Maman said crisply. 'And water.'

'Still or sparkling?'

'Sparkling, *naturellement*,' she said, as indignant as if he'd asked whether she'd prefer to drink it from a glass or a dog bowl. 'And the croque-monsieur.' She grabbed Luke's wrist. 'Is it made in the proper French way?'

He smiled good-humouredly. 'Yes, Madame. The chef is French. Would you like to meet her?'

'*Non*,' Maman said, horrified. 'I'm here to socialise with my daughter, not the staff.'

Luke took our menus and winked at me. I came to the café often enough to know that the owners were Sicilian and the head chef Nigerian.

'What has turning your tongue round got to do with me and Scott?' I asked, going back to our earlier conversation.

'All I said was that I wanted him to be at home more. But now he is, it's not how I thought it'd be.'

She narrowed her eyes at me. 'How did you imagine it would be, Marie?'

I wound my plait around my hand. 'I thought we'd talk more, I suppose. He was always too tired when he got in from Liz's, but we still watch TV in silence once Anna's in bed.'

'Perhaps your conversation is boring.'

I laughed.

She didn't. 'I am serious.'

My lower lip instinctively jutted out. What had possessed me to confide in her? I'd wanted to talk to Brigitte, but she'd been busy all morning, so in desperation I'd opened up to the least sympathetic person on the planet.

Maman crossed her arms. 'You tell too many stories about funny things Anna says and does, and the ordeal of bath and bed. If this is all Scott hears from you, no wonder he does not want to talk.'

I digested this information. *Was* that all I talked about? Had I become one of those mums so obsessed with their child that they had no other topic of conversation? I reflected on the chats I had with my clients. Weddings, mainly. Anna rarely featured. And Brigitte and I discussed everything, from serious topics – such as white privilege and the injustice of Beth's family name – to very unserious topics, such as who the next James Bond would be. So, if I didn't talk incessantly about Anna to other people, why did I with Scott?

'Maybe,' I said, reluctant to admit there could be a shred of truth in her words.

'When Anna goes to bed, put her to bed in your mind also,' Maman said. 'Run a bath for you both to share. Make Scott excited.'

I squirmed in my chair.

'Remember, you are a man and woman first; you are

parents second. Do not let the child spoil the intimacy of the marriage.'

My cheeks burnt.

'Even when your papa and I argued, it was very passionate. Once, after the most enormous of fights in the supermarket, we made love on the floor.'

I really hoped they'd waited till they got home.

She gave me a direct look. 'How often do you make love?'

'In general or with Scott?' I let out a nervous peal of laughter, which halted when I saw the glint in her eye.

'Marie! Are you visiting *le jardin secret*?'

In France, 'secret garden' was code for an affair. It explained why Maman had been surprised to find me reading Frances Hodgson Burnett's classic when I was a child. She still let me read it, though.

'Course not,' I said. 'It was a joke.'

'Oh.' She looked deflated. 'Perhaps you should.'

'I'm not going to have an affair,' I hissed. 'Now stop talking about my sex life. It's not appropriate.'

Maman shrugged. 'I'm French.'

Luke brought our food over and I smiled a thank you. Maman sniffed when he put her plate in front of her, but didn't comment, which was high praise from her.

'How is your search for Liz Clark?' she asked, placing her napkin neatly on her lap.

'I've stopped. Didn't feel right going behind Scott's back. I have to trust him to sort it out.'

Maman hovered her knife and fork over her food, as though about to perform a dissection. 'And is he? Can you meet his children now?'

I shook my head, embarrassed that I was still in this situation, despite his assurances it would change.

'So, he is doing nothing and now you are doing nothing also?'

I gave her a direct stare to show she didn't intimidate me, even though we both knew she did. 'There's nothing I

161

can do,' I said. 'I've tried everything. You and Francine are lucky you didn't kill yourselves and half of Horsham when you followed him. He doesn't have her details anywhere at home. I don't know where she lives, where she works – if she works – or what she looks like.' My throat burnt and I felt close to tears. She hadn't been in our lives for the past few weeks, but was still getting between me and Scott. 'All I know is that she has two children and is a complete bitch.'

Maman jabbed a finger at me. 'You have the information you need to find her, then.'

'Where?' I sighed. 'In a kennel?'

Maman tutted. 'I should never have had relations with an Englishman. You would not be this stupid if you had gone to school in France.'

'I wouldn't exist if you hadn't had relations with an Englishman, so I wouldn't have gone to school anywhere.'

Maman pursed her lips. 'Do you want me to help you or not?'

'Not,' I said firmly.

'*Les enfants* are the key,' she said, as though I'd answered with a resounding 'yes'. 'Go to their school and she will be there to collect them.'

I gasped. 'I'm not using his children. That's immoral.'

'Don't be so dramatic, Marie.' She waved her knife and fork in the air. 'There is no need to steal them.'

'That's good,' I drawled. 'Because in some places they consider that to be illegal.'

Maman glared at me. She was not a fan of sarcasm.

We didn't talk for the rest of the meal. Unlike at home, I welcomed the silence.

Chapter 22

'Hi, babe,' Scott said brightly into the phone when I called him from my studio after lunch.

He'd certainly perked up. That morning he hadn't bothered saying goodbye, but now I was 'babe' again. I didn't particularly like being called babe. It made me feel as though I was on some low-level reality show. Or the film about the pig. In which I was the pig.

'Hi.' I fiddled with a box of beads on my desk. 'Just checking we're OK.'

'Why wouldn't we be?' Scott clearly hadn't been dwelling on that morning's tension, as I had.

'You seemed upset with me when I suggested seeing Harry and Bella tonight.'

'No, I was upset at the thought of having to speak to Liz.'

Of course. I should have made allowances for that.

'Don't blow these things out of proportion,' he said softly. 'No point creating drama when there isn't any.'

He was right. I'd made it into a bigger deal than it was.

'So, are you seeing them tonight?' I asked.

'No. Forgot that it's curry night. I'll work late and go straight there.'

Was it really a month since the last one? Time was going scarily fast. Every month that went by was another month we could have been trying for a baby.

'I'm taking them to Maccy D's tomorrow night, though.' I could hear his smile. 'Hadn't realised how much I missed them till we spoke earlier.'

'That's great.' I took a deep breath. 'Will you ask Liz about me and Anna meeting them?'

'Give me a chance. It's the first time I've seen her for weeks. I need to build up to it.'

I looked up at the ceiling. 'Are you going to talk to her about it soon?'

'Yes. Be there in a sec,' he called to someone.

Had that been a yes to me or the person in his office?

'I have to pick the right moment or she'll just say no,' he said, to me now. 'Got to go. Love you, bye.'

I placed the phone on my desk and stared glumly at the wall. *When* would be the right moment? What would happen if Liz refused again? How many times was I prepared to be told no, Anna and I weren't allowed to meet them, and we were to stay a dirty secret?

A bolt of anger shot through me. I'd put up with this for long enough. I was trapped in a plotline that always ended the same way. It would only ever change if I made it. I snatched my phone up. Using Harry and Bella to find Liz felt very wrong, but I couldn't see another option. I wouldn't involve them, though. It was Liz I needed to get to. I'd wait to meet them under proper, happier, less legally tenuous circumstances.

A Google search revealed twenty primary schools in Guildford. Several were faith schools, which I discarded. Scott wasn't religious and had never mentioned that the children went to church. That still left fifteen schools. Driving around them all and hoping I'd recognise Harry and Bella from an old black and white photo wasn't feasible, especially when I wanted to keep my distance. I clicked on the first school on the list and pressed 'call'. My heart pounded, as an automatic message directed me to select the office or report an absence, and then a receptionist answered.

'I'm calling on behalf of Liz Clark. Her children go to your school.' My nose itched more than ever before. 'Harry and Bella Clark,' I added guiltily. This wasn't exactly keeping them out of it.

'I don't recognise those names,' the receptionist said. 'Which classes are they in?'

'She didn't say. Just asked me to get a message to them.' My cheeks burnt with shame.

A keyboard clicked down the phone. 'We don't have a record of them. Are you sure they go to this school?'

'I'll double-check. Sorry to have wasted your time.' I hung up and looked around my studio, as though expecting someone to tell me off for being so underhand. No one did, so I took a deep breath and moved on to the next school.

On the eighth school, I had success.

'Liz Clark?' the receptionist said. 'Is she all right? She hasn't collected her raffle prize from the summer fair yet.'

'She's fine,' I said. 'That's why I'm ringing, actually. To let you know she'll be in to get it soon.'

'Thank goodness. It's taking up half my office. Who knew teddy bears could be so big?'

I hadn't thought there could possibly be any similarities between myself and Liz, but I wouldn't be in a hurry to claim it either.

'It'll be out of your way soon.' An idea – a genius idea, if I did say so myself – struck me. 'If it's not too much trouble, could you bring it out to the playground after school today, please? Make it easier for her to collect.'

'Yes, that shouldn't be a problem.'

'Thank you very much. I – we – really appreciate your help.'

I hung up and exhaled loudly. I'd be able to spot Liz a mile away with a giant teddy bear tucked under her arm. It'd make a great talking point too, without involving Harry and Bella at all. I swallowed hard. This was it. I was actually going to meet her. The real one this time.

The downstairs door chimed and I rushed to the top of the stairs to tell Brigitte, who'd popped out in between clients. 'Guess what!' I said, then stopped in my tracks. 'Oh, it's you.'

Dr Greene, *Michael*, climbed the stairs with a grim expression on his face. Me greeting him as warmly as if he were Lord Voldemort – or worse, Lord Sugar – probably hadn't improved his mood.

He's my client's brother, I reminded myself, and forced a smile. 'Sorry, thought you were Brigitte. Can I help you?'

Michael looked even grimmer. 'It's rather embarrassing.'

He reached the top of the stairs. If he mentioned Scott's Viagra again, I'd push him back down them.

I crossed my arms. 'Embarrassing for whom?'

He shifted from foot to foot. 'Me. Definitely me.'

My eyes darted past him to the front door. Where was Brigitte? This deserved an audience.

He opened and closed his mouth twice, clearly wrestling with his wording. I considered suggesting he turn his tongue round seven times in his mouth, but decided that wouldn't help.

'The back of my trousers has split,' he said eventually. His Adam's apple bobbed up and down as he swallowed. 'I haven't got time to go shopping for new ones and wondered if you could do a quick repair job.'

A giggle bubbled out of me. Michael closed his eyes and I turned it into a cough.

'Of course.' My voice quivered slightly. 'I'll get you a robe to wear.'

'Thank you.' The relief on his face was comical when I handed him an oversized white, towelling dressing gown. Too bad I wasn't more traditional. It'd only add to the fun if he had to put on a pink, silk kimono.

'The loo's just there,' I said. 'Bring your trousers back when you've changed and I'll have a look at them.'

He backed away, and I grabbed my phone and texted Brigitte. *Get back ASAP!*

Michael came into the studio and handed me his trousers. 'This is really kind of you,' he said, avoiding my eye.

I took his trousers and examined the split. It was along the seam, so very easy to repair. It wouldn't even show. Unless I stitched a large, polka-dot patch over it, which I definitely would do if he mentioned Viagra.

'Take a seat.' I turned the trousers inside out. 'It'll only take five minutes.'

'Thank you,' Michael said. 'I'm due back at the practice in fifteen minutes, so that's perfect.'

He sat on the sofa, clutching the dressing gown to his knees so it didn't gape open. Despite being oversized for my female clients, it was rather undersized for him.

I sat at my desk, removed the ivory thread from my sewing machine and replaced it with navy. There was an awkward silence as I pinned the split in his trousers, but better that than an awkward conversation. We didn't have a good track record in that department. Moments later the room was filled with the sound of my sewing machine whirring. I concentrated on following the seam line to ensure a smooth, unbroken finish, going over it twice to add durability.

'There. That should last you.' I cut the threads, turned the trousers round the right way and handed them to him.

He examined the seam. 'Good as new.' He looked up and smiled, his eyes crinkling at the corners. The expression was so alien to me that my stomach contracted.

'It's interesting watching you work.' He put his head to one side. 'You seemed quite stressed to start with.' Devising a plan to intercept Liz had definitely been stress-inducing. Lunch beforehand with Maman hadn't helped. 'But as soon as you started sewing,' Michael continued, 'all the tension flooded out of you.'

I nodded. 'I could be in the middle of a war zone and switch off from it if I had a sewing machine.' I put a hand to my mouth as I remembered that Michael had worked in the middle of an actual war zone. 'Sorry. Didn't mean to sound flippant. Beth told me about your time in Syria.'

'It's OK.' Michael smiled reassuringly. 'I know what you mean. It's good to have something you can lose yourself in. I'm the same.'

'With medicine?' It was hard to imagine treating chest infections and mysterious rashes as a form of relaxation, but each to their own.

Michael chuckled. Another first. 'I'm passionate about helping to heal people, but it's not how I unwind. I play the guitar. Badly,' he added quickly, holding his hands up. 'Don't expect to see me on *Britain's Got Talent* any time soon.' He smiled and stood up. 'I'll go and get changed.'

I averted my eyes as the dressing gown gaped slightly, but not before I noticed a glimpse of navy boxer shorts. No briefs for him – which reminded me: Scott was still wearing his, after his groin strain, even though he was better. I'd have to hide them. Or burn them.

'How much do I owe you?' Michael asked.

I flapped a hand. 'On the house.'

He shook his head. 'I have to give you something.'

We walked out to the landing. 'It cost two cocktails, which you've already paid for, so we're quits. Deal?' I put my hand out.

'Deal.' He gave my hand a firm shake.

The front door chimed, and Michael and I looked down the stairs. Brigitte stared up at us, wearing an expression that could only be described as incredulous. If my understanding of the word incredulous was correct.

'Well, hello there,' she said, climbing the stairs.

Michael and I dropped our hands and stepped away from one another. Distancing ourselves in this manner did nothing to alter the fact that Michael was wearing a dressing gown.

'Michael split his trousers,' I said.

Michael held his trousers aloft, as proof.

Brigitte's eyes sparkled. 'How did you manage that?'

'Bending over,' Michael said.

Brigitte raised an eyebrow.

'A woman dropped her parcel in the post office. I picked it up for her.' Michael gestured to the toilet. 'I'll get changed.'

'What's going on?' Brigitte hissed, the moment he closed the door. 'Why is that gorgeous man half-naked?'

'Shhh.' I pulled her into my studio so that the gorgeous, half-naked man couldn't hear every word we were saying. 'We told you,' I whispered. 'I sewed his trousers up.'

'You were holding hands.' Brigitte was hopping up and down with excitement.

'We were *shaking* hands,' I corrected. 'He wanted to pay me and I said we were quits for the cocktails he bought at Heavenly Hideaway.'

Brigitte's smile dropped. 'Is that it?'

'Of course,' I hissed.

The toilet door opened and Michael came out, his trousers firmly on.

'Thank you.' He handed me the dressing gown with a smile. 'Don't know what I'd have done if you hadn't helped.'

'Any time.' I was aware of Brigitte's eyes boring into me. 'Although, hopefully, there won't be another time.'

'No.' He nodded at Brigitte, gave me another grateful smile and left. His feet hammered down the stairs and the door chimed seconds later.

Ignoring Brigitte's smirks, I sat down at my sewing machine, removed the navy cotton and rethreaded it with the original ivory. 'Don't try and make this more than it is. We don't even like each other.'

'So you keep saying.'

The needle jabbed into my finger and I winced. 'I'm married and he's gay, remember?'

Brigitte shrugged as she left, as though neither of these factors were of any consequence. Sometimes she was scarily like our mums.

Speaking of scary mums, I needed to get to the school gate to intercept Liz.

Chapter 23

I parked as close to the school as I could. Which was about a mile away, because the allocated parking bays nearby were gone and I didn't want to cause a mutiny by parking ever so slightly in front of someone's driveway.

This thwarted my plan of arriving early and casually sauntering up to the school, as though I had every right to be there. Instead, I had to run and arrived after all the other parents, coated in a layer of sweat, with Google Maps announcing loudly on my phone that I had arrived at my destination. Even Maman would have been more discreet than this.

Putting my head down, I positioned myself near the gate so I could easily spot a giant teddy bear making its way across the playground. The size and calibre of the school shocked me. My own primary had been a basic, single-storey building with a couple of Portakabin add-on classrooms. I shuddered involuntarily at the memory of being taught in one – freezing in the winter, suffocatingly hot in the summer, and smelling of socks and flatulence all year round. How we hadn't all come out with PTSD was a wonder. I'd assumed all primary schools were like this, apart from the ones that had been condemned, but this school was a vast timber-clad collection of buildings, with a play area that wouldn't look out of place at Disneyland.

Peering over the gate, my heart pounded, partly from my unexpected sprint, but mainly out of sheer terror that I'd be asked who I was and why I was there. No one paid me any attention, though, caught up in their own conversations. One woman was desperately trying to get people to join the PTA: 'Sure I can't persuade you? It's great fun and only takes up about sixteen hours a week of your time.' Another was very disapproving of her child's teacher: 'How can he teach English without involving fronted adverbials?' Another was very appreciative: 'Have you seen the new Year Six teacher? Wouldn't mind getting involved with his fronted adverbials.'

I couldn't help but giggle at this remark and glanced over at the woman who'd made it. She was someone Brigitte and I would get on with. She didn't see me, but the woman who was recruiting for the PTA did. I turned away sharply to face the gate again, cringing as I felt her approach. This was not someone Brigitte and I would get on with.

'Hi,' she said. 'I'm Alison.'

Her smile was genuinely friendly and it went completely against the grain to be rude to her, but I couldn't engage and risk blowing my cover. I gave a curt nod, hoping my lack of interest would put her off. She looked at me expectantly, presumably for me to offer my name, like a normal person would do. I pressed my lips together in case politeness took over and I blurted it out, along with my phone number, home address and a disclosure that my left boob was slightly larger than my right.

After an awkward pause, Alison continued, 'Have your children just started here? Not seen you before.'

I shook my head. 'Picking up my friend's children as a favour.' I'd pre-prepared an answer in case I was asked.

'Who are they? My two might know them.'

'I'd rather not say. It's private.' I cringed. That had sounded so much better in my head.

Alison's eyes widened. 'Is your friend famous? Is that why she can't come? Because she'd be mobbed at the gate?'

I wished desperately that I had Maman's disregard for etiquette and could tell Alison to occupy herself with her onions. But I didn't, so felt obliged to respond. Having exhausted my pre-prepared answers, and with no explanation as to why the identity of the children was private, I decided Alison's assumption was as good as any. May as well go with it.

'Yes,' I whispered. 'She doesn't want anyone to know.'

Alison gasped. 'How exciting. Who is she?' She looked over her shoulder, then lowered her voice. 'I won't tell anyone, promise.'

I shook my head. 'Can't, I'm afraid. Client confidentiality.'

'She's your client?' Alison's mouth formed an O. 'Got it. Saying you're her friend is a cover.'

I gave a brief nod and gestured to the playground. 'Don't mean to be rude, but I'd better get on.'

Alison frowned. 'Get on with waiting?'

I was saved from having to justify my stupid comment by the school bell ringing. Moments later the main door opened and many, many tiny children came out. Some dragged their bags, looking exhausted. Others looked as though they'd been mainlining energy drinks and were now ready to reap havoc after being held in captivity all day. A couple of teachers, who looked as though they needed some energy drinks themselves, made sure each child could see their responsible adult before releasing them into the wild. It was strange to think Anna would be at school in just over a year. Would she be one of the quieter children, ready for a cuddle and an early night after a long day of learning? Recalling how she'd prolonged her bedtime by an hour the previous night with a protracted series of shuttle runs around the house, I knew the answer already. She'd be the most feral of them all.

I scanned the children, wondering if the older ones had a later finish time. Alison started waving so enthusiastically, you'd think she was stranded on a desert island and a ship had come into view on the horizon. A cute little boy with a wonky tie and a weary look – caused either by a trying day or a trying mother – came over. Alison swept him up into a hug, which, remembering Anna's pretence at not knowing me at nursery, made me slightly envious.

'Let's go and meet your sister,' Alison said to him and they began to walk away. I realised that many other parents were doing the same. Where were they all going?

I hurried after Alison. 'Is there another exit?' I asked.

'Yes,' she said. 'This is just for Reception. Key Stages 1 and 2 are on the other side.'

Panic jolted through me as I realised I was in the wrong place. Liz could have collected Harry and Bella, and the giant bear, and be long gone by now. I might have missed my chance.

Alison put a calming hand on my arm. 'Don't worry. They won't let them leave without an adult, unless they're eleven and it's been agreed.' She started walking briskly. 'I'll show you where to go.' I followed, my heart pounding at the prospect of missing Liz. 'Which year are they in?'

I had no idea. The system had changed since my day and was now more in line with the US. I estimated that Harry and Bella were in what used to be third year of infants and first year primary, but what did that equate to now? I made an educated guess.

'Year Eight.'

Alison and her son exchanged a look. 'That's secondary school,' she said. 'Primary only goes up to Year Six.'

So much for my guess being educated. I forced a laugh. 'Sorry. I meant he's *age* eight. She's five.'

'They'll come out of different exits, then.' Alison quickened her pace. 'I'm going to Key Stage 1 as well, so we'll go there first, then on to Key Stage 2.'

'Thanks. You're very kind.' Or desperate to see who these kids of a celebrity were. Either way, it didn't matter as I had no intention of actually meeting the children. Just their mum, if she was still there.

As we hurried to the next exit, I mentally ran through my conversation opener with Liz. The giant bear was my way in. As she hadn't yet claimed this wondrous prize, I guessed that she didn't really want it. I'd comment on the bear and if her reaction was less than enthusiastic, I'd offer to take it off her hands to donate to a charity fundraiser I was involved with. If she seemed quite attached to it, I'd offer to give her a lift home, as it was too cumbersome to carry. The fact that my car was probably parked further away than her house was a flaw in this plan. The whole plan, in fact, had more flaws than a political party manifesto, but it was the only one I had. If all went well, I'd come across as an upstanding citizen who wanted nothing more than to help Liz in her moment of need, and she'd welcome me and Anna into the fold. If all went badly, she'd report me to the police for stalking. Or she wouldn't be there, and Alison would have me arrested for the attempted kidnapping of a minor and telling an enormous fib. My stomach tightened. Please let this go well.

We rounded the corner and were at last on the other side of this gargantuan school. Only a few children remained. They stood inside the gate with a teacher who looked so ready to go home, it possibly wouldn't matter whose home it was. I scanned the group. Was one of these Bella, or had she already been collected? Alison raised her arm in preparation for another Olympic-podium-worthy wave, but a little girl ran over before she got up much momentum.

'Sorry I was late, lovey. I've been helping this lady.' Alison turned to me. 'I'll introduce you to Mrs Evans. The office will have told her someone else is picking up . . .' She winked. 'Whoever it is you're picking up.'

I pressed my hands together. 'You've been so kind, but I can't take up any more of your time. You get home.'

Alison's face fell. 'But I need to show you the other exit.'

'I'll find it. Thank you.' I edged towards the gate. 'Bye.' I turned away, feeling guilty for dismissing her so obviously, but resolute in my mission. Aware of Alison hovering, I slipped inside the gate to talk to Mrs Evans without being overheard. 'Hi,' I said.

She looked as though she wanted to glare at me, but didn't have the energy. 'Parents aren't allowed inside the gate.'

'Sorry.' I smiled apologetically. 'I'm looking for Liz Clark. She's picking up a teddy bear that she won in the summer fair raffle.'

Mrs Evans nodded to someone who was respecting the boundaries and staying outside the gate, and let one of the children go. 'The office deals with that. Why are you asking me?'

'Isn't this the gate where Liz Clark collects her children?'

'No, they're in Key Stage 2 now. But they won't have the raffle prize either. You need to go to the office.' She sighed wearily. 'Please leave the playground.'

'Course. Sorry.' I scurried out. Maybe I'd got Bella's age wrong. Or Alison had been wrong about the Key Stages. She didn't strike me as someone who got anything to do with the school system wrong, but it had never struck me that Mark could end up being the least attractive member of Take That, so I knew my intuition wasn't always spot on.

Alison was still hovering. I pretended not to see her and walked in the opposite direction, hoping that the Key Stage 2 exit was nearby. Alison followed, pulling her children along by their hands.

'I couldn't help but overhear,' she said. I suspected this to be a lie. 'Is it Liz Clark's children you're collecting?'

'I'm not allowed to say.' I increased my walking pace.

'It must be, or you wouldn't have mentioned her.' Alison sped up also. 'But she's not famous.'

I broke into a gentle jog.

'Unless she's famous in some sphere I'm not familiar with,' Alison said, ignoring her children's protests as she ran to keep up, dragging them along with her. 'A TikTok sensation maybe? Or an influencer.'

'Please stop asking. I'm not at liberty to say.' Where was the other exit to this stupidly big school? The O2 resembled a two-up two-down in comparison.

Alison gasped loudly. 'I've got it. She's an adult actress,

isn't she? Some of them are very famous in certain circles, from what I understand.'

'No!' I exclaimed.

'That's why she doesn't want anyone to know.' Alison's face was flush with excitement. 'Can't risk that sort of talk getting back to the children. I assume they don't know.'

'No, they don't, because she's not.' I stopped abruptly. 'You mustn't tell anyone. You'd be damaging her reputation over something that's not true.'

'I won't tell a soul.' Alison criss-crossed her heart. 'Her secret's safe with me.'

I exhaled loudly. 'There is no secret. You've jumped to the wrong conclusion.'

Alison nodded. For a moment I thought she'd accepted this, but then she gave an exaggerated wink.

I groaned. Circulating a rumour that Liz was a porn star was unlikely to ingratiate me with her. 'I mean it, Alison. If you say a word about this, it will go very badly.'

'Would she turn on me?' She pulled her children close. 'Or would her bosses?' She visibly gulped. 'The fat cats using these women for monetary gain are always tyrants, prepared to do anything it takes to keep their earnings rolling in.' Her eyes widened. 'The teddy bear. Are they making her smuggle drugs in it? Are you her mule?'

I pressed my fingertips to my eyes. This was turning into a farce. 'There are no drugs in the bear. Liz is not an adult actress. There are no tyrant bosses. Please forget this entire conversation.'

Alison nodded. 'I get it. You're protecting me. Thank you.' She squeezed my arm. 'Take care of yourself.' She pasted a smile on her face and looked down at her children. 'Last one to the car's a smelly banana.' And with that, they were off.

Exhausted, I trudged on, searching for the Key Stage 2 exit, without much expectation that anyone would still be there or that it even existed. I'd almost given up hope of ever finding it – I was sure I'd passed the Lost City of Atlantis while searching – when in the distance I saw a woman talking on her phone while two children, a boy and a girl, wrestled with an enormous teddy bear. I inhaled sharply. It was her. The real Liz Clark. At last, I'd found her.

Chapter 24

I approached cautiously, as though she were a wild animal that could turn on me at any time. Which was possible, going by the tales Scott had told me of Liz's behaviour over the years.

She was medium build and height, with dark hair pulled back into a ponytail, and was wearing brightly patterned leggings, a loose yoga vest and sliders. Her cheeks were slightly flushed and she was explaining something into the phone in a measured, patient way. Measured and patient weren't adjectives Scott had ever used to describe her. The ones he used were best not repeated, especially with children nearby.

I turned my attention to the children in question. Scott's children. After years of wanting desperately to meet them, to be a part of their lives, to hug them to my bosom (the slightly larger one would be comfier), there they were. Harry and Bella. Right in front of me, having a tug of war with the bear, completely unaware of who I was or that I was there to hopefully introduce them, in time, to their half-sister. My heart pounded as I watched them play. I'd never have recognised them from the photo Scott had, but of course that was taken ages ago and had been carefully posed for. In the flesh, several years on, they were bound to look different. Taller, broader and older. Actually, they seemed a lot older. Way too grown-up for five and eight. Of course, some children were tall for their ages, but Scott was the shorter side of average, as was Liz. I studied their faces, looking for clues. Harry had a tuft of hair sticking out at an angle, just like Scott's did before he plastered it down with products. Bella had Scott's sandy hair and determination. The way she gritted her teeth to get the bear off her brother was spookily similar to Scott's demeanour when getting a stubborn cork out of a bottle of Cava.

'Right, you two, let's go.' Liz's voice made me start. I'd been so focused on Harry and Bella that I hadn't noticed her finish her call. She tucked her phone into a cross-body bag and plucked at one of the ears of the teddy bear. 'Suppose we're stuck with this now.'

This was my chance. I'd never get a better way in than this. 'Excuse me,' I said. It came out so quietly that not even I could hear it. I cleared my throat, pushing down my nerves. 'Excuse me,' I said louder. Too loud. My voice bellowed out of me as though trying to make myself heard by the referee from the back of a football stadium.

Liz instinctively stepped in front of the children. 'Yes,' she said guardedly.

I put my hands up. 'Sorry to bother you. I couldn't help but overhear.' I gestured to the teddy. 'I'm collecting raffle prizes for Children in Need. If the bear's too big for you, I could take it off your hands.'

Harry and Bella looked as though I'd asked to take one of their organs. Liz looked as though I was offering her a deal that was too good to be true.

'Children in Need?' she said.

I nodded. It had seemed the obvious choice. Race for Life and Santa Skydive didn't have much call for giant teddies. In fact, an enormous bear would be a definite hindrance.

'It's not till November. Why are you collecting now?'

'Don't like to leave things to the last minute. Fail to plan and plan to fail, and all that.' I sounded so sanctimonious. 'Always on the lookout for potential prizes. Things people don't want or need.' Now I sounded opportunist.

Bella glared at me. 'We do need it. You can't take it away.'

Harry turned to Liz. 'Tell the nasty lady she can't have it.'

I winced at the term 'nasty lady'. I was supposed to be

befriending them, not making myself even more of an enemy. This wasn't the best start to our relationship.

'Of course I won't take it without your permission.' I went to pat the bear's head, but Harry and Bella yanked it away. 'Just thought I'd ask. Not everyone likes giant bears.'

'We don't like giant idiots,' Bella sneered.

Perhaps Brigitte was right. Did I really want to open my home up to two children who would be rude to me and possibly Anna? I shook myself. I was a stranger, threatening to take away their new toy. Of course they'd react with hostility. Anna would do the same, with a few additional French swear words to round it off.

'Sorry,' I said. 'Didn't mean to upset you. Forget I asked.' Time for Plan B. 'Can I give you a lift home? Your arms will get tired, carrying such a big bear.'

As soon as the words left my mouth, I realised how wrong such an offer was. No one should accept a lift from a stranger – especially not one who'd just tried to confiscate their new toy.

I instantly backtracked. 'Ignore that. It was inappropriate. You don't know me so—'

'Actually, I think I do.' Liz gave me a long, hard look. 'Marie, isn't it?'

My insides curdled. I hadn't anticipated her knowing what I looked like. Had she demanded Scott show her a photo? Had she looked me up online? Had she followed me or shown up at places where she knew I'd be? The thought of her knowing my movements and watching me sent a shiver down my spine. But, I realised with horror, that was exactly what I was doing to her.

Liz narrowed her eyes. 'Bit of a coincidence this – you showing up at my kids' school.'

Shame coursed through me. Of course she'd seen through my façade. What was I doing? I shouldn't be here. This was intrusive and wrong. I was using the children as pawns, which was the exact thing she did to Scott. Did that make me, if not as bad, then not so very different?

Liz took her phone out. Oh God, she wasn't going to call the police, was she? Or Scott? Tell him that I'd accosted them at school, tried to steal Harry and Bella's teddy bear, then get them in my car. She'd never let me and Anna meet them properly now. And how would Scott react once he heard I'd gone behind his back and didn't trust him when he said he'd sort it out? I fought back tears. I'd ruined everything.

'I'm sorry.' My voice wobbled. 'I've overstepped the mark, I know. Just thought if I met you, we could resolve the situation once and for all. I want to build bridges, to work together for a united future.'

Liz looked up from her phone. Had that hit home?

I pressed my hands together. 'I'd love to get to know Harry and Bella. For them to meet Anna. For all of us to get along.' Liz blinked slowly. Was it possible I was getting through? Hope surged. This had been a risky gamble and I'd almost fucked up completely. But if I got Liz to listen and understand that I wanted the best for everyone, it would have been worth it. I gave a tentative smile. 'Scott has nothing to do with this. I found the school myself because I'm so desperate to make this work. I truly believe we can, if we're open and honest, and focus on Harry and Bella's best interests.' I released a shaky breath. 'This is a lot for you to take in, but perhaps we could sit down and talk in a couple of days, when you've had time to digest it? You, me and Scott. For the sake of the children.'

Liz glanced from me to Harry and Bella, who were, understandably, looking confused. I'd deliberately been vague so they wouldn't know what I was talking about. Scott and Liz needed to be the ones to tell them they had a sister, not me. Liz took a step forward. I held my breath. Did this mean she was on board? Was this the first step towards building a healthy, sustainable relationship? She placed a hand on my arm. My heart soared. It was happening!

'Can I call someone to come and get you?' she asked gently.

'Like who?' She didn't mean Scott, did she?

'A carer, perhaps? Or someone who's helped you through one of these episodes before.'

I frowned. 'Episodes?'

She gave a sympathetic smile. 'I'm sure it all seems very real, but nothing you're saying relates to me.'

I blinked at her. 'You're not Liz Clark?'

She faltered. 'Yes, I am, but I have no idea who Scott, Harry and Bella are.'

Was she playing mind games with me? I thrust a hand in the children's direction.

Liz followed my gaze. 'Why are you pointing at Lyla and Joe?'

'They're Harry and Bella,' I said.

Liz shook her head.

Oh no. Not again.

I put my hands to my head, which was starting to throb. 'I'm so sorry. I thought you were a different Liz Clark.'

'That explains it.' Liz gave a relieved laugh. 'How many of us are there?'

Seven zillion, as it so happened.

A thought struck me. 'But you knew who I was. Said it was a coincidence me turning up. You seemed a bit defensive, that's why I thought . . .' I tailed off. 'Why I thought you were a conniving, manipulative bitch' didn't seem a nice way to end the sentence.

'It *is* a coincidence,' Liz said. 'You made my friend Faye's wedding dress last year. I came to the studio with her when she collected it.'

Ah. Faye was the client who'd insisted on a low-cut dress, then got me to change it at the last minute. I'd been so stressed and sleep-deprived from working through the night to do the alterations that I could barely recognise Faye, let alone log her friend's image in my memory bank for future stalking opportunities.

'I'd better go.' I gestured in the general direction of my

car. Very general. I'd completely lost my bearings and had no idea where it was. 'Sorry about the mix-up.'

'No problem.' Liz noticed that her children had abandoned the giant bear and were now playing hopscotch. 'Quick, grab it while they're not looking,' she whispered. 'Children in Need's a great cause.'

'Oh. Thanks.' Forcing a smile, I picked the bear up and groaned under its weight. Great. I'd failed yet again to meet Liz and now I had to cart this fucking thing for miles to my car. That was the last time I listened to my mother.

Chapter 25

'Morning.' Scott slapped my bottom, as he passed me by the dishwasher, and sat next to Anna at the table. Humming, he tucked his tie in between the buttons of his shirt and poured milk on his muesli.

He'd been much happier the past three weeks, since seeing Harry and Bella again. This time, though, he was sticking to his two evenings a week, rather than dashing round when he was summoned, as he used to. He even ignored his phone beeping most of the time. Sex had gone from every night to a much more sustainable twice a week, and his previous passion and tenderness had returned. The trouble was, mine hadn't. So, on those two nights a week, I wasn't 'excited', as Maman would say. Thinking about my mum instead of focusing on Scott's lovemaking probably didn't help.

I finished unloading the dishwasher, poured milk into Anna's beaker and sat down to eat my own muesli. Scott was scrolling through his phone, but looked up and smiled. He was so handsome. I must be out of my mind not to be as into sex as I had been until very recently. Well, not out of my mind. I was no psychologist (thankfully, because I struggled to spell the word), but I didn't need to be Freud to figure out that my temporary (please, let it be temporary) failure to climax was caused by his insistence on using condoms and the lack of progress with Liz. Scott was still waiting for the 'right time' to discuss us meeting Harry and Bella. And my own pathetic attempts to meet Liz had not only failed, but had also gifted me with a new set of bruises every week from the pole dancing classes

Brigitte dragged me to, and a teddy bear so large that no charity shop would accept it. It was currently hidden in the boot of my car, but needed to go. I couldn't physically fit anything else in the boot, and if Anna ever saw it, she'd want to keep it. My protestations that it was too big would not be considered. She'd probably suggest I move out to make room.

I pushed those thoughts away. 'Busy day?' I asked.

Scott's smile broadened. 'Got an open house for a new property. Client wasn't going to go with us, but I talked them round.' He punched the air.

Anna copied him and knocked her beaker over. Scott jumped up and leapt back to protect his suit. Unfortunately, I didn't react as quickly, and Anna and I both ended up with a lap full of milk. Anna screwed her face up and cried.

'It's OK, chick. We'll wash it off.' I scooped her up and kissed her.

'No point crying over spilt milk.' Scott laughed, putting his bowl in the sink and ignoring the milk puddle forming on the floor.

I gave a polite smile to mask my frustration. Nothing like throwing an impromptu bath for Anna into the already manic morning routine.

'I'm off,' Scott said ten minutes later, poking his head around the bathroom door. Anna held up a plastic whale that sprayed so forcefully, we could use it to water the garden. Scott withdrew his head. 'Got a sec?' he called from the landing.

I stood in the doorway, so I could keep an eye on Anna.

'We haven't got plans for the weekend, have we?' Scott asked.

'I'm working Saturday.' I usually only did one Saturday a month, but the summer months were so busy that I had to do more.

'Your mum's got Anna, right?'

'Course. Can't leave her at home on her own.'

'I'm not working this weekend.' He went to smooth his tie down, realised it was still tucked inside his shirt and pulled it out. 'I did tell you.'

'Did you?' I slumped against the door. 'Can't believe I've got to work when you're off.'

'Could you rearrange your clients?'

I shook my head. This was full-on wedding season and the brides needed everything to go exactly as planned. Cancelling their appointments would unnerve them more than if one of the bridesmaids slept with the groom. They could just uninvite her.

'That's a shame.' Scott ran a hand through his sandy hair and patted it to make sure it had fallen back into place. 'Would you mind if I took Harry and Bella away for a night, as I haven't seen them much lately?'

I couldn't remember the last time the three of us had been away for a night, but voicing that would be mean, so I forced a smile and shook my head. Then a thought struck me and my smile widened.

'We could join you on the Sunday. Go to the zoo or something.' I checked Anna wasn't listening. 'Doesn't have to be a big deal. We can build up the relationship slowly.'

Scott fiddled with his tie. There was a kink where it had been in his shirt, and he twisted it back and forth to straighten it out. I watched his face for clues as to what he thought of my suggestion, but he seemed more preoccupied with the tie.

'That's a great idea,' he said eventually. My heart soared. 'I have to clear it with Liz first, though.' My heart deflated. Getting her to sanction a visit would make the Brexit negotiations seem straightforward.

'Does she have to know?' I whispered.

Scott gave me an affectionate smile. 'They'd all be calling me Daddy. Wouldn't take long for them to figure it out.'

'What if I called you Daddy as well? We'll pretend it's a game.'

Scott slapped my bottom. 'You are funny.'

I laughed along with him, even though I hadn't been completely joking, which proved how desperate I was getting.

Scott waved at Anna. 'Bye, sweetheart. Have a good day.'

'Bye, Daddy.' A jet of warm water from the whale sprayed up my back. At least it was preferable to cold milk in my knickers.

'You all right?' Brigitte asked, as we joined the queue at the café opposite work.

'Fine, thanks.' I took my reusable cup from my bag.

Brigitte rummaged through her own bag. This was purely for show, as she never remembered to bring a cup. 'Sure? You seem a bit down.'

I shrugged. 'Just disappointed that I wasn't able to find Liz. I'm back to waiting for Scott to sort it out now.'

Brigitte didn't say she'd warned me I'd be back here again, which I loved her for. 'We could have another try?' she said instead.

I shook my head. 'Liz Clark at the school thought I was mentally ill. Don't blame her. Going to the school was insane.' I reached the front of the queue and ordered our drinks. 'Things are better than they were, but now Scott doesn't want to push it, in case Liz goes back to her old demanding ways.'

Brigitte handed me a biscotti packet from a pot by the till and took one for herself. 'I saw Scott this morning, driving near the industrial estate.'

I bit into the biscuit. 'He's managing an open house. Must be on that new development.' I put the rest of the biscotti in my mouth, then realised what I'd done. 'Why did you give me that? I'm not eating sugar.'

'Notice you didn't object till after you'd eaten it.' Brigitte tapped the card machine and we walked back to work.

'Why were you at the industrial estate?' I asked.

Brigitte took a long sip through her straw, her cheeks

contracting and relaxing as she sucked. A car screeched to a halt to let us cross the road.

I put up a hand to thank the driver, although they clearly hadn't stopped for me. 'Well?'

Brigitte tossed her hair over one shoulder. Another car stopped, even though we were now on the pavement. 'I was at the sexual health clinic.' She said it as casually as though she'd mentioned stopping off for a pint of milk.

'The sex clinic?' Her life was so much more exciting than mine. I'd been mopping up spilt milk while she'd been . . . Well, I didn't want to know what she'd been mopping up. I followed her up the stairs and into her salon.

'I forgot it's been more than three months since my last contraceptive injection.' She flicked her wax heater on. 'So I went and got the morning-after pill.'

I considered scolding her for not keeping better track of her contraception, but she hadn't said 'told you so' earlier, so I needed to be equally supportive.

'Well done for remembering before it was too late,' I said, following some parenting advice I'd once read. Find something to praise, no matter how small, and ignore the bad behaviour. It was no wonder so many kids were absolute turds. 'Did you get an injection too?'

'Yes. Although, Sundeep and Ammo are staying for the rest of the week. The mood they bestow on the house is a better contraception than anything on the NHS.' Brigitte straightened a pile of waxing strips. 'I know you're desperate to meet Harry and Bella, but be prepared that it won't be happy blended families, with you all playing board games together in matching jumpers. It'll be them yelling, "You can't tell me what to do – you're not my mum!" when you've asked them to do something they deem unacceptable, such as flush the toilet.' She scraped her hair back into a ponytail, pulling so tightly that it must have hurt. 'Every child of divorce wants their parents to get back together and blames the stepmum for keeping them apart. It's shit.'

She sighed heavily. 'Maybe you're better off keeping things the way they are?'

I knew she was saying this to save me from further stress and disappointment, but I couldn't let it go. Perhaps being a stepmum would be shit, but I wanted to give it a try.

'Brigitte saw you near the industrial estate this morning,' I said to Scott that evening. 'Is the open house on the new development?'

'Hmm?' Scott flicked through the programme options on iPlayer.

'Your open house.' I hung the shirt I'd just ironed on a hanger and took another from the pile. 'Did you get lots of viewings?'

'Yeah, the owner was pleased.' Scott slowed his scrolling to read the review of a US remake of a Scandi thriller. I preferred the originals, but an English-speaking version would prevent me from ironing my fingers while reading the subtitles. 'The open house wasn't up there, though,' he said. 'That's where the physio is. Had an appointment about my groin strain.'

'Is it still sore?' I felt a stab of guilt. Scott hadn't mentioned it for a few weeks, so I'd pretty much forgotten about it.

'Nope. All better.' Scott put an arm behind his head and looked up at me, a smile playing on his lips. 'Now that everything's better in that department, I reckon it's time.'

I froze, the iron suspended in mid-air.

'Time for what?' I hardly dared ask.

Scott grinned. 'Time to start trying for a baby.'

Tears sprung to my eyes. 'Really?'

He nodded. 'Fancy trying right now?'

I nodded back, somehow laughing and crying at the same time. 'Let me switch the iron off.'

'Safety first,' Scott said solemnly. He waited till I'd unplugged it, then picked me up.

I squealed and clamped a hand over my mouth. Last thing

we needed was Anna waking and making more comments about Scott's tail.

All my reservations about our relationship melted away as he kissed me. Everything was going to be all right.

Chapter 26

I didn't just have a spring in my step. I had a hop and a jump, too. Since Scott told me we could start trying, two weeks ago, we'd had unprotected sex every night that he had been home. I was asleep by the time he got back from his evenings at Liz's, as Harry still had night terrors, but four times a week should be enough to get me pregnant soon. I'd even researched the best positions to conceive in. Scott had been thrilled to learn that the reverse cowgirl was ideal for someone with a tilted cervix and was looking forward to trying the side-by-side scissors. I'd decided against mentioning the wheelbarrow. Gardening really wasn't my thing.

I beamed as I walked Anna to nursery, taking in everything around me. The air was fresher, the flowers brighter, the birds more vibrant. Anna regarded me warily as I chatted about the wonder of nature and was very dismissive when I hugged her goodbye.

'*Tu me fais chier*,' she said grumpily, wriggling out of my embrace.

Not even being told to piss off by my three-year-old daughter could dampen my mood. It was all good parenting experience, which I'd need for the next one.

The next one! There was going to be another baby. This put everything with Liz into perspective. No more wasting time on her. I was still sad that she refused to let Harry and Bella meet Anna, but I couldn't control her behaviour. Instead of putting my energy into trying to make it happen, I'd put my energy into what I could control – my own family. I hugged myself excitedly. Anna was going to have a brother or sister! One she could actually meet.

A clap of thunder went off overhead and the mild drizzle I'd been ignoring turned into torrential rain. As with Anna's earlier verbal abuse, I was too elated to let it get me down. Instead, I turned my face to the sky and let the summer rain try, and fail, to wash the smile off my face.

'You look very pleased with yourself.'

The voice cut into my bubble of happiness. Cleo stood in front of me, an umbrella protecting her perfectly styled blonde bob. The sight of her achieved what the downpour couldn't, and my smile fell. Was the baby all right?

'How are you?' I asked tentatively.

Cleo didn't answer, but looked me up and down with disgust. I became painfully aware of how ridiculous I must look. Rain trickled down my face and my clothes stuck to my body. I crossed my arms, thankful I wasn't wearing a pale top, as this was no time for a wet T-shirt contest.

'Are you OK?' I said, releasing one arm to wipe my face before clamping it across my chest again.

Cleo glowered at me. 'Like you care.'

'Of course I do,' I said. 'I've thought about you so much since you came to my studio.' Cleo's pale blue eyes were cold, revealing nothing. I was going to have to ask if I wanted to find out. 'Is the baby OK?' I asked gently, crossing my fingers beneath my folded arms.

Cleo turned and began to walk away. Above the hammering of rain, I heard a distinct sob.

'Cleo.' I hurried after her. She quickened her pace, but I kept up. 'Is everything OK with the baby?'

Cleo mumbled something.

I put a hand on her arm. 'Sorry, I missed that. What did you say?'

'Don't touch me,' she spat.

'Sorry,' I said again. 'Please talk to me. I'm worried about you.'

Cleo spun round. 'Why? You don't know me.'

'No, but I don't want you to be upset.' I bit my lip. 'Is the baby OK?'

Cleo's face contorted. 'I lost the baby.'

My hand flew to my mouth. 'I'm so—'

'Don't say it.' Cleo threw her umbrella to the ground. 'Don't you dare say it,' she hissed. 'It's your fault.'

I went cold. 'What?'

'If it wasn't for you, I'd still be pregnant.' Cleo clutched her stomach.

My head swam as intensely as if she'd punched me. The bleeding had started at my studio when I said I didn't have time to make her dress. Had the stress of that caused her to miscarry? 'I'm so sorry,' I stammered. 'I should have made time for you.'

She shook her head vigorously. 'So self-absorbed and ignorant.' Bronze eyeliner streaked her angular cheeks. 'Don't get it, do you? That you caused it.'

I wiped my own cheeks, unsure if they were drenched with rain or tears. 'I'm sorry,' I said again, aware my words were woefully inadequate.

'I don't want your pity,' Cleo shouted. 'I hate you. Hate everything about you.'

She didn't need to say it. I could see the hatred in her face. Every vein stood out on her neck. Her eyes were full of loathing. She genuinely thought I was to blame for the loss of her baby. Perhaps I was.

A small crowd had gathered around us. Cleo was oblivious, but I was painfully aware of the whispering and nudging. Cleo continued to shout, her words growing harder to decipher. Something about opening my eyes? I strained to hear above a loud chattering noise that ricocheted around my head. I pressed a hand to my forehead, and realised my whole body was shaking and the noise was my teeth chattering.

My knees gave way beneath me and I landed hard on my bottom at Cleo's feet. She looked down at me in disgust, her mouth opening and closing as she continued to shout.

I tried to get back up, but my legs were shaking too much. Helplessly, I squinted up at her, blinking water from my eyes, as rain poured down on me.

A blurred figure positioned themselves between me and Cleo. I could make out a tall man waving his arms, shooing the voyeurs away. Like magic, they disappeared, and then Cleo was going. Turning and running away.

I bowed my head, filled with both shame and relief. A strong arm wound its way around my back and helped me to my feet.

'I've got you,' said a familiar voice.

Realising it was Michael, I tried to pull away, but my knees buckled again. Michael tightened his grip.

'Lean on me,' he said. 'Let's get to your studio.'

It was a short walk, but seemed to take forever. I'd never have made it without Michael supporting me.

'You're soaked through and have had a shock,' he said, taking the key and opening the front door as I fumbled with the lock. 'Get changed. That'll help warm you up.'

I tried to tell him I could manage on my own till Brigitte arrived, but stumbled on the very first step, so had to accept that I needed his help, at least up the stairs. At the top, he eased his feet out of his trainers, pulled my sandals off my feet and led me to my studio. There he handed me the dressing gown that he'd borrowed when I'd repaired his trousers. I opened my mouth to tell him I was all right and he could go.

'Where's your kitchen?' he asked. 'I'll make you a hot drink.'

A hot drink sounded good. I'd let him do that, then tell him to go.

'Second on the right,' I said, through chattering teeth. 'Green tea, please.' As he turned towards the door, droplets of water flew off him and I realised he was as drenched as me. He was dressed in a running top and shorts, and must have taken our shoes off to avoid making my pale grey carpet wet and dirty.

I handed the robe to him. 'Take this. I'll borrow one of Brigitte's.'

He gave a smile of thanks and went into the toilet. In Brigitte's salon, I peeled off my saturated clothes. Once in a fluffy dressing gown, I wrapped a towel round my head. Like Cleo, my face was streaked with mascara. Luckily, makeup remover was in abundance in Brigitte's salon, so I helped myself and shakily wiped away the black smears.

When Michael returned to my studio, wearing his towelling robe and carrying two mugs, I was curled up on the sofa, the dressing gown tucked around me. I wasn't going to risk flashing him like he'd unknowingly done to me. Aside from the fact it wasn't polite, his legs were supposed to be hairy; mine weren't.

'Thank you.' I took the mug gratefully and wrapped my trembling hands around it, desperate for warmth.

'How are you feeling?' Michael asked.

'Cold.' I buried my chin in my dressing gown. 'Bit sore where I fell over.'

'Want me to take a look?'

'No!' I didn't want him looking at my bruised bum. Especially, as I wasn't wearing any pants.

'Keep dry and warm.' He sat next to me and placed a cool palm on my forehead. 'You haven't got a temperature. That's good.' He gestured to my tea. 'Drink that. It'll make you feel better.'

I took a sip and grimaced. How could he have ballsed up green tea? All he had to do was pour hot water on a teabag.

'I added sugar,' Michael said. 'Helps with the shock.'

I glared at him. 'I've given up sugar, remember?'

'Right, sorry.' Michael nodded solemnly. 'How long's it been now?'

He didn't need to know about the Twix I'd had the night before. 'Never mind.' I sighed theatrically. 'I'll start again after this.' I took another sip. Green tea with sugar was all right, actually. Helped to disguise the taste of grass.

As I thawed out, my teeth stopped chattering, but my hands still trembled, as I recalled again the hatred on Cleo's face and the venom in her words. The words I'd been able to hear, anyway. No one had ever directed such anger at me before. Not even my mum, when I'd told her that champagne wasn't French, as it had in fact been invented by a man from Gloucestershire. Actually, looking back, it was pretty close.

'Want to talk about what happened?' Michael asked.

I bit my lip. I very much wanted to talk about it, but wasn't sure I wanted to with Michael. Brigitte wouldn't be in for another half an hour, though, and Scott would be at work. Speaking of which.

'Shouldn't you be at work?' I asked.

'Not till midday. I'm on the late shift.'

'Lucky for me.' I tried to smile, but it turned into a sob. What would I have done if Michael hadn't come along? Would I still be sitting in the rain with Cleo shouting at me while people watched?

'Usually, I complain when Dean makes me go running in the rain, but I'm very glad he did today.' Michael put his head to one side. 'If you do want to talk, whatever you tell me stays between us. Think of it as patient confidentiality.'

I believed him. He hadn't told Beth about our previous conversations.

'Her name's Cleo,' I said. 'She came here a few weeks ago. She was newly pregnant and asked me to make her a wedding dress by August, but I told her I didn't have time.' I felt yet another wave of shame. 'She started bleeding when she was here. Then today she told me she'd lost the baby. She blames me for making her stressed.' Tears pricked my eyes. 'If I'd helped, she wouldn't have had that pressure on her. The baby might still be OK.' I wiped a tear from my cheek.

'This isn't your fault,' Michael said. 'There's no evidence that stress results in miscarriage. If it's early on in the pregnancy, it's probably because of an abnormality.' He spoke calmly and what he said made sense, but I still felt wretched. Cleo had asked for my help and I'd said no. She'd only wanted a simple dress. I could have done that in my sleep. I overlooked the fact that to get it done on time, sleep wouldn't have featured much in my schedule.

'But if I'd said yes to making the dress—'

'Wouldn't have made any difference.' Michael passed me the box of tissues I kept for the mother of the bride. 'Chances are very high that she'll go on to have a healthy pregnancy in the future. Her GP will have explained this to her. Right now, she's distressed and her hormones are in overdrive. She possibly feels she's to blame, so is looking to divert that guilt, or needs something to pin her hurt on. That's manifested itself as anger, and the something she's taking it out on is, unfortunately, you.'

I nodded and blew my nose loudly. Just as well it was Michael I was opening up to, not Scott, with his phobia of snot. Michael didn't seem fazed.

'Are you likely to see her again?' he asked.

The prospect filled me with dread. 'She doesn't live in Horsham, but comes here for work sometimes. I wasn't expecting to see her today.'

Her put a hand on my arm. 'Avoid her if you can. When she calms down, I'm sure she'll realise she overreacted, but no point taking any chances.' His eyes were on mine, their expression thoughtful and concerned.

The front door chimed and we both jumped. Michael stood up, tightening the robe around him.

'Morning,' Brigitte called out.

'I'd better go,' Michael said. 'I hung my running gear up above the sink. Hopefully, it's dried a bit.'

'Whose are these trainers?' Brigitte's mouth dropped open when she saw Michael and me coming out of my studio in robes. If her eyes had been able to spring out of her head on curly wires, cartoon-style, they would have.

'I'll let Marie explain.' Michael went into the toilet and bolted the door.

'Have you two just . . . ?' Brigitte mouthed.

'No!' I mouthed back, bundling her into my studio. 'Long story short – Cleo, the woman I told you I was worried about, accosted me in the street. She's had a miscarriage and blames me for not making her dress and stressing her out.'

'What?' Brigitte's earlier smirk was gone. 'Sorry that's happened to her, but she can't—'

'I know.' I spoke at speed, determined to get the story out before Michael reappeared, so Brigitte didn't think anything had happened. 'She shouted at me, and I fell over and couldn't get up. Michael says I was in shock. He brought me here. He made me a hot drink – with sugar in. He forgot I can't have sugar.'

Brigitte raised an eyebrow. 'And the robes?'

'I was wet.'

'I bet you were.'

'From the rain,' I spluttered. 'We both were.' I pointed to her umbrella. 'See, it's raining.' I was talking so quickly that I was out of breath. 'He got changed in the toilet, and I got changed in your salon. This is your robe. He's wearing mine. Nothing happened. He's gay, remember. And I'm married. Happily married.' I put a hand to my stomach. So happily married that we were trying for a baby. 'He was being a good citizen. Cleo was really freaking out.'

'God.' Brigitte put an arm around me. 'Are you OK?'

'It was a bit scary.' I rested my head on her shoulder.

'You should have rung. I'd have got here sooner.'

'My hands were shaking too much.'

Brigitte hugged me tightly. 'What was Cleo saying? Was she threatening you?'

'Don't think so. I couldn't hear everything she said. The way she looked at me was the worst bit. She really hates me.'

Brigitte frowned. 'Maybe you should report her.'

I shook my head. 'She's just lost her baby. She's devastated and took it out on me. Hopefully, she didn't mean it. Probably all mouth and no trousers.'

There was a knock at the door. 'I'll be off now,' Michael called through.

'Speaking of no trousers,' Brigitte murmured.

Ignoring her, I opened the door.

'Thank you so much,' I said, taking his robe. 'Don't know what I'd have done if you hadn't come by.'

'Someone else would have helped.'

I thought back to the people staring at us. No one had exactly gone out of their way to help. Not unless I counted someone videoing the scene on their phone as help.

'But I'm glad I was there,' Michael added. He looked at me intently. 'Take it easy today. A shock takes it out of you.'

'I will.' I smiled, suddenly feeling a bit shy. 'Thanks again.'

'You're welcome.'

'Bye,' Brigitte called after him as he jogged down the stairs. She took the robe from me and pressed it to her face. 'Do you think he was naked or kept his underwear on?' She smirked. 'It don't count if the booty ain't out.'

I pointedly ignored her. 'Do you have any clothes I can borrow, please?'

'I've got a spare uniform. I'll get it for you.' Brigitte handed the robe back and I placed it on the arm of the sofa. I wasn't prepared to admit this, but when Michael had put his hand on my arm and looked into my eyes, for a brief moment, I'd wondered if he'd been naked underneath the robe too.

Chapter 27

'Are you all right, babe?'

Scott put his briefcase down and came over to the kitchen sink where I was cleaning Anna's paintbrushes. This job took longer than the amount of time she spent painting, but I didn't want to stop her creativity when inspiration took hold. Not that mixing all the colours together to make a sludgy brown and painting the paper so thickly that it disintegrated seemed particularly inspirational.

'I'm fine, don't worry.' I leant back against Scott as he wrapped his arms around me. I'd messaged him earlier, saying I'd had an incident with a client, but hadn't elaborated.

'Is Anna asleep?' he asked.

'Yes.'

'Come and sit down. Tell me what happened.' He took my hands, realised they were wet and released them again.

'It's all a bit crazy,' I said, reaching for a towel. 'This woman asked if I could make a dress for her wedding in August, but I didn't have time.' I paused, remembering another detail. 'I'd seen her in the toilet at Maman and Francine's birthday celebration, but I didn't know who she was.'

Scott frowned. 'What was she doing in the toilet?'

'A poo, I assume. She was in there for ages.'

Scott grimaced. 'I meant why was she there.'

'Course, sorry.' I shook my head. 'It's coming out a bit muddled.'

'No worries,' he said. 'Just tell me what happened today.'

'I was walking to work and she started shouting at me in the middle of the street.' Talking about it unnerved me again. 'Don't know if she was waiting or just happened to see me.' I twisted the towel in my hands. 'It was horrible.'

Scott looked appalled. 'Oh, babe.'

'Luckily, Michael – Dr Greene – was running past and stopped her.'

Scott visibly stiffened. '*Michael*, is it? How did you get on first-name terms?'

I decided to skip the part where we both ended up in dressing gowns.

'I'm making a wedding dress for his sister.' I smiled reassuringly. 'Oh, and he's gay. Not that that's relevant.'

Scott didn't look particularly comforted. 'There's something about that man I don't trust.'

'Know what you mean,' I said. 'He's a complete bell-end usually. Probably got some vigilante fantasy that he lived out today.'

Scott made a scoffing noise. 'What happened then?'

I turned back to the sink to resume cleaning the paintbrushes. 'Cleo ran off and I went to work.'

'Who?' Scott asked.

'Cleo. That's her name.' My stomach clenched at the memory of her stricken face. 'I feel so guilty, even though Michael said there's no way I'd caused her miscarriage.'

'You didn't say anything about a miscarriage.'

'Didn't I?' I scrubbed at a stubborn clump of paint in the brushes. 'That was the reason she accosted me. She thinks it's my fault, because I couldn't make her dress.' A thought struck me and I spun round. 'She said she was thinking of moving here. That'd be a nightmare. I could bump into her any time. Maybe when I'm with Anna.'

Scott sank down into a chair, clearly distressed. 'The name Cleo's ringing a bell.'

I swallowed hard. 'She's been in your estate agent's?'

He nodded grimly. 'I think so. What does she look like?'

'Petite, blonde bob, pretty.'

'That's her. Though I wouldn't call her pretty.' Scott

ran a hand across his eyes. 'You know Andy from work?'

I nodded, even though I had no idea which Andy he was referring to.

'He took her on a few viewings.' My stomach tightened. 'Andy said she's a complete fantasist.'

'A fantasist?' She hadn't looked like a geek. 'What, she plays Dungeons & Dragons and things?'

'Don't be stupid,' Scott snapped. I blanched and he put his hands up. 'Sorry, babe. A fantasist is someone who confuses real life with fantasy.'

OK, maybe I was a bit stupid.

'Andy said this woman, Cleo, told him all sorts of things that just weren't true.'

'Like what?'

Scott pulled me onto his lap. 'Said her husband was disabled: an ex-army guy who'd been wounded in battle.'

'Husband? Sure she didn't say fiancé?'

Scott shook his head. 'Definitely married. With two boys, who she claimed were both autistic.'

I put a hand to my mouth. 'Why would she say that?'

Scott shrugged. 'Attention. Sympathy. To get a good deal on the house. Who knows?' Scott pressed my head to his chest and cradled me. 'I'm just glad you're OK. Stay away from her.'

I nodded.

'But if you do see her, don't listen to a word that comes out of her mouth. Everything she says is a lie.'

I sat up. 'Why didn't she give me the same disabled fiancé story? Why make up something completely different?'

Scott pulled my head back down. 'That's what fantasists do. Part of the thrill is working out what story will get the best reaction.'

I wriggled out of his grip and sat up again. 'But there was blood on her skirt. That was real – I saw it.'

Scott sighed wearily. 'Who knows what lengths these people will go to. Maybe she put the blood there beforehand.'

I bit my lip. 'Don't know whether to feel sorry for her or scared.'

'Go with scared,' Scott said firmly. 'Then you'll be on your guard if anything ever happens again.' He tried to press my head to his chest again, but it bobbed up instantly.

'Why do it? What would she get out of it, other than a wedding dress she didn't need, if I'd had time to make it?' The whole thing was insane. I was definitely going with scared. 'None of it makes sense.'

'Because she's fucking mental.' Scott twirled his forefinger by the side of his head. Usually, I'd tell him off for such un-PC behaviour and remind him it was an illness, but I didn't have the energy.

Another question popped into my mind. One I hardly dared ask. 'Did she buy one of the houses Andy showed her round?'

Scott looked at me thoughtfully. 'Don't know.'

'Can you phone him and find out?'

Scott kissed the top of my head. 'I'll do better than that. I'll ask him in person.'

'Now?' I didn't want him to go out. My earlier unease at Cleo's behaviour was nothing compared with how anxious I felt now I knew the pregnancy hadn't been real.

Scott eased me off his lap and stood up. 'He's been nagging me to go for a beer for ages. Can't have him thinking I only get in touch when I want something. This way I can find out without pissing him off.'

'Have dinner first,' I said, desperate for him to stay as long as possible. 'There's turkey bolognaise in the fridge.'

There was a lot of turkey bolognaise in the fridge because Anna refused it at teatime. Having pretty much lived on chips at Heavenly Hideaway, this was now all she wanted to consume.

'I'll get something in the pub.' He patted his trouser pockets for his wallet and keys.

'I don't want to be on my own,' I said in a small voice.

'You're not. Anna's upstairs.'

'She's asleep. Even if she wasn't, she's not exactly the kid from *Home Alone*. If Cleo turned up, Anna's more likely to ask her for some chips than scare her away.' The thought of Cleo turning up made me physically shiver.

'Please don't worry. Being a fantasist doesn't make her a stalker.' He squeezed my hand. 'You could always invite your mum round. Her outfits scare everyone off.'

I couldn't argue with that statement. Her Aztec-print harem pants definitely scared me.

Scott left, but instead of waving at the door, as I usually did, I locked it immediately. Humming to cover my unease and disappointment with Scott for going out when I needed him, I went back into the kitchen to finish washing the paintbrushes.

Two milk bottles sat by the sink and I recalled the night they'd been knocked over outside our door. I stopped humming. Scott claimed that being a fantasist didn't make Cleo a stalker, but someone had been out there. And if it wasn't Cleo, who was it?

Chapter 28

'Sorry I missed your call last night.' Brigitte leant against the doorframe to my studio. 'I was in bed.'

I'd phoned Brigitte from my own bed, where I'd bolted the moment I remembered the milk-bottle incident. When she didn't answer, I'd resorted to calling my mum, which showed how desperate for reassurance I was. Maman told me that if anyone was a fantasist, it was me for believing excess body hair could be removed with a razor, when any woman of value (i.e. French) knew only waxing worked. It wasn't quite the reassurance I'd been hoping for.

I'd lain awake till Scott came home at midnight, growing crosser with him by the minute for leaving me on my own for so long when Crazy Cleo – I didn't have the energy to correct my own un-PC thoughts either – was on the loose. Not even the good news that Cleo hadn't bought a property relaxed me enough to sleep. Instead, I asked myself the same questions repeatedly. Why had Cleo targeted me? Did she want something or did she do this to different people all the time? Would she leave me alone now? What if she bought a house through another estate agent and moved to Horsham? How long would it take for the stubble on my legs to grow out so I could get them waxed?

I'd eventually drifted off about half an hour before Anna woke up and now felt wretched.

'Did you ring for anything specific or just a chat?' Brigitte asked.

'Cleo's a fantasist.' My lower lip wobbled. 'Make me a green tea and I'll tell you the whole story.'

'What a weirdo,' Brigitte said after I'd relayed everything

Scott had told me. She rubbed my back and I wiped my tears away with a tissue. I wouldn't have any left for mothers of the brides at this rate. 'You didn't tell her I do wedding makeup, did you?'

'No.' I blew my nose. 'Not that there is a wedding.'

'Oh, yes. Hard to remember what's real and what isn't.' Brigitte passed the bin for me to put my tissue in. 'At least you don't need to feel bad about her losing her made-up baby.'

'That's true.' It was the one good thing to come out of it. I massaged my temples. 'Got any paracetamol? My head's pounding.'

Brigitte rummaged in her bag and handed me a packet. 'Sorry you're not feeling well.'

'I didn't really sleep.' I washed the tablets down with a now-tepid mug of green tea. 'Couldn't stop thinking about Cleo.'

The front door chimed and I tensed.

'It won't be Cleo,' Brigitte said. 'We're both expecting clients.'

She peered over the top of the stairs – very cautiously, though – and I heard the relief in her voice when she called out, 'Beth. Lovely to see you.'

I let out a long, slow breath and composed myself.

'Are you sure you're all right?' Beth asked, for the third time.

I nodded weakly, as I adjusted the hem of her dress.

'You're not your usual self,' she said.

'I didn't sleep well, that's all.' I slapped myself lightly on both cheeks. It didn't help. I still felt exhausted, but now my face hurt as well.

'Maybe you need another weekend away,' she said.

'I wish.' That was *exactly* what I needed. To get away from Cleo and stalkers and milk bottles.

'You enjoyed it, then?' Beth sounded nervous.

'It was fantastic.' How rude that I hadn't mentioned Heavenly Hideaway as soon as she arrived. 'We all loved it. Even Anna, and she's very particular. She cried on our last holiday because the caravan wasn't to her standards.' I didn't add that I'd cried too. We hadn't been able to afford much, as Scott had already taken Harry and Bella away, but no matter how cheap the static home, it should have been clean. I'd spent the first three hours of our holiday cleaning. If I'd informed a botanist of what was growing behind the sink, they'd have moved in to record its evolution.

'That's a relief,' Beth said. 'I felt it went well, but you never know for sure.'

'It was brilliant,' I assured her. 'Thank you.' I put the last pin in her dress. 'You can look in the mirror now.' Beth turned and gasped. The white bodice was now adorned with tiny beads that caught the light when she moved.

'It's perfect.' She ran her fingertips across the neckline. 'I love it. Thank you.'

'Let me get the veil.' I jumped up and Beth's face swam in front of me. I sank down onto the sofa.

'Marie?' Beth crouched down next to me. 'What's wrong?'

'Feel a bit faint.' I leant my forehead on my knees. 'Be careful of your dress,' I whispered. I wasn't too weak to be concerned with the important stuff. It had taken flipping ages to sew all those beads on and if any came loose, I'd . . . Well, I'd have to sew them on again, and I really didn't want to.

'I'll call my brother,' she said.

'No. I'm just tired.' I took a deep breath, exhaled slowly and forced myself upright. 'All better now.' I didn't need another health check from Michael. He'd only tell me off for eating sugar. Or not eating sugar. I'd lost track of what he thought was best, but could guarantee it was the opposite of what I was doing.

'I may as well.' Beth already had her mobile to her ear. 'I'm meeting him for lunch shortly, anyway.' She hung up immediately. 'Engaged. He said he'd speak to my ex's solicitor this morning, so that's probably it.'

'How's that going?' I asked, draining the remains of yet

another mug of green tea. I'd had so many antioxidants that morning, I should be feeling like Wonder Woman. Instead, I felt like I'd been kicked in the head by her.

Beth rolled her eyes. 'The fight over maintenance continues. He can't seem to get it into his head that even though I'm getting married, he still has some financial responsibility for Henry and Izzy. I'm not being unreasonable; I just want him to help provide for their clothes and school trips, but his solicitor keeps blocking it. Michael's had a couple of rows with the guy, which isn't like him at all, but he's very protective of me and doesn't want my ex to take advantage.'

I remembered Michael shouting on the phone in my waiting room. Could that have been with Beth's ex's solicitor? It would explain why he'd been so angry.

'Don't want to think about my ex while I'm in my wedding dress, though.' Beth smoothed the full skirt and turned back to the mirror. Her face instantly lit up. 'It's so beautiful. Thank you.'

I beamed back. 'You're the one who makes it beautiful.'

After I'd unpinned Beth and hung the dress up carefully, we made our way down the stairs together. When we stepped out onto the pavement, I nervously looked around, in case Cleo was lurking in a doorway nearby. I wouldn't have ventured out if I hadn't promised Brigitte I'd get her a coffee and snack. She had four full-body massages booked in and needed fuel to get through them.

Michael was sat at a table outside the artisan café opposite. Luke, the waiter, was staring through the window at Michael as though he were the last flute of free champagne on a wedding tray. I could see why. Michael was exceptionally handsome. I'd kind of got used to seeing him in my robe, but today he wore a dark suit. His face was turned to the sun and his long legs were stretched out – something he couldn't do in my robe without flashing his own champagne flute. He looked the perfect combination of relaxed and shaggable. I inhaled sharply. This sleep deprivation was causing very inappropriate behaviour.

Beth put a hand on my arm. 'Are you feeling faint again?'

'No, just enjoying the fresh air.' I inhaled deeply as a bin lorry drove past. Nice. Can't beat the scent of decaying debris.

I went to say goodbye, intent on leaving before Beth insisted Michael gave me a medical examination, but her phone rang. She answered it and crossed the road, leaving me no choice but to follow.

Michael smiled and stood up when he saw Beth. I was sure I heard Luke's fingers squeak against the window as he took in Michael's height. Beth was still on the phone. She mouthed 'sorry' and gestured to me to sit down. I hesitated. I'd only planned to pop out for Brigitte's supplies, before heading back to the studio where my lunch was waiting in the fridge. Michael held a hand out to the chair opposite. I'd perch for a minute, then say goodbye and leave the moment Beth finished her call.

'Hi,' I said, sitting down. Luke's eyes bore into me through the window. I gave a sideways glance and he pretended to dust a framed menu stuck to the glass.

'How are you feeling today?' Michael asked.

'Fine, thanks,' I lied. No need to bore him with a list of my anxiety, headache, dizziness, nausea and exhaustion. He got enough of that crap at work. 'You?'

'Good. But I'm not the one who had a shock yesterday.'

I batted a hand. 'All in the past. I'm over that now.'

Luke appeared at the table. 'Ready to order?' His question was directed purely to Michael. You'd think he didn't know me, even though he saw me practically every day.

'Just waiting for . . .' Michael gestured to Beth. Luke's face fell. 'My sister.' Luke's smile snapped back into place so quickly that his jaw clicked.

'Shall I get another chair?' Luke asked.

'No need,' I said. 'I'm not staying.'

'Let me know when you're ready,' he said to Michael,

walking past me as though I didn't exist. That was the last time I put anything in his tips jar.

Beth ended her call, and Michael and I both stood up.

'That was the school. Henry's got chickenpox.' Beth kissed Michael's cheek. 'I've got to go and get him. Sorry to stand you up.' She gave me a quick hug. 'Love my dress. Thank you. See you in a couple of weeks.' She started to run down the street in the direction of the car park – no mean feat in heels – and then doubled back. 'Michael – look after Marie,' she called out. 'She nearly fainted earlier.'

Michael put his head to one side. 'You said you felt fine.'

'I am.' I hoisted my bag over my arm. 'Just tired. Nothing a walk and some lunch won't fix.'

'Maybe food before the walk would be a better idea?' Michael smiled. 'You're here anyway. Why not eat?'

'I've got something at the studio.' I waved a hand in the direction of work, and caught sight of poached eggs and avocado on sourdough toast at a neighbouring table. It looked so much nicer than my packed lunch. I wasn't sure I could face leftover turkey bolognaise for the third day in a row.

'Beth told me to look after you.' Michael held out a menu. 'I'll be in trouble if I don't.'

'OK, thank you.' We sat down and Luke raced over. 'Hi Luke,' I said. 'How are you?'

'Oh hi, didn't see you there.' Yeah, right. He looked expectantly between me and Michael, clearly awaiting an introduction. I considered ignoring him, the way he'd blanked me, but didn't want to risk him spitting into my food.

'This is Michael,' I said. 'I'm making his sister's wedding dress. Michael, this is Luke.'

The two men shook hands. Judging by the way Luke rearranged his apron afterwards, I suspected he'd got more out of the experience than Michael had. But Luke was a good-looking guy, when he wasn't visibly drooling. I glanced at Michael to see if Luke had piqued his interest but he was studying his menu, oblivious to Luke's adoration. Clearly, a loyal boyfriend. That was nice.

I ordered poached eggs, avocado and sourdough, with a side of sweet potato wedges. I'd be having turkey bolognaise for tea, so needed a good lunch to compensate. While Michael ordered his food, I went to the loo. The numerous mugs of green tea I'd had that morning were taking effect.

When I returned, Michael gave me a quizzical look. 'What's this about you fainting?'

'Only nearly.' I shook my head so vehemently that everything swam for a moment and I had to grip the table to steady myself.

Michael put a hand on my arm. 'Careful,' he said softly.

'I've had a couple of dizzy spells,' I admitted. 'I've got a constant headache and was feeling sick earlier. I couldn't sleep last night, so that'll be why.'

Michael nodded. 'Sleep deprivation impacts everything. Combined with yesterday's shock, it's no wonder you're not feeling 100 per cent.'

'More like 1 per cent at the moment.' I took a sip of water. 'Could be to do with giving up sugar, of course,' I added.

Michael grinned. 'You still kidding yourself with that one?'

My mouth dropped open in mock offence. 'I'm not kidding! Sugar no longer features in my diet.' I smiled. 'Not intentionally, anyway.'

Michael laughed. 'How often does it feature unintentionally?'

I put my hands over my face. 'Once, twice, sometimes three times . . . a day.' I peeked through my fingers. He was still laughing.

'I told you, it's all about balance. Unless those three times a day are a kilo of the stuff, don't beat yourself up.'

'Thanks.' I lowered my hands and instinctively scanned the street, checking for Cleo.

Michael's smile dropped. 'Were you worrying about Cleo last night? Is that why you couldn't sleep?'

My silence answered his question.

'Try not to,' he said softly. 'Her behaviour was a desperate attempt to alleviate her pain by inflicting some on you. Once she's processed her grief, she's unlikely to continue to blame you.'

I bit my lip. Should I tell him what I'd found out since? Did estate agents have the same confidentiality clause as doctors? If they did, Scott had broken it many times. I'd heard more 'hilarious' stories about crazy pets thwarting sales and naked houseowners being taken by surprise than I cared to. In all honesty, one story would have been too many. I decided I could trust Michael. He'd assured me that whatever I said was between us, and it'd be good to get his medical viewpoint.

'There's more to it,' I said. 'Turns out there was no miscarriage. Cleo wasn't even pregnant. She's a fantasist.'

Michael's brow furrowed.

'Scott told me last night.' I ran a hand down my plait. 'She told different lies to his colleague when he showed her round some houses.'

Before Michael had a chance to respond, Luke arrived with our food. He made a big show of laying Michael's napkin on his lap with a flourish. Michael still seemed unaware of Luke's attentions. I'd have felt sorry for him if he hadn't just tossed my napkin in my general direction.

I offered Michael a sweet potato wedge. Thankfully, he declined, because I had no intention of sharing more than one and he might have seen my offer as an open invitation to help himself to more. He'd understand if he saw the turkey bolognaise.

'Is being a fantasist an illness?' I asked.

Michael cut his panini in half. 'I'm not an expert, but fantasists are pathological liars, which is a mental illness.'

'Pathological?' I choked on my potato wedge. 'Aren't murderers pathological?'

Michael nodded.

It was my turn to grab his arm. 'So Cleo's dangerous. Possibly fatally.'

'No.' He calmly picked up his panini. 'The term pathological applies to something that's caused by a physical or mental disease, which murder can be. But someone with a pathological compulsion for cleanliness might scrub their house for hours every day. A fantasist has a pathological compulsion to lie.'

Did that mean I should be more worried about Cleo or less?

We ate in silence for a while. Each mouthful went some way to alleviating my headache, but I still felt uneasy.

'You look troubled,' Michael said.

I remembered how he'd noticed the way I relaxed when sewing. He was a very observant man. Guess he needed to be in his line of work. Wouldn't be much of a doctor if he failed to notice someone turning green or passing out in front of him.

'There's something else.' I pierced my poached egg and watched the yolk sink into the bread. 'Sounds ridiculous, though. It's probably my imagination.'

'Go on,' Michael said gently.

'I once felt as though someone was following me home from work. Then, a few weeks ago, I heard our milk bottles being knocked over outside my house, but when I looked out the window, they were standing up.' I expected Michael to laugh, but he didn't.

'Did your husband hear?' he asked.

'No. He was in bed. I thought maybe the sugar deprivation was making me paranoid, so didn't say anything. This situation with Cleo has made me wonder if it's her.' I shook my head. 'Hearing it out loud, it sounds so stupid.'

'You're not stupid,' Michael said firmly. 'But tell someone if anything else happens. It's not good to deal with these things on your own.' He reached into the inside pocket of his jacket and took out a pen, then wrote his phone number on a napkin and handed it to me. 'If your husband

214

or Brigitte aren't around to talk to, give me a call. Doesn't matter what time.'

'Thank you.' I put the napkin in my bag. 'That's really kind of you.'

He wiped his mouth on a separate napkin and placed it on his plate. Luke darted forward and whipped them both away, probably intending to take the napkin home and sleep with it under his pillow.

'Can I get a coffee and chocolate brownie to take away?' I handed Luke my reusable cup. 'Don't worry if you have to get back to work,' I said to Michael. 'I need to go to the loo anyway and don't want you to be late.' I was getting as bad as Brigitte. Two wees in forty-five minutes was some going. I unhooked my bag from the back of the chair and started to stand up.

'Dizziness, nausea, extreme hunger, exhaustion, constantly needing the loo.' Michael ticked them off on his fingers. 'If I didn't know better, I'd think you were pregnant.'

I froze halfway between standing and sitting. 'What did you say?' I whispered.

'I'm only joking. No need to get a second opinion.' Michael stood up. His face fell when he saw I was still hovering, no doubt a look of complete shock on my face. 'Sorry, I shouldn't have said that.'

I straightened up. 'It's fine. Don't apologise.' I plastered what I hoped was a casual smile on my face.

Michael shook his head. 'No, I feel terrible. That was very unprofessional of me.'

'It was a joke. It doesn't matter.'

Michael didn't look convinced. Luke appeared with the card machine. Before I realised what he was doing, Michael paid the bill with his phone.

'No,' I squealed. 'I need to pay for mine.'

Michael shook his head. 'It's my way of saying sorry for what I just said.'

'There's nothing to apologise for,' I insisted. On the contrary, his words had filled me with joy.

'And I pinched a potato wedge when you weren't looking,' Michael added.

'Well, that changes everything.' I smiled. 'Thank you.'

I waved and hurried back to my studio so I could phone Scott before my next client arrived. I needed to tell him the good news. I was pregnant!

Chapter 29

Scott's phone went to voicemail. I hesitated, not wanting to share the exciting news in a message, but desperate to tell him.

'Call me as soon as you get this,' I said. 'I really need to talk to you.'

After hanging up, I went to the closed door of Brigitte's salon and pressed my ear to it. The sign 'QUIET, MASSAGE IN PROGRESS' was on display, but she might be nearly finished. Maybe I could catch her between clients. I wasn't sure I could contain the news. If I couldn't tell Brigitte or Scott, there was a danger I'd throw my arms around my client Rebecca, who was due in any minute, and offload too many personal details. Rebecca was a lovely woman, but we'd only met twice and she might not appreciate hearing about the reverse cowgirl.

All I could hear through Brigitte's door was the soundtrack of crashing waves that she played to aid relaxation. No wonder she needed the loo every five minutes. Disappointed, I went back to my studio. I had ten minutes till Rebecca arrived to see her dress designs. Should I pop to the chemist to get a pregnancy test to confirm it? I placed a hand on my stomach. It was already slightly rounded. That, combined with the tiredness, nausea and incontinence was confirmation enough. This was exactly how I'd felt with Anna. Why hadn't I realised sooner? It was obvious even to Michael, who barely knew me. Although Michael was a doctor, so had a distinct advantage over most of us mere mortals.

Rebecca arrived at the exact moment Scott called.

'So sorry, but I've got to take this,' I said to her. 'Your designs are on the table. I'll be two minutes.'

Rebecca went into my studio, and I bolted into the tiny toilet cubicle and answered the call.

'Hi,' I whispered.

'Speak up, babe,' Scott said. 'You're on speakerphone in the car.'

I cupped my hand around my mouth and the phone. 'Can you hear me now?'

'Just about. What's up?'

I caught sight of myself in the mirror above the tiny sink. My eyes were bloodshot, with dark rings beneath them from lack of sleep; my shoulders were hunched over as I tried to get my mouth as close to the phone as possible, and there was a sign behind my head that read: 'If you sprinkle when you tinkle, please be neat and wipe the seat.' Did I really want to share this monumental news with my husband from the confines of a toilet?

'When will you be home?' I asked.

'Not till late. I'm seeing Harry and Bella.'

Of course, it was Thursday. Crap.

I straightened up and whacked my elbow against the sink. This toilet was ridiculously small. I'd had to wee with the door open when I was heavily pregnant with Anna, as I was too big to fit in otherwise. The memory made me smile and I knew I couldn't hold the news in any longer.

'I've got something to tell you.'

'Not bloody Cleo again?' Scott sounded furious.

'No, this is good news.' I giggled. 'I'm pregnant.'

'You're breaking up. What did you say?'

'I'm pregnant,' I said as loudly as I dared. 'We're going to have another baby.'

Silence.

'Are you still there?'

There was a muffled noise, then Scott's voice came through. 'You're joking.'

'No.' I did the tiniest of dances, which, due to the confined space, consisted of nothing more than a shoulder jiggle. 'Isn't it great?'

'You can't be.' Scott sounded dazed. 'It isn't possible.'

'I didn't think it'd happen this fast either.' I grinned at myself in the mirror. Why had I worried? If I could get pregnant on the pill, I could certainly get pregnant when we weren't using contraception. Scott was clearly super-virile and I was super-fertile. So much for Michael's claim that I was medically geriatric. I'd shown him. I might be forty, but my eggs were of premium quality. I should donate them to women who were struggling to conceive. It was the decent thing to do.

'I'm cancelling my next appointment and coming home,' Scott said.

'I'm not there. In fact, I'd better go. My client's waiting.'

'Get rid of her and get home,' Scott said. 'We need to talk.'

'I can't,' I said. 'She's come in specially to see her designs.'

'Make an excuse. I'll be home in an hour.'

The line went dead. I stared at my reflection, my earlier smile replaced with shock. It didn't sound as though Scott wanted to meet me at home to celebrate. He hadn't sounded elated, or as though he was struggling to get his head around it, but would be over the moon when it had sunk in. No. He'd sounded angry – with me.

Chapter 30

Scott was sitting at the kitchen table, glaring at his phone, when I got home an hour later. Thankfully, Rebecca had loved the dress design, so we only had to incorporate a few tweaks, which hadn't taken long.

'What's going on?' I asked cautiously.

Scott pushed his phone away. 'You tell me.'

I put my bag on the table. 'I already did: I'm pregnant.'

Scott scowled. 'Well, it's not mine.'

I stared, waiting for his face to break into a smile and tell me he was joking, even though it wasn't remotely funny. But his expression grew grimmer. 'How can you say that?' I eventually stammered.

'Bit bloody convenient, isn't it?' Scott snapped. 'We've only been trying for five minutes.'

'We got lucky.'

Scott shook his head. 'You expect me to believe that?'

'Yes,' I said, my voice trembling. 'I know it's a shock, but it's a good one. That reverse cowgirl really did the job.' I attempted a laugh, but it came out as a sob. I fumbled in my bag for a tissue. 'I don't understand. Why are you acting like this?'

I pulled what I thought was a tissue from my bag, but it was the napkin Michael had written his number on.

Scott snatched it out of my hand. 'What's this?'

'It's Michael's number. He gave it to me at lunchtime in case I needed to talk about Cleo.'

Scott scrunched the napkin up in his fist. 'You and Michael are having cosy lunch dates, are you? Does he like the reverse cowgirl too?'

My hands flew to my face. 'It's not like that. He's my client's brother and—'

'Oh, I get it.' Scott carried on as though I hadn't spoken. 'It was *Michael* who saved you, wasn't it?' He spat the word 'Michael'. 'What a hero. Suppose you thought it only right to thank him. Where did you do it? At your studio? At his practice? In our bed?'

I stared open-mouthed at Scott. What had happened to him? He'd never raised his voice or doubted my word before. Yes, he took me for granted sometimes, but didn't everyone in a relationship, after a while? Now he was accusing me of lying and cheating.

'I haven't done anything with Michael.' I swiped tears from my eyes. 'He's gay. Not that that makes any difference – I love *you*.'

'Don't make it worse by lying.' Scott hurled the crumpled napkin across the room. 'I've given up my life, my kids, and all I get in return is stress and aggro.' He thrust his hands in his hair. 'If it's not you, it's her.'

'Has something happened with Liz?' I asked. 'Is she stopping you seeing the kids again?' That would explain why he was angry. It wouldn't justify or explain the rest of it, but at least there would be an atom of rationale behind his behaviour. Without thinking, I blew my nose.

He looked at me with loathing. 'You're disgusting.'

Grabbing his keys, he strode towards the door.

'No.' I blocked his way. For some reason his contempt at my nose blowing riled me more than his accusation of having an affair. My earlier shock and distress had morphed into anger. 'You cannot walk out on this. I'm pregnant and it's yours. Get whatever paranoid shit you've got going on out of your head and accept that.'

Scott stared at me, his jaw clenched, his blue eyes ice-cold. 'You're the one who's full of shit.'

Stunned, I let him push past me. Moments later, the front door slammed. He was gone.

Chapter 31

I sank into a chair at the kitchen table, too dazed and confused to cry. Why wasn't Scott excited about the baby? Why was he saying it wasn't his? He didn't really believe I'd cheated, did he? I'd never even flirted with anyone else, and this idea about Michael was ridiculous. Michael was gay, for fuck's sake.

I pressed my fingertips to my eyes. What was I going to do? I had no idea where Scott had gone or how long he'd be. I wasn't sure I *wanted* him to come back if he was going to behave this way. I'd seen a different side to him, and it wasn't one I liked.

The front door clicked open and I pulled myself up tall. I would not be a persecuted, submissive woman who put up with shit. Shock had rendered me numb when he'd thrown his accusations, but I wouldn't tolerate any more abuse. I got enough of that from Anna.

My heart raced as I waited for Scott to appear at the doorway. I hated confrontation, but I needed to stand firm. He couldn't treat me like this, and I'd tell him so – when he eventually made an appearance. He was taking his time. A rustling came from the living room and I froze. This wasn't right. Scott would have come into the kitchen, not gone to another room. It had to be someone else.

Cleo's twisted, accusatory face flashed through my mind. I went cold. She was a pathological liar. Michael said that didn't make her a killer, but there was a first time for everything.

Slowly and quietly, I stood up, being careful not to scrape the chair against the floor tiles. I wouldn't confront the intruder – have-a-go heroes could do one – I'd sneak out, then phone 999.

I picked my bag up and saw Scott's phone on the table. I must have placed my bag on top of it and he'd left without realising he didn't have it. I reached out for it, my eyes on the kitchen door. I'd seen enough episodes of *Midsomer Murders* to know not to turn your back on a point of entry. My fingertips brushed the phone. BZZZT. The handset vibrated loudly against the wooden table. BZZZT. Fuck. I grabbed it and made towards the door. BZZZT. Sod stealth, I needed to get out of there. BZZZT. I ran out of the kitchen, straight into a canary-yellow obstacle. We both screamed, staring at each other, wide-eyed and petrified.

I put a hand to my chest. 'What are you doing here?'

'I could say the same about you,' Maman said indignantly.

'I live here!'

'But you should be at work, *n'est-ce pas?*' She straightened the collar of her bright yellow kimono. I wasn't sure what to be more concerned about: the fact she'd let herself into our house, when she thought we were out, or her outfit.

'Well, I'm not.' I turned and walked back into the kitchen.

Maman followed, making a strange clopping noise. Closer inspection revealed that she'd teamed the kimono with wooden clogs. This was definitely scarier than her breaking and entering.

'Why are you here?' I asked again, filling up the kettle.

'I needed something to read.' She held up one of my magazines.

'This isn't a library,' I snapped.

I put a green teabag into a mug, deliberately not offering her a drink. A petty act, but one I felt entitled to carry out. 'Do you let yourself in often?'

'*Non.*' Maman rubbed her nose.

'This stops now,' I said. 'Scott could be walking around naked.' Scott never walked around naked, hence Anna's intrigue over his tail, but Maman wasn't to know that. 'Imagine how embarrassing that would be.'

She shrugged. 'I would not be embarrassed. I'm French.'

'Well, he would, so don't do it again.'

I poured hot water onto my teabag, ignoring Maman's sniffs of disapproval that she wasn't getting one.

'Why aren't you at work?' she asked. 'Anna's at nursery.'

I looked at the clock with a start and breathed a sigh of relief to see it was only three o'clock. She wouldn't need picking up for another two hours.

'I came home to see Scott.'

'Was he naked?'

'No!'

'So, it doesn't matter that I am here too.'

I rubbed my forehand. The headache I'd had earlier was back with a vengeance.

'Where is Scott?' Maman slid open a drawer.

'He's hardly going to be in there, is he?' I snapped, sinking down into a chair at the table.

'I am looking for your manners,' Maman said tartly. 'You have left them somewhere.'

We glared at each other. I caved in first and looked away. 'You know where the coffee is,' I said sulkily. 'Help yourself. You're good at that.'

Maman opened and shut cupboard doors, taking out and putting back different mugs and tins and other paraphernalia, muttering in French, and generally making as much noise as was humanly possible while carrying out the simple task of making a cup of coffee. Eventually, she sat down opposite me, crossed her arms and sucked in her cheeks.

'What's wrong with you?' she asked. 'You have mustard rising from your nose.'

I gave her a withering look. 'If you mean that I seem pissed off, then you're right. I am.'

'*Pourquoi?*'

'Because of you, that's *pourquoi*.' I covered my face with my hands to hide the tears that had suddenly filled my eyes. 'And Scott. And other stuff.' The tears trickled down my cheeks and plopped onto the table. 'But mainly you,' I sobbed.

'*Ne pleure pas*,' Maman said.

But I couldn't stop crying. It was all such a mess. I had no idea what was going to happen. Or what I wanted to happen.

'Tell me what is wrong,' Maman said gently. 'Nothing is worth having a cockroach over.'

'I'm not depressed.' I leant my head on her shoulder, ignoring the way she stiffened. 'I'm pregnant.'

'Marie! This is wonderful.' Maman clasped my face between her hands and kissed me on both cheeks. 'But why are you crying?' She wiped my tears away with her thumbs. 'This is good news, *n'est-ce pas*?'

'It should be, but Scott's angry. He thinks I'm having an affair and the baby's not his.' I looked at her helplessly. 'He was horrible to me, Maman. Really horrible.'

If I'd thought Maman had stiffened when I showed some affection, it was nothing compared with how taut her body went now. She could have lain on a bed of nails and the nails would have come out of it worse off.

'I've been waiting for this to happen,' she said in a low voice.

'You have?' Had she picked up on something that I'd missed? Maybe she was more intuitive than I gave her credit for. 'Why?' I asked.

Maman picked up her coffee cup. 'Because he is a man. You must divorce him immediately.'

Or maybe she was a bitter, resentful man-hater.

'I don't want to divorce him after one argument. No wonder you and Dad didn't last if that's how much commitment you gave the relationship.'

'We did not divorce after one argument,' Maman said. 'There were many, many arguments. It was when the fighting stopped that I knew the marriage was over. Without passion there is nothing.'

I blinked. Was passion what Scott had just displayed? Was his ranting a sign of intense emotion rather than anger? Had I misinterpreted his actions? I replayed his behaviour in my head. No, he hadn't been passionate. He'd been a total git.

I still didn't want to write off our entire relationship based on this one incident, though. There had to be an explanation.

Maman took her phone from one of the many folds in her kimono. 'If you will not listen to reason from me, you may from your aunt and cousin.' She nodded curtly at me. 'Phone Brigitte. I am calling Francine.'

I opened my mouth to tell her there was no need to call a summit meeting; I could figure this out by myself. Then I realised that I couldn't, so I phoned Brigitte. I needed one sane person with me.

She answered straightaway. 'Where's my coffee and chocolate?' she asked.

'I left them at the café,' I said, remembering my earlier order. 'Sorry.'

Brigitte groaned into the phone.

'When's your next client?' I asked.

'Not till five. Body massage four cancelled. Thank fuck or I'd have collapsed. She's got such a wide back, it takes half an hour to get round it with both hands.'

'Can you come to mine?' I said. 'Maman's here and your mum's on her way.'

'Not Cleo again?' Brigitte's voice was full of concern.

'No, it's Scott. He's gone a bit . . .' I searched for the word. 'Arsehole-ish. I'll explain when you get here.'

'I'll be there in ten minutes.' Brigitte hesitated. 'Are you OK?'

'Yes.'

'Make it fifteen minutes, then. I'll get coffee and chocolate on the way.'

'Fucking knobhead, wanker, bastard, cu—'

'Custard cream?' I asked, offering Brigitte the packet.

She pushed it aside. 'Who the fuck does he think he is? How fucking dare he talk to you like that.'

I widened my eyes and slid them in the direction of our mothers. Grateful as I was for Brigitte's loyalty and outrage, and much as I agreed with her, I wasn't sure they'd appreciate the language. I needn't have worried. Judging by their faces, they were more offended by the custard creams than Brigitte's choice of words.

Brigitte banged her fist on the table. 'How could he do this to you? Why did he do it?'

'I don't know,' I said. 'It doesn't make any sense.'

'I've told her there is only one solution,' Maman said. 'Divorce.'

Francine nodded enthusiastically. 'End the marriage immediately.'

I gripped the sides of my chair. This was moving too fast.

Brigitte rubbed my arm. 'You don't have to make any decisions now, but, out of interest, did you ever put his name on the deeds to the house?'

I shook my head. 'We keep our money and assets separate.'

All three women nodded their approval.

'You must tell him to leave,' Maman said.

'It's not as simple as that.' I sighed. Maman and Francine looked at me aghast. I put a hand up. 'I'm not letting him get away with it. If he doesn't apologise, or if he ever behaves like that again, then of course I'll kick him out,' I said. 'But how he acted was completely out of character. If he's having some sort of mental breakdown, I need to help him through it. That's what marriage is about.' I lowered my hand to my stomach. 'And there's Anna and the baby to think about. Harry still has night terrors. Scott's sure it's because of the divorce. I don't want my children going through that if we can avoid it.'

They looked at me sceptically.

'I won't stay with him if he's horrible like that again,' I assured them. 'Wouldn't want to. But let me find out what's going on, before I pack his bags.'

Maman and Francine tutted. They'd be having a bonfire with all his belongings by now if it were left to them.

BZZZT.

Scott's phone buzzed on the table and Francine picked it up. The screen lit up, revealing a number of text messages. '*Oh là, là,*' she said. 'That is not very nice.' She showed the phone to my mum, who sucked her cheeks in so severely that it looked as though she'd been exhumed.

'What is it?' Brigitte and I said in unison.

Francine handed the phone over.

The messages were condensed, just showing the first line, some breaking mid-word.

If you don't stop ghosting me, you'll be sorry. I'll
Unfeeling fucker. No responsibility for your chil
Fuck you. Your guilt money won't help get you
You don't deserve happiness with that bitch. Yo
Don't ignore me. You can't walk out as though

I gasped, feeling sick to the stomach. 'I thought Liz had stopped sending messages.' I read them again. Their venom sent a shiver down my spine. 'This explains Scott's behaviour. If he's being sent stuff like this all the time, it's bound to make him on edge.'

'No,' all three said sharply.

Brigitte took the phone. 'These messages are unacceptable, but that's no excuse for the way he treated you. He should have told you. And the police. She's clearly deranged, and his kids are living with her.'

'The police?' I bit my lip. 'Is it a crime, though? To swear at your ex? She hasn't threatened him.'

'She might have.' Brigitte pointed to the top message. '*Stop ghosting me or you'll be sorry. I'll* . . . I'll what? Stop you seeing the kids? Turn them against you? Stick a knife in you?'

'Don't.' I covered my face with my hands. 'This is awful. It was bad enough worrying about Cleo stalking me. Not sure I can handle Liz on the loose too.'

Brigitte stared. 'Cleo's stalking you? I thought that was a one off?'

'Who's Cleo?' Maman asked.

'I had a stalker once,' Francine said. 'He came round every day. Sometimes twice.'

'He was not a stalker,' Maman snapped. 'He was a conman. He came round every day because you pretended to be interested in purchasing his Bitcoins.' She turned to me. 'Does Cleo sell Bitcoins?'

'No.' I sighed. 'I don't know for sure she was stalking me. A couple of strange things happened, then she accosted me in the street yesterday.' I glanced warily at Scott's phone. 'Now this. I don't know what to think.'

'Call the police,' Maman said firmly.

Francine nodded her agreement. The pair were practically rubbing their hands with glee at the drama of it all.

'It's not an emergency,' I protested.

'Ring 101,' Brigitte said. 'Explain what's going on and ask their advice.'

'I don't know. It feels overdramatic.' I tilted Scott's phone and read the messages again. They *were* verging on abuse. It wasn't right that Liz vented her unjustified resentment on Scott whenever she felt like it. He must have dreaded hearing his phone beep. Not wanting to check it, but having to, in case the message was from me or was genuinely about Harry and Bella. I felt a surge of anger. Liz had to be stopped.

'I'll do it.' I picked up my phone before I could change my mind, pressed call and gave my name, address, date of birth and location. When it came to the nature of the incident, instead of criticising me for phoning about such a trivial matter, the PC I spoke to echoed my family's thoughts that this was something to be taken seriously. Relief flooded through me – until she said she needed to talk to Scott too and would call back if she didn't hear from him. I wrote her name and number down, on the magazine my mum had tried to steal, and hung up.

'They want to talk to Scott.' I bit my lip. 'He's not going to be pleased that I've interfered.'

Maman tutted. 'He's the one who should worry about his carrots being cooked, not you.'

'Don't forget his behaviour this afternoon,' Brigitte said. 'You contacted the police to help him, despite that. He should be crawling at your feet with gratitude.'

Francine nodded. 'All men should crawl. It is what they deserve.'

I put my hands on my stomach. Was it my imagination or did it already feel rounder?

'I haven't said congratulations yet,' Brigitte squealed. 'Whatever happens, this is great. It's what you wanted.' She gave me a huge hug. 'How far along are you?'

'I don't know.' I started counting on my fingers. 'Need to work it out from my last period.'

'Shame the pregnancy test doesn't tell you that.'

'I haven't done a test.'

'How do you know you're pregnant, then?'

'I just know,' I said. 'I've got all the symptoms – tired, dizzy, weeing all the time.'

'That's how I feel practically every day,' Brigitte said. 'Especially after back-to-back massages.'

'Have you been sick?' Maman asked.

That was how I'd eventually realised I was pregnant with Anna. The out-of-date pot of hummus I'd been blaming my vomiting on couldn't be held accountable three weeks after consumption.

'No,' I admitted. 'But I *felt* sick earlier.'

No one said anything. Given the amount of non-stop crap that spewed from my family's mouths, this was cause for concern.

'It just so happens I have a pregnancy test.' Brigitte took a thin, oblong box from her bag. I remembered her telling me they gave her a spare one at the sexual health clinic.

'Why do you have a pregnancy test?' Francine demanded.

Brigitte faltered for a moment, then shrugged. 'I'm French,' she said.

Maman and Francine accepted her explanation with a proud nod.

Brigitte handed me the test and I took it to the bathroom, weed on the stick and returned, clutching it in my hand.

Maman shooed me away. 'Leave it in the toilet. Urine doesn't belong in the kitchen.'

'How long do you have to wait?' Brigitte asked when I came back.

'Four minutes.' I set a timer on my phone, then sat down, my heart racing. I knew I was pregnant, but it was still nerve-racking waiting to have it confirmed.

Francine tilted Scott's phone back and forth, so the messages kept flashing up.

I swallowed hard, wondering how Scott would react when he heard I'd spoken to the police. 'What's the best way to tell Scott?' I asked.

'Tell me what?'

We all jumped and turned. Scott stood at the kitchen door. His eyes scanned the four of us, then fell on his phone in Francine's hand. His jaw tightened.

At that exact moment, the timer went off on my phone. My pregnancy test was ready.

Chapter 32

Scott strode over to Francine. 'What are you doing with my phone?'

Most people, having been caught snooping, would return it meekly. Not Francine. She dropped the phone into Scott's outstretched palm with such a look of disdain that you'd think he'd been upskirting her with it.

The screen flashed on as he took it. He scanned the messages and his face went pale. He thrust the phone in his pocket and looked at the four of us staring up at him.

'So you know, then,' he said quietly.

'Why didn't you tell me?' I asked.

He regarded me warily. I felt equally conflicted. I was hurt, angry and confused by his earlier accusation, but I was also sad and worried that he'd been receiving these hateful messages and hadn't felt he could burden me with it. I decided to deal with the current situation first.

'Those messages from Liz are poisonous,' I said. 'You should have told me, so we can deal with them together.'

A muscle pounded in Scott's cheek, but he didn't say anything.

'Enough of this English politeness.' Maman stood and jabbed a finger at Scott. 'How dare you accuse my daughter of visiting *le jardin secret*.'

Scott frowned, understandably baffled by this accusation. 'What's she talking about?' he said out of the side of his mouth.

My earlier hurt and humiliation overrode my concern about the messages. 'She's saying, how dare you accuse me of cheating on you,' I said coldly. 'It's bullshit. You must know that.' Scott's jaw tightened.

'Marie.' Brigitte gestured to me behind Scott. I hadn't noticed her leave the room, but she must have, as she was clutching my pregnancy test in her hand.

I sidestepped Scott, took it from her and brandished it at him. 'This baby is yours. You have no reason to think otherwise.'

'Marie,' Brigitte whispered.

'What about your cosy little lunches with the doctor?' Scott's face, which had been ashen earlier, was now flushed.

'Lunch doesn't mean sex.' I looked him straight in the eye. 'If you're going to continue being an arse, you can leave. I'll bring the baby up myself. I'm practically raising Anna on my own already.'

'Marie,' Brigitte said sharply. 'Look at the test.'

I shot her a look. Why was she interrupting, when I was taking control of my destiny? Brigitte pressed her lips together and shook her head. My bravado ebbed away as I looked down at the test in my hand and focused on the small white screen in the centre of the oblong. It only contained one line. I shook it hard and checked again. Still one line. This couldn't be right. According to the test, I wasn't pregnant.

Brigitte put her arms around me. 'I'm so sorry,' she whispered.

'What is it?' Scott asked guardedly.

'I'm not pregnant.' A hollow laugh made its way out of me. 'After all that, I'm not pregnant.'

'Oh, babe.' Scott reached for me, but I turned my head and clung on to Brigitte, disappointment coursing through me.

'I don't understand,' I said quietly. 'I've got all the symptoms.'

Brigitte stroked my hair. 'They're also the symptoms of stress and lack of sleep.'

Scott placed a hand on the base of my spine. 'Can we talk?' he asked. 'Without an audience?'

'What do you want to do?' Brigitte asked softly. 'We won't leave if you don't want to be on your own with him.'

I didn't particularly want to be on my own with Scott after the way he'd behaved. But I needed to find out what was going on and he wouldn't talk freely with anyone else around. Particularly, when two of those people insisted on chipping in with their own contradictory views, as though on the panel of *Question Time*.

'No, go,' I said. 'I'll call you later.'

Brigitte released me and instructed Maman and Francine to leave. Obviously, they ignored her, and she physically had to hoist her mother to her feet. Tutting, Francine smoothed her navy shift dress down. Maman did the same with her canary-yellow kimono. They kissed me on both cheeks as they left and Maman patted my arm. It was possibly the most tactile she'd been since giving birth to me.

They glared at Scott as they passed and then started jabbering away in French when they reached the hall. You didn't need to be bilingual to understand the meaning, especially as the word *bâtard* came up several times.

As soon as the front door shut, Scott pulled me to him. 'So sorry, babe,' he murmured into my hair. 'I know how much you wanted this.'

I wriggled out of his grip. 'What are you sorry for? Accusing me of cheating? Taking your frustration with Liz out on me?' Tears pricked my eyes. 'You're certainly not sorry about the baby. You were horrified when I said I was pregnant.' I put my hands on my stomach, searching for the bump I'd felt earlier. It was still there, but was clearly nothing more than the sweet potato wedges I'd had for lunch. I remembered Michael's words: 'If I didn't know better.' His diagnosis was right – I was medically geriatric. More likely to need a hip replacement as the result of a fall than fall pregnant.

Scott ran a hand through his hair. 'Don't say that. I was in shock and overreacted.'

'You accused me of screwing the doctor.' I swiped my tears away. 'What the fuck was that about? You can't honestly think I would?'

'Course I don't.' Scott shook his head. 'You saw those messages from Liz. They're doing my head in.' His voice trembled. 'Can't believe I accused you like that. She's driving me mad, actually mad.'

'Did she ever stop sending messages?' I demanded.

'No.' He slumped down at the kitchen table. 'Sorry I didn't tell you, but stress is the last thing you need when we're trying for a baby. You saw how aggressive the messages are. They're out of control and I don't know what to do.'

My anger towards him lifted slightly. We still needed to address the affair accusation – he couldn't say a simple sorry and expect me to just dismiss it – but protecting me from Liz's abusive messages and dealing with them on his own must have been hard.

'You don't have to worry about the messages anymore,' I said. 'I called the police for advice and they're taking them very seriously.' Scott's head whipped up. 'They want to speak to you,' I continued. 'And Liz.' The colour drained from Scott's face. 'She can't behave in this way and threaten to stop you seeing your children.' I handed him the magazine on which I'd written the PC's contact details. 'This is the name and number of the officer I spoke to. She agreed it's not right and wants some more details from you. Said she'd go and speak to Liz if necessary.'

Scott stared at the magazine, aghast. 'You called the police?'

'Yes. She needs to be stopped.'

Scott's jaw tightened. 'You had no right to call the police behind my back. If I wanted them involved, I'd have rung them myself.'

'Those messages are toxic.' I wanted to shake him. 'What else is she capable of? Your children might not be safe with her. I had a duty of care to call the police.'

'Get real,' Scott snapped. 'The messages don't mean anything. It's just words. Stupid words.' He gripped the magazine so tightly that the front cover started to come away from the spine. 'You've made everything worse.'

'How can it be worse?' Scott's unjustified anger was fuelling my own. 'We need help. That's all the police want to do – help.'

Scott scowled. 'It's none of their business. If they contact Liz, the whole thing will blow up.'

'Not with the police on our side.' Why couldn't he see this? 'It's the only way to get her behaviour to change.'

'It's none of your business either.' Scott slammed the magazine down on the table. 'I told you I'd deal with it.'

I inhaled sharply. Not my business? His ex-wife was controlling our lives and he was allowing it to happen, then criticising me for finding a solution. Four years of suppressed frustration erupted out of me. 'But you're not dealing with it, are you?' I shouted. 'Nothing's changed the whole time we've been together. If anything, it's got worse, and I've had enough.' My words were coming out faster than my brain could keep up with them. 'While you've been sitting around, hoping things will magically improve, I've been out there, trying to find her and sort this mess out.'

Scott's eyes narrowed. 'Find who?'

I threw my hands in the air. 'Liz, of course. The person we're talking about. Who else would I be trying to find?'

Scott's mouth dropped open. 'You've been trying to find Liz?'

'Yes.' I jutted my chin out defiantly.

'Are you fucking mad?'

'No, I'm desperate.'

Scott grabbed my shoulders. 'Did you find her?'

I wrenched free of his grip. 'No.'

'You're not to go looking for her.' Scott glowered at me. 'I mean it. She'd stop me ever seeing the kids if she knew.'

I'd already decided not to look anymore, but I wasn't ready to give in yet. I pointed at a photo of Anna on the fridge. 'How else are they going to meet their sister?'

Scott thrust his hands in his hair. 'Why can't you let it go? You're obsessed. Things are fine as they are.'

Shards of fury pulsed through me. 'They are *not* fine. They're crap. This situation isn't normal. I've made so many allowances over the years and I've had enough.' I glared at him and he glared back.

'You think it's easy for me, do you?' he snapped. 'Trying to keep everyone happy?'

'We're not happy, though, are we?'

'I thought we were, but I guess I'm not enough for you. All you care about is having another baby.'

I shook my head. 'That's not *all* I care about, but yes, it's important. I thought it was to you too, until you flipped out this afternoon.'

Scott's hands clenched into fists. 'I said I was sorry. Are you going to throw it in my face every time we have a row?'

I looked at him in disbelief. 'It's just happened. You haven't even explained why you thought the baby wasn't yours.'

'The messages—' Scott started.

'No.' I put a hand up. 'The messages made you freak out, I get that. But why jump to that ridiculous conclusion?' My heart pounded. 'It doesn't make sense.'

A muscle pulsed in Scott's cheek. He stared at the table long and hard before raising his eyes to meet mine.

'We've only just started trying,' he said. 'It wouldn't happen this fast.'

'So you instantly thought I was shagging someone else?' I folded my arms. 'That's how little you trust me?'

Scott moved towards me, but knocked one of the chairs and it fell to the floor with a loud bang. 'I told you: Liz's messages made me act crazy. I know you wouldn't, but all I could think was that if it was mine, it wouldn't show on a test yet. It's too soon.'

I opened my mouth to fire back a retort, then his words sank in. 'You're right,' I gasped. 'It's too soon to show up on a test. Which means there's still a possibility I'm pregnant.' My head spun and I lowered myself into a chair. Was I being silly, still hoping for this, or could it be a reality? Could those microscopic cells be multiplying within me right now? My heart pounded. If I was pregnant, this level of stress wasn't good for me or the baby. I closed my eyes and took a deep breath. I was so wound up that this was as effective as trying to mop up the Indian Ocean with a flannel.

Scott let out a frustrated wail.

My eyes sprung open. 'Stop that,' I hissed. 'I need a calm environment, just in case.'

Scott stepped back and stumbled on the chair that he'd knocked over. He picked it up angrily. 'We can't go through these dramatics every month.'

'I'm not being dramatic. I'm being cautious.'

'You've called the police, tried to find Liz behind my back and now you're saying you're pregnant, even though there's a negative test in front of you.' Scott slammed the chair down. 'How much more dramatic could you be?'

'Stop shouting,' I shouted, before realising what I was doing and lowering my voice. 'It's not good for the baby.'

Scott gritted his teeth. 'There isn't a baby.'

I placed my hands on my stomach. 'There might be.'

'Stop saying that.' His body was completely taut, every vein in his neck straining against the skin, and his hands were in such tight fists that his knuckles had turned white. 'You're not pregnant.'

'I could be. Why are you being so negative?'

'I'm being realistic. You're forty.'

I winced. He was right, though. I stood up and strode across the kitchen. 'There's only one thing for it. We're getting ourselves checked out.'

Scott frowned. 'What do you mean?'

'If I can't conceive, I need to know.' I opened the contacts in my phone. 'I'll make an appointment with the doctor.'

Scott tutted. 'Any excuse to see your doctor friend.'

'Obviously, I won't see *him*,' I said through gritted teeth. 'I'll request another doctor and book us both in for a fertility test.'

Scott did a double take. 'Don't get me involved. I'm not having one.'

I gave him a withering look. 'There's no point just me having a test. We need to know we're both OK.' He rolled his eyes, which infuriated me even more. 'It's not exactly a tough gig for you,' I snapped. 'You only have to wank into a jar.'

Scott shook his head. 'I'm not doing it.'

I glared at him. 'Yes, you are.'

He glared back. 'No, I'm not.'

'We're getting that test done,' I hissed. 'You don't have a choice.'

'Not going to happen.' He grabbed his car keys from the table.

I ran to the kitchen door and stood in front of it, blocking his path. 'You're not walking out on me again.'

Scott released a suppressed roar. 'I'm not doing a stupid test.'

'Why? Why won't you do it?'

'Because there's no point,' he shouted.

'There's every point.' I jabbed my finger into his chest.

'No, there isn't.' He swatted my hand away.

'Why?' I screamed.

His face was contorted with rage, his cheeks flushed, his eyes dark.

'Tell me, Scott,' I screamed again. 'Why isn't there any point?'

The words exploded out of him. 'Because I've had a vasectomy.'

Chapter 33

I slumped back against the door. An icy chill like nothing I'd experienced before ran through me. He hadn't said that, had he? He couldn't have done. My mouth opened and shut a few times before I was able to stammer, 'What?'

Scott stared at me, horror etched on his face. There was no doubting it. The words may have come out in anger, but they were the truth. He'd had a vasectomy. He'd taken away my chance of having a baby.

Bile rose in my throat. Turning, I wrenched the door open and ran to the downstairs cloakroom. I just made it to the toilet before throwing up. Tears streamed down my face as I heaved again and again, until there was nothing more to bring up. Twisting away from the toilet, I pulled my knees up to my chest and sobbed, wails ricocheting out of my body. One word went round and round my head: why? Why? Why?

Eventually, my tears subsided. Not because I was no longer upset – far from it – but because my body wasn't physically able to sustain that level of turmoil. I flushed the toilet, splashed water on my face and swilled toothpaste round my mouth, before sinking back down onto the floor. Despite the warm July day, I shivered uncontrollably. I pressed my face into my knees. White spots exploded behind my eye sockets. Each one represented an unborn child. A baby that I'd never be able to have. A long, agonised whimper escaped me. Why? Why? Why?

A blanket was placed around my shoulders and a hand stroked my hair. I jerked away, unable to bear his touch.

'Babe,' Scott said softly. 'I'm so sorry. I never wanted to hurt you. Please, hear me out.'

I shook my head. Moments ago, I'd been desperate to find out why, but now that he was offering to tell me, I didn't want him anywhere near me. It didn't matter why. He'd done it. He'd pretended we could try for a baby, knowing it couldn't possibly happen. The situation with Liz was crap, but that could be dealt with and hopefully fixed, if not by us then by legalities. Nothing could fix this. Not police intervention. Not a court order. Nothing.

'Let's get you out of here.' Scott's hands went around me and he pulled me up to standing. I tried to resist, but he was stronger and I was devoid of energy, every part of my body trembling. He carried me to the sofa, where he placed me gently, pulling the blanket firmly around me. He knelt down on the floor. I turned my head, unwilling to look at him.

'I'm so sorry,' he said again. 'That was an unforgiveable way to tell you.'

'It was an unforgiveable thing to do,' I croaked. His apologies meant nothing. They didn't alter what he'd done. What he'd taken away from me. 'How could you? You knew how much I wanted a baby. A sibling for Anna.'

'I know that's important to you,' Scott said. 'But don't forget she's got two already.'

I turned and stared at him in disbelief. 'How does that help? She's not allowed to meet them.'

'She will, now the police are involved.' Scott held up his hands. 'I shouldn't have got angry earlier. It threw me, but you did the right thing. A call from the police is exactly what's needed. Liz will have to be reasonable from now on.'

My hands curled into fists. 'I don't give a fuck about Liz anymore. You can move in with her for all I care.' I meant it. I'd never forgive him for this. Never.

Scott's face crumpled. 'Don't say that.' He tried to take my hand again, but I jerked away. 'You can't make Anna the victim of a broken home. It'd destroy her.' He began to cry, which made me even angrier. He had no right to be upset after what he'd done.

I looked at him with disgust. 'You've destroyed our marriage.'

He shook his head furiously. 'No. You and Anna are my world. This can't be the end of us. I did it *for* us.'

'You had a vasectomy in secret,' I spat. 'How can that possibly be for us?'

'I should have talked to you. I see that now. I went about it the wrong way and I'm sorry.' Tears rolled down his cheeks. 'But I did it for the right reasons. For our family. For love.'

'This isn't how you treat people you love. You don't know what love is.'

'I do,' Scott sobbed, clutching the hem of my blanket. 'I love you and Anna more than anything. I can't lose you . . . I can't.'

I pressed myself into the sofa, wanting to get as much distance between us as possible. I willed my body to stop trembling so that I could get up and walk out. Walk away from Scott.

Scott's shoulders shook as he continued to cry, his forehead resting on the edge of the sofa. I watched him with contempt. This man, who until an hour ago I had loved completely, now repulsed me. He'd done the cruellest thing ever and would have continued to be cruel if the truth hadn't been blurted out in a fit of rage. And now he was acting like the wounded party. The anger festering exploded out of me.

'Why did you do it?' I shouted.

Scott raised his head and looked at me imploringly. 'For Anna,' he said quietly.

I glared at him. That made no sense.

Scott wiped his eyes. 'I didn't want to tell you, to make you feel bad.'

I shook my head. '*I'm* not the one who should feel bad.'

He knelt upright, so his face was level with mine, and released a shaky breath. 'I feel guilty admitting it, but I see Anna differently than the way you do.'

What was he going on about?

Scott laid a hand across his heart. 'To me, Anna's amazing.'

He wasn't making sense. Why would I see Anna any differently? Opinionated, demanding, and a bit too free and easy with French swear words, but amazing nonetheless.

'She's one of a kind.' Scott smiled with pride. 'Don't get me wrong, Harry and Bella are great, but they're not like Anna. She's fun and cheeky and super-smart. Don't you think?'

I nodded, confused about where he was going with this. Of course I thought that; it went without saying.

Scott grabbed handfuls of air. 'I love her so, so much. It's like the line from *Jerry Maguire* – "you complete me". That's how I feel about Anna.'

I didn't know how to respond. I actually thought that was a crap line. No one should complete anyone, not a partner nor a child. Enhance them, yes. Make them happier, yes. But not complete them. That insinuated we were partial beings until someone else came along and fixed us.

Scott misinterpreted my silence. 'You mustn't feel guilty that you don't feel the same. I know you love her too, in your own way.'

'I don't feel guilty,' I snapped. 'I love Anna with all my heart.'

'If that's true,' Scott said softly, 'how would it be possible to love another child as much?'

'It's nature,' I said indignantly. 'We don't have an allocated amount of love in us. It grows to let in more people.'

Scott nodded. 'That's the theory. But can you honestly imagine feeling as strongly for anyone else as you do for Anna?'

'No,' I admitted. Even when Anna was driving me insane with a tantrum, or prising my eyes open with her fingers at five in the morning, I'd put my life on the line for her without hesitation. It was hard to envisage the intensity of that love for someone else. I bit my lip. I assumed I would, but there was no guarantee. Suppose I didn't? It'd show. They'd know. And how screwed up would they be, knowing I didn't love them as much as their sister?

Scott leant forward, his hands pressed together. 'Why, when you love Anna so much, do you feel unfulfilled?'

I shook my head. 'I'm not unfulfilled.'

'Then why are you so desperate to have another baby?'

'Because it'd be nice.'

It sounded so flat when I said it out loud. It'd be *nice*. Having fish and chips on a Friday night was *nice*. Watching the latest Chris Hemsworth film with Brigitte was *nice*. I shouldn't be categorising having a baby in the same way.

'Another baby would turn Anna's life upside down,' Scott said. 'I saw it happen with Harry when Bella arrived. He went from being a happy, confident kid to tormented by nightmares and abandonment issues.' His face was full of remorse. 'It's not possible to give both kids the same amount of attention. The eldest one suffers.' Tears filled his eyes. 'I don't want Anna to go through that. At the moment we can give her everything, help her progress and develop emotionally and mentally. Couldn't do that if you're juggling feeds and working when the baby naps.' He pressed a fist to his lips. 'She'd lose her confidence, knowing that the baby's needs always came first. That she was second best.'

'She wouldn't be second best,' I protested.

'*I* know that.' Scott looked at me imploringly. 'But Anna wouldn't. She already feels that your work means more to you than she does.'

'What?' I sat upright. 'Has she said that?'

Scott looked down. 'I didn't want to tell you, because your job's very important and Anna's too young to understand. But she sometimes says, "Mama likes sewing more than playing with me," or, "Mama's too busy for me."'

My stomach twisted. Poor Anna. How terrible to think

your parent prioritised their job over you. I had no idea she felt neglected. I hadn't thought I could spend any more time with her than I currently did, but I was working Saturdays at the moment and often sewed while we watched her programmes together. I'd taught her some basic stitches and thought she enjoyed sewing alongside me, but perhaps it was the only way she felt she could connect with me. I'd have to stop doing that, and sew in the evenings instead. Anna needed to know I was fully there for her, not as an afterthought.

'How do you think she'd feel if a baby was monopolising your attention?' Scott asked softly. 'You'd be even busier then. She'd feel you didn't care at all.'

'I wouldn't let that happen,' I said, but it wasn't with conviction. I already struggled to run a business and give Anna everything she needed. Turned out, I wasn't giving her enough. Much as I hated to admit it, Scott was right; she'd get even less with a baby around.

Scott moved so that he was sitting next to me on the sofa and took my hand. 'She gives me everything I could possibly need or want from a child,' he said. 'It's a real shame you don't feel the same,' he added quietly.

'I do!' I twisted round to face him. 'Like you said, she's amazing.'

Scott paused, as though summoning up the courage to speak. 'What is she lacking that you think another child would give you?' he asked gently.

Guilt clawed at me. 'She doesn't lack anything. She's brimming over with everything that's good in the world.' I thought of her gorgeous smile, her infectious giggle, her smart-arse retorts. 'She *is* my world,' I whispered.

Scott gazed at me earnestly. 'What are you looking for, then? What's missing?'

I searched my mind for an answer. Earlier, I'd been overjoyed to be pregnant, then devastated to discover I wasn't and never would be. Why was that? Why was I so determined to have another baby? Scott had used the words unfulfilled, lacking and missing. None of those applied to me. I was happy with Anna and the balance I had in my life. I swallowed hard. Scott was right: another child would alter that completely, especially with Anna already doubting my commitment to her. I hadn't thought this through at all. I'd automatically subscribed to society's norms of 2.4 children, without taking into account the impact it'd have on my own family. How it would affect my daughter: my precious, wondrous little Anna. Guilt coursed through me at how little I'd considered her in this. How I'd taken for granted the gift I'd been given and greedily expected more. I didn't need another baby. Anna was enough for me.

I turned to face Scott. 'Nothing's missing.'

Scott clasped my hand tightly between both of his. 'What I did was unforgiveable. But I'm going to ask anyway: please, please forgive me. For Anna's sake, if not mine? She needs both her parents. Let's not turn her life upside down because of this one mistake.'

I stared at him. What he'd done was wrong. So very, very wrong. I wasn't sure I'd ever get over it. But I'd been wrong too. Dismissing Anna's security, development and wellbeing for a baby that just five minutes of analysis revealed I didn't even need.

'It's going to take time,' I said shakily. 'But I'll try.'

Scott pulled me into his arms. 'Thank God,' he said, his voice cracking. 'I don't know what I'd do without you.'

My arms hung by my sides. I wasn't ready to hug him back yet. 'Promise me something,' I said.

'Anything,' he said, kissing my forehead. 'Anything.'

I tried to ignore the way my body stiffened at the touch of his lips. 'Promise you'll never lie to me again.'

'I promise.' Scott tightened his embrace. 'Anna will be the happiest, most secure little girl ever. We'll all be happy. Together, as a family.'

I gazed blankly over his shoulder. Family. Providing a

secure environment for Anna. That was all that mattered. My disappointment would fade. My yearning for another baby would lessen. It'd take time to forgive Scott's deception, even longer to forget, but, for Anna's sake, I would. I had to.

Chapter 34

'Are you sure you're OK?' Brigitte asked for about the fourteenth time.

'Yes,' I lied, also for about the fourteenth time. I moved the phone to my other ear, as I power-walked to nursery. I couldn't wait to scoop Anna up, hold her tight and show her that she was the most important thing in the world to me. The knowledge that she believed my work was more important than her horrified me. I prayed it wasn't too late to undo the damage I'd already done.

'But he was so out of order.' Brigitte let out a frustrated wail. 'I don't care how abusive the messages from Liz were. That doesn't give him the right to abuse *you*.'

'He didn't abuse me.' I used a sing-song voice to demonstrate how silly her accusation was. 'He was in shock, jumped to the wrong conclusion and got a bit shouty.' I forced a laugh to mask the anguish I felt. 'Don't worry, I shouted back.'

'You were justified – he wasn't.' Brigitte exhaled loudly. 'I can't believe he accused you of an affair.'

'He admits it was a stupid thing to say. The messages really got to him.' The messages, the messages – I felt like a broken record. 'We all say things we don't mean sometimes,' I added. 'I just have to get over it and move on.'

'But you were so upset.' I could hear the confusion in Brigitte's voice.

'I still am,' I admitted, allowing one sliver of truth to escape. 'But he's apologised, explained why it happened and promised it'll never happen again.'

'It had better not.' Brigitte tutted. 'What about the police? He seemed pretty pissed off about that too.'

'Shock again. Said it was a great idea when he'd calmed down. He now thinks this is the answer to finally getting Liz off our backs.' I released a slow breath, thankful that part at least was true.

'So, what now?' Brigitte asked.

'I'm picking Anna up from nursery.'

'No,' Brigitte said. 'With you two trying for a baby.'

My stomach twisted. 'What do you mean?' I asked, hoping my voice didn't quiver.

'Is he going to react like that every month? Has it put you off, in case he blows up again?'

I blinked hard to prevent tears from escaping. It went against my very nature to hide something from Brigitte. We told each other everything. But I couldn't tell her Scott'd had a vasectomy. She'd hate him. She'd hate that I was putting up with what he'd done. She didn't have children. She didn't understand the sheer force of love that was so strong, you'd put up with crap you wouldn't normally to guarantee them a better life. Some women turned to prostitution or crime to provide for their family. They'd give anything to be in my situation, living in a nice house, with food on the table, a healthy daughter, a job I loved and a decent husband. Because Scott was, fundamentally, a decent man. Yes, he'd made a mistake, a gut-wrenchingly painful mistake, but he hadn't done it out of malice or to hurt me. He'd done it to stop *me* hurting Anna.

I swallowed hard. 'We've decided to wait a while before trying again.'

'What?' Brigitte shouted so loudly that I had to hold the phone away from my ear. 'You've spent two years trying to persuade him, then you try for less than a month and give up again?'

'Not giving up,' I lied. 'Just waiting till Anna's a bit older.'

'Why?' Brigitte sounded shell-shocked.

'Because it's the right thing to do.' I didn't need to lie now. 'I'm so busy, working weekends and evenings. I don't spend as much time with her as I should. If I had a baby, she'd be neglected. It wouldn't be fair on her.'

'You're not serious?' Brigitte gave a mocking laugh. 'You always put Anna first. You're forever on the floor, playing with her and involving her in everything you do.'

'And I want to carry on doing that.' I increased my speed. 'I wouldn't be able to if I had a baby to look after. Something would have to give. You don't want me to give up my business that's taken twenty years to build, do you?'

'Course not,' Brigitte said. 'But—'

'This is the right thing to do,' I repeated. 'For Anna.'

'If that's what you want.' Brigitte's voice was full of uncertainty.

'It is,' I said firmly.

I reached the nursery and was about to tell Brigitte I had to go, when I heard Anna calling: 'Mama!'

She was at the window, waving frantically. Her key worker stood next to her. 'Can we go to the splash park?' Anna called through the gap in the window. Usually, I'd say no. I'd be shattered from work, and eager to get back to make Anna's tea and start the three-hour wind-down to bedtime before I got back to sewing. Guiltily, I realised that this was the exact kind of behaviour Scott had referred to. Putting my work before Anna. Well, not anymore. I wouldn't work less; I'd just work differently. Later into the night. Skipping lunch breaks. Not going out with Brigitte so much.

I waved at Anna and nodded. She jumped up and down, and my heart soared. This was what mattered, nothing else.

'Give Anna my love,' Brigitte said down the phone.

'I will.' I walked around the side of the nursery to the front door. 'Got to go.'

'Lunch tomorrow?'

I hesitated. Lying to Brigitte over the phone was hard enough. How could I do it to her face? She'd be able to tell at a glance that I was hiding something. Even if I tied my hands behind my back to avoid rubbing my nose, she'd see it in my eyes. She knew me so well. And I knew her. I'd be able to read her emotions – the disbelief, the concern, maybe even disappointment. The only way to ensure it didn't drive a wedge between us was to avoid her for now.

'I won't have time,' I said. 'Sorry.'

'I'll catch up with you in between clients, then.'

'Hopefully.' I pushed open the gate leading to the nursery's front door. 'But I'll be working flat out for the next few weeks. Won't have much time for chatting.'

'Thank goodness for pole dancing or I'd never see you.'

I took a deep breath, ignoring the burning in my throat. 'Been meaning to say, I'm not going to come anymore.'

'You're not?' Brigitte's voice was uncharacteristically small.

'No.' I blinked hard. 'I'm useless at it and I'm sure Maman gets Anna out of bed after I've gone. She's always grumpy the next day.'

'That's a shame. I'll miss you.' Her voice caught and tears sprang to my eyes.

'Got to go.' I gulped. 'Love you.'

'Love you too,' Brigitte whispered hoarsely.

I hung up and clasped a hand to my mouth. The thought of not talking to her constantly – at work, on the phone, while attempting a bootie jump – was unbearable. But it wouldn't be forever. I composed myself and rang the front doorbell. As soon as I was confident Brigitte wouldn't ask me about Scott's behaviour or trying for another baby, everything could go back to exactly how it used to be.

The door buzzed and I pushed it open, with a heavy heart. I had a horrible feeling that things wouldn't ever be exactly how they used to be.

Chapter 35

'Seen anything more of wassername?' Scott asked, putting on a tie in front of the bedroom's full-length mirror.

'Who?' I looked over from the edge of the bed where I was sitting, applying mascara while checking myself in a hand-held mirror.

Scott undid the tie and swapped it for one of the many hanging inside the wardrobe door. Ties to him were what shoes were to many women. Or dress patterns to me. Or dick pics to Brigitte.

'Cleo,' he said.

Hearing her name made my stomach clench. 'No.' My hand shook as I replaced the mascara wand.

'Good.' Scott stood back to admire his appearance. There was much to admire: chiselled jaw, bright blue eyes, dazzling smile, full head of hair. Just a shame he was on the short side.

I gave myself a mental telling-off. These kinds of uncharitable thoughts had been happening frequently, since that shitty day two weeks ago, and weren't helping me move forward.

I examined my makeup in the tiny compact.

'Why are you all dolled up?' Scott asked.

'I'm taking Anna to Brighton for the day.' I knew he hadn't been listening when I'd told him. Although, in his defence, hearing would be last on the list of senses required when watching the 'essential to the plot' nudity of last night's episode of *Game of Thrones*. Afterwards, Scott had been keen for us to go to bed, but I'd stayed up working, as I had every night for the last two weeks. Sewing till midnight was standard during wedding season, but this year I was working even later. Partly because I was finishing in the studio earlier to spend more of the evening with Anna. Partly as an excuse not to go to bed with Scott. Guilt pricked at me. It seemed my sex drive had taken a sabbatical and I wasn't sure when it'd be back. It needed to be soon. Sex was an integral part of our lives and I missed experiencing those emotions. Plus, it was a natural part of a healthy relationship and that's what I was striving to have.

Apart from the lack of sex, by all appearances, I'd moved on. Scott and I went about our everyday routines in an amiable way. There wasn't an atmosphere. We never talked about his vasectomy or the fact that another baby had ever been a consideration. I didn't ask about Liz or when we could meet Harry and Bella. I didn't even ask how they were when Scott got back from an evening with them. Scott had spoken to the police and their involvement had, as intended, shaken Liz into behaving in a more measured way. He no longer received constant texts or summons at all hours. Instead, he saw the kids on his two allocated evenings. Which were now my two favourite evenings of the week.

I knew maintaining a façade, acting as though everything was fine, wasn't sustainable. But it wouldn't be for much longer. I'd received a blow and was in a period of adjustment. Once I'd got through it, everything would return to normal. I'd stop finding faults where there weren't any, and Scott's annoying habits would return to being merely annoying, as opposed to driving me to the brink of murder. No matter how masterful a lawyer I hired, it was unlikely I'd walk free after bludgeoning my husband to death for not mopping up a puddle on the kitchen worktop. When I'd made peace with my issues and my affection for Scott had returned, my sex drive would be back with a vengeance. Scott wouldn't know what had hit him. Unless he still hadn't mopped up the puddle, in which case it'd probably be a saucepan.

Anna giggled at something and the joyous sound carried

up the stairs. Quite possibly caused by how many pieces came out of the remote control when she took it apart, but that didn't matter. All that mattered was that she was her usual happy, carefree, diva self, totally oblivious to my conflicting emotions about her father. He's a good man, I reminded myself. He'd made an error of judgement, but it had come from a place of love. This was my new mantra and it ran on a loop through my head. It was getting on my nerves, to be honest, so hopefully it'd sink in soon.

Someone who wasn't oblivious to my inner turmoil was Brigitte. She'd given up asking me if I was OK, as I gave stock answers – 'Yes, fine. Honestly. You don't need to worry . . .' – every time. But she wasn't fooled and I'd sometimes look up from my sewing machine or mannequin to catch her peering into my studio with a frown on her face. She'd swap it instantly for a smile and ask if I wanted to pop out to the café or to get some fresh air. I'd said I was too busy every day for two weeks now and I missed her. But until my 'He's a good man . . .' mantra evolved from an inspirational quote to my sincere feelings, I couldn't risk the truth bursting out of me. It had better happen before Beth's hag do the following week. Brigitte and I had an entire evening together, and alcohol would be involved. She could wheedle anything out of me once I'd had a cocktail, especially if she was buying.

Scott went to his bedside table to rummage for cufflinks and I nipped in front of the mirror, while it was free, to straighten the full skirt of my red and white floral halterneck dress.

'Why are you going to Brighton?' he asked. 'It's a shithole. Can't move for seagulls.'

I ignored his description of Brighton as a shithole. I loved the Lanes and North Laine and the onion-domed Pavilion, and the colourful people and vibrant atmosphere. It was my favourite seaside destination. Although, admittedly, I'd never been to the Maldives.

'Thought you were too busy to do anything but work,' he added.

He was right. I couldn't really afford to miss a whole day during wedding season, but I'd learnt my lesson and wasn't going to prioritise work over Anna anymore.

'I am, but she's been asking to go to the seaside since our weekend at Heavenly Hideaway. I'll catch up with work when she's in bed.'

Scott slipped his arms around me from behind. 'It'd be nice if you caught up with me in bed instead.' He cupped my breasts and traced the outline of my nipples with his thumbs. That move had always been an instant knicker-loosener, but now I flinched. Scott nuzzled my neck. His lips felt like moist rubber against my skin.

I feigned a giggle. 'Your stubble's tickling me.' Scott slapped my bottom as I pulled away. My hands curled into fists.

Anna was waiting for me at the bottom of the stairs, wearing a green summer dress, a sun hat over her dark curls, and wellies. She jumped up, clutching a bucket and spade. On the mornings I had to get to work, it'd be easier to coax a newborn back into the womb than get Anna out the door, but today, when we had all the time in the world, she was of course ready and waiting.

'Let's swap your wellies for sandals,' I said. 'It's warm enough to paddle barefoot.'

Anna frowned. 'I haven't got a bear foot. I've got a people foot.'

'That's my girl. Bright as a button.' Scott patted Anna's head as he walked to the front door. 'Gets her brains from me.'

Scott had believed nuns were made-up purely for TV and film entertainment, till he was in his twenties, so his brain – singular, not plural – was indeed on par with a three-year-old's. I bit my lip. I had to stop finding fault. Scott wasn't behaving any differently to the way he always had.

'Why not take the day off and come with us?' I asked, to alleviate my guilt.

Scott shook his head, drained his coffee cup and put it on the stairs. 'Places to go, people to see.' He kissed me goodbye and I lowered my chin so that his lips landed on my forehead rather than my mouth. As soon as the door closed, I wiped his coffee imprint away.

There was already a queue when we reached the bus stop. Anna waved at the children waiting. I smiled at their parents, but didn't engage in conversation. I'd quickly realised at antenatal class that having had a shag within the same cycle of your period didn't automatically mean you were destined to be lifelong friends. Not all the women realised this. One mum tried phoning daily to enquire about Anna's stool consistency and frequency. This was clearly an excuse to relay her own daughter's bowel movements and then, disgustingly, detail how they compared to her own. There were enough shit conversations going on in the world without having to create conversations about actual shit. After a few days of this, I blocked her. Judging by her lurid descriptions, her toilet wouldn't have been far behind me.

The bus arrived and we boarded. I let Anna choose our seats, as I didn't mind where we sat. I was so happy to pass control of the journey to the driver that I'd have travelled on the parcel shelf if need be.

Anna and I grinned at each other in a 'this is a bit of an adventure' way. She knelt up and pulled my hair away from my face to whisper in my ear. I bent my head, eagerly awaiting the secret she was about to tell me.

'Can I play with your phone?'

'No! You can play with me.'

Anna looked me up and down. 'That's a bit boring.'

I looked out of the window. 'I spy with my little eye, something the colour blue.'

'The sea!' Anna squealed, looking out of the window, then down the bus at the windscreen.

A view of the sea was impossible, as we were still in

Horsham, but I followed her gaze anyway. Walking up the aisle towards us was Michael. My stomach somersaulted.

'It's the man who's not a doctor,' Anna said loudly.

Michael looked momentarily surprised, then smiled broadly. 'You've rumbled me. I'm well and truly off duty today.' He gestured to the empty seats across from us. 'Mind if I sit here?'

'Course not.' I went to move my highly impractical, but gorgeous, vintage wicker bag, but Michael got there first and carefully transferred it to the overhead shelf, along with his rucksack, before sitting down. He was dressed in teal-blue, fitted shorts and a white short-sleeved shirt covered in tiny blue anchors.

Anna leant around me and openly stared at him.

He waved. 'Hello again.'

'Still no steth-ah-scope.' Anna narrowed her eyes at him. 'Do you have a phone, at least?'

Michael looked confused. 'Yes, but I can't listen to heartbeats with it.'

Anna sighed heavily, as though she were talking to a complete moron as opposed to someone with a doctorate. '*Bon dieu*,' she tutted. I had to find a new babysitter. It'd been bad enough living with Maman the first time around. I didn't want to go through the whole thing again with a mini version of her. 'I want to *play* with your phone,' she said. 'Not do doctor stuff with it.'

'Anna,' I said sharply, mortified at her rudeness.

Anna had the good grace to look ashamed. 'Sorry,' she said, her eyes downturned.

'Sorry,' I echoed.

'I've got a niece and nephew, remember. I'm used to it.' Michael smiled. 'That's why I'm going to Brighton. School's got an inset day and Beth's working, so I'm meeting them at the bus stop, and taking Henry and Izzy to the seaside.' He pointed at the bucket on Anna's lap. 'Might see you on the beach.'

'There's no sand on Brighton beach. Just stones.' Anna spoke into her bucket, unsure if she was forgiven. I should enjoy this rare contriteness while it lasted. She'd be back to bolshie in approximately two minutes, if past behaviour was anything to go by.

'And shells,' Michael said. 'Henry and Izzy love collecting the shells.'

'So do I.' Anna gave him a sideways glance. 'How old are they?'

'Henry's eight and Izzy's five. How old are you?'

'*J'ai trois ans,*' Anna said. Michael looked impressed and I couldn't help but feel proud. Maman could babysit after all. 'Can I see a photo?' Anna asked.

'Course.' Michael slid his phone from the pocket of his shorts, opened his photo library and passed the handset to Anna. She took it and thrust her bucket at me.

'You'll never get that back,' I said. 'She knows what she's doing.'

Michael smiled. 'A true pro.' He lowered his voice. 'How are you? Any more dizzy spells?'

My throat tightened. The last time we'd seen each other had been that hideous day. He'd joked that if he didn't know better, he'd think I was pregnant, then regretted his words. No wonder. He must know about Scott's vasectomy. He'd assumed I knew too. My cheeks burnt with sadness, embarrassment and shame.

'Marie,' Michael said softly. 'Are you all right?'

I nodded sharply. 'Yes, fine, thanks.' Thank goodness I hadn't told him I was pregnant. He'd have thought I was mad.

'Sure?' he asked.

I forced a smile. 'Yes.' Fake it till you make it.

Michael didn't look convinced, but nodded a pretend acceptance. It was like being with Brigitte. His eyes darted to Anna. She'd found a game on his phone and was engrossed.

'Any sign of Cleo?' he whispered.

I shook my head.

'And the feeling of being watched?'

'Nothing.' I tapped the side of Anna's bucket, as though it'd stop me jinxing it. 'If it was real it's stopped, and if it wasn't . . . then I'm well and truly bonkers.'

'Or overworked, stressed and sleep-deprived,' Michael said. 'Or chocolate deprived,' he added, his eyes sparkling mischievously. I swallowed hard, suddenly feeling very deprived of something. 'How's work going?' he continued. 'Beth loves her dress.'

I seized the change of topic. 'She looks stunning.' I swung the bucket excitedly. 'Brigitte and I are going to hers the morning of the wedding. Brigitte's doing her makeup and I'll help her get dressed.'

'Do you do that for all your clients?'

I shook my head. 'Brigitte does if they've hired her, but I don't usually. Beth's become a friend, though, so I want to. She's invited us to the hen and stag do—'

'Hag do.' Michael smiled.

'That's it. And her wedding reception, which is really nice of her. Brigitte and I have booked a hotel, so we can make the most of the party.' I gave the bucket such an enthusiastic swing that some sand from a previous trip scattered over Michael. I swallowed a smile. 'Sorry.'

'I'll be getting covered in a lot more later.' Michael brushed his shorts down, good-humouredly. 'It'll be nice to see you at the reception. Are your husband and Anna coming too?'

Anna looked up briefly when she heard her name, decided the conversation wasn't interesting and went back to her game. I should take the phone away, and engage in a bonding activity that promoted her development and interest in the world around her, but she was content and we'd play together all day when we got to the beach. And I couldn't be arsed.

'No, just me and Brigitte,' I told Michael. 'Anna's too young and Scott won't know anyone. Brigitte and I won't either, but we're happy meeting people and dancing.' I had invited Scott, but as he hated Brighton and I'd arranged for Anna to go to Maman's, he chose not to come. I'd been relieved.

Michael crossed one leg, so his foot was resting on his other knee. His knee jutted out into the aisle, just centimetres from where my hand rested on Anna's bucket. 'Scott's not a fan of meeting people and dancing, then?' he asked.

The bus swung round a sharp corner and he lurched to the side. His bare knee brushed my arm. A jolt shot through me.

I cleared my throat, pretending the jolt hadn't happened. 'He meets people all day in his job, so likes to chill out in his free time.'

'He's an estate agent,' Michael said.

I nodded. He had a good memory. 'And he spends a lot of time with . . .' I shielded my face from Anna and mouthed, 'His children from his first marriage. Anna doesn't know.'

Michael looked between the two of us with raised eyebrows – still hadn't cracked the one-eyebrowed arch, then.

'Long story,' I whispered. 'I'll tell you later.' My cheeks flushed. Why had I said 'later'? It wasn't as though we were friends who hung out together. Were we? I lowered my hand. 'How are you, anyway? Busy with holiday jabs?'

'The nurse deals with immunisations, not me,' Michael said. 'Summer's marginally quieter than winter. Not so many cold and flu bugs, but people come about other things. Hay fever, sunburn.' He stifled a smirk. 'Shouldn't tell you this . . .' He looked over his shoulder and scanned the other passengers on the bus, then leant towards me. I leant in too, to hear his hushed voice. 'One patient made the mistake of sunbathing naked in his garden after shaving his genitals. Had blisters in places you really wouldn't want chafing.' He struggled to contain a laugh. 'Poor man. They'd swollen to the size of oranges. Had to take a week off work because he couldn't wear anything on his lower half. He wore his wife's sarong to the appointment.'

I giggled. 'Did you give him a medical certificate?'

'Saying what? This man's unfit for work because he's burnt his balls?'

We laughed loudly, clamping our hands over our mouths to avoid disapproving looks from the other passengers. Anna, mainly. I realised I had missed laughing.

Michael wiped his eyes. 'I told him to apply cold, damp compresses, take Ibuprofen and avoid sun exposure. Not that I think he'd ever do that again.'

'His neighbours must be relieved.'

Our laughter fizzled away naturally and I became aware that we were still leaning towards each other, our foreheads almost touching, his mouth by my ear.

I sat back and searched for another topic. 'Dean still putting you through your paces?' I asked. 'In the gym,' I added hastily, in case Michael thought the subject of overexposed balls had caused my mind to leap to his boyfriend.

'Not too much. I run most days anyway and sometimes we go together. He uses me as a guinea pig for personal training programmes he's putting together, but he's building up a good client base, so inflicts pain on them rather than me.' He patted his stomach, which was so taut beneath his shirt that it was a wonder he didn't injure his hand. 'Not sure if that's good or bad.'

'The sea!' Anna squealed, and I reluctantly tore my eyes away from Michael's toned torso.

People gathered their things together as we neared the bus stop. Anna dropped Michael's phone into her bucket, no longer needing it now that she had the sea to entertain her. I fished it out, dusted the sand off and hoped it was still working. Michael got my wicker bag down from the parcel shelf and handed it to me. The bus pulled up and, through the window, we saw Beth waiting with Henry and Izzy.

'Come and say hi,' Michael said.

He stepped off the bus first, and the children charged over and threw their arms around him. Laughing, he hunched over to hug them both. Beth walked up behind, looking beautiful in a fitted green dress.

'Thanks for this.' She kissed Michael's cheek. 'Don't know what I'd have done otherwise.'

'It's a pleasure. Glad I can help.' Michael put a hand on Henry's and Izzy's heads. 'Look who I bumped into on the bus.'

They all turned to see me and Anna standing a few feet back. Izzy waved shyly, and Beth strode over and hugged me.

'What a lovely surprise. Henry, I don't think you've met Marie, have you? She's made me and Izzy the most beautiful dresses.'

Henry looked as interested as I would be if someone explained the inner workings of a carburettor, but smiled politely all the same. In contrast to Izzy's blue eyes, his were deep brown like Beth's. He was tall for eight years old, with broad shoulders, like Michael.

'Hi,' I said brightly. 'This is Anna.' I motioned to Anna, but she needed no introduction.

'Hello.' She dropped my hand, marched over to Izzy and took hers instead.

'I'd better get to work.' Beth kissed Izzy and Henry. 'Wish I could come with you. The beach will be much more fun than my meetings.' She took a voucher from her bag and handed it to Michael. 'Here's 20 per cent off fish and chips at The Codfather. I did a promotion for them recently.' She smiled at me. 'You too. I like to share my good fortune.'

'I don't think—' I started, but Michael interrupted.

'We're all going to the beach anyway. May as well go together and share the fish and chips.'

I bit my lip. It was kind of Michael, but he'd been put on the spot. Conversation had flowed on the bus, but we'd talked about everything now and ran the risk of a day of awkward silence. Unless he had any more stories about sunburnt goolies – which I hoped, for the owners' sakes, he hadn't.

Anna tugged on Izzy's hand. '*On y va*,' she said. 'Let's go.'

It seemed I didn't have a choice. We were spending the day with Michael.

Chapter 36

'I need a break. My arm's killing me.' Michael handed a smooth stone to each of the three children. Anna hurled hers straight into the water, rather than twisting her arm to get it to skim, as Michael had demonstrated. But she was only three, and as long as she was having fun and didn't hit anyone, that was fine. Hit anyone *else*, that is. A man further down the beach was still massaging the back of his neck.

Michael flopped down next to me. 'Where do they get their energy from?' He wiggled uncomfortably. Stones weren't comfortable to flop down on.

'They don't have to work, or do laundry or housework or cooking.' Or even wipe their arse, in Anna's case, but loyalty prevented me from adding this to the list. 'Think how much energy we'd have if someone else did the boring jobs and we could just play.'

'I am just playing and I'm still knackered.' Michael rubbed his eyes.

'Have an afternoon nap if you want,' I said. 'I'll watch them. Just be careful you don't get burnt.'

Michael covered the fly of his shorts with his hands and we both laughed.

'No, I'm all right,' he said. 'I'll finish the chips. That'll energise me. Don't tell Dean. They're not part of the protein plan he's got me on.'

I pulled an apologetic face. 'The seagulls pinched them. I wrapped them back up, but they ripped through the bag. The way they fought over them, you'd think they were in some impoverished war-torn country.' I cringed as I remembered that Michael had lived and worked in an impoverished war-torn country, which I doubted bore much resemblance to Brighton Beach. 'Sorry,' I said. 'That was insensitive.'

Michael shook his head. 'You're fine. Don't worry about it.' He plunged his hands into the stones by his thighs, then let them trickle through his fingers.

I watched the children playing for a moment. Henry was showing Anna how to skim a stone. She listened intently, nodded, then chucked the stone in the water in exactly the same way as before.

'Beth said you went to Syria for a few months and ended up staying nine years,' I said. 'How did that happen?'

'There was so much to do,' Michael said simply. 'I couldn't walk away and leave them to it.' He sighed heavily. 'The situation out there is dire. Very little food or medicine or basic aid. Bombs being dropped on a daily basis. Not where I was,' he added when I gasped. 'I was in Damascus. We treated the people who'd been medically evacuated from Ghouta. They were exhausted, starving, injured. And they were the lucky ones. They'd been rescued.' His jaw tightened. 'It's so wrong. Hundreds of thousands of people are suffering. Not just in Syria. In other places too. At the mercy of the tyrants running their countries when all they want to do is work, have families, live their lives.' He nodded towards Izzy, Henry and Anna. 'Watch their children live theirs.

'I often think I should have stayed,' he continued. 'But I was at breaking point, emotionally and physically. Dean would suggest going on holiday, but taking a break felt selfish and self-indulgent. The people out there don't get a two-week respite when they've had enough. They're stuck with it day in, day out for the foreseeable future. Which, for many of them, isn't very long.'

He drew his knees up and rested his elbows on them. His eyes glistened behind his sunglasses. 'I missed Beth's wedding, and Henry and Izzy being born. Never even met her ex. Just as well, as it turns out. Not sure I could resist punching him for the way he treated her.' He took his sunglasses off and rubbed his eyes. 'I still feel bad about not being here when they broke up. I almost came home, but knew that as soon as I saw her and met the kids, I wouldn't want to leave them. They're so desperate for medics in Syria, I'd have dropped them right in it if I'd left.' His voice was so soft now that I had to strain to hear him over the excited cries from the children and the seagulls' squawks. 'I have dropped them in it now, though. I'm living my cushy little life a million miles away from the devastation they're still going through.'

Anguish was etched on his face. I wanted to hug him, but we were only just forming a friendship, and it felt too intrusive, so instead I gently patted his back.

'You mustn't feel bad after sacrificing your own family and life for nine years to help others. You gave everything you had. Must have been exhausting.'

Michael nodded. 'I'd burnt out. Dean told me I had to come back or there'd be nothing left of me. He couldn't face being in medicine anymore after what we'd seen. He wanted to help people be healthy for the long term, not just fix them up and dispatch them, never knowing if what he'd done had made a difference. That's why being a GP appealed to me. I want to build relationships with my patients; go back to the days when doctors treated whole generations of a family. More chance of being able to do that in a small town like Horsham than in Brighton.'

'That's very commendable, but you might not want to treat my whole family,' I said. 'My mum's French and doesn't think it qualifies as a proper appointment if she hasn't taken all her clothes off.'

Michael grinned. 'Mademoiselle Dubois, of course. Should have made the connection. It's an unusual surname.'

'Oh God.' I cringed. 'What's she done?'

Michael put his hands up. 'Can't say – patient confidentiality. Nothing to worry about, though. It only involved removing her socks.'

'Ugh. Not that toenail infection.' I shuddered. 'She's had it for years.' It'd clear up if she applied the anti-fungal lacquer she'd been prescribed. But Maman viewed unpainted toenails as a form of self-abuse, so ended up in a dodgy nail bar within twenty-four hours of starting the treatment. Brigitte refused to go near her feet after a nail fell off during a pedicure. 'I'm surprised that wasn't enough to put you off Horsham,' I added.

Michael chuckled. 'No, I think I'll stay. The town's got character and I like the people.'

Our eyes met and I realised I was still rubbing his back. But the rhythmic technique I also used to comfort Anna after a fall or bad dream had slowed to a much slower, intense, almost intimate motion. I snatched my hand away and turned to watch the kids. Which I should have been doing anyway, the vast ocean being a slight hazard for unsupervised young children.

Michael cleared his throat. 'Beth's pleased I moved to Horsham. She didn't know where to start with wedding-dress shops in Brighton, as there are so many. Couldn't believe it when I said there was someone making bespoke dresses on Horsham High Street.'

'You recommended me?' I looked back to him. The lifeguard's whistle and screams of terror would alert me if the children got into trouble. 'How did you know about my studio?'

'One of my patients said you were amazing and she couldn't wait to wear her dress. Beth feels the same.'

'Ah, that's nice.' I wiggled my toes in appreciation. 'How about you? Ever thought about marriage? Not that I'm suggesting I make you a dress.'

'No, not sure I'd suit one.' Michael smiled. 'It'd be nice to get married someday. Maybe have kids. Or have kids in my life in some capacity. There's a bit of a hurdle to leap first.'

I nodded. It would be trickier, but plenty of gay couples had children now, either through surrogacy or adoption.

'Does Dean feel the same way?'

Michael shrugged. 'He's a few years younger, so in no rush. We're both mindful of the shit Beth went through. *Is* going through.' He corrected himself. 'Don't want to risk something similar happening to us.'

That surprised me. I'd assumed Michael and Dean were solid, not warily wondering if the other was going to cheat, and ditch them and any kids.

'Beth's ex sounds horrific,' I said. 'How could anyone not want to see their children? Scott has constant fights with his ex about theirs.'

Michael cocked his head. 'What's going on there?'

'He's got two kids from his first marriage, but his ex won't let them meet me and Anna,' I explained. 'I met him after they'd divorced, so it's not as if I caused the breakup, but she's adamant. Whenever Scott talks to her about it, she blows up and makes it hard for him to see them.'

'He's got legal rights,' Michael said. 'She's not allowed to withhold visiting.'

'I know.' I sighed. 'She gets round it by pretending they have something on. It'd cost a fortune to get a solicitor involved every time. And there's no legal requirement for them to meet me and Anna. We've got to hope that, in time, she'll agree.'

Michael nodded towards Anna. 'Why the big secret?'

I opened my mouth to reply but realised I didn't have an answer. Scott said it was to protect Anna, but protect her from what? We had to tell her some time and the older she got, the harder it'd be. We needed to be honest with her.

'Won't be for much longer,' I said feebly, turning my attention to the children. They stood at the water's edge, holding hands, jumping over the foamy waves when they hit the shore. It was a beautiful sight, but one that almost felt cruel. This was what I wanted for Anna. A sibling to play with. But she'd never have it now. A sob threatened to escape, but at that moment, Anna ran over and threw her arms around me. I hugged her tightly back, enjoying the rare moment of affection.

'Today is a perfect day.' She smiled.

I smothered her face in kisses. 'Know what would make it even more perfect?'

'Chocolate ice cream,' we squealed in unison and grinned at each other.

'Brilliant idea.' Michael stood up, brushed sand from the back of his shorts, and called Henry and Izzy over. 'Sugar-free chocolate ice cream, here we come.'

Anna snuggled into Michael on the bus journey home, completely at ease after our day together. Michael had an arm loosely around her shoulders and chatted about the landmarks that we passed. I grinned at the sight, but my smile faded as I realised that I couldn't recall seeing Anna snuggled up to Scott like that. We *had* to do more together as a family. It'd benefit Anna and help me reconnect with Scott. The most interaction we had at home was when we all needed the loo and couldn't be bothered to go downstairs, so fought to get in the bathroom first. We always let Anna win to avoid a dirty protest.

I now had a list of things to talk to Scott about – spending time together, and telling Anna the truth about her half-siblings. Should I also mention that I only pretended to enjoy *Clarkson's Farm* or would that be pushing it?

Anna's eyes closed, and Michael and I exchanged a smile.

'I got you a little something,' he said.

My stomach fluttered with anticipation. I'd like to be one of those people who'd grown out of presents and requested charity donations when it was their birthday, but I wasn't. Being given a present, no matter how big or small, was exciting. Especially if it was big.

Michael handed me a Montezuma's bag and I looked at him questioningly. If this was a test to see whether I could resist sugar, he surely knew by now that I'd not only fail, but was capable of gnawing my way through the packaging to get to the chocolate faster. I put my hand in the bag and felt the contents. Michael grinned as I squeezed the squishy bag inside. It wasn't one of the luxuriously wrapped boxes I'd eyed in the window many times, so what was it? I bit my lip. Perhaps the gift was a set of worry beads to turn to when I had a chocolate craving. If that were the case, this present would only be one step down from Maman's fanny tightener.

Warily, I took the present out and gasped with delight. It was a large bag of giant dark-chocolate buttons. They looked good enough to eat. Which, ironically, I couldn't if I was serious about quitting sugar.

'They're 100 per cent dark chocolate,' Michael said.

I frowned. 'Didn't you say that tasted like a bull's scrotum?'

Michael laughed. 'I've done some research and these are the exception to the rule. You need to nibble them, as they're much more bitter than normal chocolate, but I tried one in the shop and they're surprisingly nice, considering they don't have a single grain of sugar inside.'

'I can eat them guilt-free?' I beamed at him. 'Thank you!' I tore open the bag, offered it to Michael and took one for myself. As instructed, I nibbled a slither off and let it melt on my tongue. Delicious. I closed my eyes and sighed contentedly.

'This is the best present I've ever had.' I took another tiny bite. 'Thank you so much.'

'You're welcome.'

Anna mumbled something and my eyes snapped open, but she was fast asleep. Good. Didn't want her pinching my chocolates.

'She's a great kid,' Michael said, smiling down at her. He wouldn't say that if he'd had to clear up after one of her dirty protests. 'Really blossomed with Henry and Izzy.'

I put the last of my button in my mouth and nodded. 'You're brilliant with children. Hope you and Dean do have them.' Michael had been about to bite into his own button, but his hand paused mid-air. 'Shame I can't be a surrogate for you,' I added.

Michael frowned. 'A surrogate?'

I flushed. I'd got too personal. Maybe they'd tried that route and it hadn't worked. 'Well, as you said, there's a hurdle to leap. Surrogacy's one option, isn't it? Or adoption.' I put my hands up. 'None of my business, though.'

Michael cocked his head. 'The hurdle is that I'm single.'

I put a hand to my mouth. 'I'm so sorry. Why didn't you say?' He'd talked freely about Dean all day. Even said that he hoped to get married someday, but Dean was younger. 'I thought you were happy together. Is it because he's not ready for a family yet?'

Michael looked bewildered. 'What are you talking about?'

'You and Dean,' I said. 'I didn't know you'd broken up.'

'We haven't.'

Now I was confused. 'So, he is still your boyfriend?'

'No!' Anna jumped in her sleep and Michael stroked her hair to calm her. 'Why did you think that?'

'Beth said you got together in Syria. And you live together.'

Michael's face went through a series of expressions, ranging from disbelief, to incredulity, to horror. 'He's my best mate,' he spluttered. 'We met at uni, but he was a few years behind me. He came out to Syria to help. The least I could do was let him use my spare room when we got back.' He shook his head vigorously, perhaps trying to dislodge the notion of him and Dean as a couple, trying for a baby.

'But Beth called him your partner,' I said.

Michael raised his eyes to the ceiling. 'I invested in his personal training business. He needed a backer to get started.'

'Ah.' I smiled an apology. 'Was your boyfriend another one of the men that were at the bar, then?'

Michael's eyebrows shot up. 'What men? What bar?'

'The one at Heavenly Hideaway. You were with a group of men.'

'That doesn't mean one of them's my boyfriend.' He massaged his temples.

'You haven't got a boyfriend, then?' I felt terrible. I'd been banging on about marriage and children, and he wasn't even dating.

'No.' Michael took a deep breath. 'I haven't got a boyfriend.'

'Sorry,' I said, my face on fire.

Michael burst out laughing. 'Don't be sorry. There's a very good reason I haven't got a boyfriend.' He looked me in the eye. 'I'm not gay.'

Chapter 37

'Told you he wasn't gay.' Brigitte's smugness oozed down the phone.

I hadn't been able to resist phoning her. Having a fun-filled day full of laughter had reinforced how much I missed her. I couldn't tell her what Scott had done, but that didn't mean I had to avoid her. She'd sounded thrilled to hear from me, but hadn't asked why I'd been keeping my distance, which I was thankful for.

'Yes, you were right,' I said. 'Not that it matters either way.' I flopped down on the sofa and shot upright again when I encountered the handle of Anna's spade. I picked it up and sat down again. The Montezuma's buttons poked enticingly out of my bag. I put a whole one in my mouth. So much for nibbling on them. I'd have finished the entire bag by bedtime at this rate.

'Sounds like you had a good day,' Brigitte said.

'We did. He bought me some 100 per cent chocolate. Because I can't eat sugar.'

'Doesn't sound like something a bell-end would do.'

'Turns out he's not.' I popped another chocolate in my mouth. 'He's actually a very nice man.'

'Told you. Just like *Pride and Prejudice*.' That smug tone was back. 'You started off thinking he was a knob, but he's the exact opposite.'

'Lizzie wasn't married to someone else, and Darcy wasn't gay,' I pointed out.

'Neither is Michael.'

Oh yes. Had to get my head around that.

'You are married, though,' Brigitte conceded, somewhat

reluctantly. 'How are things at home? Has Scott had any more abusive texts?'

'No.' I reached into the Montezuma's bag again. 'He says the call from the police put the wind up Liz. She only messages to confirm arrangements with the kids now.'

'I hope Scott's grovelling, after the way he treated you.'

The chocolate button got stuck in my throat. 'Yes,' I coughed. 'Bending over backwards to make up for it.'

The better Brigitte thought things were, the less she'd ask.

'So he should.' She tutted. I could sense her bursting to say more – none of it complimentary – but her front door opened and Sanjay called out hello before she could utter a single expletive.

'I'll let you go,' I said. 'Catch-up cuppa tomorrow in the kitchen?'

'Definitely.' I could hear Brigitte's smile down the phone. 'Love you.'

'Love you too.' I hung up, popped another chocolate button, and lay back on the sofa. I should work, as I had so much to do, but was too tired. Lazing around on the beach had taken it out of me. Even Anna had gone straight to sleep, despite her nap on the bus and Michael giving her a piggyback ride home from the stop. I'd protested, but we both knew I didn't mean it. I could barely carry all the shells she'd collected, let alone Anna.

The chocolate button melted slowly on my tongue and I smiled at the memory of Anna's shrieks of delight when Michael had galloped along the street, her dark, curly bunches bobbing up and down as she'd clutched his broad shoulders. It had been hard not to notice how well-defined Michael's arms were, when he'd supported Anna with them, or how deftly he'd sprung up after crouching down so she could climb on his back.

My eyes grew heavy and I was on the verge of falling asleep when the doorbell rang. Groggily, I went to the window. It couldn't be Scott, as he'd have his key, and it was unlikely to be Maman, as she let herself in even more freely than Scott. My stomach somersaulted when I saw Michael outside. Still dressed in his shirt and shorts, he shuffled from foot to foot, as though nervous about something. He wasn't going to ask for the chocolate buttons back, was he? He had good cause to look nervous if he were. I'd fight him to the death for them. The thought of wrestling Michael made my stomach flip even more. It had a definite, not unwelcome, impact on my fanny too. Pushing the image from my mind, I went and opened the front door.

'Sorry to just turn up,' Michael said. 'I don't have your number or I'd have called.' He took a smooth stone from his pocket and handed it to me. 'Anna asked me to look after this and I forgot to give it back. Wasn't sure when I'd next be seeing you, so . . .'

'Thank you, that's really kind.' I stood aside. 'Come on in.'

'Thanks.' Michael followed me into the kitchen.

'Would you like a beer?'

'That'd be great, thanks.' Michael looked around. 'Lovely house. It's got so much character.'

I grinned with pride, as I took two bottles of Peroni from my pale blue Smeg fridge. I'd owned the house for four years and still loved it. Surprisingly, given his job, Scott had no interest in décor, so I'd never had to compromise my taste when he'd moved in. Everything, from the pop art wallpaper in the bedroom to the American diner-inspired kitchen had been chosen by me. Scott's personality didn't feature at all in the house. It was all me and Anna. Although, Anna's contribution was mainly large wooden toys and a big pile of crap.

'My place looks more like a gym than a home. Dean's always got his junk out.' Michael grimaced. 'Not his actual junk,' he added quickly. 'We really aren't together.'

I smiled. 'It doesn't matter to me if you're gay or not.'

Michael didn't return my smile. Instead, he stared intensely at me, his eyes searching mine. 'It matters very much to me that you know I'm not.'

My stomach did a seat drop. What was he saying? Why did it matter what I thought? And why was I gazing at his full lips, wondering how they would feel on mine?

'Beer!' I said, realising I was still holding both bottles. I flipped the lids using the bottle opener on the wall – I was wrong: Scott had contributed something – and stepped towards Michael.

Something sharp pierced the sole of my foot, and I shrieked with pain and lurched forward. Almost the entire contents of one of the bottles flew through the air and soaked Michael's shirt. He jumped as the icy liquid seeped through to his skin while I hopped up and down, scattering more beer, this time mostly on me. A small green Lego brick sat innocently on the floor, as though it had played no part in this brutal attack.

'Flipping Lego,' I whimpered, immensely proud of myself for being so restrained. If Michael hadn't been there, I'd definitely have used the other F-word.

'Let me see.' Michael took the bottles and put them on the side, then lowered me onto a kitchen chair. Kneeling down, he lifted my foot to examine it. I pinned my full skirt down around my thighs.

'There's a bruise, but it hasn't broken the skin.' He ran his thumb over the tender spot, and a spasm travelled through my foot and up to the insides of my thighs. I clamped my knees tightly together.

Michael smiled. 'I think you'll survive. Feel free to get a second opinion, though.'

'No, your esteemed opinion's good enough for me.' Our eyes met and we held each other's gaze. My breath caught in my throat and I looked down. My eyes only made it as far as his chest. The beer had left a brown stain on his white shirt with tiny blue anchors. That'd be a sod to get out if we didn't treat it now. 'Let me give your shirt a quick rinse,' I said. 'I'll try and get the beer out.'

'Thanks.' Michael undid his buttons, revealing his

smooth, toned skin inch by tantalising inch. I swallowed hard, knowing I shouldn't stare, but unable to look away. He slipped the shirt off his shoulders and I actually gasped out loud.

'How did you get so fit?' My voice was an octave lower than usual, and breathless. Husky, some might say. Nasally, other, less kind people, would claim. Maman, for example.

Michael shook his head, embarrassed. 'It's living with Dean. I didn't look like this in Syria. Had a full beard, didn't eat properly, never had time to exercise. You wouldn't have given me a second glance.' He held his hands up. 'Not that I expect you to now. Sorry, don't know where that came from.'

Possibly from the way my eyes were roaming up and down his torso with undisguised lust. And now, entirely of their own accord, my hands were reaching out and touching his chest. They started at the base of his neck, ran down over his firm pecs, then trailed slowly down to his navel. I had no control over them and could only watch, with a mixture of mortification at my daring and unadulterated desire.

'Marie,' Michael said huskily. Definitely husky. Even Maman would grant me that one. 'I can't deny this isn't everything I've wanted since we met, but what about your husband?'

I whipped my hands away, heat flooding my cheeks. 'I'm so sorry. Things aren't good with Scott, but that's no excuse. I shouldn't be doing this.' I walked to the sink, unable to look Michael in the face. Not that it was his face I'd been paying much attention to.

He stood behind me and I felt his hands on my upper arms. I trembled beneath his touch and could swear my bosom heaved inside my halterneck bodice. Admittedly, you'd have to look closely to notice, as I hadn't been blessed with Brigitte's charms, but there was definitely a quiver caused by my thumping heart. Goodness. I was behaving like a character in a Barbara Cartland novel. Although, I doubted Lego featured in her stories.

'Why aren't things good with Scott?' Michael asked softly.

'I don't like him anymore.' The words came out before I could filter them. 'He didn't tell me he was getting a vasectomy.' Michael's grip tightened on my arms. 'I've tried to forgive him,' I continued. 'But I can't.' Michael's breath quickened and it brushed the back of my neck. 'If I loved him like I used to, maybe I could move on. But the longer we're together, the more I get to know him, the less I like.' Guilt flooded through me. I shouldn't be saying these things.

Michael loosened his hold on my upper arms and turned me around. His bare chest was millimetres from my face, but I somehow forced myself to look up into his eyes.

'You deserve to be with someone that you like more, not less, as you get to know them,' he said firmly. 'Someone who would never lie or do something so disgustingly deceitful.' He stared at me intently. 'Someone who cares about you more than they care about themselves.'

'Someone who buys me 100 per cent chocolate buttons,' I murmured.

'Yes.' His eyes dropped to my lips. 'You definitely deserve those.'

For a moment I panicked that I had chocolate round my mouth, but before I had time to check, he was kissing me. I moaned with pleasure as his tongue explored mine, and he ran his hands up and down my back.

'Your dress is soaking wet,' he whispered.

'I'd better take it off, then.' I loosened the tie of my halterneck. 'Can you get the zip for me?'

His eyes widened but he didn't need asking twice. Reaching round, he eased the zip down my back and slowly peeled my dress off, his eyes never leaving mine. Only when my dress fell to the floor did he allow himself to look.

'You're so beautiful.' He bent and kissed me, pulling me to him tightly so my breasts squashed against his chest. Our hands roamed up and down one another's backs, then he slid his round to my breasts and massaged them gently, tugging at my nipples playfully.

'I want you so much, Marie,' he said breathlessly.

I undid the button on his fly. 'So do I.'

There was no going back now. I was going to cheat on Scott. I was powerless to resist. Call it animal magnetism, primal instincts, the fact I was a bit of a slag – it was going to happen.

Kissing passionately, I unzipped Michael's shorts and they fell to the floor next to my dress. He was naked underneath, which surprised me. I'd have thought a doctor would view underwear as the more sanitary option. Before I could kill the mood by asking, he lifted me up onto the work surface and wrapped my legs around him. Greedily, I pressed myself against his erection and rotated my hips, gasping at the sensations surging through me.

Michael pulled away. 'I don't have a condom.' His voice was full of regret.

'It's OK. I want a baby.' I pulled his face back to mine and he smiled as we kissed.

Taking him in my hand, I guided him, throwing my head back and crying out with pleasure as he edged slowly in.

'Oh, Michael,' I gasped.

'Marie.' He pulled me tightly to him and kissed me intently. 'Marie.'

The front door banged shut and I jumped.

I was lying on the sofa, the handle of Anna's spade clasped tightly in my hand.

'Hi, babe.' Scott appeared in the doorway. 'Sorry, my last viewing overran.' He frowned down at me. 'You all right?'

'Yes,' I stammered, pushing myself up to sitting. My heart pounded and my face was burning. 'Just had a weird dream.'

'About digging for treasure?' Scott gestured to the spade I was holding. I dropped it guiltily. Thank Christ it was only in my hand.

'Can't remember now.' I swallowed hard. The chocolate button was still in my mouth. I couldn't have been asleep for more than a few minutes. How had Michael and I gone from talking to having sex so quickly? I shook my head. The timescale wasn't what I should be questioning! Why was I dreaming about having sex with him at all?

'Give us a chocolate.' Scott picked up the bag of buttons, tipped his head back and poured a few into his mouth. Instantly, he screwed his face up and spat them into his hand. 'Ugh. What are these?'

'They're too bitter to eat like that.' Annoyed at his lack of respect for my precious dark chocolate, I took the bag back.

'Give them to your mum and aunt,' Scott said. 'They're bitter enough to appreciate them.' He went into the kitchen to wash his hands.

I clenched my own into balls. Brigitte and I were allowed to moan about our mums, but Scott had no right to. It wasn't as though they were rude to his face. Well, not every time. Even so, out of respect to his in-laws, he shouldn't bad-mouth them.

Although I wasn't one to talk. In my dream, my mouth had been worse than bad; it had been downright wicked. Along with the rest of me. My cheeks flushed at the memory. I'd never be able to face Michael again. I'd have to avoid him at Beth's hag do on Saturday and the reception two weeks after that. And sign up to a different doctor's surgery. And stay away from Horsham High Street, the bus and the café opposite work. Their profits were set to plummet.

Racked with guilt, I joined Scott in the kitchen.

'Anna and I had fun today,' I said. 'The three of us should do something like that soon. Go to Bournemouth, maybe.' It was now fortuitous that Scott didn't like Brighton, as I'd never be able to go again in case I saw Michael. I realised I'd better tell Scott we'd seen him, in case Anna mentioned it. 'We bumped into my client with her children and brother,' I said casually. No need to mention that her brother was the doctor that Scott didn't like and had accused me of having an affair with.

My hands trembled as I mopped up the puddle Scott had left by the sink. Behind me, he opened a beer. The sound triggered a montage of images from my dream, starting with me offering Michael a beer and ending with me . . . well, offering him a lot more than that.

'Think I'll go to bed,' I said. 'Sea air wore me out.'

'Mind if I don't come up?' Scott said. 'The doctor needs a night off.'

I froze. 'What?'

'Dr Indiana Jones.' Scott slapped my bottom. 'He'll be back on duty when Elsa's ready.'

'Oh right, yes.' I wrung out the dishcloth and turned to leave. 'Night, then.'

'Not so fast.' Scott grabbed my arm. 'There's something you haven't told me.'

I blinked at him. Had he figured out that I'd spent the day with Michael?

'Christ, you are dozy tonight, aren't you?' Scott said. '*I love you* ring any bells?'

'Sorry.' I affected a dozy face. 'Told you I was tired.' I gave him a quick peck. 'Love you,' I said, before hurrying out of the room and up the stairs into the bathroom.

It was the first time since reaching the 'I love you' stage of our relationship that I hadn't told him that when saying goodnight. Another image from my dream came into my mind. 'I don't like him anymore,' I'd told Michael.

I gave my reflection a stern look. That statement, like the rest of my dream, was fictitious. Admittedly, I didn't like some of Scott's behaviours, but that was an entirely different thing. Yes, it was taking time to overcome the hurt and disappointment following his vasectomy, but that didn't mean I no longer loved Scott.

I stared at my reflection, a sense of unease growing within me. If that was the case, if I did still love Scott, then why had it felt so forced just now when I told him?

Chapter 38

'What time does your film finish?' Brigitte asked Sanjay.

He was dropping us off in Brighton for Beth's hag do, and going for food and to the cinema while we were at the party, then picking us up. He was a gorgeous guy and would do anything for Brigitte. Rumour had it that included in the bedroom. I was prone to believe this particular rumour, as it came directly from the horse's mouth. The word horse had also been used.

'About midnight,' Sanjay said. 'But I can pick you up earlier if you've had enough.'

The three of us laughed. A night out was such a rare treat that there was no way Brigitte and I would leave early. Although, that meant having to avoid Michael for several hours. It wouldn't have been an issue if Beth and James had been having traditionally separate hen and stag dos, but because Beth and her ex had led such separate lives, she and James wanted to start their union with a joint celebration. It was very romantic. And a cunning way of avoiding the usual willy straws.

'I'll message you. Enjoy the film.' Brigitte leant across and kissed Sanjay. I fiddled with the hem of my wiggle dress, while I waited for their smooch to end. It was the green dress I'd made for the date that Scott had cancelled all those weeks ago. At the time I'd been so disappointed. Now, the thought of a date with him filled me with dread. I had no idea what we'd talk about. Knowing he'd expect sex afterwards made it even less appealing. I'd still managed to evade his advances, but I couldn't forever. Not without it driving even more of a wedge between us.

Brigitte and Sanjay eventually stopped snogging and we all got out of the car. Sanjay extended a hand to help me, because my fitted wiggle dress was living up to its name and only allowing me wiggle manoeuvrability.

'Thanks, Sanjay.' I put my arms around him and he hugged me. It was like being wrapped in an enormous duvet. A duvet that was ripped to perfection. 'Really kind of you to do this.' I kissed his cheek, wishing he was coming with us. If I stood behind him, Michael wouldn't be able to see me. My stomach flipped over at the prospect of seeing Michael. Perhaps it would be easier if I pretended he was gay. Although, my dream suggested I'd take some convincing.

Sanjay released me and kissed Brigitte again. 'Don't forget, we're kid-free tonight,' he said with an enormous smile.

She grinned back. 'I'll thank you properly for the lift later, then.'

I hoped they'd remember to drop me home first.

Sanjay left, and Brigitte looked me up and down and whistled. 'Look at you.' I'd teamed my wiggle dress with black strappy sandals and tonged my hair into loose curls.

I giggled. 'Right back atcha.'

Brigitte had also curled her hair, but backcombed it to add volume. She wore a black strapless bodice with faux leather, spray-on trousers. The overall effect was a dark-haired, modern version of Sandy in *Grease*. She looked breathtaking, although her trousers were so tight, I was slightly concerned she'd have a yeast infection by the end of the evening. Brigitte linked her arm through mine and took a step towards the bar where the hag do was taking place.

'Mind if we go somewhere else and have a catch-up first?' I asked.

'Course.'

We went to the nearest bar, ordered a cocktail each and slipped into a booth. Brigitte's trousers were so shiny that she almost slid under the table, but thankfully her buxom boobs lodged themselves on the tabletop and she was able to lever herself up without undue embarrassment. With my less ample bust, I'd have slipped straight under like a toddler down a water chute.

'I'm glad you suggested this,' Brigitte said when she'd composed herself. 'I was worried you were avoiding me.'

I stared into my drink. 'I have been, a bit,' I confessed. 'Needed some time to get my head round the argument the other week.'

I wasn't ready to talk about the vasectomy. She'd tell me to kick Scott out. Actually, she'd go round and kick him out herself, then kick him all the way down the street. Part of me would buy tickets to watch that spectacle, but I had to think of Anna. I didn't want her to go through a divorce and be split between two parents. I knew from experience how horrible that was.

'How do you feel now that you've had time to reflect?' Brigitte asked.

Pretty shitty, was the truth. But as soon as the affection I'd once felt for Scott returned, we'd be fine. All marriages went through blips and this was one of ours. Besides, I had another dilemma to discuss with Brigitte – my dream. We'd been too busy at work to talk, and Scott had been home the past two evenings. He didn't pay much attention to my conversations with Brigitte, but his ears would have pricked up when I relayed how another man had rogered me senseless on our kitchen worktop. Especially, when I was so particular about oiling it with a microfibre cloth every few months to protect it from water damage.

'I'm nervous about seeing Michael,' I said.

'Because you fancy him,' Brigitte said.

'No!' I ignored Brigitte's arched eyebrow. 'Because I had this stupid dream.'

Brigitte grinned. 'An erotic dream?'

'No.' My nose tingled and I sat on my hands so I couldn't rub it.

Brigitte looked disappointed. 'Why are you nervous, then?'

I lowered my voice. 'We had sex in my dream.'

'Can't have been any good if the dream wasn't erotic.'

I gave in. 'OK, it *was* erotic. But that doesn't mean I fancy him. It was some stupid psychological reaction to finding out he's straight. Or because Scott and I haven't done it since the row.' Looking at Brigitte, I realised how much I needed to talk to her. I could do it without mentioning the vasectomy. There'd be no coming back from that. 'Things aren't great with Scott,' I admitted. 'I can't get past the way he reacted. I keep remembering his face when he accused me of cheating and the horrible things he said.' I bit my lip. 'I know he didn't mean it – he was stressed by Liz's vile messages. They'd upset anyone. So why can't I put it behind me and move on?'

Brigitte regarded me thoughtfully. 'Do you want me to say what I honestly think?' I nodded. 'I don't like the way Scott treats you,' she said. 'He always gets his own way. I've lost count of the number of times he's talked you round to his way of thinking. He always does what he wants, when he wants.'

'Does what *Liz* wants,' I corrected. 'He doesn't do anything for himself.'

'What about his curry nights? They're definitely more than once a month.' Brigitte tutted. 'He never helps out around the house or with Anna.'

I fiddled with a beer mat. 'He works hard. He's tired.'

'You work harder than him – practically all night in your busiest weeks of the year – but you do everything else as well.'

'He's under a lot of stress,' I said weakly.

'And you're not?' Brigitte shook her head. 'You make so many allowances. I love that you're thoughtful and kind, but Scott takes advantage of that. Even tonight, Anna's gone to your mum's, so Scott doesn't have the hassle of putting his own daughter to bed.' Brigitte slapped the table. 'The way he behaved when you thought you were pregnant was disgusting. I don't care how stressed he was by those messages. He should never speak to you like that.'

I nodded. 'He was completely out of order, but he's apologised and is back to his usual self.' I grimaced. 'Trouble is, his "usual self" irritates the hell out of me now. All the little things he does, which I've always put up with, make me want to scream.'

'The arse slapping?' Brigitte asked. 'That would wind me up big time.'

I nodded. 'And calling me babe. I hate it.' We stared at each other. 'What am I going to do?' I whispered. 'I don't want us to break up.'

Brigitte exhaled loudly. 'I don't think he deserves you, but if you really want to make it work, then you have to start being honest with him.'

My face grew warm. I wasn't being entirely honest with Brigitte, but one shitshow at a time.

'Tell him when he does something you don't like. Make him help you more.' Brigitte gave me a stern look. 'And don't let him get away with that affair bullshit. He can't say a quick sorry and expect you to forget it.'

She was right. If we got these issues ironed out, then I could move on. But there was something else. It had been nagging away at me for a while now. Before the row even.

I cleared my throat. 'I'm scared.'

Brigitte gripped her cocktail glass so tightly that it was a wonder it didn't shatter. 'Of him?'

I shook my head. 'If he ever talks to me like that again I'll tell him to leave.'

'Good.' Brigitte nudged my drink towards me. 'What, then?'

I picked up my glass and realised my hand was shaking. 'I'm scared that I made a mistake in marrying him.' I took a large mouthful. 'We'd only been together a few months when I fell pregnant. If it wasn't for that, we might not have lasted. Things were great at the time, but new relationships are when all you do is shag. When that initial passion wears off, you need something else, a common interest. Scott and I have Anna, but what else do we have?'

Brigitte gazed at me, her face full of compassion.

'It was crazy to get together so quickly,' I continued. 'I never would have done if I hadn't been thirty-six and ready to have a baby.'

I remembered the thrill of meeting Scott when he'd showed me round the house I now owned. After years of living in a one-bed flat after a failed relationship in my twenties, and saving every penny I could, I was ecstatic when I saw the Victorian terraced house and my offer was accepted. Scott was new to the area, and I'd babbled away about the best bars and restaurants to go to. When I moved in, Scott sent a bouquet of flowers with a note asking if he could take me out to celebrate. He was charming and good-looking. Of course I'd said yes.

Those first few months were a constant high. I was thrilled with the house and how it was taking shape, thanks to the hours I spent painting and sanding and sewing. Sanjay put up shelves and made a window seat for the living room. Another reason I loved him – my carpentry skills were crap at best, potentially lethal at worst. Scott and I saw each other a couple of nights a week and had fun, without any real thought of where it might go, when I discovered I was pregnant.

Scott had been horrified – who wouldn't be? – but after a few weeks, he came around to the idea. It made sense for him to move out of his rented flat and in with me, and he proposed the day Anna was born. Who knew if without her we'd have gone on to get married and have children, or if it would have fizzled out. If I analysed it, there hadn't been any great substance to the relationship. We'd had a laugh and fancied each other. It wasn't a bad basis for a marriage, but it wasn't the best either.

'Having Anna and marrying Scott was the right thing for you at the time,' Brigitte said softly.

I swallowed hard. 'So why doesn't it seem so right now?'

Brigitte hesitated. I could see her wrestling between an

answer that would label Scott a selfish, undeserving wanker, and one that would be kinder. Thankfully, she went for the latter. 'There's a lot going on – work, Liz, Cleo, looking after a child who's three-going-on-thirteen, trying for a baby, not trying for a baby . . .' My throat tightened. 'It's too much. It'll be better with Scott when things calm down and you've put some boundaries in place.'

I nodded. She was right. I was bound to get irritated when I was on overload. Things would be fine when wedding season eased in a few weeks.

'Thank you,' I said.

Brigitte winked. 'Now, tell me about this dream.'

Over another cocktail, I told Brigitte the full details, which had a much-needed therapeutic result. After we'd giggled about my overly detailed imagination – 'Think of what you could have got up to if you hadn't wasted time treading on Lego . . .' – we finished our drinks and made our way to the hag do.

The cocktails had relaxed me, so I didn't feel too nervous walking in, especially as I couldn't see Michael. Brigitte and I found Beth and were welcomed with a huge hug. She was wearing the obligatory bride-to-be sash and tiara. As was James, although the word 'bride' had been crossed out and replaced with 'groom'. Grinning from ear to ear, he couldn't take his eyes off Beth, who looked stunning in a blue off-the-shoulder dress.

'Come and dance,' she said, beckoning us to the dance floor.

'I'll get a drink first.' I loved dancing but it took more than two cocktails to give me the courage to do it in public. Brigitte had no such inhibitions and was on the floor within seconds, her arms in the air, her hips twirling an imaginary hula hoop. She was taking the 'it don't count if the booty ain't out' motto very seriously.

The bar was rammed, so I resigned myself to a long wait. One of the bartenders was creating my much-loved espresso martini. I watched with longing as she poured the liquid into two glasses and topped each with three coffee beans. To my surprise, she placed them in front of me.

'From the gentleman over there,' she said.

I looked across to where she was pointing. Michael held up a bottle of beer in greeting and smiled. My stomach somersaulted. Oh no.

Chapter 39

Michael gestured with his head to a corner of the room. I hesitated. I was supposed to be avoiding him. But he didn't know about my stupid dream and it wasn't as if I planned to attempt a re-enactment. It'd be rude not to say thank you after he'd gone to the trouble of getting me and Brigitte drinks. I didn't have to spend the entire evening with him.

Clutching our cocktails as protectively as if they were newborn babies, I edged around the dance floor and made my way to Michael. He'd secured a table with two bar stools and helped me with the drinks when I reached him.

'Sorry,' he said. 'Should have got Brigitte's delivered to me.'

'It's fine.' I held my glass up to show that not a single drop had been spilt. 'Not my first time.'

Michael raised his bottle. 'Handled like a pro.'

We smiled and sipped our drinks. Why had I worried? We were just two adults talking. All very appropriate. No awkwardness. No flirting. No wondering if he was commando beneath his dark blue jeans, as he had been in my dream.

Heat flooded my cheeks. That was *not* very appropriate. I scanned the room for a subject that was. Brigitte's dancing definitely didn't qualify. She seemed to be pole dancing without a pole and her jiggling bosom was so spectacular that it warranted its own *Carry On* film.

'Beth looks like she's having a good time,' I said, finding a safe topic. Beth and James were talking, their heads together, their smiles contagious. They looked exactly how a couple about to marry should look: excited, radiant and randy. 'James seems nice,' I added.

Michael nodded. 'He's great. Always a relief when you

like your in-laws. Must be horrible spending Christmas with people that you'd rather avoid.'

'It definitely has its challenges,' I said.

The music grew louder and Michael leant closer. 'Scott's family?'

'No, he doesn't have any. I was talking about my mum and aunt.'

We both laughed.

'I'm sure she's great, despite her quirks,' Michael said.

I winced. 'She hasn't been to see you about those too, has she?'

A tall, extremely good-looking man made his way towards us. He was the same height as Michael, with one of those upside-down triangular bodies that comes from many, many hours of disciplined weight training. I didn't think it was possible for another human being to have wider shoulders than Sanjay, but this man made Sanjay look as though he'd merely borrowed Joan Collins's shoulder pads.

'All right, mate?' the very attractive man said to Michael, giving me an inquisitive smile.

I smiled nervously back. He was too sculpted and handsome for me to be worthy of being addressed.

Michael handed the man a beer. 'Dean, this is Marie. Marie, this is Dean.'

Of course. The personal trainer, who used to be a doctor. An unusual blend of brains and brawn. Although Michael was brawn enough for me, and brainy too. My cheeks grew warm. What had that stupid dream done to me? I was confusing reality with fantasy. If this kept up, I'd have to see a doctor. Michael smiled and I swallowed hard. Not this doctor, though.

'Lovely to meet you, Marie,' Dean said. 'I hear you're to thank for Beth's wedding dress.'

'I hear you're to thank for Michael's physique,' I replied, then immediately wanted to die. Why did I say that? I may as well have announced that I thought Michael was hot. Which I didn't. I *really* didn't.

'That's right.' Dean playfully squeezed Michael's bicep. 'All thanks to me.' He winked. 'Looks like you work out too. Do you swim?'

Bloody wide shoulders. 'No, I lug a three-year-old around.'

Dean smiled, then nudged Michael. 'Know who she is?' he asked, nodding towards the dance floor.

'That's Marie's cousin, Brigitte,' Michael said. 'Their parents are both identical twins, so Marie and Brigitte are genetically as close as sisters.'

Dean nodded politely. He clearly had an interest in Brigitte's relations, but the Bill Clinton variety, not those involving her family tree.

'She's married,' I said, before Dean got his hopes up. Although, as replacements for Sanjay went, Dean looked as though he'd be handy for future carpentry jobs. He'd only have to look at a nail and it would embed itself into a wall with more force than a power tool could ever hope to harness.

Dean scanned the dance floor. 'Got any other cousins? Good looks clearly run in the family.'

I felt myself blush. Was it my imagination or was Michael nodding? 'No, just us,' I said.

'Shame.' Dean gestured to Michael's beer. 'Same again?'

'Please. And two espresso martinis. Decaf,' he added pointedly, grinning at me.

I swallowed my smile and turned to Dean. 'Please don't. They're expensive and Brigitte hasn't even had hers yet.'

Dean waved a hand. 'It's a pleasure,' he said. 'You can buy me a beer later.'

'Thank you. That's really kind.' I raised my glass, only to discover it was empty. I'd made fast work of that.

Michael swapped my empty glass for Brigitte's full one. 'So, what did you think of my boyfriend?' His chuckle turned into a grimace. 'Sorry, too hideous to think about. If you saw Dean neck a raw-egg smoothie you'd understand.'

I sipped Brigitte's cocktail. 'Think I'll stick with this.'

Michael swigged from his bottle. 'Which series of *Game of Thrones* are you up to?'

'That reminds me!' I exclaimed. 'You said you fancied Sean Bean in *Lady Chatterley's Lover*.'

Michael spluttered. 'I wanted to be Sean Bean, not be with him. He spent the whole series shagging Joely Richardson. At fifteen, that's pretty much all I wanted to do too.'

I giggled. 'So you weren't devoting every waking moment to studying medicine?'

'Many waking hours were devoted to biology of a kind, but not one that'd benefit my future career.'

We laughed, and our eyes locked for a significant moment before I looked away. I cleared my throat. We shouldn't be sharing a moment. Especially not when talking about his teenage wanking habits.

'Any more funny patient stories to tell?' I asked, changing the subject. 'Anonymously, of course.'

'No.' Michael held his hands up. 'I feel bad that I told you about the burnt balls. It was very unprofessional.'

We looked at each other and burst out laughing. Anyone who didn't find the words 'burnt balls' hilarious was dead inside.

'When Anna first saw Scott naked, she said "Ooh, a tail."' I wasn't sure why that story had sprung to mind when discussing amusing genitals.

Michael frowned. 'A snail?'

Laughter exploded out of me. 'A tail, not a snail.'

Michael chuckled into his beer. 'Thank God for that.'

I wiped a tear from my eye. 'I wouldn't have married him if it had resembled a snail.' I giggled. 'It would have been me needing Viagra, not Scott.'

Michael raised his eyebrows.

I smiled. 'It's OK, you don't need to worry about patient confidentiality.'

Michael shook his head, seeming genuinely perplexed. He was good.

'Scott's Viagra.' I giggled. 'Don't know why I'm laughing. I was so insulted when you told me he was taking it because of my age.'

Michael frowned. 'I never—'

'Medically geriatric, you called me.' I clutched my side. 'Said forty was too old to have a baby.'

Michael shook his head. 'I wouldn't have said that, because it's not true. If there aren't complications or health issues, it's very possible to conceive when you're forty.'

'Unless your husband's had a vasectomy.' I guffawed. 'Not much chance of it then.' I bent over, great bellows of laughter exploding from me. I clutched my mouth to hold it in, but the laughter kept coming, my whole body convulsing with it.

'How much has she had?' I heard someone say.

'*What* has she had?' came the reply.

Tears streamed down my face, as I sank to my knees. Why was I laughing? This wasn't funny. Nothing was funny. Everything was shit.

Michael took my hand. I hadn't noticed him crouch down. 'Take deep breaths through your nose,' he said.

I tried, but the laughter was controlling me. It wouldn't let me breathe properly. I gripped his hand tightly, panic rising. Why couldn't I stop laughing? What was happening to me?

'You're having an anxiety attack,' Michael said, as though reading my mind. 'Don't worry, it'll pass.' His fingers closed around mine and he placed his other hand on my back. It felt warm, comforting, secure. 'I need you to close your mouth, and breathe in and out of your nose,' he said gently. 'Bite the inside of your cheek if that helps, but not too hard.' I did as he said. Laughter was still bubbling out of me, but not as intensely as before. 'I'm going to breathe with you. Remember, through your nose, not your mouth. Focus on my words.' I listened to his soft, melodic voice and followed his counting, inhaling and exhaling as instructed.

I didn't know how long we crouched together on the

floor, his arm around me, shielding me from the hustle and bustle of the bar, his other hand holding mine. But it must have been a while. Long enough for my tears of maniacal laughter to turn to tears of heart-wrenching grief.

Chapter 40

'Let's get some fresh air,' Michael said.

I let him ease me up to standing and lead me out of the bar to an outside table. I took a tissue from my bag and blew my nose, then wiped my tears away. Not very hygienic to use the same tissue for both actions – Scott would have been retching – but Michael seemed unfazed. Given the sights he must have seen over the years – Maman's gammy toe for one – a bit of snot was nothing.

I tucked the soiled tissue back in my bag. 'Sorry. Not sure what happened back there.'

'Don't apologise,' Michael said. 'Panic attacks aren't within your control.'

'I wasn't panicking, though. We were having fun. I was laughing.' But then I hadn't been able to stop. I shuddered at the memory of how powerless I'd been.

'Anxiety manifests itself in many forms,' Michael said. 'Laughter is often the brain's way of avoiding a trauma. It tries to fool you into feeling better.'

'I feel like a fool.' I winced, recalling my helplessness.

'You mustn't. It's nothing to be ashamed of.' He looked down at his hands. 'Panic or anxiety attacks tend to be triggered by something.' His eyes flicked up to mine. 'Scott's vasectomy seems to be what triggered yours.'

My cheeks burnt. I hated that Michael knew. It was my shameful secret and I didn't want anyone else to know.

'You didn't come to the appointment with him,' he said quietly.

I swallowed hard. 'Did you do the surgery?' The thought of Michael performing the vasectomy made it even worse.

'No.' Michael also sounded relieved. 'It's a small procedure, rather than an operation. He'd have had it done at the sexual health clinic.'

Brigitte had seen Scott on the industrial estate where the clinic was. He'd told me he had a physio appointment.

'His referral appointment was with my colleague, a junior doctor,' Michael said. 'I only knew because she asked my advice. Usually, when a man's in a relationship, his partner accompanies him. Scott said it wasn't necessary for you to be there.'

Of course he had. My knowing it was even happening wasn't necessary in his eyes.

'It's not a legal requirement,' Michael continued. 'We can't force the issue; we can only recommend it. Scott was adamant you didn't need to come, but it didn't sit right with me.' He looked at me questioningly. 'You'd told me you hoped to be pregnant soon. When I saw you with Scott and realised you were married, it didn't make sense.' He shifted in his chair. 'That's why I went against my oath and tried to talk to you at the studio. To make sure you were comfortable with it.'

So that's what he'd been intimating. Not that Scott shouldn't be needing Viagra at his age, or that I was too old to have children. The complete opposite – that I was still young enough. I hadn't deciphered the clues. But why would I? The idea of Scott having the snip was nowhere on my radar.

'I need to apologise about something else as well.' Michael looked genuinely pained. 'When we went for lunch, I jokingly said that if I didn't know better, I'd think you were pregnant. I shouldn't have said that. It was unprofessional and insensitive, and I've felt terrible ever since.' He reached across as though to take my hand, then thought better of it. 'My only consolation was that you seemed happy. I assumed you couldn't have any regrets about the vasectomy or you wouldn't have been.'

I had been happy. I'd been overjoyed. My stomach twisted

with the painful memory of thinking I was pregnant, then having that hope taken away from me in the cruellest way possible.

Michael gestured towards the bar. 'Seeing your reaction in there makes me worry that you do regret it.' He rested a hand lightly on my arm. 'You don't have to tell me anything; it's none of my business. But as a concerned friend, as someone who cares about you . . . Are you all right?'

No, I wasn't all right. I had to tell someone or it'd destroy me.

'I didn't know about the vasectomy.' The words burst out of me. Michael's eyes widened in shock. 'I was desperate for another baby. After years of saying we had to wait for the right time, he'd at last said we could start trying.' My voice cracked. 'But it was because he knew we *couldn't* have one.'

Michael wrapped his arms around me. 'I'm so sorry.' He sounded dazed. 'Can't believe he did that to you.'

I let him rock me back and forth. Numbly, I watched people in the bar, chatting, laughing and dancing. Each of them encased in their own happy bubble, oblivious to the fact mine had burst.

'Easy, tiger,' Dean boomed behind me.

Michael and I leapt apart.

'Marie's not feeling well,' Michael said. 'I was checking she's OK.'

Dean winked at me, as he placed a beer and two espresso martinis on the table. 'I used to be a doctor too, if you want a second opinion.'

Michael shook his head at him and Dean mouthed 'sorry'.

'Ooh, are those our drinks?' Brigitte appeared at our table, her cheeks flushed from dancing. 'Thank you whoever bought them.'

'You're welcome,' Dean said, with a little bow. 'You might be able to have both. Your cousin's not feeling well.'

Brigitte had been on the brink of full-on flirt mode, but abandoned that immediately when she saw my face. 'You look terrible. Have you been doing shots?'

'No.' I hesitated, embarrassed to explain what had happened and dreading telling her why.

'She had a panic attack,' Michael said calmly. 'We came outside to get some fresh air.'

'Oh, Marie.' Brigitte sat down on the other side of me and took my hand. 'You should have come and got me. Are you OK now?'

I nodded. 'Michael talked me through it.'

Brigitte shot him a grateful smile. 'Where did it come from? You've never had one before.'

'No.' I stared at the table, my face hot.

Michael stood up. 'We'll go inside. Give you some space.' Picking up his beer, he nodded to Dean and the two of them headed back to the bar. It was testament to Brigitte's concern for me that she didn't ogle Dean's chiselled derrière as he walked away.

'Did something happen with Michael?' she asked. 'Was he inappropriate?'

'No!'

She raised one eyebrow. 'Were you?'

I almost laughed. If only that was it.

'It's Scott.' I released a shaky breath. 'He's had a vasectomy.'

Brigitte shook her head. 'Sorry, say that again. It sounded like you said "vasectomy".'

I pressed my lips together and nodded.

'But you want a baby.' Brigitte was looking at me as though I were insane. 'Why have you done that?'

'*I* haven't,' I said shakily. 'He did it without telling me.'

Brigitte stared at me in disbelief. 'He fucking what?'

'The weekend we went to Heavenly Hideaway. He told me he had a groin strain from playing football.' I blinked away angry tears. 'I nursed him back to health.'

Brigitte's hands tightened into fists. I winced and she loosened her grip on the one holding mine. 'You had no idea?'

I shook my head. 'I honestly thought we were trying for a baby.'

'That absolute fucker,' she growled. 'Why didn't you tell me?'

I grimaced. 'I knew you'd hate Scott for it.'

'You're right. I do hate him.' Her body was trembling with rage. 'Why did he do it?'

'For Anna. I was neglecting her. She thinks I care more about my work than her.' Guilt crept in. 'If we had another baby, she'd have been even more left out.'

'He's had a vasectomy behind your back, and convinced you that you're a bad mum and that having another baby would make you even worse?' Brigitte's face was contorted with anger. 'This is gaslighting.'

I shook my head. 'Since Scott told me, I've focused on Anna completely and she's really happy. We can see it.'

'Since *Scott* told you,' Brigitte emphasised. 'Not Anna.'

'But—'

'No,' Brigitte said sharply. 'If Anna wasn't happy, she'd tell you. She's got enough of our mums in her for that.'

That was true. Anna complained daily about the time I hadn't allowed her inside the lion enclosure at the safari park.

'He's even more of a shit than I realised.' Brigitte shook with anger. 'How could he do this to you?'

'He thought he was doing the best thing for the family,' I said, but I didn't sound convinced.

'The only person he does the best thing for is himself.' Brigitte's eyes filled with tears, which filled me with alarm. She never cried, unlike me, who welled up at everything from *News at Ten* to *Bake Off*. 'I already thought he treated you badly, but this is way beyond that.' She blinked hard. 'Please don't stay with him. He's a toxic, gaslighting fucker and you need to get him out of your life.'

I pressed my fingertips to my eyes. Guilt ripped through me at the thought of how emotionally distressing a divorce would be for Anna, but the alternative was far more upsetting. I couldn't go back to exchanging pleasantries with Scott every day, sitting side-by-side on the sofa watching

Game of Thrones, mopping up that bloody puddle by the sink, sharing a bed. The thought of him touching me made me want to rip my skin from my body. And that was never a good sign.

I looked up. Brigitte was staring at me, her hands clasped together, mascara smudged beneath her eyes.

'Anna's the most important person in all of this,' I said. 'But I can't stay with Scott, not even for her.'

'Thank God.' Brigitte threw her arms around me. 'You're so much better off without him.'

I nodded glumly. 'When shall I tell him?'

'The sooner, the better.' Brigitte picked our glasses up and handed me mine. 'If you ring him now, he'll be gone by the time you get home.'

'I can't do that. I owe it to him to tell him face-to-face.'

Brigitte's eyes flashed. 'After what he's done to you, you don't owe him anything.'

Her anger was contagious. Scott's vasectomy, and then him convincing me I was a bad mum, stung afresh. I took a large mouthful of espresso martini. 'Fuck him. I'm doing it.'

Scott's phone rang for so long that I thought I was going to have to end our marriage with a voicemail, but eventually he answered, sounding slightly breathless.

'Has something happened?' he asked.

I was taken aback by his astuteness. 'How did you know?'

'You never ring when I'm out.' It was true, I didn't. And he didn't ring me. Further proof of how shit our relationship was. 'Is Anna all right?' he asked.

'Yes.' I paused, replaying his words. 'Did you say you're out? I thought you were having a night in.'

'Change of plan. Andy invited a few of us over to watch the game.'

'He's at his friend's,' I mouthed to Brigitte, wondering whether I should wait till he was somewhere private.

'He's got somewhere to stay, then,' she mouthed back. Good point.

'So why did you ring?' he asked.

I sat up tall. I could do this. 'I can't get over the vasectomy,' I said bluntly. 'I've tried to forgive and forget, but it's gone beyond that.' Brigitte nodded encouragingly. 'I don't want to be with you anymore.'

'Babe?' Scott sounded confused. 'What are you saying?'

My heart pounded. 'Our marriage is over. Sorry.'

There was a long pause down the phone, then: 'Have you been drinking?'

'Yes.' I held my head up high. 'Why shouldn't I drink? It's not as if I'm pregnant.'

Brigitte looked as though she might burst with pride.

Scott winced. 'Things always seem worse after a few drinks. Let's sit down and talk.'

The thought filled me with dread. 'There's no point. I'm not going to change my mind.'

'This is Brigitte's doing, isn't it?' Scott exhaled loudly. 'She's turned you against me.'

'No.' I gritted my teeth. 'You did that by lying to me in the cruellest way imaginable.'

'You know why, though, babe. It was for Anna.'

Bringing Anna into it fuelled my hatred. 'You made me believe I was neglecting her.'

Scott inhaled sharply. 'You're twisting my words. I never said neglected – that's come from you.' He paused and I scrambled to recall our conversation. Maybe he hadn't said that exactly, but it's what he'd implied. 'You're a fantastic mum,' he said. 'Doesn't matter how much you used to work – you're prioritising Anna now and she's happy. That's what counts, isn't it?'

'Of course,' I said. 'But—'

'And I'm home more now,' he continued. 'Which is what you've wanted the whole time we've been together. Yes?'

I massaged my temples, suddenly confused. 'Yes,' was the only answer I could give.

'So, what's the problem?' he asked softly.

I hesitated. What was the problem again?

'Let's go home and talk about this,' he said. 'Don't throw away the past four years in a drunken phone call.' When he put it like that, it did seem I was being a little hasty. 'We owe it to Anna,' he whispered. 'You want to do what's best for her, don't you?' He was right. We should talk – for Anna's sake. 'Where are you?' he asked.

'At The Mesmerist.'

Brigitte frantically criss-crossed her hands.

'I'll come and get you,' Scott said.

The thought of a thirty-minute car journey, followed by a lengthy discussion and bed, filled me with dread. As though snapping out of a trance, I remembered that I didn't want to be anywhere near him.

'Sanjay's picking us up,' I said. 'You don't need to drive out. We'll talk tomorrow.'

'I'm at Andy's, remember? I'll be there in about ten minutes.'

He hung up and I looked at Brigitte with horror. 'He's coming to get me in ten minutes.'

Chapter 41

'Sanjay can be here quicker than that.' Brigitte took her phone from her bag. 'Shit, it's gone to voicemail,' she said a minute later. 'I'll message him. Let's wait inside.'

Downing our drinks – even in an emergency, we weren't prepared to waste them – we hurried back into the bar.

'What happened?' Brigitte asked. 'One minute you were telling him it was over, the next you were telling him where we are.'

'I don't know.' I shook my head. 'Everything he said made more sense than what I was saying. I started to think I was being unreasonable, till he said he'd pick me up and I knew I didn't want that.'

I realised with a jolt that Brigitte's earlier accusation was spot on. He *was* gaslighting me. He'd just done it again. Manipulated the conversation so that I doubted my thoughts, even my feelings. And now he was coming to get me.

Brigitte held up her phone. 'Sanjay's just replied. We'll tell Scott together that he's not taking you home.'

'Yay, you're still here.' Beth appeared, her bride-to-be sash hanging off her shoulder and a shot in each hand.

'We are, but we're about to go. Sorry.'

Beth pulled a sad face and thrust the shots at us. 'Have a drink before you go. People keep buying them for me and I can't have any more.'

The waft of peach schnapps turned my stomach. 'No thanks. It'll make me sick.' Brigitte knocked hers back without any such concerns.

'You're sick?' Beth looked around wildly. 'Where's Michael? He can give you a once-over.'

Brigitte nudged me with her elbow and I ignored her. 'Thanks for inviting us,' I said, shouting over the music. 'You picked a great spot.'

'Scott's picking you up?' Beth smiled broadly. 'I need to meet this amazing man who fights so hard to see his children.'

'No, he—'

'Do you think he'd have a word with my ex?' Beth swayed in her heels. 'Tell him he can't just abandon his kids because his new wife doesn't want them around.'

'You're better off without him,' Brigitte said.

She'd just said the same to me about Scott. Which reminded me, we needed to plan our exit strategy before he arrived.

'Shall we go to the loo before we leave?'

Brigitte nodded. 'Definitely.'

We said goodbye again, several times – and Brigitte downed the other shot at Beth's insistence – and then we made our way through the throng towards the ladies. The queue snaked out of the door and along one wall of the bar.

'Let's try the gents.' Brigitte pointed me in the opposite direction.

Usually, I'd prefer to queue than suffer the squalor of the men's toilets, but my evening had already been shat on. What did it matter if my shoes were too.

We'd almost got there, when Beth popped up again. 'Don't let me drink any more. I'm so pissed, I thought I saw my bastard ex-husband.' She hiccupped. 'Rick was completely bald, though. This guy had loads of hair, so it couldn't be him, could it?'

Brigitte and I shook our heads in unison.

Beth smiled with relief. 'So glad you decided to stay. Did Michael make you better?'

'Did I make who better?' Michael appeared beside us, and Beth slumped against him and closed her eyes.

'Sorry, but I really need the loo,' Brigitte said. 'I'll be back in two minutes.' She darted off, leaving me with Michael and a comatose Beth.

'How are you?' he asked.

'I've had better nights, but I'll be OK.' I gave a small smile, embarrassed by everything he'd witnessed. 'Thank you for earlier. That was above and beyond the call of duty. I'm sorry for involving you.'

'Don't be. That's what friends are for.' Our eyes met. His, full of compassion and kindness. Mine, probably bloodshot and full of mascara. He held my gaze. I swallowed hard, my inner turmoil subsiding and being replaced with a different feeling entirely.

'There you are.' Scott's voice in my ear made me jump and I leant away, not wanting to be anywhere near him. Scott noticed Michael. 'What's he doing here?'

That's why Scott had been so against me befriending Michael. Because he knew about his vasectomy.

'It's his sister's party,' I said, tearing my eyes away from Michael's kind, concerned, handsome face to look at Scott. Scott, who was staring at Michael, seemed like a weasel in comparison. Or a stoat. Maybe a ferret. One of the creatures from that rat-like family. His eyes had widened to comical proportions, while his head seemed to shrink into his body.

He took my hand. 'Let's go.' I jerked forward, as he stepped away, pulling me with him.

'No.' I pulled my hand out of his and wiped it on my dress.

'I mean it,' Scott hissed.

'She doesn't have to go if she doesn't want to.' Michael stepped forward and Beth jolted awake. She blinked and looked around, as though wondering where she was, then did a double take at me and Scott. Her mouth dropped open and she staggered forward.

'It *is* you, isn't it?' she gasped.

The colour drained from Scott's face.

'How dare you.' Beth's hand went to her throat. 'How fucking dare you show up at my party after ignoring me and the kids for years?'

Scott grabbed my wrist and pulled me towards the door.

I dug my heels into the ground. 'What's going on? Do you know Beth?'

Scott didn't answer, but quickened his pace, dragging me along.

I tried to prise my arm free, but he had too tight a grip. 'Stop,' I yelled.

'The lady said stop.' The bouncer at the door stepped in front of Scott.

'Thank you,' I said, wrenching myself free. The bouncer ushered Scott outside and I turned back to where Beth and Michael stood. Beth was still clasping her throat, her eyes wide. Michael's face was a mixture of shock and outrage.

Brigitte returned from the toilet and looked between the three of us. 'What's happened?' she asked.

'Why was Rick here?' Beth's earlier tipsiness had gone in an instant, as had her friendly demeanour. 'How do you know him?'

I shook my head. 'I don't. That was Scott.'

Beth's eyes narrowed. 'Scott? Your husband?'

'Yes,' I said, a feeling of unease growing within me.

Beth whimpered. 'What sort of sick game are you playing?'

I looked to Brigitte for help. She put her hand on Beth's shoulder. 'What's going on?'

Beth looked at me with such hatred that I froze, unable to breathe even. 'You tell me,' she said. 'You're the one married to my ex-husband.'

Chapter 42

I was too stunned to speak.

'Scott and Rick are the same person?' Michael looked dubious. 'How is that possible?'

Beth was staring daggers at me. 'I don't know, but it is.'

'Are you sure?' Michael asked.

Beth nodded slowly, not taking her eyes off me. 'Don't know where the hair came from, but the rest is definitely him.'

'Right.' Michael's face was thunder. 'He and I are going to talk.' He strode towards the door, collecting Dean en route.

Beth looked at me with such contempt that it chilled me to the bone. 'How could you stop him seeing his own kids?'

I gasped. 'I don't. Scott sees his children all the time.'

'*Rick*,' Beth spat, 'hasn't seen Henry and Izzy for years.'

My head swam. None of this made any sense.

Brigitte put her hands up. 'Marie's telling the truth,' she said. 'She's desperate to meet her stepchildren, but Scott's ex-wife won't let her.' She peered out of the window, trying to spot Scott through the throng of customers. 'Is it possible Rick and Scott look very similar? You said Rick was bald.'

Beth crossed her arms. 'I was with him for ten years. It's definitely him.'

I wanted to believe she was mistaken . . . It was possible: she hadn't seen Rick since Izzy was a baby, she'd been drinking, it was dark in the bar. But the gnawing feeling in my stomach was growing. Scott's birth name, the name he'd changed because he didn't want any connection with the father who'd cheated on his mother, was Richard Clark. It could be shortened to Rick. Beth used her maiden name, so I'd never have been able to find her when tracking down Liz Clarks. But that didn't explain why her name was Beth, not Liz.

Beth, Liz. Liz, Beth. The truth had been staring me in the face all along.

'Beth,' I said shakily. 'Short for Elizabeth?'

She gave an abrupt nod.

'Did Rick call you Liz?'

Beth grimaced. 'He tried to, but I hated it. So he called me babe instead. Wasn't much better.'

Brigitte and I exchanged a horrified look.

'And Henry and Izzy?' I asked.

'Izzy's short for Isabella. Rick insisted on calling her Bella and nicknamed Henry, Harry.' Her face hardened. 'Not that he calls them anything now, of course. They never hear from him, because of you.'

I shook my head manically. 'Scott visits his children – Harry and Bella – all the time. His ex – Liz Clark – won't let me, or Anna, meet them. But that doesn't make sense if . . . if you're Liz Clark.'

'I'm not Liz Clark.' Beth pursed her lips. 'Suppose I would have been if I'd taken his surname and nickname for me.'

'What about the abusive messages you sent him?' Brigitte asked. 'They were so bad that Marie phoned the police.'

'They weren't from me,' Beth said flatly. 'Wouldn't waste my time. Not that I have his number. That's how little contact he has with his children.'

My head pounded as I tried to make sense of this senseless situation. Beth was the polar opposite of the woman Scott had led me to believe Liz was. And why did she say Scott never saw the children, when he was with them all the time? Unless . . . My blood went cold. Unless Scott was lying about everything.

I felt as though I'd been punched in the stomach.

'He lied about seeing them.' I looked at Beth and Brigitte helplessly. 'It's the only explanation.'

'You never suspected anything?' Beth didn't look convinced. 'You've been with him all these years and didn't think it odd he didn't bring his kids round?'

'I told you when we were away that I was desperate to meet them. He always had some reason from Liz that meant we couldn't.' Shame oozed from my every pore. How could I have been so gullible? So willing to accept every lie he told me. What else had he lied about? I scanned my memory for details Beth had revealed about her ex and landed on one.

'Scott told me he and Liz broke up because she had an affair, but you said Rick cheated on you.' My voice was hoarse and I cleared my throat. 'I think I know the answer to this question, but—'

'He said I cheated on him?' Beth exhaled loudly. 'Izzy was just a few months old. It was a difficult birth. I wasn't ready emotionally or physically to have sex with Rick, let alone someone else.' She tutted. 'He didn't have the same problem.'

My head spun. There was too much to take in. Beth was Liz. Scott had lied about who she was. He'd lied about his vasectomy. He'd lied about seeing his children. So where was he when he went out? What lies was he up to then?

'Beth.' James came over and Beth leant into him.

'Take me away from this madness,' she murmured.

James, completely oblivious, smiled at her fondly. 'Just two weeks to go, then I'll take you to Barbados.' He nodded towards the window. 'What's going on outside? Your brother's talking to some bloke. Looks a bit heated.'

We all looked over to see Scott, with his back pressed up against his car. Dean stood with his arms crossed tightly across his chest and Michael was talking animatedly.

'It must be taking all their self-restraint not to punch

him,' Beth said to James. 'You know how much they hate Rick for what he did to me.'

'Not sure it comes close to how much I hate him,' Brigitte muttered.

James registered Beth's words. 'That's Rick?' He handed her his beer. 'If they won't hit him, I will.'

Beth put a hand on his arm. 'Don't you get involved too. They can handle it.'

James frowned, but respected her enough to listen. He couldn't be more different from Scott, who didn't listen to anyone.

I bit my lip, wondering what Michael was saying to Scott. As we watched, Sanjay approached Scott's car.

'Shit. I don't want Sanjay to get involved.' Brigitte hurried to the door and I followed, aware of Beth and James behind us.

Sanjay reached the three men and put his hands up. 'Don't know what's going on, but I'm sure we can resolve this like gentlemen,' he said calmly.

'Deck them, Sanj,' Scott shouted. 'They're trying to steal my car.'

Michael and Dean looked at each other in surprise and Scott seized the opportunity to throw a punch, launching himself forward so his fist landed squarely on Michael's jaw.

'Get the other one,' he shrieked to Sanjay, shunting Michael with his shoulder so that he staggered back, as he scrabbled for the car door.

Sanjay stepped towards Dean, balling his hands into fists and hunching his shoulders, ready to tackle him. Dean mirrored his stance.

I ran over and wedged myself between the two men. 'Scott's lying,' I said to Sanjay. 'You don't need to defend him.' I turned to Dean. 'This is Brigitte's husband. He's got nothing to do with it.'

'Oh, sorry, mate.' They straightened up and shook hands,

as though each apologising for taking the last protein shake, rather than preparing to be locked in combat.

There was a clatter, followed by the words, 'Fuck, fuck, fuck,' as Scott dropped his car keys. Kneeling on the pavement, he felt under the car for them.

Michael stood with Beth and James, his back to me. Beth was dabbing his chin with a tissue.

'Michael?' I said. 'Are you all right?'

He turned around and I winced. Blood dripped onto his shirt from a deep cut on his chin.

'Bastard had a key in his hand.' Michael pressed the tissue to his chin. 'I was only talking to him. Telling him he had to stop avoiding the solicitor and pay the child maintenance he owes.'

I took a clean tissue from my bag. The one Michael held was already drenched with blood. 'I'm so sorry.'

'He's the one who should be sorry,' Michael said gruffly, balling the first tissue in his fist and replacing it with the one I handed him. 'The way he treated Beth and the kids, and now you. All those lies . . .' He shook his head. 'I've been trying to get hold of him to pay what he's been owing for years. Can't believe I'd met him and had no idea.'

'I can't believe I married him.' I shuddered at the thought of being with this horrible, horrible excuse for a human being.

'Rick?' Beth walked over to Scott. He'd managed to locate his keys and was fumbling with the lock. 'Where did all that hair come from?'

Scott self-consciously smoothed his second crown down.

'Plugs,' Brigitte squealed. Scott glared at her. 'Told you he'd had plugs,' she whispered to me.

'Is that what you spent the child maintenance on?' Beth snapped.

'I'll backdate the payments. Already told your brother I would.'

'What about Henry and Izzy?' Beth's voice shook. 'Aren't

you going to ask how they are? Don't you want to see them?'

'Course I do.' Scott dropped his keys again and swore. 'I'll be in touch. Sort something out.'

Beth gave him a look of contempt. 'You know what, Rick – or Scott, or whatever your name is. Don't bother. You don't deserve to see them. They're better off without you.'

Scott pressed his lips together but didn't respond.

The bar door swung open behind us and the bouncer sauntered over. 'Everything OK?' he asked.

'Where were you five minutes ago when my brother was getting punched?' Beth snapped.

He held up his mobile phone. 'Got everything on here if you want to report him to the police for assault.'

'Can you forward that video to me?' Brigitte asked.

I gave her a questioning look, as she told the bouncer her number. Her phone beeped. 'Just in case Scott tries denying this too,' she said.

Beth walked back to James and Michael, and Scott swooped down on his keys. He opened the car door and extended a hand in my direction. 'Come on, babe. Let's go home.'

Out of the corner of my eye I saw Michael press another tissue to his chin, which was still pouring with blood. James was cradling Beth, who was sobbing into his chest. This was supposed to be a night of celebration for them. Instead, they were reeling from the shock of Scott's appearance. His lies and duplicity had cost me these new friends, but that was nothing compared with the anguish he'd caused them. Worst of all, Michael had been physically assaulted by him.

I walked up to Scott and he smiled at me.

I'd always loved his smile. One flash of it and I'd forgive him for dumping me and Anna to go and see his other kids, or for working late, or for leaving a puddle by the sink, even though he knew it would warp the wood. Even when I was exhausted from having worked late into the night, that smile coerced me to find the energy for sex. I shuddered. That smile no longer had any of those powers over me. Instead, it made me want to punch him in the face. So I did.

Chapter 43

'I'm so proud.' Brigitte grinned over her shoulder to where I sat in the back of Sanjay's car. 'You really showed him.'

I didn't feel worthy of praise or as though I'd got my revenge. The punch hadn't felt cathartic or redeeming. I felt . . . What was the word? Oh, yes: shit. I felt shit.

'Told you he'd had plugs,' Brigitte continued. 'His hair was like Astroturf.' She ran her fingers over Sanjay's cropped black hair, flecked with grey. 'Don't you ever get plugs. Nothing wrong with a receding hairline.'

Sanjay jerked his head away. 'I'm not receding.' He tutted, finger-combing the front of his hair.

Brigitte winked over her shoulder at me. Her face fell when she noticed how miserable I was. 'I'm so sorry. Wittering away when you're feeling like shit.' Good to know I'd chosen the correct term. 'Are you sure about going home? The spare room's yours if you want it.'

I shook my head. 'I want to hear what he's got to say. Find out why he told so many lies. The longer I give him, the more time he has to concoct some ridiculous excuse. He's clearly good at it.'

'We'll come in with you,' Sanjay said. 'Don't trust him after the stunt he pulled back there.'

'Thanks, but he'll go on the defensive if you're there and I won't get any answers. Don't worry, he won't hurt me.' He might sulk and have a strop, but he wouldn't turn on me physically, and he couldn't hurt me emotionally any more than he already had.

My throat burnt. Poor Anna was going to be the victim of a broken family. I swallowed down my tears. No, I needed

317

to reframe this. Anna was not a victim, any more than I was. Scott was around so rarely that his absence wouldn't have much impact on our day-to-day lives. If he devoted one evening each week and one day of the weekend to Anna, she'd see him more than she did now.

'Don't let him gaslight you,' Brigitte said. 'If you start to doubt yourself, call me.'

'I won't fall for that again,' I said firmly. 'After I've found out what I want to know, I'll tell him to leave. I want him out before Maman brings Anna back tomorrow. She doesn't need to see him packing his bags and going.'

'But she'd love to see that,' Brigitte said.

'I meant Anna, not Maman.'

'Oh, right. Sorry.'

When we arrived at my house, they both hugged me.

'If he gives you any grief, punch him again,' Sanjay said. 'Then ring me, and I'll come and finish him off.' He clenched his jaw.

'Good luck,' Brigitte said, reluctantly letting me go. 'We can be here in five minutes,' she added.

'Thanks. I'll call you later.'

'He'd better not lay a finger on her,' I heard her say, as I closed the front door.

'More likely to be the other way around,' Sanjay replied. 'Scott's punch was crap. It was the key that did the damage. Marie's had power. It's all in the shoulders.'

Maybe having broad shoulders wasn't so bad after all.

I went into the kitchen, poured myself a glass of water and sat down at the table. I briefly contemplated getting changed. Usually, I got straight into my PJs when I got in, but a Barbie onesie didn't have the *gravitas* I needed for this situation. My green dress was splattered with Michael's blood. I wondered again how he was. After I'd hit Scott, Brigitte had led me to Sanjay's car. Saying goodbye to Michael and Beth hadn't seemed appropriate. What would I have said? 'Sorry I ruined your special night by involving your ex-husband, who, it turns out, is my current husband. My bad. Let's do lunch sometime.' My stomach twisted. He and Beth must hate me. The thought hurt almost as much as Scott's betrayal.

The front door opened and I tensed. Scott's footsteps padded across the hall, then he walked into the kitchen. The sight of him unnerved me more than I thought it would. Not because I was afraid, but because I hated everything about him. He sat down next to me and took my hand. I snatched it away and crossed my arms.

He took on a pained expression. 'Don't be like that, babe.'

Anger surged through me. 'How the fuck do you expect me to be? Everything you've told me is a lie. Everything. About who Liz is, her not letting you see your kids.'

Scott's brow furrowed. 'You have every right to be angry. There's a lot to take in.'

'Explain it to me,' I snapped. 'Why don't you see Harry and Bella – or Henry and Izzy, as they prefer to be called?'

'Because of you.' Scott leant forward. 'You offered me a new chance at happiness. A fresh start. It wouldn't have worked if I'd been tied to my old life and the baggage that came with it.'

I thought of Henry and Izzy skimming stones at the beach with Anna. How could he view them as baggage?

'I wanted them to be part of our life.'

'Wouldn't have been a proper fresh start, though. They've got new dad now anyway.' His jaw tightened. 'She didn't hang around.' His audacity was astounding. He made Donald Trump look humble.

'Who were the children in that photo you showed me? It wasn't Henry and Izzy.'

Scott's brow furrowed, then he seemed to remember. 'I got it out of a picture frame in a shop. You wanted to know what they looked like and I didn't have an up-to-date photo.'

There was so much I could say, but I moved on to my next

question. I wanted this over as quickly as possible. 'Where do you go when you're supposed to be with them?'

Scott shrugged. 'I drive around, try to clear my head. Life gets stressful sometimes.'

'The abusive messages. Who are they from?'

Scott twisted his wedding ring around his finger.

'It's not possible for me to hate you any more than I already do, so just say it,' I said coldly.

Scott flinched. 'What I'm about to tell you is going to hurt,' he said. 'I really regret it, but it's important I'm honest with you.'

Honest? Was he having a fucking laugh? The man didn't know the meaning of the word.

'I did something I shouldn't have done.' His Adam's apple bulged as he swallowed. 'We were going through a bad patch.'

I frowned. I couldn't remember a bad patch. Then I remembered that our entire relationship was a bad patch. Scott could be referring to any time in the last four years. I didn't care enough to ask him to specify which year.

'I showed a client – a female client – round a house and we, er . . . became friends.'

I stiffened. Seemed I did care a little bit.

'She was thinking of moving to Horsham and asked my advice about the town, so we went for lunch a couple of times and, well, you know how it is.'

'I don't, actually.' I reached for my glass of water but my hand was shaking too much to lift it.

'It should never have happened. I regretted it straightaway.' His voice broke. 'I'm sorry. It was a moment of madness.'

'Were you with her when you said you were with Harry and Bella?' I asked.

'Sometimes.' He couldn't meet my eye.

'So, you weren't always driving around?'

'No,' he said quietly. 'I tried to end it and she went crazy. Threatened to tell you, bombarded me with messages, called me constantly.' He released a shaky breath. 'I had to keep seeing her, so she wouldn't tell you. It was a nightmare.'

Being forced to screw someone wasn't the most chilling nightmare scenario I'd heard of. It was unlikely to replace the pit of snakes on *I'm a Celebrity* as their deadliest challenge.

'You've been getting messages from *Liz*,' I emphasised her name, 'since Anna was born. Have you been having an affair with this woman all this time?'

'No!' He looked genuinely surprised at my suggestion. 'It was just a few months.'

We'd gone from a moment of madness to a few months. I couldn't believe a word that came out of his mouth.

'Are you still seeing her?'

He shook his head. 'I ended it back in June. Told her I loved you and it had to stop. That's when the messages became abusive.'

'The ones I told the police about?'

Scott nodded.

'But they were sent from Liz. Why . . .' I trailed off as I'd answered my own question. Scott must have put the details of whoever he was seeing in his phone as Liz to cover his tracks. A professional liar. I wasn't, though, and I'd inadvertently misled the police. 'I told the police the messages were from Liz. How did you explain that?'

'Best thing you ever did, phoning the police.' Scott gave me a grateful smile. 'I told them the situation, that I'd been a naughty boy.' I shot him a look of disgust and he hurried on. 'They spoke to Cleo. Told her to stop or they'd press charges.'

A whimper escaped me. 'Cleo? The woman you had an affair with is Cleo?'

Scott's cheeks flooded with colour.

I thought back to Cleo being in the toilet at the hotel, then turning up at the studio. All the questions she'd asked about my wedding day, my marriage, my husband. And all along they'd been screwing behind my back.

'She came and saw me at work. She wanted me to make her a wedding dress.' My hand flew to my mouth. 'Did you ask her to marry you?'

'No! She's delusional. Crazy. You saw that when she attacked you in the street.'

I remembered Cleo's tortured face as she stood over me, screaming that I was to blame. That I was the reason she'd lost her baby. Her baby. A chill ran down my spine. 'She was pregnant,' I whispered. 'Were you the father?'

Beads of sweat formed at his hairline. 'The condom split,' he said quietly. 'I told her to take the morning-after pill, but she didn't.' He ran a hand over his brow. 'She sent me a message that night we went out, saying she was pregnant. I told you Bella was ill, went straight round and told her it was over. That's when she turned nasty. Before that she'd just sent the odd message telling me I should be with her, not you – nothing too wacky. It was after that that things got out of hand.'

'She told you she was pregnant and you dumped her?'

'Course I did,' Scott said. 'It had never meant anything. I wasn't going to let one stupid mistake ruin my marriage. But then she threatened to tell you.' His jaw tightened. 'When she lost the baby, I thought that'd be the end of it, but she didn't stop. Accosting you in the street. Sending me those threatening messages over and over. It was like being tortured, feeling my phone vibrate, knowing another would come through minutes later. I was terrified you'd find out and I'd lose you.' He looked up. 'But then you rang the police and they sorted it. It's over now. We'll never hear from her again. We can forget about her and move on.' He put a hand tentatively on my arm.

He wasn't serious? He couldn't possibly believe that we'd ever move on from this.

Scott misread the fact I hadn't flicked his hand away, or put a knife through it, as acceptance of his explanation. 'There'll never be anyone else, I promise.' He squeezed my arm.

'Get off me,' I hissed.

He jumped back and held his hands up. 'It'll take time. I get that.'

'You told me Liz had an affair.' I looked him in the eye. 'But Beth's ex cheated on *her*. And *you're* her ex.'

Scott rubbed a hand across his eyes. 'Things changed after Bella arrived. Liz had no time for me. It was all about the kids, and she never wanted to have sex. But it's not like that with you.' He gave me a small smile. 'We always have fun in the bedroom, don't we?'

The memory of Scott kissing me, touching me, being inside me made me want to vomit. Thank God he'd had a vasectomy. If he hadn't, I could be pregnant now. I'd be happy, oblivious to the fact he'd lied to me the whole time I'd known him, betrayed his children and got another woman pregnant. At least he wouldn't be able to do that again.

My eyes widened, as another realisation dawned. 'Your vasectomy.' I banged my fist on the table. 'It was so you'd never get caught out like you did with Cleo.'

'No!' Scott put a hand to his chest. 'I did it for Anna. She's happy and settled. Another kid would mess that up. Take you away from her even more.'

This was the reason he'd gaslit me with before. My shame at believing him fused with my fury. 'Don't pretend you did it for her,' I snapped.

'Not just Anna – you as well. The two of you are my world.' His eyes pleaded with me. 'I know I've messed up. If I could take it back, I would.' He pulled at his tie, as though it were choking him. 'Please forgive me.'

For the first time that evening, I took in what he was wearing. His favourite navy suit, with a pale blue shirt and a tie.

'Why are you so dressed up to watch football at Andy's?'

Scott blinked several times. It was a cliché to say I could see the cogs turning, and he wasn't intelligent enough to have more than a couple of cogs, but there was a definite thought process taking place.

Scott cleared his throat. 'I wasn't at Andy's tonight. I was having dinner with a friend. A female friend, but it's perfectly innocent, I swear.'

I gave him a withering look.

'It's true,' he said, but even he didn't seem convinced.

'Why didn't you tell me earlier?'

'All right,' he snapped. 'She's more than a friend.' His shoulders slumped. 'You won't have sex with me anymore. What am I supposed to do?'

My mouth dropped open. He was blaming this on *me*?

'You forced me out of the house,' he said wearily. 'Going on and on about the kids. Why wasn't I seeing them? Didn't I miss them? I had to keep going out to shut you up. You can only sit in a bar on your own for so long before a conversation strikes up with someone.'

I'd thought he couldn't hurt me any more, but he'd found a way. 'Has this been going on the whole time we've been together?' I asked shakily.

He hung his head.

'All those times you said you were with your children, picking them up, helping with homework, taking them away for the weekend – you weren't driving around; you were with other women.'

'Not *all* the times,' Scott said indignantly, as though offended by the suggestion. 'Just the odd fling. They never lasted long. Never meant anything. Never changed how I feel about you. The Cleo situation got out of hand.' He ran a hand through his hair. His stupid hair. Even that wasn't authentic.

'Stop talking.' I put a hand up. 'I don't want to hear anymore.'

'That's everything, I swear.' He exhaled loudly, sounding relieved he'd got it off his chest. 'I'm sorry,' he added. 'I really do love you.'

I looked at him in disbelief. 'You're not capable of loving anyone but yourself.'

Scott adopted a wide-eyed, wounded expression. How could I have ever thought him handsome? He was a caricature. A grotesque compilation of well-practised smiles and amusing mannerisms. Strip those away and all that was left was a vacuous, puerile, sorry excuse for a human being.

I curled my hands into fists. 'Get out.'

'Please don't do this,' he said.

'I should have told you to go when you had a vasectomy without telling me. When you let me believe we were trying for a baby.' Anger powered the last words out of me. 'You made me doubt myself as a mother. You should be thankful I'm not punching you again.'

'I deserved that.' Scott rubbed his chin. 'But there's no need to throw me out. You've shown everyone you're not a pushover. They'll see that you taught me a lesson, I apologised and we moved on. Because that's what married people do.'

'I don't want to be married to you,' I said simply. 'I want a divorce.'

Scott shook his head. 'Babe, no.'

'My name's Marie. Although, I guess "babe" is easier, so you don't accidentally say the wrong name. Beth said that's what you called her too.' I shook my head. 'Just go.'

Scott's face crumpled. He grabbed my left hand and pointed to my wedding band. 'For better or worse, remember? This is the worst it'll ever get, but it's all out in the open now. We can have a do-over. No more secrets, no more lies. We'll make it better again.'

I wrenched my wedding ring off and threw it across the room. 'Get out of my house,' I said through gritted teeth. 'Go to Cleo or whoever you've got on the go at the moment. She's welcome to you.'

'You can't do this,' Scott sobbed. 'Think of Anna. How will she cope without her dad? She needs me.'

Using Anna as emotional blackmail just made me hate

him more. 'Bringing up a child takes commitment, love and sacrifice,' I said. 'You're not capable of those things. Now go.'

Scott scrambled to his feet. 'I'll stay at the office. We'll talk tomorrow.'

'There's no point.' I followed him to the front door so I could lock it after him. 'We're done.'

'I'll tell Anna you ripped her family apart. I wanted to stay, but you wouldn't let me.' He glared at me accusingly. 'This is going to fuck her up, and that's on you.' He turned and walked away.

I slammed the door and double-locked it, my fingers trembling as I secured the bolts. I hated him. I wanted him out of my life. And out of Anna's life. The question was, how did I do that?

Chapter 44

'Murder,' Maman said simply. 'You hire a special person and they murder him.'

'I have a number for someone,' Francine said.

Brigitte looked at her mum in alarm. 'Why do you have a hitman's number?'

Francine peered into her espresso cup. 'Your papa was behind with his maintenance payments once.'

'He was off work with a slipped disc.' Brigitte glared at her. 'He's my dad. I can't believe you considered having him killed.'

'*Pour l'amour de Dieu*. I didn't call the man, did I, or he would be dead already.' Francine's eyes glazed over and a faint smile played on her lips. This was a fantasy she'd indulged in before.

I rubbed my eyes. I was exhausted. After Scott had left, I'd showered and gone to bed, but I hadn't slept. Instead, I'd fretted about the future. Anna was going to want to see her dad, that was natural. It would be wrong of me to try and prevent it – illegal, even – but how was I going to smile and wave her off every week, sometimes for whole weekends, sometimes for Christmas, knowing what a conniving, egotistical, selfish man he was. And don't get me started on the fact he was also a massive turd.

'Let me see it again.' Maman flapped her hand impatiently till Brigitte handed her phone over. Unbeknown to me, the bouncer at the bar had not only filmed Scott punching Michael, but he'd also filmed me punching Scott and forwarded it to Brigitte. I couldn't bring myself to watch it, but my family had no such apprehension – it had been viewed more times today in my house than *The Sound of Music* had globally in its sixty-year history.

'*Superbe*,' Maman said proudly, as she rewatched me punch Scott hard in the face. She hadn't been this elated when I'd been awarded my degree. Instead, she'd announced loudly that *le spectacle* was boring and that the man next to her had been featured on *Crimewatch*. That man being my dad.

Brigitte put an arm around me. 'How are you doing?'

I glanced towards the door to make sure Anna was engrossed in her programme in the living room. 'I can't take it all in,' I said. 'Don't know which bit to be most upset or pissed off about. His lying . . . His cheating . . . The vasectomy.'

'Yeah.' Brigitte sighed. 'Each is fucked up in its own right. To have to deal with them en masse is too much.'

I nodded. 'And how must Beth feel? She must think I betrayed her.' And Michael, I thought sadly. A huge sob bubbled out of me. I clung to Brigitte, and she hugged me tightly and rubbed my back. The same way I'd rubbed Michael's back when we'd sat on the beach together. When we'd been friends. When he'd liked me enough to buy me chocolates I could eat and noticed how much sewing meant to me after watching me work for only a few minutes.

Scott had never commented about my sewing, other than to complain about tulle drying over the bath or my machine making too much noise. He had no interest in me or my work. He didn't love me. He loved having a wife to keep house and cook for him and have sex with, when he wasn't getting it elsewhere. Which explained why sometimes he was rampant, and other times disinterested. Everything was great when I lived up to his expectations. But if I was ill or on a deadline, and the house wasn't spotless, or dinner was a ready meal, and I couldn't go to bed because I was working, then he became resentful and sulky. Instead of offering to make dinner, or put Anna to bed, he made me feel guilty, as though I were neglecting him. Neglecting my duties.

My tears continued to flow. Why hadn't I realised this sooner? Why had I allowed him to treat me with indifference and, at times, unkindness? I'd made so many allowances, assuming it was natural to be taken for granted in a marriage. I'd mistaken keeping the peace for putting up with his crap. I'd been a fool.

'Enough of this,' Maman exclaimed. 'It's not as if you have to drink the sea.'

Francine nodded. 'Better to be alone than accompanied badly.'

'Yeah, whatever.' Brigitte turned to me. 'They're right, though. It's not the end of the world. You will get through this – I'll make sure you do – and you're definitely better off without him.'

I nodded, my sobs easing till I was able to breathe normally.

Brigitte handed me a tissue and I blew my nose noisily.

'At least I won't have to go in the garden every time I want to blow my nose from now on,' I said, attempting a smile.

'That's the attitude.' Brigitte clapped her hands together. 'Right. Let's pack the wanker's stuff up.'

The four of us went up to my room – *my* room again, not mine and Scott's – and chucked Scott's clothes and belongings in bin liners. I wasn't giving him my suitcases. I used them for work and would need them for all the holidays I intended to take Anna on. Scott had claimed we couldn't afford a holiday, blaming it on the extras his kids needed and for which he paid on top of maintenance. Instead, he must have spent the money on mini-breaks with his latest squeeze or getting his thatch reseeded. I scrunched Scott's precious ties into a tight ball, before pushing them into a bag.

When everything was bagged up, we threw it all down the stairs, giggling if something clanged or cracked on the way down. The sound of laughter enticed Anna away from the TV and she joined in, kicking the bags around the hall. Eventually, one of the bags ripped and she plonked herself down on the suit jackets that spilt out over the floor.

'Need a wee,' she declared.

I went to pick her up and whisk her into the toilet, then stopped.

'Just do it there,' I said.

She looked at me questioningly.

'This is a one-off,' I said sternly.

Brigitte, Maman and Francine nodded approvingly. We couldn't abide toilet humour usually, but everyone had to lower their standards in times of crisis.

'What shall we do with them?' Brigitte asked, looking at the bin liners cluttering the hall.

'Put them outside, on the pavement,' Maman said.

'Someone might nick them if we leave them outside.'

'*Bien sûr*,' Maman said, as though that were the sole objective.

I bit my lip. I wanted Scott's stuff out of my house, but I wasn't sure about leaving it outside to be stolen. I couldn't be dealing with the subsequent whinging and insurance claim. The less I had to speak to him, the better.

I was saved from making a decision by a key turning in the lock and Scott coming through the front door. He froze when he saw the four of us standing in the hall and looked over his shoulder, clearly wondering if he could get away with backing out and pretending his entrance had never happened.

Maman stepped forward, her petite frame as stiff as a board. Pulling herself up tall, she jabbed a finger at Scott and volleyed a stream of French in his face. She was talking too fast for me to fully understand what she was saying, but judging by the glee on my aunt's face, he was getting a right bollocking.

Scott hung his head. 'Don't know what you said, but I'm sure I deserved it,' he said when she eventually finished. 'I've behaved terribly. It's the biggest regret of my life.' He glanced at me. 'Babe. I mean, Marie. Can we talk on our own?'

'No,' I said sharply, then remembered Anna was there, taking everything in. Scott hadn't even acknowledged her. I lowered my voice. 'From now on, everything goes through a solicitor.'

'Surely we can—' Scott started.

'No,' I said again, through gritted teeth. 'We said everything we needed to last night. I'm not changing my mind.' I nudged the nearest bin liner towards him with my toe. 'Take your stuff and leave your key.'

'Where's Daddy going?' Anna asked, still nestled on top of Scott's suit jackets. 'A conference?' It was telling of their relationship that she directed this question to me, not him. I nodded and Anna waved at Scott, unconcerned. '*À bientôt.*'

If he'd hoped Anna would be his trump card, he was wrong. He'd got back from that relationship exactly what he'd put in.

'Your key,' Brigitte said coldly.

Scott made a performance of easing it from his key ring. Brigitte yawned loudly and Maman started muttering in French again. Eventually, he got it off and placed it on the windowsill, then bent down and scooped up some of the bags. One of them rattled with the sound of broken glass. Brigitte suppressed a giggle.

'Be back for the rest in a sec,' he said, backing out of the front door.

I unwound another liner from the roll to put his suit jackets in.

'Up you get, chick,' I said, crouching down next to Anna.

She stood up, wiggled and looked down between her legs. '*Merde*,' she said. 'A poo came out.'

I'd never loved her more.

Brigitte took Anna to the toilet to get cleaned up while I bundled the jackets, along with Anna's gift, into the new bin liner and tied it very, very tightly.

Scott came back in, scooped up the remaining bags and

looked forlornly at me from the front step. 'Marie,' he said softly. 'Please, can we talk?'

'No. My solicitor will be in touch. Don't come to the house again.' Walking over, I slammed the front door and leant against it.

Maman patted my shoulder. '*Je suis fière de toi*. Very proud.'

'*Moi aussi*,' Francine said.

'I bet you two are happy,' I said glumly. 'You never wanted me to get married.'

'Not true,' Maman said. 'I didn't want you to marry *him*.'

I looked at her in surprise. 'Why not?'

'He wasn't right for you.' She adjusted the ruff of her starched purple blouse. 'Knew it the moment you told me about his cheating papa. Dogs do not make cats.'

Brigitte came back into the hall with Anna.

Maman caressed Anna's cheek. 'But good comes from bad. We learnt a song last night, didn't we?'

Anna nodded enthusiastically and launched into a very loud rendition of *Frère Jacques*, complete with hand and arm gestures that a three-year-old really shouldn't know, let alone use.

I frowned at Maman. 'That's not the version I learnt at school.'

Maman shrugged. 'While the cat's away, the mice will dance.'

Of course.

Anna looked up at the four of us. 'I'm bored now,' she announced and went back into the living room. She was so French.

Outside, we heard Scott's car start up and he drove away. I'd thought his departure would be distressing, but instead I felt as though a weight had been lifted.

'Ooh, forgot to tell you,' Brigitte said to Maman and Francine. 'Scott had plugs. Used to be completely bald.'

Maman and Francine nodded, as though receiving confirmation of something they'd always known.

'The way it stuck up made him look like *un imbecile*,' Maman said.

Francine nodded. 'He looked like the creature in the game where you hit with a hammer to make it go down.'

I giggled. 'Whack-a-mole.' The vision of Scott's head being repeatedly pummelled with a mallet by my closest relatives was an endearing thought.

Maman looked at her watch and nudged Francine. They picked up their bags – Francine's a chic, leather square; Maman's an embroidered teapot – and air-kissed Brigitte and me.

'Where are you going?' Brigitte asked.

'Occupy yourself with your onions,' Francine said. 'We do not have to tell you everything.'

Brigitte shrugged. 'Fair enough.'

Francine pressed her lips together. She'd clearly hoped to frustrate Brigitte more than that.

'What are they up to?' I asked Brigitte after they'd gone.

'The French market's on today.'

'Ah.' The market was a monthly highlight for Maman and Francine. Not because they could go and buy their much-loved cheeses, olives and bread. It was because they loved criticising everything and explaining to the formerly buoyant stallholders, in great detail, why genuine French produce was far *supérieur*. Then they'd buy their much-loved cheeses, olives and bread.

I smiled at Brigitte. 'Please don't feel you have to stay. I'll take Anna to the park. We can walk you home on the way.'

'No rush. Sanjay said he'd pick me up when I'm ready.' She examined her nails. 'We're taking Ammo and Sundeep out for lunch.' She shrugged, as if it wasn't a big deal.

'That's a first, isn't it?'

'Sanjay and I had an in-depth tête-à-tête last night.' Brigitte held up her hands. I hoped she'd washed them since then. 'Been thinking a lot about how hard you tried to have Harry and Bella in your life. I thought you were lucky not to be lumbered with them. Sundeep and Ammo just cause friction between me and Sanjay. When we row, it's always about them.' Her cheeks grew pink. 'But I haven't been as welcoming or patient as I could be. They're part of Sanjay and I need to accept that. He and Pooja are going to talk to the kids together and insist they're polite to me. If I make more of an effort with them, hopefully they'll make an effort with me too.' She crossed her fingers.

I smiled. 'I'm really glad. It'd be great to have a good relationship with them.'

'What about Henry and Izzy?' she asked. 'Are you going to ask Beth about meeting up with Anna?'

'I doubt she'll want to see me again. She'll probably ask me to courier the dresses, rather than come in and collect them.' I blinked hard. 'I'd become really fond of Izzy, and Henry's lovely, which makes it even worse. I couldn't have wished for nicer siblings for Anna, but the way Beth looked at me last night . . .' My stomach tightened as I recalled the hatred in her eyes.

'She was in shock. Her reaction was understandable. Bet she'll want to talk when she's calmed down.' Brigitte raised one eyebrow. 'You could always get in touch through her brother.'

My stomach tightened even more.

Chapter 45

I hung Izzy's bridesmaid's dress up, ready to be collected. She was going to look stunning in the silk gown with tulle cap sleeves and matching headband. The jewel-green fabric brought out the blue in her eyes. Izzy's eyes were the same colour as Scott's, I realised, my stomach clenching at yet another discovery.

We hadn't seen Scott since I'd kicked him out almost two weeks before. Well, told him to leave – not literally kicked him, although apparently Maman had tried as he went past. I'd appointed a solicitor the next day – a client Brigitte recommended. 'She doesn't even flinch when I hot-wax her bikini line,' Brigitte had said. 'You need someone tough like that.' She was liaising with Scott's solicitor about the legalities, not that there was much to sort out. My house and business were in my name and, as we'd kept our finances completely separate, he wouldn't be able to make a claim on them. He had nothing of worth, apart from his car and a thick head of hair, neither of which I wanted.

We'd spoken once. I'd felt physically sick when his name flashed up on my phone and I'd steeled myself for another futile plea to take him back. Instead, he told me he was transferring to another branch – in Herefordshire, 200 miles away. The position came with an option to rent a flat above the shop. It was a one-bed, so he couldn't have Anna to stay, but said he'd visit regularly. He was currently down the road in the Premier Inn and hadn't visited yet, so our interpretation of the word 'regularly' clearly differed.

I felt sad for Anna, but also relieved. Living in the same town, knowing I could bump into him at any time, would have been unsettling. A 200-mile distance was much more manageable. I'd make sure Anna FaceTimed him and I would never criticise him in front of her. If, when she was older, Anna reviewed the facts and reached the conclusion that her dad was a bit of a git, then that was down to her. It wouldn't be influenced by me. Although, I wouldn't disagree.

Beth's dress was on the mannequin in the centre of the studio. I felt a glow of excitement and pride when I looked at it. The full skirt of the pure white gown hung perfectly; the lace back was both sensual and romantic; and the beads on the bodice sparkled in the sunlight. My excitement was clouded by nerves, though. The only contact with Beth since her hag do had been a text I'd sent the day before, reminding her of her final appointment to fit and collect the dress, and hers in return confirming that she'd be with me by eleven.

The front door chimed and I jumped. Beth wasn't due for half an hour, but perhaps in her eagerness to get the appointment out of the way, so she never had to see me again, she'd come early. Or it could be Cleo. She wouldn't know Scott and I had broken up. Even if she did, that didn't mean she'd forgiven me for her miscarriage.

'Morning,' Brigitte called out and I breathed a sigh of relief. Her feet ran up the stairs and she appeared in my doorway. 'How are you?' she asked, concern etched on her face, as it had been every day for the past two weeks.

'Fine, thanks.' I *was* surprisingly fine. Scott's absence had far less impact than I could have envisaged. It confirmed how little he'd been at home physically, and emotionally, when he was there. Anna had only mentioned him once, when the bath got blocked and I'd used a coat hanger to fish a tiny plastic toy out of the plughole. 'Daddy should have done that,' she'd said, watching the water swirl away. Even she associated him with plugs.

'Good.' Brigitte smiled as she handed me my post.

'How's it going with Sundeep and Ammo?' I asked.

'Better,' she said, clearly also surprised. 'The three of us ate together last night while Sanjay was at work.'

'That's brilliant. Do you feel you're getting to know them more?'

'It's a slow process. They're not exactly chatty, but they're not telling me to get lost either.' She shrugged. 'I'll take that. Want a green tea?' she added.

'Got anything stronger? Beth's coming in soon.'

'She'll be cool. Especially when she sees how amazing her dress looks.' She stepped towards it.

'Don't take a photo!' I threw a muslin sheet over Beth's dress.

'All right, all right. Keep your hair on.' Brigitte's grin changed to a grimace. 'Sorry.'

I laughed and flicked through the post she'd given me. One envelope was handwritten. Many brides sent thank-you notes, which were lovely to receive, especially if they contained a photo for my portfolio. I sat down on the sofa and opened it. Inside was a sheet of paper covered in neat handwriting. The name at the bottom made my stomach tightened. Cleo.

Dear Marie,

I'm writing to tell you how sorry I am for the upset I must have caused you. My accusation that you caused my miscarriage was inexcusable. It had nothing to do with you. In my distress, I was desperate to blame someone. I'm sorry that you were that someone.

My behaviour since meeting Scott has been very out of character. My therapist believes the pregnancy affected my hormones to such an extent that I acted in ways that I wouldn't usually. I became fixated with Scott. I believed we belonged together and that you stood in our way.

I'm ashamed to admit that I followed you several times and even came to your house one evening. I then pretended I was getting married so I had an excuse to meet you. I'm not sure what I hoped to achieve, but my therapist says that I don't need to give explanations; I just need to take ownership of what I've done, so that I can move on.

After my miscarriage, Scott wanted nothing more to do with me. Instead of supporting me in my hour of need, he turned away, saying he needed to focus on his marriage. This made me truly hate you and led me to accuse you of causing the loss of my baby. I followed this up with a series of aggressive text messages to Scott.

It was only when the police became involved that I realised how out of control I had spiralled and that I needed help. On the police's recommendation, I sought counselling, and am now coming to terms with my situation and the understanding that you played no part in my miscarriage.

I no longer need to come to Horsham for work, so you won't see me again.

I'm sorry for any pain and distress caused by my actions and wish you well.

Regards,
Cleo

I read the letter again, my heart pounding. Just as well I knew about their affair or this letter would have floored me. Was that her intention? A final act of revenge? Or did she assume only an idiot wouldn't realise her husband was cheating? I put the letter in a drawer to show Brigitte later. Whatever Cleo's reason for writing, it was reassuring to know she wasn't out to get me. I didn't need to look over my shoulder anymore or jump when the door chimed. I could leave that to Brigitte for the days she had a back, sack and crack wax booked in.

As if to taunt me, the door chimed. I automatically tensed. Who was scarier at this point – Cleo or Beth? I went to the top of the stairs and called out a nervous hello.

'Hi,' an equally nervous voice came back.

I looked down in surprise. The last time I'd seen Beth, she'd looked at me with utter hatred, which I didn't blame her for. I'd steeled myself for a similar treatment today, or a stony silence as she took the dresses and left. Instead, the expression on her face was one of apprehension and concern.

'Sorry I haven't been in touch,' she said, reaching the top of the stairs. 'Wasn't sure you wanted to hear from me.'

I gasped with relief. 'I thought you wouldn't want anything to do with me, once you knew who I was. Not that *I* knew who I was . . . If that makes sense.'

She gave a small smile. 'It was obvious you were as shocked as me. And I know you'd never stop Rick seeing his children. You're not that sort of person.'

It took me a moment to appreciate that Rick was Scott. I nodded. 'I was desperate to meet them. Still don't fully understand why he wouldn't let me.' I rolled my eyes. 'Actually, I don't understand anything that he did. Turns out he cheated on me too. Constantly. His latest acquisition fell pregnant, so he had a vasectomy without telling me, so it couldn't happen again.' I grimaced. 'What a guy, eh?'

'That absolute shit.' Beth shook her head. 'I'm so sorry.'

'No, I'm sorry.' I led her to my studio and we sank into the sofa. 'We ruined your hag do. Scott showing up like that was terrible.'

Beth's eyes flashed. 'You have nothing to be sorry for. This is all on him.'

I nodded. 'I told him to leave that night. He got his clothes the next day. Haven't seen him since.' Beth squeezed my arm. 'It's OK.' I gave her a reassuring smile. 'Things hadn't been good for a while. All of this was a shock, but it would have been far worse if I'd thought we were happy.' It was true. I could have done without the distress and drama, but if it hadn't happened, I'd still be with Scott. Pretending everything was good and determinedly ignoring the warning signs – I'd have probably done that for years. Possibly until Anna was an adult. I suppressed a shudder. The prospect of being with Scott for all that time didn't bear thinking about. We'd be like a long-running sitcom that had stopped being funny years before, but doggedly limped on. *Last of the Summer Wine* sprang to mind, although I couldn't envisage that ever having been funny.

Beth put her head to one side. 'How's Anna taking it?'

'So far, so good.' My eyes flitted to a photo of her on the windowsill. She'd made a veil out of a tea towel and was wearing my wedding shoes. She'd never been inspired enough by anything Scott did to imitate him. Thankfully – I didn't want his behaviour inspiring anyone. 'He was hardly ever home anyway,' I continued. 'Always visiting Harry and Bella. Or so he said.' I shook my head. 'Still can't believe he told so many lies or that he didn't want to see your gorgeous children.' I looked again at the photo. 'Not sure he wants to see Anna either. He's moving to Herefordshire.'

Beth tutted. 'Selfish bastard. We're all better off without him.' She followed my gaze to Anna's photo. 'I hear the three of them got on brilliantly in Brighton.'

I nodded, smiling at the memory of the children laughing as they tried to jump over the waves. 'Crazy that Anna was with her brother and sister, and we had no idea.'

'She's got the same butter-wouldn't-melt smile as Henry,' Beth said. 'When I see that, I know he's up to something.'

'Definitely! And her eyes are like Izzy's.'

'So, how are we going to tell them?'

My heart soared. 'They can meet?'

'Of course!' Beth grinned. 'The children have a right to know each other.'

Tears sprang to my eyes. 'I want that more than anything, but wasn't sure you would.'

Beth shook her head. 'Are you crazy? Henry and Izzy haven't stopped going on about Anna since they met her. They're going to go wild when they find out she's their sister.' Her voice cracked. 'You two are part of our family now. Christmas, birthdays, holidays – the whole shebang. You'll be sick of the sight of us.'

'Oh, thank you.' Tears ran down my cheeks. 'I've always wanted Anna to have a brother or sister. Now she has both.'

We hugged each other tightly. I could tell by the way Beth shook that she was crying too. We didn't speak for a few minutes, each absorbing the magnitude of our fortuitous meeting and how our children would benefit from it. Eventually, Beth gave me a final squeeze and let go. I passed her the tissue box on the table and took one myself. We blew our noses loudly. Scott would have been vomiting in the corner if he'd been there.

'Do you mind if we wait till I get back from honeymoon?' Beth asked, taking another tissue and wiping her cheeks. 'Don't want to drop that bombshell and then disappear for a week. Especially, as they're staying at Michael's. They'd nag him constantly to take them to see Anna.'

My stomach flipped over at the sound of his name.

'If we'd known earlier, you and Anna would be guests of honour at the wedding. But it's too late to add any day guests and there's no guarantee I wouldn't tell everyone after a glass of fizz.' Beth smiled. 'Don't let me blurt it out at the reception.'

I fiddled with the hem of my skirt. 'I'm not sure I should come to the evening.'

Beth's face fell. 'Why not?'

'I don't want there to be any awkwardness.'

'There won't be,' Beth said firmly. 'He wants you to come.'

'Really?' Relief and excitement flooded through me. I'd been so worried Michael hated me that I hadn't dared ask about him.

Beth nodded enthusiastically. 'He's looking forward to getting to know you better.'

I managed to hold in a squeal, but couldn't contain a huge smile spreading across my face. 'How's his chin?' I asked as casually as I could.

Beth frowned. 'Fine.'

'That's a relief,' I said. 'It looked pretty bad after Scott hit him.'

'Scott didn't hit James.'

Disappointment coursed through me. She was talking about her fiancé, not her brother.

'Michael had to have stitches, though,' Beth said.

'Is he all right now?' I asked in a small voice.

Beth nodded. 'Annoyed that he's going to have tape on his face in the wedding pics, but OK other than that.' She clapped her hands together. 'Now, please put me out of my misery and let me see my wedding dress.'

'Of course.' I pushed my disappointment aside and forced a smile.

I'd have to go to the reception, it'd be too rude not to, but I'd avoid Michael. Shouldn't be too difficult, as everything indicated that he was avoiding me. Once I'd shown my face, I'd leave, having done my duty. Only then could I be put out of my misery too.

Chapter 46

Brigitte and I stood at the entrance to the wedding venue. Fairy lights twinkled on the oak-framed door, and the sound of music, laughter and general merriment came from within.

'How do I look?' I asked Brigitte, checking my strapless red dress hadn't ridden down when I was clambering out of the cab.

'Stop fishing,' Brigitte said. 'You know you look amazing.'

'No, I don't.' I did, actually. My dress was a new purchase – I'd been too busy with work to make anything. Fitted to just below the knee, I'd emphasised my waist with a black belt, and wore chunky black bangles and sandals. My hair was swept over one shoulder and Brigitte had done my makeup – black liquid liner, lashings of mascara and postbox-red lips, which she'd painstakingly painted with a tiny brush consisting of about three hairs to ensure longevity. Brigitte looked amazing too, in a strappy navy silk jumpsuit with gold accessories and her hair piled on top of her head. But looking amazing was the norm for Brigitte, so she didn't deserve as much praise as me.

'Come on,' Brigitte said. '*On y va.*' She linked her arm through mine, and we went into the barn and helped ourselves to a glass of fizz from a tray inside the door.

Beth was on the dance floor, dancing to 'Copacabana' with Henry and Izzy. She looked stunning in her white gown and Izzy was radiant in emerald green. I was slightly disappointed to see that Henry had been talked out of the Superman outfit and was wearing the same as the ushers. Too bad it hadn't worked the other way around and he'd persuaded the ushers to wear superhero outfits. Many, many fantasies would have been fulfilled with Michael and Dean in tight-fitting Lycra.

'Shall we go and say hello?' Brigitte asked.

'Let's wait till she's finished dancing,' I said. 'I'm not ready for Barry Manilow yet.'

We stayed near the barn door. There was a lovely breeze coming through and, more importantly, we were near the tray of fizz.

'Hi ladies. So glad you could make it.' Beth's husband, James, came over and kissed us both on the cheek.

'Congratulations,' we chorused. 'Are you having a lovely day?' we said, also in unison, then glanced at each other with alarm. Please don't let us be turning into our mums.

'Best day ever.' James beamed from ear to ear. 'I mean, look at her. She's incredible.'

We turned to watch Beth on the dance floor. She twirled in time to the music, her skirt fanning out around her, her beaded bodice shimmering in the lights from the disco. Already naturally beautiful without makeup (the cow), Brigitte hadn't needed to apply much earlier, but had instead enhanced Beth's large eyes, long lashes and full mouth. Her hair was a mass of curls pinned into a side bun. She looked both demure and sexy.

'And now,' said the DJ into her microphone. 'It's time for the happy couple's first dance.'

'That's my cue.' James looked around for somewhere to put his pint glass and I took it from him. 'Thank you,' he said gratefully.

'Have fun,' Brigitte and I said together. We glared at one another. We *had* to stop doing that.

On the dance floor, James slipped his hands around Beth's waist and pulled her close to him. We 'aahed' with the rest of the crowd, as James and Beth swayed and gazed at each other with a mixture of tenderness and yearning that left no one wondering if they'd be consummating their marriage that night.

Beth's parents and another couple, presumably James's mum and dad, joined them on the floor.

'Would you like to dance?' Brigitte asked.

I choked on my champagne. 'You're asking me to slow dance?'

'No, I'm preparing you.'

'For what?'

'Would you like to dance?' said a voice behind me.

My stomach catapulted, as Michael smiled down at me. Wearing a dress shirt and tailored trousers, he looked more handsome than any other man I'd ever seen. And that included Idris Elba – something I didn't think humanly possible.

'Yes, please,' I said, attempting a smooth, sophisticated delivery.

I stepped forward, then realised I had a glass of fizz in one hand and a pint in the other. So much for smooth and sophisticated.

'Thirsty?' he asked with a smile.

'Here, let me.' Brigitte took both drinks and Michael took my hand, lacing his fingers through mine. A quiver ran up my arm, across my shoulders and straight down my torso to between my legs, where it decided to stay. On the dance floor, Michael clasped my hand to his chest and slipped his other hand around my waist. I reached up and placed my free hand on his shoulder.

'Having a good day?' I asked. It was the most boring and predictable question to ask someone at a wedding, but it guaranteed a feel-good answer. They'd have to be a real wanker to say no. Or Maman. She hadn't even pretended to enjoy my wedding, although she had said afterwards it was a lovely day, apart from my dad's and Scott's presence. Knowing what I knew now, it would have been considerably better without Scott there.

'Sorry to hear about you and Scott.' Michael's lips brushed against my ear as he spoke. I hoped he couldn't feel my heart hammering through his waistcoat.

'It's not an ideal situation,' I said, very much referring to the situation with Scott, not the one I was in at that exact moment with Michael. 'But things weren't good between us. In some ways, this has given me the out I needed. Bit extreme, but it avoided a protracted, painful break-up.'

'Like pulling a plaster off?' Michael said.

'Exactly. Speaking of which, Beth said you'd be wearing one today.' My eyes went to his plaster-less chin, but rested on his mouth.

Michael smiled. 'Luckily, it's pretty much healed up, so I didn't need to wear one. The butterfly strips they gave me at the hospital didn't exactly look cool.'

'If anyone could pull that look off, I'm sure you could.' Oh God. Was I flirting? It had been so long, I wasn't sure I was doing it properly. 'I'm so sorry about everything that happened that night,' I said hastily. 'You were so kind to me, then Scott turned up, ruined Beth's night and punched you.'

'You don't need to be sorry. You're not the one who hit me.'

'I know, but . . .' I trailed off, unwilling to bring Scott into the conversation.

'Glad you didn't,' Michael continued. 'You've got a great right hook. It's all in the—'

'Broad shoulders.' I sighed. 'I've heard.'

'Upper body strength, I was going to say.' Michael cleared his throat. 'Yes, you've got strong shoulders, but you've also got defined arms and, I'm guessing from your posture, a great core.'

Defined arms and a great core? He wasn't exactly saying I had great tits and an arse to die for, but I'd take what I could get.

Michael frowned. 'I have a question. How did two strong, independent, intelligent, beautiful women get taken in by that lying piece of shit?' He shook his head. 'Beggars belief.'

'I don't know.' I bit my lip, remembered my painstakingly applied red lipstick and discreetly ran my tongue over my teeth to clean them. 'I'm embarrassed and ashamed and—'

'No, you mustn't be,' Michael interrupted. 'That's not how I meant you to feel. I just can't figure it out. He must be extremely clever.'

I thought back to Scott's insistence that dinosaurs weren't extinct, but rather they'd just downsized to become lizards. Extreme dickhead was more of an apt description for him.

The song ended and we clapped Beth and James, who did a little bow and curtsey before swapping partners for the next song, so that Beth danced with James's dad and he danced with her mum. 'Come Fly with Me' started up and Michael raised his eyebrows, questioning. I smiled and he took me in his arms again, putting both hands around my waist this time. I placed my hands on his shoulders, sliding them further around his neck as the dance progressed. He rested his cheek against my forehead and we rocked from side to side, without talking. My skin tingled at his touch. I ached for him to bend his head and place his lips on mine. But I also relished the anticipation and the dizzying possibilities that lay ahead. It was quite possibly the most exciting few minutes of my life. Even with Brigitte doing comedy blow-job faces from the side of the dance floor.

When the song ended, Beth came over and draped her arms around us.

'I love this woman,' she said to Michael. I suspected she'd had quite a lot to drink. 'Little Anna's Henry and Izzy's sister.' She put a finger to her lips. 'Don't tell them, though. It's a surprise.'

'I won't,' Michael said solemnly.

'They're going to spend Christmas with us,' Beth continued. 'We'll be one big, happy family.'

'Beth, come and dance.' Brigitte appeared and led Beth off towards Dean. I gave her a grateful smile. Blow-job faces aside, she was the best.

'Christmas, eh?' Michael still had his hands around my waist and we swayed out of time to the music. Elton John's 'Don't Go Breaking My Heart' was considerably faster than the previous two songs and we probably looked ridiculous, trying to slow dance to it, but I didn't care.

I smiled up at him. 'She might retract that offer once she's met my mother.'

'You haven't met ours yet.' He nodded towards a tall, slim woman on the dance floor, wearing a cerise peplum jacket and pencil skirt. She and Brigitte had joined forces and were recreating Beyoncé's 'Single Ladies' routine. 'Should be an interesting Christmas Day,' Michael said.

This talk of family get-togethers was nice, but not as nice as the touchy-feely dancing had been. It was tricky to recreate the sensuality of our slow dances, though, with Elton John and Kiki Dee singing at top volume, and Brigitte hollering, 'It don't count if the booty ain't out!'

Michael must have felt the same, because he took my hand and led me to the side. 'I've got to go soon,' he said.

'What?' It was his sister's wedding. Why was he leaving?

'Uncle duty.' He nodded to Henry and Izzy, who were trying to keep up with their extremely energetic grandma, but clearly flagging. 'They're staying at mine tonight.'

'Oh.' I felt ridiculously disappointed. And ridiculous. I'd been fantasising about him kissing me, while he'd been killing time until he had to go home and babysit. 'Well, it was nice to see you.'

Michael cleared his throat. 'I wondered if we could get together some time.'

He was looking after the children while Beth was on her honeymoon. It was understandable that he'd like to arrange a playdate to take the pressure off in her absence. It wasn't exactly what I'd hoped for, but it'd be lovely for Anna to see Henry and Izzy.

'Sure,' I said. 'We can take them to Brighton again, if you like.'

'Great.' Michael smiled then shook his head. 'Sorry, what?'

'Brighton,' I said slowly. 'On the bus. Like we did before.'

'That's not what I meant,' Michael said.

Maybe a whole day with me was too much. 'How about the park in Horsham, then?' I suggested.

Michael leant closer. His lips were by my ear again, sending waves of desire pulsing through me. I forced myself to remember that all he wanted was someone to babysit with him.

'I meant me and you,' he said.

'Well, of course we'd go too.' Surely he was aware they were too young to go to the park by themselves. He was a healthcare professional, for goodness' sake.

A car horn beeped outside.

Michael sighed. 'The cab's here. I'd better get Henry and Izzy.'

I nodded glumly. This night hadn't ended as promisingly as it had started. But what did I expect? Michael was fit, handsome, intelligent, kind and funny. He was hardly going to make a beeline for a woman with an erratic estranged husband. Especially when that man was also his sister's erratic ex-husband.

Brigitte came over. 'Why are you looking so fed up? You and Michael were on the verge of snogging a minute ago.'

'Mixed messages,' I sighed. 'He just wants to get the kids together while Beth's away.'

Brigitte raised an eyebrow. 'Bullshit,' she said. 'He fancies you. The playdate must be a ruse.' She glanced over her shoulder to where Michael was lifting Izzy up to kiss her grandma goodbye. 'I thought he'd ask you out, though. Didn't have him pegged as someone who'd pussyfoot around.' She winked. 'Not when he could be doing other things with your pus—'

'Shush,' I said sharply, as Michael approached us, Izzy in one arm, Henry holding his hand.

'Thanks for coming,' he said. 'And for helping Beth look so beautiful.'

'It was a pleasure,' we chorused, then cringed.

Gazing at me, he seemed on the verge of saying something, but Izzy yawned loudly in his ear.

'That's my cue to go.' Michael smiled. 'Hopefully see you soon.' His eyes held mine.

I nodded. 'Let me know when you want to take the kids out.'

'Sure. Thanks.' He gave a final smile and led Henry out the door.

Brigitte and I watched them leave. 'See,' I said. 'He doesn't fancy me. Whatever chemistry we had on the dance floor fizzled out as soon as we stopped.'

Brigitte groaned. 'It's so obvious that he likes you. Why can't you see it?'

I shook my head. Brigitte needed to let it go. I'd made a complete fool of myself with Scott. I wasn't going to do that with Michael too.

Brigitte eyed me thoughtfully. 'Have you seen the video of you punching Scott yet?'

'No, and I don't intend to.'

She took her phone from her bag. 'You need to.'

I opened my mouth to protest but she gave me such a determined look that it'd have made even our mums acquiesce, so I didn't even try.

'I'll skip through the part where you hit Scott, but you have to watch the end.' She fast-forwarded the clip, then handed her phone to me. Reluctantly, I watched. There I was, my back to the camera. Scott was slumped against his car, clutching his face. Brigitte ran over, put an arm around me and led me towards Sanjay's car. I frowned at Brigitte. What was the point of this?

'Keep watching,' she said.

The camera scanned the crowd. There was Dean, shaking his head in disbelief. There was Beth, her hand pressed to her mouth, her eyes wide. There was James, wrapping a comforting arm around her. And there was Michael, blood pouring from his chin, staring out, past the camera, to where

Sanjay's car was parked. To where I was. And on his face was an expression I'd seen before. I'd seen it on Sanjay's face when he looked at Brigitte and I'd seen it earlier that evening when James looked at Beth on the dance floor. It was a look that combined affection and pride and, yes, I had to admit it, longing. And he was looking at me.

'He fancies me!' I squealed.

'At last.' Brigitte raised her hands to the ceiling. 'She gets it.'

A car door slammed outside and we looked at each other in horror.

'He's leaving,' I gasped.

'Stop him!' Brigitte pushed me towards the door. 'Quick!'

I ran out of the barn and towards the parked car, holding my hand up to shield my eyes from the headlamps. They were so bright, I couldn't see beyond them. Were they about to drive off? Would they swerve dramatically around me or was there a risk they wouldn't see me and mow me down? I hesitated. Much as I wanted to talk to Michael, I wasn't prepared to die trying. Not when I could ring him tomorrow.

I stopped in my tracks. I could ring him tomorrow. There was no need to throw myself in front of the car, when I could say everything I needed to in a much calmer, safer environment the next day. I turned back towards the barn.

'Marie?' Michael's voice cut through the darkness.

His silhouette emerged from behind the headlamps.

'Hi,' I stammered. My heart pounded as he smiled down at me, his dark eyes sparkling in the light from the car. 'When you said you and me, did you mean just you and me? Not with the kids?'

Michael's face split into an enormous grin. 'At last, she gets it!' He took my hands. 'Yes, Marie. Just you and me. Not a bucket and spade in sight.'

I giggled. 'Sorry. Bit slow tonight.' I hoped this didn't mean he'd strike intelligent off my list of attributes.

'Slow is fine with me.' He slipped his hands up my bare arms and bent his head – and at last, at long bloody last, I

351

totally got it. His lips pressed against mine and the sparks of anticipation that had been coursing around my body gathered and plunged straight to between my legs, causing me to groan with longing and desire. Maybe we wouldn't need to take it slow for too long.

'Uncle Michael,' came a voice from the car.

Michael's mouth smiled against mine and he slowly pulled away.

'I've been thinking about doing that since we first met,' he whispered.

I'd been thinking he was a total bell-end when we first met, but I decided not to mention it. There was a risk it'd spoil the mood.

'I'll call you in the morning.' He kissed me again and walked towards the cab.

I pressed my fingertips to my lips, willing myself not to squeal out loud.

'Marie?' he called, just before he got in the car.

'Yes.'

'What made you finally realise?'

I thought back to Brigitte and smiled. 'I got a second opinion.'

A Note from the Author

Dear reader,

THANK YOU so much for reading *Has Anyone Seen My Husband?* I hope you enjoyed reading it as much as I enjoyed writing it (but without the stress and swearing).

My books are inspired by my own feeble attempt to juggle a career with childcare, life admin and never-ending laundry. I'm still struggling, despite the fact my children are now teenagers. (Any tips on how to cope would be much appreciated.)

As a humorous fiction writer, I aim to provide witty, warm, uplifting stories. If I've failed miserably, please don't tell me – I prefer to remain deluded. In addition to the Laugh out Loud moments (you're humouring me, remember?), there are also serious themes within my books. Serious stuff happens in life and I think it's important not to shy away from it. The subjects I've touched on may give you something to think about and perhaps spark some conversations. Please let me know if you chose *Has Anyone Seen My Husband?* for your book club and what you thought about it.

If you have enjoyed the book, I'd be extremely grateful if you could post a review please. On social media, Amazon, Goodreads or wherever you bought the book. Reviews make a massive difference to authors and are so appreciated. I know it can be a pain, but taking a couple of minutes to post something will bring much joy and, hopefully, more publishing contracts, so that I can write more books. My future career is basically in your hands. Not that I'm trying to guilt trip you or anything. Much.

For more info about my writing life, book news, author events, and to see occasional photos of me hanging out with my family/friends/cat/Han Solo figure, you can follow me on social media via the links below. You can also sign up to my newsletter at www.kathleenwhyman.com to receive very irregular updates. No fear of being spammed here!

Thank you again for reading *Has Anyone Seen My Husband?*. If you enjoyed this, please check out my other books – *Wife Support System* and *Would You Ask My Husband That?* Even better, please buy them for everyone you know!

Take care and happy reading!

Kathleen x

Website – www.kathleenwhyman.com
Instagram – @kathleenwhymanauthor
LinkedIn – @kathleenwhyman
X – @kathleenwhyman1
Facebook – @kathleenwhymanauthor

Acknowledgements

It's hard to know what to write in my acknowledgements, as every thank you I have written before still stands. I'm very fortunate that the same incredible people continue to support, motivate and champion me and I am eternally grateful. I honestly don't know what I'd do without you all. I'd possibly have less hangovers, but where's the fun in that?

As I sat at my desk, gazing out of the window debating if those are rain clouds on the horizon and if I should get the washing in or risk leaving it out (the life of a published author is glamour personified) and wondering where to start, my husband, James, came into my study. He'd just bought a digital label maker and had made me a label with 'Kathleen' on. Not sure whether this was to remind me or him of my name, but it was very thoughtful and I shall wear it at all times. Well, for the rest of the day anyway. So, this unexpected act of kindness has earned him first place in my list of thanks. Thank you James for reading my books even though they're not your thing (the reference to Einstein's theory of relativity is my gift to you), for looking at me with such pride during my book launch party speech last year (and thank you Kate Lowe for telling me, as a combination of fear and alcohol had temporarily disabled my ability to focus), and for making me a name label. Not many authors get such gifts bestowed upon them.

The even greater gift you have bestowed upon me is our incredible daughters Eve and Elena. Girls – I know my regular, er, let's call it 'encouragement' to revise, get enough sleep (preferably at night time), eat broccoli, and not turn the bathroom floor into a paddling pool is massively annoying, but please know that the words come from a place of love. They may be spoken through gritted teeth, but they're with love! Thank you both for being the best thing that has ever happened to me. (Don't worry James – the name label is a close second.)

You can't choose your family, but if you could, then I'd have chosen this lot anyway. (Out of love, not a lack of imagination.) Thank you to my amazing mum, Susan, for her never-ending support and energy and for not being Maman. My brother, Adam, is a constant source of joy and beer, both of which are always welcome. My in-laws Linda, Jed, Laura, Andy and Deryn, plus all my aunts, uncles and cousins, both related and inherited, are all phenomenal and I'm lucky to have them in my life. Ditto my gorgeous nieces and nephews, Brady, Charlie, Isla and Holly.

You wouldn't be reading this book if it wasn't for my writing family, who I did choose (or gratefully latched on to when they graciously offered to represent me). Emily Glenister continues to be an agenting legend. Her hard work, dedication, belief, encouragement and support are the stuff writers can only dream of. She's also a blooming good laugh. They say you should never mix business with pleasure, but when your agent is this much fun, it'd be foolish not to. Thank you Emily for everything. And thank you David Headley for letting me join your gang!

You may have spotted from the cover that this book was shortlisted for the Comedy Women in Print (CWIP) prize. CWIP is an organisation founded and run by the absolutely fabulous Helen Lederer. As well as being an incredibly talented writer, actress and comedian, Helen somehow finds time to champion female witty writers. I'm not sure I'd be where I am without CWIP and am so grateful to Helen for her tireless work in supporting authors, and for inviting us to her parties so that we can gawp in awe at her celebrity friends. At the book launch for her memoir (*Not That I'm*

Bitter – treat yourself to a copy; it's brilliant!), I resisted photobombing Vanessa Feltz, and held the door open for Robert Bathurst, who politely thanked me. I've got this 'mingling with the stars' thing nailed.

Thank you to the dream team at Embla for investing in me and helping shape *Has Anyone Seen My Husband?* into the best version it can be: Cara Chimirri, Melanie Hayes, Anna Perkins, Emma Wilson, Daniela Nava (I love the GIFs you inserted alongside the editing notes!), Danielle Clahar-Raymond, Emilie Marneur, Katie Williams, and Beth Free (another fab cover design!).

Thank you to my gorgeous friends who gave up their time to read *Has Anyone Seen My husband?*. In alphabetical order – Brigid Gannon, Catherine Bennetto (I'm working on that world tour so that I can come and visit you and Jason Momoa in NZ), Jo Carnegie, Kate Lowe, Sarah Johnson, Sarah Tomlin, Sinéad Cree, Vicky Bradford and Zoë Folbigg – thank you for your fab feedback and even more fab friendship.

Marie Holbrook– thank you for letting me borrow your name. (Note to all – any similarities to the character is purely coincidental!) Susan Patel – thank you for letting me borrow your husband. I don't really try and stroke him whenever he walks past – honest! Sarah Braddock and Hayley Jade – thank you for letting me borrow Dolly's as the setting for the salon and studio. Becky Page – thank you for taking on all of Eve's driving test admin (and teaching her to drive!), so that I could crack on with my deadlines. Tonya Mascoll – thank you letting me share the story of your surname's origin. It makes up a very small part of my book, but I hope it'll make people think. Pauline Minnis, Geoff Brazier and Magali Robathan (aka Maggie Bates) – merci beaucoup for all the French phrases and mannerisms. That's the extent of my French, which is why I had to lean so heavily on you! Thank you Ellie Thomas for inventing the word keefy. Thirty years on, I'm still using it! Alison Brooker, Hannah Brown, Danny

Pearson and Pip Akram – thank you for being the heart of Hitchin and championing all things creative. Wendy Clark and Sandra Clarke, take no notice of what I said in the book – your surnames *are* cool! Faye Brann and Nancy Peach – burlesque and pole dancing? You two certainly liven up a Dishoom lunch! Speaking of pole dancing, thank you Xaghra Stevens and Lauren Green at The Pole Hub for your helpful, friendly advice. If only I were braver (and younger) to give it a go myself!

I'm very fortunate to have lots of lovely writer friends who are so generous with their time, support and words of wisdom (apologies for not being intelligent enough to be able to reciprocate). In addition to those I've already named, I'd like to give a shout out to Jill Dawson, Holly June Smith, Lorraine Brown, Laura Pearson and Caroline Khoury. I also want to send a virtual hug to my *Strictly* sisters, the Readers' Wives book club, Flapping Flaps (don't ask), Socially Isolated, my RNA buddies, the CWIPesses, and everyone in the Hermitage Café Writers' Room.

Writing can be a solitary occupation and while this is often exactly what's needed, sometimes it's nice to go and write with others, or in a location where you're not responsible for answering the door or doing the laundry. My places of escape are my local library, Hermitage Rd Café and David's Bookshop Café. Thank you Bekah and Alex Nicolas, Ruth Nye and the brilliant team, and Rachel Bagenall and Steph Collis for always looking after me and championing my books. The same thanks goes to Liz Tye and Julie Anderson at Next Page Books, Jo Weaver at Treat Yo' Self gifts and Martyn Boyle at Waterstones Hitchin.

Being part of a writing community is great for sharing experiences and advice, bouncing ideas off each other and generally avoiding life admin and housework. Going to a writing retreat or festival is an even better way to do this and I highly recommend the Bournemouth Writing Festival. Held each April, it's three days of back-to-back workshops, events, activities and networking opportunities. It's run by Dominic Wong, who is possibly the most hard-working person I've ever met and certainly knows how to get his money's worth out of a logoed T-shirt. Thank you Dominic for creating such a fantastic resource for writers of all levels, genres and ages, and for entrusting me with a workshop on writing comedy. Hopefully everyone laughed for the right reasons!

I've now gone from not knowing where to start with my acknowledgements to not knowing where to end. Listing them all has made me realise how incredibly lucky I am to have so many wonderful people in my life, who do lovely things for me. So, thank you. Again!

There's just one more thank you to include (I promise!) and that's to everyone who has read the book. Thank you for investing your time in me. I really hope you enjoyed reading it as much as I enjoyed writing it. And as much as my husband is enjoying his label maker!

About the Author

Kathleen Whyman is an author, a journalist, a knackered mum and an Espresso Martini fan. These may be linked.

Kathleen's humorous women's fiction books are inspired by her feeble attempt to juggle a career with childcare, life admin and never-ending laundry. She's still struggling. (Any tips on how to cope would be much appreciated.)

Has Anyone Seen My Husband? was shortlisted for the Comedy Women in Print prize. Her previous novels include *Would You Ask My Husband That?* and *Wife Support System*. She's starting to sense a theme.

As well as writing, Kathleen runs comedy writing workshops, hosts author events and loves interviewing authors, either for print/digital media or in person for events. Halfway through an interview about her memoir, Susannah Constantine told Kathleen and the audience: 'I thought you were going to be crap, but you're actually brilliant.' Kathleen has chosen to take this as a compliment.

Kathleen lives in Hertfordshire with her husband and two teenage daughters. There's a lot of door slamming.

Website – www.kathleenwhyman.com
Instagram – @kathleenwhymanauthor
LinkedIn – @kathleenwhyman
X – @kathleenwhyman1
Facebook – @kathleenwhymanauthor

About Embla Books

Embla Books is a digital-first publisher of standout commercial adult fiction. Passionate about storytelling, the team at Embla publish books that will make you 'laugh, love, look over your shoulder and lose sleep'. Launched by Bonnier Books UK in 2021, the imprint is named after the first woman from the creation myth in Norse mythology, who was carved by the gods from a tree trunk found on the seashore – an image of the kind of creative work and crafting that writers do, and a symbol of how stories shape our lives.

Find out about some of our other books and stay in touch:

X, Facebook, Instagram: @emblabooks
Newsletter: https://bit.ly/emblanewsletter

Printed in Great Britain
by Amazon

47266717R00209